Lizzie Lane was born and brought up in South Bristol an[...]
worked in law, the probation service, tourism and as a[...]
porting artiste in such TV dramas as *Casualty* and *Holby*[...]
which are both set in Bristol.

She is married with one daughter and currently live[...]
her husband on a 46-foot sailing yacht, dividing he[...]
between Bath and the Med. Sometimes they mix with[...]
set and sometimes they just chill out in a bay with a con[...]
a warm breeze and a gin and tonic!

Also by Lizzie Lane:

Wartime Brides

Coronation Wives

LIZZIE LANE

A Christmas Wish

EBURY
PRESS

3 5 7 9 10 8 6 4 2

First published in 2013 by Ebury Press, an imprint of
Ebury Publishing

A Random House Group Company

The Random House Group Limited Reg. No. 954009

Addresses for companies within the Random House Group can
be found at: www.randomhouse.co.uk

A CIP catalogue record for this book is
available from the British Library

The Random House Group Limited supports The Forest Stewardship
Council® (FSC®), the leading international forest-certification
organisation. Our books carrying the FSC label are printed on FSC®-
certified paper. FSC is the only forest-certification scheme supported
by the leading environmental organisations, including Greenpeace.
Our paper procurement policy can be found at:
www.randomhouse.co.uk/environment

Printed and bound by CPI Group (UK) Ltd, Croydon, CR0 4YY

ISBN 9780091953362

To buy books by your favourite authors and register for offers visit:
www.randomhouse.co.uk

My thanks to Mary for being a friend in the habit of providing lemon curd on toast with champagne. It helps a lot

Chapter One

Magda
January, 1927

'Your Aunt Bridget never had bairns of her own. She'll appreciate having you come to stay with her. You'll be happy there. Trust me.'

Although she was only ten years old Magda Brodie knew her father could tell lies as though they were the absolute truth. So many times he'd promised he'd be home from the sea, but didn't appear; so many times he'd promised his wife Isabella Brodie the world and barely delivered a wage.

Her young legs ached with the effort of keeping up with his long strides. Her heart ached with the pain of being parted from her twin sisters, Venetia and Anna Marie. And when would she hear her baby brother Michael chuckle again?

'And didn't you have a good Christmas,' her father went on as though the memory would help her adjust to a different life away from her siblings. 'A lovely Christmas.'

She whispered an acknowledgement that was lost against the woollen scarf covering the lower half of her face. Things had been wonderful at Christmas despite her mother dying just a few weeks before.

An elderly lamplighter on the other side of the road wished them a happy 1927.

Joseph Brodie raised his free hand. 'Same to you, old timer.' His other hand remained clamped around his daughter's wrist as though fearing she'd run away if he let go.

'Got to be better than 1926,' cried the old man seemingly unwilling to let go of them and be left alone with his task. 'What with General Strikes and all that. Would never have happened in my young day.'

'Aye! Let's hope it's better for us all,' said Joseph Brodie without slowing his pace.

'What about our Anna Marie and Venetia? What about Mikey?' asked Magda.

'They'll be fine. Once I've got you settled then I'll do something about them. I'm waiting to hear, so I am. I'm waiting to hear before I take them to where they're to live.'

'I wish it was Christmas again,' she said. He didn't appear to hear her or if he did he chose to ignore what she said. 'I wish it was,' Magda repeated, breathing the heartfelt words into the thick muffler.

It had been the beginning of a grey, wet November when her mother had taken Magda, her twin sisters and baby Michael to the workhouse in East London. She'd coughed violently between telling them it would only be temporary.

'Only until your father comes home from the sea. Everything will be better then.'

Nothing was better, and certainly not Isabella Brodie. The cough that she'd had for as long as Magda could remember worsened until she was coughing blood. The decision was made to take her from the workhouse to somewhere called a sanatorium. All this happened in a maelstrom of activity, with people bustling around whilst speaking in low voices and entreating the children to stay out of the way. The latter was uttered with misted eyes and a shaking of heads.

The wetness of late November departed, December bringing an east wind and grey fog that softened the harsh lines of grime-covered brick and sludge-coloured stone of the East End of London.

The damp fog had a sickly yellow tinge and a gritty taste, suffused as it was with smoke from a million coal-fired chimneys. The workhouse kept the windows closed, the stuffiness inside preferable to the wicked weather outside.

Magda asked when they could see their mother again, but was told that the disease spoiling her mother's lungs was highly contagious and the sanatorium discouraged visitors, especially children.

Halfway through December, when snow had fallen, melted, and froze again over an iron-hard ground, a kindly lady at the workhouse had called them into the kitchen. The workhouse kitchen was a warm place where great copper pans bubbled away on a big black range, the steam smelling of good things to eat.

The woman had gathered the four of them around her, Magda with her baby brother Michael in her arms. Her sisters Venetia and Anna Marie had stood so closely together it seemed they were joined at the hip and shoulder. In fact they were twins, though Venetia had dark, Mediterranean looks like Magda and their mother, and Anna Marie was fair and blue eyed like her father.

'I'm sorry to say that your mother has passed away.'

Three pairs of innocent young eyes had stared back at her, baby Michael, uncomprehending of the family tragedy, gurgling with laughter.

Anna Marie, always a little more sensitive than the others, had been the first to cry. Unwilling to show weakness to strangers, Venetia had hung her head.

Magda's bottom lip had trembled whilst her dark grey eyes studied the top of Michael's head.

'Is our father coming to fetch us? Will we be with him for Christmas?'

Her voice had been small, but steady when she'd asked the question.

The kindly lady, who had dedicated her life to helping the less fortunate, placed a hand over her chest as though she'd been struck with a sudden pain.

She'd explained to Magda that the workhouse only catered for children when they were part of a family. It was customary for those with absent parents who could not be traced to be placed in a home for abandoned children.

The kind lady, whose name was Miss Burton, couldn't help feeling sorry for the poor mites. It wasn't normal procedure, but she had come to an abrupt conclusion.

'I tell you what, my dears. You can all stay here while we try and locate your father to tell him of this tragedy. Now how would that be?'

Magda had been forthright. 'We will only stay until our father comes to fetch us and have us all live together. That's why he went away on ships. To earn enough money to buy us a nice house by the sea. That's where we'll live.'

'I'm sure you will,' Miss Burton had responded, her generous heart touched by the child's trust in the absent parent.

'Is our mother going to be an angel?' Anna Marie had asked, her blue eyes like china saucers in her heart-shaped face.

'Yes. And just in time for Christmas,' Magda had answered with a determined set of her jaw, her little head held high.

At Christmas there had been presents for all the children, and a festive feast of sorts including a slice of chicken, crisp roast potatoes, plum pudding, and jelly and blancmange just for the children.

'This is the best Christmas ever,' Venetia had proclaimed, her dark eyes bright with excitement and her mouth full of pudding.

Magda's first inclination had been to say that it couldn't be the best; not with their mother lately buried. But on reflection she'd decided not to. Instead she'd said, 'When we're rich and living by the sea, we'll have the best Christmas ever. You just see if we don't.'

'Promise?' Anna Marie had lisped, having just lost a front milk tooth the night before.

'Hope springs eternal,' her sister had responded. She didn't know where she'd read that, but it sounded good – and certainly hopeful.

The twins had been given a game of snakes and ladders for Christmas. It was whilst the three of them were playing the game, Venetia declaring hotly that it was her turn and that her sisters were cheating, that a shadow had fallen over them.

Tall, dark and smelling of black tobacco and sea salt, her father had finally arrived, his presence as big as his body and the smile on his bluff and bonny face.

'Your father's home from the sea,' he'd proclaimed. 'So how are my darling kids?'

The dice had rolled with the counters across the game board as the twins jumped to their feet, throwing their arms around him with such gusto that he staggered backwards.

Only Magda had held back, half fearing it was a mirage and he would vanish if she dared acknowledge that he was there – finally there.

'Our mother's gone to be a Christmas angel,' Anna Marie had declared once she'd unwrapped her arms from around his waist.

Her father had looked down at Michael who looked back at him warily, not sure at all who this strange man could be.

'Son,' their father had said.

He had made no attempt to pick the baby up.

'Magda,' he'd said finally, turning to her once he'd brushed the twins from his side. 'My. How you've grown. Aren't you going to give your old dad a hug, now?'

Young as she was, she'd heard his warm regards every time he came home from the sea and made excuses to their mother as to why there wasn't much money for all his efforts.

Once he'd realised he was not going to get the welcome from her that he'd had from the others, he took her to one side and told her of where she would be living now that her mother was dead.

Whilst she was still trying to take it in, he had said to her, 'Magda, you have to be brave. For the little ones' sake, you have to be brave, my girl.'

Even now his words jarred. She closed her eyes and thought about making a Christmas wish. Her wish was that her father had never come home and that she was still with her sisters and little brother.

When she opened her eyes again nothing had changed. The weather was still bitingly cold though her father, Joseph Brodie, strode along as though the day was fine and a bitter wind was not beating into their faces.

The small girl at his side would only come to know when she was older that confidence was her father's shield against the world and the guilt within him. He was ripping the family apart, but Joseph Brodie was a selfish man who people – especially women – found easy to love. Besides that, he was not a man ever to admit that what he was doing was wrong.

She saw the grim surroundings, the alleys piercing between terraces of dirty red brick houses, the smell of dirt, drains and smoke from chimneys. It was hard to be brave. She didn't feel brave. She felt helpless.

Finally she found her voice. 'When will I see our Venetia again?'

'In time. In time.' His response was curt though bright as though everything in the world was lovely.

His grip on her hand tightened. Perhaps he suspected she had it in mind to run away, but she was a child. It was in her nature to love those close to her, to trust her father just as she had her mother.

'When will I see my sisters and brother again?'

'When things are better. I've told you. All the details of where they'll be living are in yer mother's Bible. Still, you saw them at Christmas. Despite everything you had Christmas together. Now wasn't that a good thing?'

Magda had to concede that it was. The family had clung together and she'd tried her best, as the eldest, to reassure them that everything would be fine.

'When you come home again, will you buy that house by the sea that our mama talked about where we can all be together?'

'Is that what she told you?' He sounded more than surprised; perhaps a little taken aback.

'Yes. And we'll all live with you, together, and next Christmas I shall cook us all Christmas dinner with a turkey – or perhaps a chicken,' she added, changing her mind because he might think a turkey too expensive. And after all, if he was going to buy a cottage by the sea, wouldn't that be better than a turkey? And houses cost money. Her mother had told her so when she'd questioned why they lived in two cold rooms in a shared house.

She swiped a hand at the tears clinging to her lashes, her fingers cold despite the thickness of her knitted mitten. The New Year had blown in bitterly cold with the threat of snow.

The sky was no more than a ribbon between the cramped roofs and crooked chimneys of the narrow streets they trod.

7

She noticed that some windows in the tiny houses still had paper chains or pretend snow, no more than bits of cotton wool stuck to the panes. A few more days, perhaps only hours, and the real thing would start to fall. It was that cold.

Every so often her father, Joe Brodie, would glance at her, see that she was far from happy, and then commence to tell her how grand things would be when he once again returned from sea.

'And I'll buy you a dolly with eyes that close and she'll be wearing a pink dress.'

The rag doll she was carrying beneath her arm was the one thing connecting her present with her past and had been given to her by a kindly neighbour some years before. This year's Christmas present had been a colouring book and some crayons. It was stuffed into the paper carrier bag that swung from her father's left hand along with the few bits of clothes she owned.

The cobbles were slippery underfoot, the afternoon fast turning into a wintry twilight.

Magda shivered. She was the eldest so her father had told her to be his big brave girl and to be an example to the little ones. Being brave, she'd decided, wasn't easy and she didn't like this place he'd brought her to. At least the workhouse had become familiar territory even though she had only resided there for a few months.

Despite the biting wind, Magda raised her head, narrowing her eyes as she took in the drab surroundings with increasing dismay. Her nose wrinkled at the smell of old drains, decay and dirt.

'Dad. I don't like it here. This place stinks.'

Though her mouth was muffled by her scarf, her voice was clear.

Her father shook his head, refusing to admit that things

were bad because that's the way he was. The arrangements he'd made for his children suited him and that was all that mattered. He was blind to anything else.

'Now, now, Magda my girl. You're overreacting. It's poor but honest around here and your aunt will be good to you. You just see. Everything will be fine, my girl.'

Her mother had come from Italy, a place, she'd told Magda, where the sun always shone.

Joseph Brodie had sailed into Naples and charmed the dark-haired, dark-eyed young girl into marrying him. With his melodic voice, his broad shoulders and his dancing blue eyes, the handsome Irishman had stolen her heart away. 'Love at first sight,' she'd said to her children in her lilting voice before a sad look had come over her features. 'I loved him despite all his faults, his many faults, and I love him still.'

The fact was that for all his charm, Joseph Brodie was feckless; there was no way he could settle down to a life with a wife and children, tied to the land. He reckoned the sea was in his blood. The fortune he'd promised his bride never came their way.

Isabella Julieta Brodie had worked at anything and everything she could to keep a roof over their heads and bread on the table. Eventually the hard work and starvation rations had caught up with her. Eventually they were turned out of their lodgings and sent to the workhouse. Though the diet was basic it was better than they'd had and her mother had promised there were better times to come once she was back on her feet. 'Especially when your father comes home. We will all be happy then.'

With her last breath her mother had expressed her love for her husband and asked the nice nurse to tell the children to behave for him.

It wasn't to say that Joseph Brodie wasn't upset by his

wife's death. He was, though the fact that his children needed him was not something he wished to face. Going to sea was a habit he found difficult to break. It was as though he had two lives – one with his wife and one with his shipmates, visiting one port after another all over the world. 'Anyway,' he said to those who would listen. 'What would I be doing living on the land, working in a factory or a mine, even on me father's farm? It wouldn't suit. That it wouldn't. Not at all.'

Just for a while though, his exuberance for life at sea was temporarily jettisoned in favour of a brief mourning.

On the day of Magda's departure, the three older children had clasped their arms around each other, shivering and sobbing into each other's shoulders. Baby Michael had looked up at them wide eyed and frightened until he too was crying for someone he didn't yet know that he'd lost. Magda had exchanged a soft whisper with her twin sisters. *No matter what, we must be strong for each other.*

She also promised them that one day they would have that Christmas dinner in a place to call home. She didn't know when it would be, but it would happen. 'I swear to you it will. And I'll send you a Christmas card every year and write you letters. That's what people do when they're not together.'

Daring to hope that things really would be better, Magda had asked her father couldn't he reconsider and all of them live together and he not go to sea any more?

He'd shaken his head.

'I can't stay, Magda. I have to go. I have a living to make. But first I'll make arrangements for you all. You'll all be fine. You'll be sorted. I promise.'

'And all the places where each of you are living are in yer mother's Bible,' he said. 'Magda's the eldest. Magda will keep it with her. Right, Magda?'

For his part, Joseph Brodie told himself he was doing the

right thing, though deep down, if he was honest, he would have to admit that he was behaving as he'd always behaved. No matter who loved him and who he loved – in his own way of course – he tended to do things to suit himself. Yes, he felt grieved that he hadn't been there for his wife, but he blamed others for that; the wages on board every ship he'd ever worked on, every far-flung port where the bartenders relieved him of his hard-earned cash, and – once drunk as a lord – every dock-side whore who'd reminded him of his wife.

Close to the city docks, terraced houses, crumbling from years of neglect by absentee landlords, lined cobbled streets.

This part of London was home to all manner of folk, poor, honest and dishonest. Poverty and crime rubbed shoulders out of necessity. Making a living by any means possible meant holding onto life. Only the coffin maker on the corner of Cocks Passage and Edward Street, the street they were heading for, had an unending source of business.

Creaking signs above lopsided doorways advertised chimney sweeps and cobblers. Old inns rubbed shoulders with rope makers, coopers and tenements housing at least one family on each floor.

Pale-faced children peered from dark interiors or played out in the street with bits of wood or stones. The former were floated on sooty puddles, the fallout from the smoking chimney pots, the gas works and the coal yard at the end of the street where it abutted the river. Little had changed since the Great War.

A man sitting against the wall outside the pub begged them for alms. He was wearing the top half of an old navy uniform. Three or four medals dangled from the breast pocket.

Her father stopped. 'Where did you serve?'

'Jutland. German eight inch took me legs off.'

Magda noticed the man was sitting on a wooden board that

had wheels on. She noticed with the fascination a child feels for the unusual that he had no legs.

Her father tossed him a coin. 'Have a half on me, old fellah. I wasn't so far from there meself.'

The man's face lit up. 'You're an officer and a gentleman.'

Joseph laughed. 'Sure I am. How did you guess?'

The man disappeared into the pub, the door swinging shut behind him, though not before a hubbub of conversation, stale smells and amber light had fallen out onto the pavement.

In an oppressive street beneath an oppressive January sky, Joseph Brodie knocked at the battered door of his sister-in-law.

The house was a straightforward two-up, two-down terraced, one of about eight all strung together, and it looked the poorest in the street.

Aunt Bridget was married to James Brodie, Joseph's brother, who worked as an able seaman on the pig boats that plied between London and Cork. Irish pork was best, according to Bridget Brodie, leanest and freshest. 'Sure, isn't it slaughtered just on down the road here?'

Joseph Brodie knew this was true. Depending on the wind, the screams of the pigs smelling blood and death travelled from the slaughterhouse with unnerving regularity.

Bridget Brodie did not possess the same calm tone as her brother-in-law. Neither was she purposeful in her movements; darting around and doing everything at breakneck, slapdash speed. Being bereft of children had made her bitter, though perhaps because he was a man, Joseph Brodie couldn't see what she'd become. If he had perhaps he would have thought twice about leaving his daughter there.

Her sharp eyes, blue in a complexion that erred towards pink, as though she'd been toasted in front of the fire, fixed on Magda. 'She has her mother's colouring. The others had yours. I saw them once.'

'Would you hold that against her?'

She shrugged. 'I'll not speak ill of the dead, though you know my thoughts on foreigners.' She crossed her flat chest in a swift, stabbing movement. 'We've got enough of them in this place as it is. Jews one end, blacks the other – God knows but this place is going downhill.'

''Tis only to be expected, you living so close to the docks, ships come into London from all over the world. You're bound to get people here from all over.'

Bridget Brodie eyed him sharply. 'That don't mean they have to stay here. I see them go in across the way there too,' she said, nodding towards the house across the street. ''Tis a whorehouse, you know. My God,' she said, crossing herself again, 'what would my old mother think if she knew her daughter was living opposite a whorehouse?'

'Sure you don't know that for sure.'

'Too right I do, Joe Brodie. Men, mostly sailors, going in and out of there at all hours. 'Tis disgraceful I say. Plain disgraceful!'

Controlling any hint of guilt, Brodie looked across to a gabled building, its upper floor overhanging the lower. It had likely been there since the first sailor sauntered past smoking a rolled-up leaf of best Virginian tobacco and wondering what he could do with the potatoes he'd also brought back with him.

For the first time since laying his plan, he experienced a twinge of doubt, but beggars couldn't be choosers. He firmly believed that in a few years, the ten-year-old Magda would be close to being a woman and as such needed female guidance and certainly not the likes of him. She might find it hard at first, perhaps, but she'd thank him for it later. Sure she would, and wasn't his sister-in-law an upright, God-fearing woman?

'You'll do the Christian thing?' he said as he counted out

13

ten shillings into her waiting palm. 'There's some to be going on with. I'll get more to you later.'

Her sharp eyes softened at the sight of coins tumbling into her palm. 'That I will,' she said, a smile curving her lips. If he'd looked closer he would have seen that her smile did not travel to her eyes. She tucked the coins down the neck of her cheap dress between her breasts and sighed with satisfaction.

She saw his eyes follow the progress of the money into her cleavage and it warmed her. Suddenly her attitude changed. The red-faced woman with her squinty eyes and overblown figure took on the simpering attributes of a streetwise girl, one whose sole purpose in life was seducing a man she had a fancy for.

'Will you stay and have a cup of tea with me? Or stay a bit longer and go to the pub tonight?'

He shook his head. 'I've got to go and deliver my other kids to where they're going. The addresses where they'll be found are all in here.'

He lifted the Bible then looked at Magda, the doubt about leaving her still in evidence, but slowly retreating in the face of expediency.

'Isabella's Bible is to go into my Magda's keeping. I've listed the addresses of those who know where the others can be found at the front of this book and also there's details of how to get hold of me. Magda will take care of it so that even if I drown at sea, she can take over and get the family back together. Can you do that for me, Magda? I promise you, it won't be for long. We'll all be together in no time once I've made me fortune and returned from the sea for good. No time at all.'

'Yes, Dad,' Magda said, though she said it softly, the words sticking in the dryness of her throat. He was leaving again. Leaving her, leaving the others, just as he'd left her mother.

During all this time of listening to him and his brother's

wife, she'd felt her body growing colder and colder. The chill was only partly down to the dampness of the house where she'd already noticed fungus growing in one corner. The fire in the grate did little to warm the room, a spiral of damp-looking smoke rising lazily from solid black coal.

The fact was, she did not want to be here but was too young, too weak to disobey her father's wishes.

With trembling hands, she took her mother's Bible from her father and clasped it to her breast.

Satisfied that all appeared to be well, Brodie took Magda to one side and bowed to her level.

'I've given your aunt money for your needs. You'll be safe till I come back. Now I'll be off to take care of the others. Remember, they're all written in here.' He tapped the Bible that she was hugging as tightly as a more favoured child would a doll or a teddy bear.

Magda felt her eyes fill with tears. Her father, Joseph Brodie, was the lynchpin between her past and her future – whatever that was likely to be. And he was leaving.

Aunt Bridget took hold of her shoulders. 'Come on, Magda,' she said soothingly, the dampness of her hands permeating through Magda's coat. 'Be a good girl and let your father go now. He's work to do and you, my girl, have to be brave.'

Joe Brodie ducked out of the door. Once outside, he stopped and turned.

'Be a good girl for your Aunt Bridget. I'll be in touch soon.'

Together they watched him stride off down the street, Magda frozen to the spot, her Aunt Bridget still holding on to her shoulders.

The women in the house across the road were leering out of their windows, calling at him to come back and stay with them awhile.

'You won't regret it, sweetheart,' one of them called.

Aunt Bridget turned a thunderous expression in their direction and brandished a threatening fist at them. 'Sluts! You're all sluts and the sooner you all burn in hell the better this world will be.'

'Don't tell us, Bridget Brodie. You're as pure as the driven snow? Or perhaps the Virgin Mary?'

The woman's words brought laughter from the other women gathered with her – women of every colour, every shape and size.

'Foul-mouthed trollops!' Aunt Bridget shouted back.

'Been to the Red Cow of late, have you Bridget? Drank only milk and sat with your legs crossed, did you?'

Aunt Bridget scowled in their direction. 'Hussies. Hussies, all of them.'

Magda looked up at her. 'What do they mean?'

'Wave to yer father,' growled Bridget Brodie, her tone altered and her fist thudding into Magda's back. 'Show yer gratefulness, darkie,' she said.

Alarmed by the form of address, Magda turned and looked into Bridget Brodie's face. The blue eyes were sharp as bits of broken glass, the mouth that had smiled now pursed into self-righteous tightness.

Fear flooded Magda's stout young heart. Lunging for the street, she shouted, 'Dad! Come back!'

She only managed one shout before she was pulled back into the mean room, the door slamming tightly shut.

Her eyes remained fixed on that closed door. Had her father heard her? Was he coming back? She wished that he would.

'Well,' said Bridget Brodie, fists fixed on her hips, her expression dark and evil. 'You've got no family now. No stuck-up foreign mother around to spoil you with 'er foreign ways. Four children living and her ungrateful enough to go and die.

And here's me with no child to call my own. Now you've to rough it, my girl, just like everybody else around here.'

Magda's eyes filled with tears, but still clutching her mother's Bible, she held her head high. She would not cry. All this would pass as all things pass, just like her time in the workhouse.

'I'm Magdalena Brodie, and one day I'll be a lady.'

Bridget Brodie looked amused. 'Well, will ya now! Well, there's pride fer you, and pride is one of the deadly sins. Do you not know that?' Her aunt's expression turned sour.

Magda cried out as rough hands marched her to the other side of the room where she was forced to kneel before a plaster statue with a pale face and even paler hands. The statue stood in a roughly formed alcove behind which light shone from the outside through a small glass pane.

'There. Now ask the Blessed Virgin for forgiveness. And don't get up till you're sorry fer yer ways. And bow yer head respectfully,' she said, landing a parting blow at the back of her head, forcing it forward.

Magda squeezed her eyes tightly shut and prayed as never before to the Mother of God, all the time clutching the Bible tightly to her chest.

Bridget Brodie saw how attached Magda was to that Bible and decided she was not finished with the girl yet.

Twisted with hate, she wrenched the Bible from Magda's grasp. 'I'll take that, me girl! You'll have it back when I say so and not before.'

'That was my mother's. My father said I was to take care of it.'

Another slap around the head. 'Are you deaf, girl? You'll have it when I say so. Isn't that what I just told you? Now get back to asking the Blessed Virgin for forgiveness. And don't get up till I tell you to.'

She pushed her back to where she'd been and kicked into the back of the child's knees so that they buckled under her.

Bridget Brodie's eyes glittered with satisfaction. At long last she had some power over Joseph Brodie, or at least over one of his brats. She would enjoy this time. She was determined to do so.

Damn Joseph Brodie. Damn his foreign wife. If he'd kept his promise to her, when she'd been single and plain old Bridget McCarthy, then perhaps she might have had babies with him. As it was she'd been rejected and in being rejected had married his brother and had no babies.

It was all Isabella's fault, but now Isabella was gone. The sin of the mother had fallen onto the daughter and Bridget Brodie would make her pay for it.

Chapter Two

The Twins

'I liked the boat,' said Venetia to her sister. 'It was the best part.'

Anna Marie eyed her twin with frightened eyes that shone like glass in a face that was paler than normal.

Her lips were still blue even though they'd long left the boat that had brought them across the Irish Sea.

They'd caught a train then a bus to Dunavon, a town that would have been swallowed up as a suburb in London. Anna Marie wished desperately that she was still in London simply because it was all that she'd ever known.

They made their way to where a pony and trap waited for them. Not a bus. A horse-drawn vehicle. They'd seen horse-drawn brewery drays back in London, but never a pony pulling a cart meant for passengers.

'There. Now this is your grandfather. Say hello to him.' Their father sounded bright and breezy but his manner was deferential as though he feared the man sitting up front in the trap.

The twins eyed the white-haired man who likewise eyed them. His eyes were a frightening blue, perhaps because he didn't blink but looked at each of them as though in two minds whether he liked them or not.

Even their father, who never seemed afraid of anyone, had taken off his cap, screwing it around in his hands like a school-boy about to be caned.

The girls dutifully muttered a muted hello, their voices tinny like the sound of clockwork when it's fast running down.

Their grandfather grunted in a gravelly voice. 'Well, get aboard. I haven't got all day.'

Joseph Brodie hoisted the two girls and their meagre luggage into the back of the cart.

'Be good,' he whispered.

The cart dipped to one side as he got up into the front seat alongside his father.

'Giddup!'

The girls started at the command as much as the pony between the shafts.

It began to rain, a soft, incessant drizzle for which Ireland, as they later came to find out, was famous.

Their father half turned in his seat. 'Pull the tarpaulin up over you. That'll keep you dry.'

He helped them do it.

Out of the rain but not liking the smell, the two girls wrinkled their noses.

'It stinks,' whispered Venetia.

Anna Marie just stared at her, fearing that if she opened her mouth to comment, the white-haired man with the fierce blue eyes might hear. She hadn't liked the sound of his voice. She could never imagine herself ever speaking to him just in case she said the wrong thing. He was too frightening.

The two men up front also pulled bits of tarpaulin up over their shoulders. Both stared silently ahead, eyes narrowed against the icy beat of the needle-fine rain.

Water trickled from their eyebrows, their noses and their chins and down their necks, soaking their clothes.

Each man smouldered with his own thoughts, though one more angrily than the other.

'I do mean it, Father,' Joseph Brodie began hesitantly. 'I've got the wanderlust out of my system, honest I have.'

Dermot Brodie grunted.

He didn't sound convinced.

His son swiped the water away from his eyes, thinking how he could convince the old man that he was a reformed character, deserving to be applauded for his efforts.

'I know I've let you down, you and Mother, but I mean what I say. And don't I have the children to consider, now that Isabella is gone?'

His father grunted again.

'As soon as I've settled the girls, I'll go back over to England and fetch Magda. After all I can't expect Bridget to look after her forever. And then there's Michael – little Mikey. I was thinking he was too young for the crossing, him just a baby and all that. The good folk I've left him with will make sure he's well taken care of until I go back for him too. And then won't that be grand! The whole family back together again!'

He glanced at his father's bearish profile, the white eyebrows, the hair, the grim set of the mouth. He wanted a sign that he'd been believed even though, as usual, he'd somewhat embellished the truth. He'd taken money for Michael and most of that was already gone.

With little coinage left in his pockets he had no choice but to return to sea. The truth was that he had no intention of bringing either his eldest daughter or his baby son over to Ireland.

Magda would be all right – she'd be grown soon. As for Michael, well, the Darbys had made him an offer he couldn't refuse. They were without children and he had children in need of a home and a mother. If he delved deeply into his heart of hearts, he might admit to himself that he'd never wanted children. He'd wanted Isabella, his Italian beauty, and the only way he could have her was to marry her; she'd made that pretty plain from the start. He wouldn't have done it for any other woman, but Isabella. He'd done it for her, the love of his life.

The town of Dunavon was left behind, the plain, no non-sense facades of downmarket Victorian buildings and squat cottages giving way to hedgerows and fields.

Damp, cold and frightened, the girls peered out from beneath their covering, cowering together for comfort as well as warmth.

The sight of so much greenery was new to them; London just couldn't compete. Anna Marie eyed it with interest, Venetia with dismay. Venetia had liked the shops and bustle of a big city. She didn't like the look of this at all.

Anna Marie, however, was beginning to relax. She was still frightened of the old man sitting up front, but if she could only escape into those fields now and again she might forget he existed.

They turned off the narrow road into one that was no more than a lane, its surface pitted with stones and craters that were presently full of water. They were about to arrive at Loskeran Bridge Farm.

Their father, sitting up front, locked his gaze on the old farmhouse, the only one of two storeys in the whole area.

Though better than most, it still looked mean when compared to buildings he'd seen all over the world. Not that he could voice his opinion; his father was a proud man and would hit him down for it.

Smoke curled lazily from the chimney as though fighting against the rain in its efforts to reach the sky.

Nothing much had changed since he'd left; the pigs still smelled the way he'd remembered them, the chickens still clucked around the yard, and the few cows his father owned stared at him as they chewed cud in rain-soaked fields.

Joseph Brodie could always be counted on to put a brave face on things. He could also charm the birds off the trees, or so his shipmates often said, and indeed he believed this to be true. He could charm anybody – with one exception.

His father spit on the ground before stepping down from the gig.

'I don't believe a bloody word you're saying.'

His son had already alighted, leaving him with the pony and trap.

'My darling Joe!'

Molly Brodie's arms were locked tight around the broad back of her favourite son, her firstborn, her lovely boy and the light of her life.

Dermot grimaced. From the moment they'd received the letter telling them their son's intentions, Molly had been over the moon, springing about the place sprightlier than she'd done in years.

'You have to give the boy a chance,' she'd said when he'd voiced his opinion that their son was lying and would leave them literally holding the baby. Not that he minded having his granddaughters under his roof, but they'd be little help around the farm, nothing like a strong son, that was for sure. But was Joe telling the truth? Would he stay and work on the farm?

Molly had pleaded with Dermot the same way she used to plead when his sons were boys and he'd taken off his belt. Not enough times, in his opinion, but for the most part he'd given in to her – just as he was doing now.

'Well, will you look at you now,' said the kindly woman whom the twins were told was their grandmother. 'Soaked through. Let's get you inside and out of those wet things. After that, I've mutton stew simmering, fresh bread and our own butter. And a cake. Do either of you girls like cake?'

That night the girls snuggled up together in a double bed in a room they'd been told was theirs and theirs alone.

'That cake was lovely,' said Venetia. 'And so was the stew. I heard our dad say that he's bringing over Magda and Michael soon. Then we'll all be together.'

'I like it here,' murmured Anna Marie, barely able to keep her eyes open. She was so warm, so tired and so full of good food. 'I like the pony. He's called Merrylegs. And we're to call our grandfather Granfer. Gran said that he'd like that.'

Venetia hugged her sister closer. 'We won't be here forever. One day we'll go back to London. I'm going to ask Dad when he's going back to bring our Magda and Michael over. I'm going to ask him if I can go with him.'

'I'm not. I'm going to stay here and play with the animals.'

Venetia said that farm animals were for eating not playing with, but Anna Marie was fast asleep.

In the morning Venetia got up with the sound of chickens out in the yard and somebody shouting, 'I told you so, woman. I told you so!'

She dressed quickly, at the same time hissing at her sister that she was off downstairs to ask their father if she could go to England with him.

Anna Marie eyed her sleepily. 'You go. I'll stay here.'

Venetia almost tumbled down the stairs in her haste to get hold of her father and ask him to take her with him.

The warmth of the kitchen, the smell of bread baking and thick slices of bacon sizzling in the pan was like heaven on a damp Irish morning.

Gran was clattering dishes and pans around and looked upset.

'Where's my dad?'

The question was heard by her grandfather as he came in from outside bringing a mist of dampness with him.

'Gone!'

His boots clumped on the scrubbed flagstones as he made a move to wash his hands before breakfast.

Venetia, her dark eyes filling with fear for what she was about to hear, stood with her mouth open.

'Is he coming back?' she asked.

Dermot Brodie wasn't listening. He was shaking a finger in front of his wife's face as she dished up his bacon and eggs, and shouting at the top of his voice.

'Didn't I tell you so? Didn't I?'

Venetia felt her legs go weak.

Her grandmother saw her and cast anxious eyes at her husband.

'Have a care for the child, Dermot. She's been through enough, losing her mother and all that.'

Dermot Brodie straightened and looked at Venetia.

'Your father lied to me, girl. His own father. He never meant to stay. He's always gone his own way and he's no different now than he's ever been. Your father's gone back to sea. You might see him again, or you might not. Either way it looks as though we're stuck with the pair of you!'

Chapter Three

Magda

Magda Brodie watched as her aunt locked the front door behind her. She was off to the pub – to see her friend, as she put it.

Magda sighed. Her world had become very small seen only via the small windows at the front of the house.

She had a good view of the grander house across the way where gentlemen callers arrived by taxi or chauffeur-driven car and mostly at night. Only a few came on foot and then furtively, their coat collars turned up as though reluctant to be recognised.

Sometimes one of the girls living across the road would see her looking out and would wave to her. She would wave back, the small action raising her spirits.

Sometimes she would see one of the girls talking to an old woman who limped. She saw their eyes stray across to her and knew she was the subject of their conversation.

On these occasions she shrank back into the gloomy room, fearful lest they tell her aunt that she spent time between chores gazing out at a world that she was forbidden to join.

There were no books in Aunt Bridget's sorry abode, except for the Bible kept enticingly high above her head. Magda missed the books she'd once read. They had been borrowed from an old man who kept a second-hand shop on the Fulham Road. His main merchandise had been second-hand furniture. He'd lent her those books in part exchange for her mother's sewing box.

'But only to lend,' he'd said to her. 'Might have a paying customer with a library one day.'

She'd loved those books; fairy stories and adventures, books full of magic, beautiful princesses and honourable princes. And there were always bad fairies and witches, though none of them frightened her, not like her Aunt Bridget.

In the absence of books, she made up stories about the young women in the house across the road, the old lady, the gentlemen callers.

The girls were captive princesses, all waiting for the right prince to answer the right riddle. So far none of the gentlemen callers had answered the riddle correctly, which was why all the princesses were still there, none of them leaving on a white horse with their favoured Prince Charming.

As for the witch, well, there was no doubt who that was and she herself was the most beautiful captive princess of all, subject of a wicked curse and sealed in a cold dark prison.

Spring came and the weather turned warmer. The girls opposite were wearing prettier dresses of all different colours. They looked like butterflies. Sometimes they looked very happy. Sometimes they looked sad or tired of the world at large, but at least they were free to come and go, Magda thought, and for a while she envied them.

It was a sunny morning, a fresh breeze blowing dust and paper along the street, when Magda saw the dark side of the life of the girls across the road.

One of the girls was shouting and screaming, hanging onto

a man for all she was worth. When he pushed her, she fell to the ground, her hands curling protectively across her belly.

The older woman, the one Magda viewed as the Fairy Godmother in her story, came out of the house.

She couldn't hear the words clearly, just enough to know that the younger one was being encouraged to leave the man and go into the house.

The girl, who looked quite plump to Magda's eyes, shook her head, her hair flying wildly around her face.

She lunged at the man, trying to hold onto him. He pushed her again, this time so violently that she fell backwards and fell full stretch on the ground.

Then he kicked her.

Magda covered her mouth with both hands, her eyes wide with horror.

Other women came out of the house to help the injured girl inside. They disappeared. Only the older woman remained, her face like marble, staring in the direction the man had taken.

The old woman caught sight of Magda watching from her puny window and shook her head again as though sharing a sad thought before retiring.

A few days later Magda saw two men arrive in a hearse. A long black car like this had taken her mother away to the cemetery. Had the man pushed the girl hard enough to kill her?

One of the black-clothed men in the hearse went into the house with something tucked beneath his arm.

The man in black came back out, his head tilted forward, eyes fixed on the tiny white box he carried. That's what he'd taken into the house, though covered then. Now it was obvious. The parcel beneath his arm had contained a tiny coffin.

She saw the women dabbing their eyes as they followed the hearse. There were only three of them, the mother of the child, another girl supporting her and the Fairy Godmother.

Seeing the small coffin Magda's thoughts turned to her baby brother. Was he still alive?

When her aunt rolled in from her favourite drinking haunt, her face redder than usual, her clothes dishevelled and her breath smelling of brown ale, Magda dared ask her about contacting her family.

'I could write to them,' she said hopefully, glancing up to where her mother's Bible sat on the high shelf.

Aunt Bridget slumped heavily into a chair. 'Your father didn't leave enough money for feeding you, my girl, let alone writing letters. Heat up that stew. You'll get no pampering here. Not in this house.'

Magda sighed. Food was mostly thin soups, stews and hunks of bread thickly spread with pork dripping or plum jam.

Not that Aunt Bridget denied herself a decent meal; pigs' tails, ox tongue, lamb chops and pork sausages. She devoured them all, the scraps left to the child whose big eyes were beginning to look even bigger in her heart-shaped face due to lack of sustenance.

Aunt Bridget fell into a deep sleep, her head back, her mouth open and emitting a full-bodied snore.

The steam from the soup misted the windows.

Whilst her aunt lay snoring in the chair, Magda wrote the initials of her sisters' names with her fingernail in the condensation. Then she wrote a large 'M' for Michael.

'I miss you,' she whispered. 'I miss all of you.'

Behind her, Aunt Bridget let out a resounding snore that almost woke her up.

Magda froze. The moment of fear passed. The snoring continued unabated.

The fire was as mean and smoky as ever and there was no point in piling on any more coal. The coal itself was contained in a pine box to one side of the grate. A cardboard box holding

29

newspapers and bits of kindling sat the other side. The kettle, its spout black and its handle grease-covered, hummed like a pet cat on the hob.

Magda shivered. No matter the time of year, the house was damp. It paid to keep moving about in order to stay warm. Even in bed Magda shivered beneath the thin, smelly blanket that Bridget had rejoiced in telling her had once covered a horse.

She eyed the cardboard box, the newspapers and the pieces of butcher's paper in which her aunt's supper had been wrapped.

The misted window panes, the butcher's paper, and even the box containing it, had given her an idea.

Being careful not to make a noise, she slid each piece of paper out of the box and smoothed it flat. Those that were too smeared with blood, she put back into the box. She was left with two good sheets that weren't too crumpled.

Sucking in her lips, she eyed each carefully. They'd do very well for writing paper and would give her something to do during the day. And not just letters. She thought about that last Christmas they'd been together.

Miss Burton at the workhouse had received lots of Christmas cards decorated with snow scenes, jolly snowmen or red-breasted robins. The kindly Miss Burton had let her look at one that she'd received. Inside it had said 'Merry Christmas'.

Magda glanced over her shoulder to make sure Aunt Bridget still slept soundly. The open mouth, the dribble running through the hairs of her chin along with the recurring noises, declared that she was.

Magda folded both sheets of paper in half, then in half again. There were scissors in the dresser drawer. Again she had to be careful, easing the stiff old drawer out of its cavity bit by squeaky bit.

By the time she'd finished, she had four pieces of paper from the two sheets. These she folded in half, flattening them again as best she could. Sucking in her bottom lip, she eyed the creamy coloured paper, and the wrinkles that were still there though not so obvious as they had been. They were not as stiff as proper shop-bought cards, but she told herself that her sisters and little brother wouldn't mind that. It would be good to hear from her and that was really all that mattered.

A snort from Aunt Bridget made her start and hug the pieces of paper to her chest. Nothing would give her aunt greater pleasure than guessing her plan and throwing the lot into the fire.

'We'll be having none of that,' she would sneer. 'No writing in this house.' Indeed, Bridget Brodie did not own a pencil, let alone a book.

Leaving her aunt sleeping, Magda stole up to bed, hid the paper beneath her pillow and said a little prayer.

'Please God, I'm going to write letters, a diary and make cards for my sisters and brother. I can't remember their birthdays, so I'll just make Christmas cards if that's all right with you. Those old crayons from the workhouse are a bit worn down but will do for the colouring in. As for the writing, well, I would prefer to write with a pencil. Please, God, I need a pencil.'

Chapter Four

The Twins
1929

Molly Brodie glanced out of the kitchen window, saw the pony and trap turn at the end of the lane, and watched until it was out of sight. The girls had been living with her and her husband for nearly two years now and she was enjoying their company, more so when Dermot was not around. He was growing older and grumpier, disappointed with his sons and dissatisfied with the world at large. Molly enjoyed having her granddaughters to herself.

'Right,' she said, turning round to her granddaughters. 'It's time for us girls to have some fun.'

The twins exchanged looks of excitement and giggled, Anna Marie's face turning pink because going behind her grandfather's back was always a little frightening.

Eyes bright with anticipation, Molly Brodie bent her head to the gramophone and, after winding it up, placed the needle onto the edge of the record.

'Charleston!' she shouted gleefully and proceeded to dance. The girls joined in. This, they'd discovered, was their grandmother's secret sin. She loved to dance. She'd always loved to dance, so she'd told them.

'But your grandfather thinks it's heathen because it came from America some years ago and although all those Irish people have gone over there and say how grand it is, he doesn't think anywhere can be as good as Ireland.'

It had become their habit to wait until he was off into Dunavon to fetch supplies and drink with Roger Casey, the builder. Out would come the record from its secret hiding place, the needle would be inserted and the handle wound up.

Once they'd danced themselves breathless, they collapsed with laughter; the girls huddled around their grandmother's legs.

That's when she would tell them about America and her wish, as a young girl, to go there.

'I thought your grandfather would take me there, but he had a glib tongue. What he promised and his real intentions were two entirely different things.'

The two girls listened avidly; their grandmother was good at describing what this other country was like and they lapped it up.

'Do you know they have the highest buildings in the world? Great big towering things that look as though they're stabbing the passing clouds. And a big statue at the entrance to New York harbour. That's what people have told me and I've no reason to doubt the truth of what they say.'

Sighing with the sadness of unachieved dreams, she laid her head back against the chair and closed her eyes.

'I wonder what my life would have turned out like if your grandfather had been true to his word? Folk that have been there tell me the streets are paved with gold. And that's where they make the pictures you know. That's where Clara Bow, Mary Pickford and Charlie Chaplin live. Not in New York mind you. I hear they live in a place called Hollywood.'

'I think I would like to go there, to America,' said Venetia, her small hand covering the work-worn fingers of her grandmother. 'I think I'd like to be a film star – like Clara Bow.'

She remembered the posters outside the picture houses in London. 'I don't want to stay in Ireland,' she added. 'I want excitement. I want adventure. I want to dance and sing on the stage and in the films.'

Anna Marie eyed her sister timidly. 'I couldn't do that. Sing and dance in front of people.'

'You don't need to,' said Venetia. 'You can come with me. We have to stay together. Always!'

Anna Marie sucked in her lips. Unlike her sister she was predisposed to staying in one place, but her sister was of strong character. Whatever she said, Anna Marie couldn't help falling in with her plans.

'Wait a while and I'll take you to the pictures. I've heard we're going to have a picture show in Dunavon just before Easter. I'll ask your grandfather.'

Their grandmother's promise was forgotten in the work around the farm. First there were spring lambs to take to market and a fresh spring turning into a typical summer of warm days interspersed by rain. The land turned verdant, the animals gave birth to their young and the smell of all things growing made the air rich enough to taste.

Autumn saw the harvesting of the fields, the laying in of winter fodder for the bad weather to come when the grass held no goodness.

Anna Marie loved life on the farm though she tried not to show it to her sister. Venetia had never adjusted to the countryside, but what she did love were her grandmother's tales of a place called Hollywood in a magic land called America.

I'm going to go there one day. I tell you I am,' Venetia declared.

Anna Marie worshipped her sister and always went along with whatever she said. Though they were chalk and cheese, they rarely argued, mainly because Anna Marie always let Venetia have her own way.

Just before Christmas the travelling film show came to town. It was called *The Jazz Singer* and it was the first 'talkie' ever made.

'It was made nearly two years ago back in 1926 and people thought the talkies would never catch on, though apparently all films being made are now talkies. Now there's a thing! I didn't realise we were going to see people actually talking,' their grandmother whispered to them. 'That was what persuaded your grandfather to let us see it. He can't believe it's true and won't believe it until he sees it with his own eyes.'

'Or hears it with his ears,' said Venetia.

Anna Marie was wistful. 'Is it really nearly two years since our mother died?'

She whispered her question, unwilling to upset her grandmother whom she'd grown inordinately fond of.

'Yes,' Venetia snapped. 'Two years living on a farm.'

'It's not so bad.'

'It's not like London.'

'There are no animals in London.'

'There are lights. I like lights,' Venetia countered.

Anna Marie sighed. Sometimes she found it difficult to cope with her sister's attitude. She loved the farm, loved her grandmother and loved the animals. Not that she often admitted the fact to Venetia.

Their grandmother shouted up the stairs that they were ready to see the film show.

'Get down here now or you won't be going.'

Anna Marie immediately set off for the stairs, pausing there to look at her sister.

'Well? Are you coming or not?'

Venetia sucked in her lips.

Anna Marie breathed in deeply, fearing one of her sister's rebellious moods might be coming on.

Venetia sprang into sudden life. 'You wouldn't think I'd want to stay here would you? I'll never want to stay here. I'll tell you that for nothing. We'll leave here. We'll both leave here.'

Anna Marie made no comment. She had no real wish to leave the farm and Ireland, but if Venetia ever did insist on them leaving, she knew she would not have the strength to resist.

Chapter Five

Magda
1929

Snow began falling two days before Christmas. By morning it had thrown a thick blanket over a hushed neighbourhood. Just for once the old houses in Edward Street looked beautiful, like brides attired in wedding finery.

Bridget Brodie's heart was still as frozen as the weather and Magda still hadn't found a pencil in the house, and she so badly wanted to draw a Christmas scene and write a Christmas message. The old crayons were fine for drawing pictures, but she considered writing was best done with a pencil.

Magda had just finished getting the fire to light, when a blow from a chilblained hand flung her away from the feeble flames.

'Bread! We need bread.'

Aunt Bridget pointed at the ill-fitting door. 'Will you git going now and stop staring at me like an ijit?'

The door had twisted with age and barely reached the floor. Snow drifted through the gaps onto the flagstone floor where it melted, and turned into ice overnight.

Magda was beginning to get the measure of her aunt, and although she knew what it might earn her, her eyes flared with loathing.

Bridget saw the look. A face creased with care and cruelty became like an evil mask, all pity devoured by poverty; compassion drowned by selfishness.

Her lips curled back from twisted teeth yellowed with nicotine.

She raised her hand. 'Don't you look at me with yer evil eyes, you dark witch, you.'

'A witch can put a curse on you,' Magda growled.

Her aunt looked at her dumbstruck – and it suddenly occurred to Magda that her aunt was superstitious; she actually believed her.

The moment was short lived. 'Bread!'

A threepenny piece hit the side of her cheek.

'It's snowing again.'

'Never mind the snow, you lazy little foreigner. What's a bit of snow? The likes of me are used to it, and you should get used to it too.'

'You never let me out other times.'

'Less of your back chat!'

'You're only letting me out because it's snowing.'

'Well, the ungratefulness of the child!'

'If I go out in this, then I'm going out other times too.'

Picking up the same blanket that covered her at night, she wound it around her thin form. The blanket had replaced her coat, which Aunt Bridget had decided was too small.

'Sure I'll give it to the nuns down at the convent. They'll give it to someone deserving they will.'

The blanket was old, unwashed and rough against her skin. She didn't care about its roughness, the ragged strips trailing along behind her or the stink of dirt and smoke. It would keep

38

her warm. It would hide who she was and the shame she felt at being so dirty, so shabbily dressed.

Pressing her face against the gap at the side of the door, she felt the chill scything through, frosting her face like a thousand needles. She was aching to get out, but she wasn't going to let her Aunt Bridget know that. She'd been kept a virtual prisoner for a whole year.

The snow came up to her knees, soaking her skirt, her worn stockings and her canvas boots. The boots were suitable for summer or a clement climate, not for an English winter. Her winter boots had gone the same way as her coat in reality, paying for a second-hand fox fur for her aunt that stunk like a skunk and had rabid glass eyes.

Warily, like a rabbit emerging from a burrow, Magda scrutinised her surroundings. Being locked up for so long had made her nervous of going out.

Thanks to the snowfall, the alley was deserted. There were no gentlemen callers across the way and there would be none until the snow had melted and the roads were passable.

The sound of trams running on their twisted rails came from some way off on the main road into East London. Except for a few horse-drawn delivery carts, the trams had the road to themselves without the hindrance of the buses, which were gradually taking their place.

Hurrying was difficult, each step taking a great deal of effort, raising one leg out of the snow, down into it again, repeating the process with aching legs and chilled bones. Her breath came in hot steaming gasps. Her chest tightened with each cold breath and the snow fell heavier like a curtain of thick lace before her eyes.

*

Winnie One Leg hated cold weather. It made her bad leg ache even if she wasn't moving around or out in it.

Pursing her upper lip she removed a heated penny from the window pane and looked out. What she saw caused her to hold her breath. The snow was embellishing the mean buildings with an elegance they did not usually possess. Crumbling buildings with jutting first floors suddenly looked magical.

'Like an old woman in a fine white cloak,' she murmured to herself.

It wasn't as though she hadn't seen such a scene before and she'd expected the whiteness, the grey sky, and the sudden beautification of lop-sided houses and grim narrow streets. She had not expected to see a monstrous cloak, moving seemingly of its own accord.

What she'd perceived to be a cloak was, on reflection, a blanket. The figure struggling to get itself and the blanket through the snow was far from adult.

The pretty little girl living with Bridget Brodie.

So the Connemara mare, the name they all knew Bridget Brodie by, had let the girl out. Somebody pointed out that the breed was one of the prettiest ponies in the British Isles and it was an insult to compare the two. Somebody else had remarked that the child's name was Magda.

Bridget Brodie was a hard woman. Winnie had seen her screaming and beating her husband James Brodie with a broken chair leg. It wouldn't come as any surprise that the child was receiving the same treatment. For one solitary moment she shared the child's pain, rubbing at her twisted leg, rueing the day she'd ever got involved with the likes of Reuben Fitts.

She blinked away the memory. What was done was done, though she bitterly regretted what had happened. If only she'd had the courage to stand up to him and demanded he called a doctor when she was screaming in labour, unable to bring the child forth. But there. Water under Waterloo Bridge. All in the past.

Her thoughts and her eyes went back to the Brodie child. What kind of future could she look forward to? Not one she deserved if Bridget Brodie had anything to do with it.

None of your business, Winnie One Leg.

Hugging the warmth of the loaf close to her ribs beneath the scruffy blanket, Magda pressed on. The snow was deep on the ground, each step painfully slow. Her calves ached with the effort. Her eyes were blinded by snow and a biting wind.

Narrowing her eyes she looked for a landmark pointing the way back to her aunt's house. There to her right was the Red Cow, to her left the coffin makers, a light shining from a small window, snow heaped up in drifts against the door.

There was not another soul in sight and the whole world seemed to have fallen silent; no sound from the pub, none from the workshops of the coffin maker.

A drift of snow, pure white and unsullied by footprints or cart tracks, suddenly moved then split open. Four ragged figures emerged like carrion chicks from a single, shattered egg. Boys. Four boys.

Magda backed away, her small hand held high, palm facing her attackers. 'Touch me and I curse you.'

Her voice was true and clear, slicing through the cold air like a meat cleaver through butter.

She wasn't sure she could curse them, but her aunt had told her she was cursed; cursed with foreign blood and the daughter of a witch. So what if she played the part? Well, if these louts believed it too, so much the better.

Moving sharply to avoid her attackers she dislodged the hood of torn blanket that had covered her head.

No longer covered by the scrap of blanket, a shock of silky

black hair fanned out around the girl's face, the wind making it into long, gauzy streamers, as fine and floating as butterfly wings. The boys paused, their rags blown aside by the wind exposing dirty knees and thin legs. One of the boys was wearing what looked like the coat of a merchant seaman with brass buttons and a torn hem. It reached to his grey socks, which lay in folds around his ankles.

Watching from her window, Winnie shook her head. If the girl would just throw the bread down, they might leave her alone. With the exception of the Fitts boy, the tallest and strongest of the group, the others were from poor families. Fitts's son would be their ringleader, of stockier build than the others and possessing his father's arrogant gait, his shoulders rolling from side to side as he took measured paces towards the girl.

There was no reason for Winnie to be noticed for she made no sound and barely moved.

'None of my business,' she muttered and spit into a lace-edged handkerchief.

She was about to turn away, to go into the parlour and tidy it up ready for visitors when a memory came to her.

The vision was familiar, though usually it only surfaced in the dead of night.

Shaking her head she mopped the sweat from her brow with the back of her mitten-clad hand. Why had it suddenly come to her and why did it make her feel this way? What did that snippet of a girl and her own long-endured nightmare have in common?

Her eyes, blurred with sudden moistness, went back to the window. The frost curtailed clear vision, the small hole too small to see much, but she knew what was happening out there. The weak would be in danger of going under. The loaf would be taken from her and she'd be left cut and bruised, and that was before Bridget Brodie got hold of her. And as for that brat Bradley Fitts . . .

Before she even had time to consider what she was doing, her gnarled fingers, as knobbly and thin as winter twigs, were wrestling with the door bolt.

Liberally smeared with goose grease, the bolt slid back easily, the door flung open and the snow and cold of the outside, plus a small girl wrapped in a worn blanket, fell in, still clutching a loaf of bread.

Winnie waved her stick at some of the poorest, most wretched boys in the city, and that singularly wicked one, Bradley Fitts. Like his father he bullied the destitute with promises of taking whatever they wanted from them that had.

Winnie was like a fury in old-fashioned black shawl and dark purple dress, waving her stick and yelling at the top of her voice.

'Away with you devils or I'll be setting the Peelers on you.'

At the sight of her, it was Bradley Fitts who shot off first. One thing he didn't do was take the blame for anything. He left lesser mortals to do that.

'Bread, Winnie. Bread!'

The boy who shouted wore a navy blue coat, had tousled hair and a little more meat on his bones than the others.

She started to close the door.

'Anything . . .'

His voice was pleading. She knew his name was Edward Shellard and that his father worked on the docks unloading ships from all over the empire. She also knew there were ten children in the family and that his mother seemed to have spent most of her life with a pregnant belly. If that wasn't problem enough, when he wasn't working, George Shellard could be found in the Shipwrights Arms down by the East India Docks.

She reached for the remains of a heel of a loaf, returned to the door and threw it out, crumbs and all, making indents in the snow. The boys fell on the scraps, shouting and scrabbling in the snow. Winnie shut the door, feeling strange, wondering if she was getting softer in her old age.

The same grey eyes that had regarded her earlier regarded her once again. Magda seemed all eyes looking up at her.

'That was kind of you. Good fortune happens to people who are kind.' Her voice was clear and pure, and so very much more confident than she'd expected it to be.

Placing her gnarled fists on her hips, Winnie looked the girl up and down admiringly, then nodded like the wise old bird some said she was. 'Your eyes will be your fortune, my girl. Magda Brodie, isn't it?'

Magda nodded, her gaze drawn to the obvious deformity of Winnie's hands.

'Your hands are painful. I expect they're worse at night.'

It occurred to her that the child had spoken as though she was years older than either of them.

'And you're skinny. The Connemara mare doesn't feed you enough,' said Winnie.

Magda frowned. 'Is that what you call her?'

Winnie threw back her head and laughed. 'An Irish nag, and I think your Uncle Jim would confirm that your aunt Bridget Brodie is both a nag and a mare and that's the truth!'

'My aunt hates me and hated my mother. If my mother hadn't died I wouldn't be here.'

The child's grey eyes seemed to fill her face; such a forth-right look, her chin uplifted and jutting forward.

'My full name is Magdalena Brodie. My mother came from Italy where it's sunny all the time and people sing and dance on saints' days. I'm not staying here forever. My father will come for me – soon – and one day I shall be a lady.'

Winnie stared in wonder at the sudden brightness in the

child's face. Such a lovely face. Such a lovely child.

In her mind she was already assessing the wealth such a girl could bring to her establishment, catering to the men callers like the other girls. It was, well, worth thinking about.

'Do you wish to be a lady?'

The dark grey eyes turned thoughtful. 'That depends. I would like to be clean and have nice things. And be kind to people. And make sick people well again. Yes,' she said, nodding resolutely.

'You don't have to live with her if you don't want to. How would it be if I had a word with your aunt and got her to agree to you moving in here?' Her voice was as smooth as oil as she watched the girl with one eye shut.

The girl gave her such a direct look that would be more at home on somebody three times her age.

'It's much warmer here and you're very kind, but my father told me to stay with her and when he comes back he'll expect me to be there.'

Magda's strong little chin jerked forward. 'Anyway, I couldn't possibly move in here unless she gives me my mother's Bible. It's got the addresses of my sisters and brother.'

Winnie nodded slowly. 'Of course. Would you like some mutton stew?'

Magda nodded.

'Sit you down,' said Winnie, the last traces of a Liverpool accent still in her voice.

Magda sat on a balloon-backed chair pulled up to the table whilst Winnie ladled hot stew from black saucepan to white china dish.

Winnie watched as she ate.

'Is it good?'

Her mouth full of food, Magda nodded and finally managed to mumble that yes, it was good. Very good.

Winnie continued to eye the child, loving the way she

smiled at her between each mouthful, finding a strange peace in the joyfulness of Magda's face.

Some deep-seated instinct told Winnie to ignore her plan to bring the child into her house even though her virginity alone would bring a small fortune. And she knew many men who would pay that fortune, though not yet, not until the girl had become a young woman – fourteen at least.

It had been this way for a long while. Once her own beauty and thus her means of making money had gone, she'd employed the beauty of others to make her a living. This girl was already a beauty. How long would it take to subdue her to the rules of the house – if she could be coerced into submission that is?

Magda, she decided, was strong willed, just as she had been. She found herself wondering whether her own baby daughter would have been so. A sudden tightness seemed to claw at her heart as the painful memory bloomed large and beautiful in her mind.

Reuben Fitts hadn't cared a toss about their dead child and once he'd seen her hip, damaged as a result of the difficult labour, he'd lost interest.

He'd used her and abused her. Love didn't come into it, though power and having control over another human being did.

He'd said he'd loved her and that if she loved him, she would lay with other men. But the child had been his though he chose to deny it.

Losing him, losing a baby and losing her living had made her harder and deeper of thought. That was when it had come to her that the twentieth century, with its motor cars, its aeroplanes and other wondrous things, was little different than other centuries. As in the past, women were either servants or chattels and it had to be worse for women who were different. They could opt to be servants all their lives or opt to be wives and mothers, worn out by the time they were thirty and never in charge of their lives. What if she gave them another option?

'You're welcome to move in any time you like and free to leave when you like. As my girls will tell you, 'tis safe under my roof. They're doted on by their gentlemen callers and dressed in the finest clothes – ladies every one.'

Winnie waited, unsure whether the girl was hers just yet, though not sure she wanted her to be. Something else was eating at her. The memory of her baby daughter's death had never plagued her before as it did now. It had happened such a long time ago, when she was young and beautiful with her whole life ahead of her. She wasn't that old now, though she certainly looked it. The years had not been kind and some had been downright cruel.

Magda finally finished eating, put down the spoon and rubbed at her full belly.

'My mother cooked stews like this before she got sick.'

'Is that so,' said Winnie, leaning forward, both gnarled hands resting on her walking stick. 'Tell me about your mother and your family. I'd love to hear all about them.'

At first it seemed as though Magda was unwilling, but then it all came out. Magda told her about her mother, about her absent father and the sisters and brother that she badly missed and the wonderful Christmas that they'd had and would have again.

As she listened, Winnie's thoughts returned to that dead baby, born in pieces into a harsh, unforgiving world. If the child – a girl – had lived, she might well have been like Magda – not so much in looks perhaps, but lost. Alone. At the mercy of others . . .

Magda tossed her head. Her look was forthright. 'My father

left enough money with Mrs Brodie to keep me until he comes back. There's not much left. If he doesn't come back quickly she'll throw me out on the street.'

Pushing compassion to the back of her mind, a slow smile crossed the wrinkled old face of Winnie One Leg. 'Well. We can't let that happen, my dear, can we?'

Chapter Six

Michael
1929

Aubrey and Eleanor Darby looked at each other as though they were the luckiest people on earth.

'Mr Brodie has signed the necessary papers at long last. As you no doubt appreciate, being a seagoing man, it was difficult tracking him down. But everything is now in order. The child is legally yours.'

Samuel Lehman, the dark small man who had handled their transaction, eyed them from over the top of half-moon spectacles. Not entirely happy with the conditions of the transaction, he considered the middle-aged and childless couple would work out the kindest parents an adopted toddler could ever have.

'I've sent the money to the address Mr Brodie gave me – a sailors' home in Dover. I must reiterate what I already told you: that you didn't have to hand over any more money. You could have used a suitable adoption society – and I know that as a man of the cloth you should have access to such organisations.'

'The money was inherited from my father,' explained Eleanor Darby. 'I'm sure he would approve of the transaction.

He so wanted a grandchild. We couldn't give him one whilst he was alive, but now he's procured one for us.'

Samuel nodded. 'I quite understand.'

Actually he understood them very well, but what he couldn't understand was how the father of the child, Joseph Brodie, could have sold his son as one might sell a tract of land, a house or a bicycle.

Samuel himself had two sons and a daughter. He'd never dream of selling any of them; he'd rather sell the blood from his veins than the fruit of his loins.

'I take it the boy is doing well?'

Reverend and Mrs Darby exchanged looks, joy shining in their eyes.

'Very well indeed.'

'And the move?'

'Excellent,' said Aubrey Darby. 'I think we've been extremely lucky. Blessed with a child and a move to a new parish in the country. I think God has indeed smiled on us.'

Samuel Lehman came from behind his desk and offered his hand.

'Reverend Darby. Mrs Darby. I wish you all the luck in the world. May God bless your family. May Michael grow up fit, strong and a credit to you – as I am sure he will.'

As they hailed a taxi, Eleanor Darby squeezed her husband's hand.

'I'm so glad that's over with. Michael is ours now, isn't he?'

Aubrey Darby opened the door of the taxi so his wife could get in first.

'Of course he is.'

His wife looked at him with worried eyes. 'And no one will ever take him away from us? His father has no further claim on him?'

'Of course not.' Her husband assured her, relieved though

that he had privately instructed Samuel about their change of address and received the gentleman's assurance of client confidentiality. He had never met Joseph Brodie but the type of man who would sell his own child was probably one ruthless enough to try to extort more money in time. He was glad that he was removing his new family out of Brodie's reach.

Chapter Seven

Magda
1928

Days of freedom were too few and far between for Magda's liking. It occurred to her that she could make use of her aunt's superstitious nature, though that by itself might not be enough. The fact was she had to play on what her aunt had turned her into – a weak, starved, scruffy creature who was getting thinner day by day.

On a night when her aunt had wolfed down a mutton chop for her supper and Magda had eaten precious little all day, she fainted.

She heard her aunt screech. 'Mary, Mother of God!'

She lay inert. Only when she was sure she had her aunt's total attention did she deign to open her eyes.

'What's the matter with you? What's the matter?'

Although she could get up if she wanted to, Magda chose not to. 'I'm . . . so . . . hungry . . .'

'Oh my God, oh my God, oh my God. Get up girl. Get up.'

'I feel so faint,' Magda whispered. 'I think . . . I'm . . . dying . . . and I may curse . . .'

Her aunt's eyes flickered with a mix of fear and concern. She was scared. Scared Magda was going to die, scared of what Joseph Brodie would say if she did and just as frightened of being cursed from beyond the grave.

'There's a mutton chop left. I'll cook it up for you. That I will.'

She was off in a whirl of nervous movement, muttering prayers and expletives that cursed Joseph Brodie and the fact that the lard in the frying pan smelled of fish.

Magda lay almost inert, not pulling herself up into a sitting position until she could smell the chop cooking. She wouldn't care a jot if the mutton was tinged with a fishy taste; she'd enjoy it just the same, but more than that; she'd scored a small triumph over her selfish Aunt Bridget.

'It'll have to be bread with it,' said Aunt Bridget as she sawed away at a day-old loaf. 'And I'll pour the juices into it. That should bring her round,' she was saying to herself. 'That'll put her to rights.'

It was undoubtedly the best meal Magda had had since moving in with her aunt.

The Connemara mare, she thought, as she eyed her aunt over the doorstep of chewy mutton and bread soaked in the meat juices.

That night she slept soundly and in the morning her aunt was making tea, scraping dripping onto toast and sprinkling it with salt.

'Get that down you. Now look,' she said, holding the carving knife as though it were a sword. 'I can't feed you much on what yer father sends me. When he sends it! So you'll have to scavenge for bits and pieces under the carts and stalls up in the square.'

'Square?' Magda said weakly, her movements painfully slow as though she had no energy left in her body.

53

'End of the street goes into the square. There's a bit of a market there. All you have to do is crawl under the stalls and pick up the stuff that's fallen underneath. Bring back enough to make a stew. Now get that dripping inside you and git going.'

Magda could barely believe what she was hearing; after all this time she was being given a bit of freedom.

The very thought of going outside gave her new strength. Her blood flowed to her legs, which before had felt weak as though her bones had turned to mashed potato.

Just as she was thinking that she needn't come back at all, Aunt Bridget caught hold of her arm.

'In case you're thinking of doing a runner, remember the other brats and your mother's Bible. It's under lock and key. I've hid it.'

It was true. The old cow – or old mare according to Winnie One Leg, had recently hidden the Bible. Magda couldn't – wouldn't – leave until she had that in her hands.

The wind was cold and Magda threw back her head and took great gulps of air. Freedom. What a heady taste it was!

Edward Street came out into Beatrice Place, which in turn came out onto Victoria Square. The whole area was awash with people ebbing backwards and forwards in an endless tide. And the noise! The noise was lively and seemed almost to warm the very air.

At the centre of the square was a small park enclosed by green painted railings – nothing much more than a lawn, a few bushes and a couple of benches.

Two shops, a barber and a haberdasher, were on one side of the square and a pub was at each corner. One of them was the Red Cow, much frequented by her Aunt Bridget. The other, the Coopers Arms.

All around the park, squashed between the buildings and a sliver of road, were all manner of stalls run by barrow boys, all shouting out for custom whilst tossing a cabbage from hand to hand or, in the case of the man selling fish, a whole herring.

For a moment she stood in wonder drinking in the colour, the noise and the cheerful smiles and nods of loud-voiced men and demanding women.

So engrossed was she, that she was only faintly aware of someone watching her.

'Hey little lady. Can I interest you in a pound of Cox's?'

The boy who addressed her was a few years older than Magda, with dancing blue eyes and hair that was thick and dark and curled over his collar. He was tossing a small apple from one hand to another.

An older man was at the other end of the stall serving a fat woman in a tight-fitting coat and a battered old hat.

The boy saw her look at the stuff beneath his stall; the discarded cabbage leaves, the escaped potatoes and carrots, some bruised and unfit to be sold.

Despite her hunger, Magda's pride got the better of her. No way would she become a beggar, scrabbling on all fours in front of the dark-haired boy with the dancing eyes.

'Off for a pint, Danny,' said the older man on the stall with him, pulling his cap more firmly onto his head.

'Safe in me 'ands, Dad. Safe as 'ouses in me 'ands.'

The boy's father ambled off in the direction of the Red Cow. Once he was safely out of sight, Danny called her over.

'You look as though you could do with a plate of King Edwards,' he said to her.

'King Edwards?'

'Spuds. Taters. In fact by the looks of you, it's more than spuds you need.'

He glanced in the direction his father had gone, the apple still in his hand. 'If you can catch this, I won't say a word if you take what you want from beneath the stall. 'Ere, you can even 'ave a sack to put it all in. And I'll add a bit to it. Nearly the end of the morning and we leave 'ere at one. No point letting it go to waste is there?'

He lifted up a sack that looked to be made of orange string.

'Well?' he said.

Her eyes fixed on the apple. When he threw it, she caught it easily.

His grin was wide. 'There you are. Take what you like.'

He threw her the sack. She caught that too. She could have bitten into the apple straightaway, but she didn't. The thought of all the discarded vegetables turned into soup made her mouth water but her stubborn pride held her back.

'Come on, little 'un. I'll give you a hand.'

'I'm not that little.'

'How old are you?'

'Eleven.'

'I'm nearly fourteen, so to me you're only a little 'un. Nice little 'un though,' he said with a grin.

His grin was so reassuring that she didn't hesitate then to scrabble around with him beneath the stall.

Cabbage leaves, potatoes, carrots, onions, turnips and cauliflower – it all went into the sack. So did some fruit, though only items that hadn't got too squashed.

He got out from beneath the stall before she did, but before she popped out, his face appeared again, hanging upside down. He had something in his hand.

'Pig's tail,' he said to her. 'My old mum makes a nice stew with a few of these.'

She crawled out and faced him. He was rubbing the pig's tail against the zig-zag pattern of his Fair Isle pullover.

'It got pinched by a dog from the butcher over there, but I chased 'im off. Was going to give it to me old mum, but she wouldn't like the fact that the dog 'ad it in 'is mouth or that I picked it up from the ground. Fussy, my old mum. I ain't so fussy. I'd eat it without a second thought. You ain't so fussy, are ya?'

He winked at her.

His cheek made her smile.

'Beggars can't be choosers.'

'You ain't a beggar. You're too pretty and speak too nicely to ever be a beggar.'

'P'raps I am for now. You have to do what you have to do,' she replied. The words fell out and she suddenly recalled where she'd heard them before. They were her mother's words. Thinking of her made her eyes sting.

The pig's tail was shoved into her bag and Danny followed it up with a couple of oranges.

She felt shy thanking him. 'You're very kind.'

'I'm only kind to people I like. Any time you're down 'ere, you come and see me. Danny Rossi. Always 'ere, girl. Every day.'

'Isn't that an Italian name?'

He looked surprised. 'Yeah. Now 'ow would you know that?'

'My mother was Italian.'

Magda decided that one look at Danny Rossi and the most miserable person couldn't help but smile, though perhaps with the exception of Aunt Bridget.

'Is this your stall?' she asked him.

'My dad's.'

'So you help him out.'

'For the moment. I have to do what I have to do and this is what I have to do right now. Won't always do it though. I've got plans. Believe me I've got plans.'

'What plans?'

'Plans to be better than what I am. Plans to be important and useful.' He winked. 'And to wear a uniform. I want to be like 'im.'

He pulled a battered novel from his back pocket and flicked his fingers at the lurid cover. Magda read the title.

Barton on the Beat.

'I read loads of Bob Barton books. He's a London copper.'

'So you want to be a policeman?'

'Shhh,' he hissed, placing a finger before his lips. 'Not so loud. Don't let anyone round 'ere hear you saying that. They'd think me a traitor – selling 'em out so to speak. Still, beats selling fruit and vegetables.'

'Selling fruit and vegetables is useful – where would we be without them?'

He threw back his head and laughed, which had the effect of sending his overlong hair spreading around his neck like a collar.

Magda frowned as a very serious thought occurred to her. 'Will you find missing persons, things like that?'

'You bet I will, though to start off with it'll probably be just lost dogs. Why do you ask?'

She told him about wanting to find her family.

'Could you help me find them?'

He looked taken aback. Reading about being a police detective and actually playing the part were two different things.

Magda misinterpreted. 'I can't pay you anything so can't ask you to look for them for me, but if you could tell me what to do, how to find missing people, I would be really grateful.'

'I'm not a policeman yet.'

'No, but you will be. And you're sure to be good at it after reading all those Bob Barton books.'

'Well.' He scratched the back of his head as he thought about it. 'I s'pose it wouldn't hurt to get me hand in so to speak. Tell you what, let me 'ave a think and I'll see what I can come up with. Trot along 'ere tomorrow about half an hour earlier than now. I'll take my break and we can 'ave a bite to eat together over on the seat there. 'Ow would that be?'

She eyed him warily, wondering if he was making fun or really serious.

'You mean it? You're not making fun of me because I'm only a child and a lot younger than you?'

Looking seriously impressed, he shook his head. 'No. Of course not. Now go on, clear off before I change me mind.'

She thought about asking if he had a pencil she could borrow, but didn't want to push her luck.

She dashed round the corner into Beatrice Street so fast that she collided with what seemed like a green wall in front of her.

'Blimey, you're in a hurry. Been a fire or something?'

Magda looked up into a face that was round as a pumpkin above a dark green jacket and knee-length pleated skirt. There was something youthful about that face, as though the owner wasn't much more than a child forced through circumstance to grow up too early.

Magda recognised her as one of the girls from the grand house across the road.

'Looks like you done all right for yourself,' said the girl, nodding down at the orange string sack.

'It was all free. From underneath the stall. I didn't pinch anything and Danny Rossi gave me a pig's tail. I'm going to make a stew.'

'Well, aren't you the one! Going back now are ya?'

Magda nodded and thought how beautiful the young woman smelt. Roses. Flowers anyway.

'My mother used to wear a hat like yours,' said Magda, glad of someone to talk to besides Bridget Brodie. Not that she ever talked – not really. Just shouted.

'Do you like it?'

Magda nodded.

The mustard hat reminded Magda of one her mother used to wear – a cloche she'd called it, but Magda had always called it her tulip hat because that's what the shape reminded her of – a tulip – a dark red one in her mother's case, not mustard like this one.

'Your name's Magda, innit?'

Magda nodded. 'It's short for Magdalena. Magdalena Brodie.'

'Mine's Emily. Emily Crocker. I'll walk back with you if you like. That sack looks a bit heavy. Wanna hand?'

Magda shook her head and cradled the sack in her arms.

'Looks a nice lot you've got there. Bet you got everything you wanted.'

Magda chewed her lip. 'Everything except a pencil. I really do need a pencil. And some new crayons if I could get some, but I can manage with my old ones though they are a bit worn down.'

She didn't add that even if she had located a pencil, she hadn't any money to pay for it.

'Is that all? I think I could find you one. You live over in the house opposite with that old . . .'

'Connemara mare.'

'Oh. So you already know what we all call her. Old cow if what I heard about her is right. Been carrying on with the landlord of the Red Cow, and 'im with a sick wife upstairs and likely put away before long.'

'What does that mean? Carrying on?'

'Well,' said Emily taking a deep breath. 'It's like skipping with somebody else's skipping rope when you don't have their permission to use it.'

Magda eyed her, open mouthed. 'Shouldn't she be confessing all that to the priest?'

Emily burst out laughing. 'Well, I should think it would

give the old priest something to entertain his quiet moments.'

Magda laughed with her. It just seemed the right thing to do.

'I've seen you looking out of the window,' said Emily. 'Don't go out much do you?'

Despite her threadbare appearance, Magda held her head high. 'My aunt wouldn't let me but I will do from now on. I pretended to faint from hunger so she told me to go out and find some food for myself. She told me my father hadn't left enough to feed me on. Mind you, she makes sure she don't go hungry.'

'Yeah, and she gets that for free, down at the Red Cow, food and drink for services rendered,' Emily said with a laugh. 'So. What do you want the pencil for? Writing to somebody are you?'

It all came flooding out. Magda told her about her family and how they'd last been together at Christmas last year. She also told her about the letters she wrote regularly on sausage paper and her plan to make her own Christmas cards to send to her siblings.

'I can't really send them because I don't know where they are without their addresses. But I thought I could keep them for when we do eventually meet up.'

Emily smiled down at her. 'I think that's a lovely idea. I'm surprised that old . . .' She checked herself. 'Your aunt . . .'

'It's all right. You can call her an old cow or the Connemara mare. She calls you tarts. Sluts and whores who sell their bodies to men that they might fornicate with them in unholy nakedness.'

Emily's jaw dropped. 'Bloody hell. Sounds like a sermon from the pulpit don't it. And like the pot calling the kettle black. Reckon it don't matter if I call 'er names then does it?'

Magda shook her head. 'What does fornicate mean?'

Emily burst out laughing.

'It's something men think they're good at.'

'But they're not?'

Emily was still grinning. 'No, they just like to think they are.'

'I'm glad to have somebody to converse with.'

'Converse? Well, that's a long word.'

'I like words. I'm glad I've spoken to you. Because I haven't been out of the house, I haven't spoken to anyone else in ages. I thought I might never be able to speak again, but I have and that's good.'

Emily cocked her head to one side and her face was all smiles.

'Don't ever lose your voice, girl. You've got a pretty voice. Different than what I 'ear round 'ere. I thought you'd speak a bit Irish like yer aunt, but you don't.'

'My mother was Italian. She was careful how she spoke English because she wasn't born to it.'

Emily nodded carefully as though she were thinking deep thoughts.

'I can find you a pencil,' she said at last. 'How about I pop it over to you when the old cow's gone to the pub?'

'She locks the door when she goes out,' Magda said, her tone not so merry as they got closer to the gloomy house in Edward Street.

'Never mind. I can pass it under the door to you. How would that be?'

In her mind's eye, Magda visualised the ill-fitting door.

'The gap beneath the door is big enough to push a pencil under.'

'Big enough to push a bit of decent paper and card under too? Paper for your letters, card for your cards.'

Magda was staring into the street, her stomach churning.

Her steps slowed. She really didn't want to go back into that house, but the Bible with those addresses inside was there.

Seeing the stiffening of Magda's face, Emily slowed her steps too.

'How come you're not at school?'

Magda hunched her shoulders and heaved a big sigh. 'She won't let me go. She won't let me read either. Says all I'm fit for is to scrub floors. Mostly her floors. But I'm working on getting her to let me go to school. There has to be somebody who can make her let me go, don't you think?'

Emily Crocker narrowed her eyes. She had a mind to inter- fere, but no doubt Winnie One Leg would tell her to mind her own business. Out of the corner of her eyes she could see Winnie now, trying not to be seen but there all the same, sneaking a peek out of the window.

'Leave the pencils and stuff with me. I can find something a bit better than the paper used to wrap sausages. Bit smelly,' she said, her dark eyes shining as she wrinkled her nose.

Despite the cold wind and her grumbling stomach, Magda suddenly felt warmer.

'That would be lovely. Really lovely. Thank you.'

True to her promise, Emily Crocker waited until she saw Bridget Brodie on her way to the Red Cow. Her lips were red, her cheeks were rouged and she was wearing a fur coat that Emily reckoned really belonged to the invalid landlady of the Red Cow.

'Look at 'er,' she said to the other girls. 'Done up like a dog's dinner. And she got the nerve to call us slappers!'

'Fur coat and no knickers,' said her best friend Betty Cooper and went back to fastening a sequin-covered hair net over her crinkly dark hair.

'I'm no expert, but I reckon that kid should be at school,' said Emily. 'I weren't going to say anything because . . .'

'It's none of your business,' said Winnie One Leg.

'I knew you'd say that,' muttered Emily. 'I'm nipping over there in a minute to shove this under the door.'

Winnie peered at the pencil and paper and sniffed. 'Can't do no harm. Just make sure the Connemara mare's left the end of the street before you do it. You know how she is; any excuse to call the rozzers.'

'Shouldn't we be calling somebody out to sort her – you know – the people who deal with child welfare?'

Winnie One Leg didn't respond straight away. She was looking across the street, aware of a small shadow impairing the light from within.

'Very likely,' she said thoughtfully.

The girls exchanged shrugs and pulled faces. Winnie had something on her mind. Winnie could pull strings.

By the light of a street lamp Magda saw Emily Crocker sprinting across the road as fast as her court shoes could carry her.

Magda pulled the draught excluder – no more than an old stocking smelling of her aunt and stuffed with newspaper – away from the bottom of the door.

A cold draught came in first. Her eyes opened wide with delight as not one but three pencils were pushed underneath it, rolling around on top of a piece of stiff white cardboard and a writing pad. To her great joy an unopened box of crayons came in behind it.

It didn't matter that the cardboard looked as though it had once been part of a shoe or shirt box. It didn't matter that she'd have to cut the bits of card into shape just as she had the butcher's paper. She had everything she wanted.

Wiser than to leave it downstairs in case her aunt returned unexpectedly, she went upstairs and replaced the butcher's paper beneath her pillow with some of the card.

Lizzie Lane

After cutting and folding a piece of card in half, she drew a fat robin on the front and wrote 'Merry Christmas' across the top.

What to write inside took more thought. Whilst thinking about it, she coloured in the robin; brown feathers, a red breast, black dot eyes and little yellow legs. Making the white background look like snow was more difficult, but patches of blue crayon seemed to work.

At last she opened up the card, picked up her pencil and wrote simply but sincerely.

'To my sisters, Venetia and Anna Marie and my little brother, Mikey. I'm missing you very much. I can't send this card today cos I have no stamps and don't know where you are. I will keep it safe until I can give it to you. Love, Magda.'

Chapter Eight

Magda

'You need to make a list,' said Danny. 'A list of the facts as you know them and the people connected with the last time you saw your family.'

They were sitting on a bench in the middle of Victoria Square sharing Danny's cheese sandwiches.

Magda swallowed the very tasty piece of bread and cheese she'd been chewing.

'The facts?'

'Like your old man leaving you with your aunt. That's a fact. Likewise 'im going off to sea. That's a fact too. Then there's the money he's supposed to be sending – or not sending as the case may be. How does she receive it? Does it come through the post? Is there a return address? Or does somebody deliver it direct into her hands? Or does she collect it from somewhere or somebody? That's the facts you've got to find out.'

'That seems very wise.'

Danny looked pleased. 'It's the way Bob Barton does it. Set out the facts and deduce the evidence.'

'I see.'

Danny passed her another sandwich.

'Once we've sorted that out, we think about the people most likely to know the whereabouts of your sisters and brother – that's besides the old witch you live with. Right?'

She nodded. 'There's Uncle James. He might know. I've not met him yet.'

'I'll make a note of that.'

Danny flicked the bread and cheese crumbs off the piece of paper on which he'd written his analysis of Magda's situation.

'Next I think we need to make enquiries at the workhouse you were in. They might have some idea.'

Magda swallowed and set her sandwich down. Suddenly she didn't feel like eating.

'My mother died there.'

He patted her hand then gave it a squeeze.

'There were nice people there too. I remember a lady. Miss Burton. She was kind to us. She told me that normally we would have had to go to the orphanage, but seeing as it was Christmas she arranged for us to stay there until our father came to fetch us.'

'And last but not least, we come to your father,' said Danny after ticking off the former deduction. 'Is there some way of finding out what ship he was on?'

Magda shrugged. 'I don't know.'

Daniel glanced around him as though afraid of some menacing presence overhearing what he was about to say.

'I've had a word with somebody in the know,' he said, tapping the side of his nose. 'He reckons that if you know the name of the ship or even the shipping company, they will let relatives know the name of the ship said relative has signed on. This last course of action is only to be resorted to if all the others run up against the buffers. I mean, there's a chance your aunt receives the money through a shipping company. If that's the case, then we've got 'im cornered.'

Magda sat quietly thoughtful, her sandwich lying untouched on her lap.

'I'm not sure my father sends any money and I've heard Aunt Bridget say that she never knows from one week to the next what ship Uncle James is on, so it would be the same for my father.'

'Ah!'

'I need to go there.'

'You do? Um. Where exactly?'

'The workhouse. I want to go there and ask them if they know anything.'

'Great. I've got the afternoon off, we can both go there if you like,' said Danny, brimming with enthusiasm. 'Right. Now which workhouse would we be talking about?'

Magda looked at him startled. 'Is there more than one?'

Danny rubbed at his eyes. 'I'm afraid so. There's a lot of poor in London and I did 'ear that a lot of them 'ave closed down. Still, we can always check can't we – as long as we know the name. Do you know the name?'

Hearing Danny's plans had raised her spirits. Those spirits were now dashed. She shook her head, tears of anguish stinging her eyes.

'I can't remember.'

They arranged to meet again once she'd had time to think things over. Her new friend was reassuring.

'Memory is a funny thing. You think you've forgotten something and suddenly it pops up when you least expect it. It'll 'appen to you, girl. No doubt about it.'

Danny was so self-assured she couldn't help but believe him.

The day after it really did seem as though things were changing for the better. It began with a loud hammering on the front door.

Bridget Brodie wasn't expecting anyone, so assumed who-ever it was had got the wrong house.

'Go away. This is a respectable house. You'll be wanting over the road.'

Whoever it was took no notice but gave the door another series of knocks that reverberated throughout the house.

'Whoever you are, you're going to get a piece of my mind,' snarled Aunt Bridget finally raising herself from her chair where she'd been picking horses from the newspaper for that afternoon's racing at Kempton Park.

Head bristling with steel curlers and a cigarette hanging from her mouth, she dragged open the door.

The man standing there was slight of stature, had sharp fea-tures and the expression a wasp might have when it felt the urge to sting.

He wore a bowler hat, a dull beige trench coat and smelled of mothballs.

With an air of authority, he brought out a leather-bound folder from beneath his arm.

'Mrs Brodie? I'm Mr Archibald Campion, inspector for the local school board. I understand there's a child in here that is not attending school. I trust you can give me a good reason for her non-attendance at Prewett Lane School?'

Aunt Bridget's jaw dropped like a two-pound iron and her metal curlers rattled as she opened her mouth to splutter a lie.

'You've been misinformed. There's no girl . . .'

The lie might have gone on if she hadn't realised that Magda was standing behind her, just visible in the gloomily drab interior.

She gave it another try.

'Sure, it's my niece and she's only here for a short while until her father comes back from the sea.'

The school inspector fixed her with shrewish eyes that

narrowed beneath hairless eyebrows above a long, hooked nose.

'That's not what I've been told, Mrs Brodie and I will caution you here and now that you will be summoned to court if you continue to keep the child from school. Now if you will please confirm her name . . .'

'Her name's Magda . . . as if that's important . . .'

'Very important. In fact from information received, I understand that her full name is Magdalena Brodie and that her mother is deceased. Is that right?'

Bridget Brodie's mouth gulped open and shut like a fish out of water.

She did not give in easily to intimidation, but people in authority were the notable exception. They were better educated than her, better dressed and spoke as though their tongues were laced with honey. They also had the law on their side.

'Are you listening to what I'm saying, Mrs Brodie? The school term starts next Wednesday. Be sure that she's there. In the event of non-compliance, we would have to seriously consider taking the child into care and looking to you for the cost of her keep, that's besides fining you for disobeying the law. Now what's it to be?'

Magda heard it all, relishing her aunt's discomfort and the wonderful news that she would be going to school. Her aunt dare not defy the School Board.

A chance glance across the street, and she saw the gleam of faces bobbing in and out of focus. Her quick little mind worked it all out. God bless Emily Crocker.

'Do I have your assurances, Mrs Brodie?'

'Yes sir. Of course sir.'

'Good. Just so we understand each other. Next week, without fail. And woe betide any shirking on your part.'

Once she'd agreed that Magda would attend the local school, the door was eased, creaking, back into its opening.

Bracing herself for what she knew would come next, Magda took slow backward steps towards the darkest corner of the room.

Bridget Brodie turned from the door, crouching like a cat about to pounce on a defenceless sparrow. Fingernails of chipped red polish clawed at her shoulders, gripped her and shook her like a cat does a mouse. She was shaken so violently, it felt as though her brains were spilling out of her ears.

'You ungrateful brat! Went behind my back, did ya! Went and reported me to the school board, did ya!'

The room was filled with her screaming voice.

Magda kicked out in protest.

'I didn't tell anyone.'

'Where's my cane?' Bridget yelled. 'Six of the best, for you my girl. Six of the best for telling lies about me . . .'

'No! You're not caning me for something I did not do. Now let me go, you Connemara mare!'

Aunt Bridget's eyes nearly popped out of her head.

'You little heathen! What was that you called me?'

Magda kicked at her shins.

'Animal!' screamed her aunt.

Magda backed away. 'How could I tell anyone? I've not been out of this house until now and then it's only to run errands or pick up the leavings from beneath the market stalls, or fetch half a pound of scraps for Captain.'

Captain was Aunt Bridget's cat. Not that he always got all the scraps the butcher gave her. They tasted fine in a stew. The cat made do with mice.

Bridget screwed up her face until her eyes were mere slits beneath her brows.

'I'll find out who told on me. Mark my words! And when I

71

do, they'll be for it. I swear that by Mother Mary herself. D'ya hear me?'

Magda heard, but she didn't care. That night she did as she did every night, knelt at the side of her bed and implored God to keep her family safe. Tonight she added, 'And God, will you please bless Emily Crocker. She may be a whore – whatever that is – but basically she's a good person.'

Before lying down to sleep, she got out her pencils and paper and the new crayons Emily had given her. She also fondled what was left of the crayons she'd received that Christmas at the workhouse.

They were in the original box along with the original gift tag. The writing on it said 'To Magdalena Brodie, from everyone at Sycamore Lane Workhouse'.

Chapter Nine

Magda

The following morning Magda raced into Victoria Square barely able to contain her excitement.

Danny was serving a customer so she had to wait – a difficult thing to do seeing as she felt about to explode with excitement.

The first thing she did was tell Danny that she was finally going to school. Her aunt would be in dire trouble if she didn't turn up. The second thing was that she knew the name of the workhouse.

'Sycamore Lane,' she exclaimed, bubbling with excitement.

Danny shoved his stub of a pencil behind his ear and looked thoughtful.

'I know where that is. We could go there on Wednesday if you like.'

Magda bit her lip. 'Is it far?'

He grinned. 'If you're asking whether it's too far to walk, yes, it is. If you're angling for the fare so we can both take the bus, then I have to say no.'

Magda's face fell. 'Oh!'

Danny pointed to a bicycle behind the stall. 'We can go on that. See? I can pedal, and you can ride in the basket. I use it for special deliveries. Be 'ere about eleven in the morning. Sharp! Remember, Bob Barton, the bad blokes' enemy, don't stand slackers.'

She arrived on time. Because she was about to start school, her aunt had purchased a few items from the pawn shop. They weren't that special, but better than what she had been wearing, which she'd now grown out of.

She'd also washed her hair and brushed it until it gleamed. The sash from her old checked dress was frayed at one end, but made a passable headband. On the whole she felt respectable enough to present herself at the workhouse.

She'd also brought some of the letters and cards she'd written in the hope that Miss Burton – the kind lady she remembered – would still be there and able to pass them on.

Danny was already astride his bike waiting for her.

'Hop in then,' he said.

By bracing herself against the handlebars and springing from the front wheel on one foot, she just about managed to fit into the basket.

For the most part they kept to the road that flowed with the river, still in the East End of London but further in than Edward Street and Victoria Square.

The leaves on the trees were turning to orange, brown and yellow, raining down on them when the wind blew, the bicycle wheels churning them up like a rustling sea.

The branches of a solitary sycamore were all that remained of what must once have been an avenue.

The brisk wind turned Magda's cheeks pink. Her hair flew in her eyes. Her gaze remained steady.

There ahead of her were the gates of Sycamore Lane Workhouse. The sign to the right of the gates fixed high on the wall was still there, but it looked dirty and the paint was scabbed.

Dead leaves were beginning to pile up in front of the gates and what could be seen of the building looked dead and dark.

Danny brought the bike to a halt. For a moment he didn't say anything.

'Don't look too promising.'

Magda nodded mutely. She had a terrible feeling about this but kept it to herself.

Taking a deep breath she heaved herself out of the basket.

After leaning the bike against a tree, Danny stood beside her.

Though the wind blew her hair around her head in a knotted frenzy, Magda did not move.

'There's no one here.'

Danny shrugged. 'Closed down I suppose. I did 'ear they were doing away with them. Horrible places – for the most part.'

'She was nice. Miss Burton.'

'Can I help you now?'

Whilst they'd been looking, a figure had appeared behind the padlocked gates.

'The watchman,' whispered Danny. To the watchman he said, 'Excuse us, but we were looking for somebody who used to work here, a Miss Burton. My friend has business with her.' He sounded very official.

The man had the looks of the military about him, standing ramrod straight, his cheeks wreathed in old-fashioned whiskers.

'There's nobody here. Best you leave.'

His accent was Scottish and as broad as his shoulders.

Danny breathed a heartfelt sigh. 'I s'pose we'd better.'

Magda ignored him. 'Please,' she said, one hand in her pocket, fingering the letters and the cards she'd brought with her, plus a letter to Miss Burton. 'I was here for a time with my sisters and brother. They went to live somewhere else and I'm desperate to find them.'

The man's countenance remained stiff when his eyes fell on her.

'I told you. There's nobody here. It's all shut down.'

'Is there anyone who might pass the letter on to her and the few things with it? I would so appreciate it. I've no other family left in the world.'

It wasn't strictly true. She did have Aunt Bridget, but she didn't count; a relative nobody wanted.

The man seemed to reconsider.

'There is a clerk who comes along here to collect the post. I suppose I could pass it to him.'

'That would be wonderful!'

Magda flashed him her most captivating smile as she handed him the letter to Miss Burton plus the few cards and letters to her siblings. Dear Emily had even provided envelopes, just a few tucked inside the writing pad she'd pushed beneath the door.

'I put my address at the top of the letter,' Magda enthused to Danny.

'Was that wise?' he said, his voice almost lost in the wind as they cycled back to Victoria Square.

Magda knew what he meant. Aunt Bridget would destroy a reply purely out of spite.

'I'll make sure I'm up before her. I usually am.'

Chapter Ten

Miss Burton
1930

'Rest. That's what I advise. Plenty of rest.'

Miss Burton fixed the rotund man who had just examined her, with eyes warm with compassion but also bright with intelligence.

'I'm not a fool, doctor. I know my days are numbered.'

She was lying in the same bed she'd slept in since childhood. Her mother had slept in the next room, though once her father had passed on and she'd turned sick herself, her mother had expected her to share her bed. 'I'm so cold sleeping alone,' she'd complained.

For the most part Elizabeth Burton had done everything possible to make her mother's last years comfortable. However, that did not mean she'd neglected her duty, as she saw it, to those who had far less than the Burton family.

Her father had been a sergeant in the Salvation Army, caring for anyone who was destitute and down on their luck and his wife had done her duty providing solace and soup to those who needed it.

It was always to be expected that Elizabeth would follow

in their charitable footsteps, and indeed she had, though rather than deal with the homeless and abandoned, she'd applied for and got a position in the workhouse.

She'd never regretted staying at Sycamore Lane so long. In fact, it had filled her heart with joy to see the sunken faces of starving people fill out as a result of wholesome food and the abandonment of drink.

'Now promise me you'll be a good girl and stay there for the rest of the day. No reading. No writing. No doing anything at all. Patience is here to prepare your food.' The doctor attempted a fatherly tone, which Elizabeth found irritating.

'I know, I know.'

Being a righteous woman, Miss Burton had not been drawn into telling a lie. If the doctor noticed she hadn't actually promised a thing, then he made no comment. Like many others, including her sister, Patience, a missionary lately returned from China, he knew her to be strong minded. No matter what he said, ultimately she would please herself.

Patience came clumping up the stairs after the doctor had gone.

'I've brought you a cup of beef tea and some bread and butter.'

Miss Burton often wondered how the Chinese had coped with a woman who clumped about in heavy boots. The fact was that Patience had been born with a deformed leg and wore a calliper. The boots were a necessity; the Chinese, their women hardly able to walk on what was left of their poor feet, must have thought her something of a monster. Not that Patience would have let that worry her. Patience never let other people's opinions worry her; she marched on determined to do the Lord's work no matter what.

Although the two sisters were united in doing good works, they were distinctly dissimilar in looks. Elizabeth Burton was tall, her hair the consistency of candy floss and coaxed into a cottage-loaf style. When up and about she favoured twinsets, a single set of pearls at her throat, a present from a young man she'd once known who'd been killed by the Dervishes in the Sudan. Patience wore her hair cut short, an odd array of linen blouses and big skirts and a wedding ring on her finger. Her husband, Charles Armitage, an American pastor, was still out in China. She would be rejoining him once she'd collected funds from the good folk at the Baptist church and a few Methodist businessmen that she knew.

'You've received some letters and cards,' said Patience once she'd set the tray on the bed just as she liked it, and fussed with the curtains until they too suited her. 'I've got them here. Mr Collier, the clerk from Fair Mount House, brought them.'

Fair Mount House was a shelter for those who had nowhere to go. With the demise of Sycamore Lane Workhouse, it was stretched to capacity. It was Mr Collier who went to pick up any stray post arriving at the old workhouse.

With the aid of her spectacles Elizabeth Burton studied the envelope. 'This is a child's hand. And look at these cards. Christmas cards drawn in crayon. Yes. A child. Well, how delightful.'

Patience handed her the letter opener, a lovely thing she herself had brought back from China. The blade was of ivory, the handle inlaid with tiny flowers made from mother of pearl.

Patience stood by, not asking the contents of the letter, but curious anyway.

'The letter too is from a child,' said Elizabeth. 'Her name's Magdalena Brodie. Her mother died. She stayed with us for a while, over Christmas in fact.'

'You recall this child?'

Patience sounded surprised. So many children, so many

families had passed through Sycamore Lane when her sister was principal there.

'I do indeed. After her mother died, the whole family should have gone to the orphanage, but it was Christmas. I just couldn't do it. I let them stay. After Christmas their father, a seaman of unreliable character, came to fetch them. This girl, Magdalena, was sent to live with an aunt. She's asking if I know the whereabouts of her twin sisters and her baby brother and can I pass on her letters and cards to them. She explains that there are more but didn't wish to burden me with too many. She's had no word of the whereabouts of her family and no contact with her father.'

Elizabeth Burton turned to face the light coming in from the window, her head full of diverse thoughts. She remembered those children and the day their father had come in to tell them of the arrangements he'd made for their futures. Not with him. He'd told her about the girl being sent to live with an aunt, the twins to his parents in Ireland, and the offer of adoption he'd had for the baby.

She watched as the daylight gradually died. Autumn was coming to a close. A few leaves clung to the tree outside her window. Soon even these would be gone and so, my dear, will you, she thought to herself. Even though Patience bustled around expressing her confidence that God would see her through, never mind Doctor Jones, for all his good intentions.

Whatever time she had left, she was going to put to good use. No matter what the doctor had said about no reading and writing, she had read a letter and now she was going to write a few.

'Are you going to drink that beef tea or do I have to spoon feed you?'

'Of course I will. It looks and smells quite delicious. Do you think while I'm consuming this delicious repast, you could fetch me my writing slope from the study? There's a few letters I need to write urgently. Can you do that?'

Waiting until Patience had clumped halfway down those stairs, Elizabeth took the soup and poured half of it into the plant pot beside her bed. Two hyacinth bulbs were planted in the pot. She hoped she would smell their intoxicating scent before she died.

By the time Patience returned, she'd drunk most of the remaining beef tea and eaten one piece of bread and butter.

'I don't think I can manage any more,' she said, handing her sister the tray.

Patience noted the remaining slice of bread and butter and the dregs of the beef tea.

'Well. You've managed something. Not much though, Elizabeth.'

'I've done much better than yesterday.'

'That wouldn't be difficult. Yesterday you ate nothing,' Patience reminded her – as if she needed reminding. Eating wasn't something she needed to do.

Elizabeth gratefully accepted her writing slope, and even if her thin legs ached a little under its weight, she determined to bear it. A young girl's hopes and dreams depended on the letters she was about to write to be given to Mr Collier, the very good man who collected the letters and kept the records and archives of Sycamore Lane Workhouse. All being well, he would send them on, one to Ireland, one to the Reverend Darby and one to be sent to Miss Magdalena Brodie.

Chapter Eleven

Magda

Although Magda watched for the postman every day, there was nothing for her.

'Was she very old?' Danny asked her.

'I suppose so.'

She knew he was hinting gently that Miss Burton was dead.

'Chin up. What else you got on yer list?'

Magda got the piece of paper out of her pocket and smoothed it flat on her lap.

'Relatives. The only one I can ask is Uncle James, but he's still at sea.'

'When's he next due?'

She shrugged. 'I don't know. He doesn't come home that much.'

Danny grinned. 'Neither would I if I was married to a woman like yer Aunt Bridget.'

Magda grinned at him. 'You're a wicked boy, Danny Rossi. Three Hail Marys for you . . .'

'Yeah, and a bloody Norah!'

They laughed. Her neck stretched like a swan he'd once

seen on the Thames when she laughed. She wasn't quite as skinny as she used to be and there was more colour in her face since she'd started school.

Magda sighed. 'I wonder if I'll ever find them.'

He patted her hand. 'You will. Now. What about grand-parents? You must have some. Somewhere.'

'There must be some in Italy, but I don't think my mother's parents spoke to her when she insisted on marrying my father. As for Ireland – yes – I suppose there must be, but I doubt Aunt Bridget would tell me where.'

'And that Bible. Do you know where she's hidden it?'

She nodded. 'There's a door set into the wall in her bed-room. It's like a meat safe with a metal door and it's padlocked. I think it's in there.'

'Hmm. We could give it a try – when she's out I mean.'

'She locks the front door when she goes out.'

'Always?'

'Always.'

She wanted to reach out and smooth away the frown that came to Danny's forehead. He was so good to her; feeding her and being her friend, helping her with the big mission of her life – finding her family.

'Sad,' he said. 'You having no family. Might 'ave been different if your mother was still alive.'

'She would be if we'd been able to afford a doctor.'

'Well, I blame yer father for that. He should 'ave been there, not gallivanting off around the world. Downright irresponsible that is. Downright irresponsible. And he should be here now. Getting it all sorted.'

Although she accepted deep down that her father was feck-less and indifferent to his family's suffering, Magda could not find it in herself to condemn him. To hear Danny doing it hit a raw nerve.

'What's it to you, Danny Rossi? What do you know about anything?'

She sprang to her feet; flinging the sandwich he'd given her back at him. Crumbs and crusts flew everywhere, bringing a flock of pigeons homing in on the treat.

She stalked off, tears stinging her eyes. At the same time she listened for the sound of his footsteps running after her. It didn't happen.

Stubborn pride kept her away from the square for a few days. When she went back, there was a space where his father's stall used to be.

She asked the fishmonger why they weren't there.

'Came into some money and moved away. That's all I know, love. Sorry.'

Chapter Twelve

Magda
1931

Danny moving away left a big void in Magda's life and, in the absence of anything else, she threw herself into her school work, achieving high marks and enjoying her time there. Christmas was the only time when she became melancholy, wondering what had happened to her family and the cards and letters she'd sent them.

Schooldays were coming to an end and Magda's good looks were starting to turn heads.

Most of the girls were leaving school at fourteen. A few, like Magda, had been selected for a scholarship, a further two years' study. The scholarship girls were educated in a separate annexe to the main school. Her aunt had protested that she needed to be out earning, not sat in a school room.

''Tis time you repaid me for looking after you.'

'I'll get a job as well as remain at school. The market's open at five. I'll work there before I go to school and weekends too.'

Aunt Bridget didn't look convinced, but Magda didn't care. She glared at her aunt unblinking, daring her to forbid her to stay at school. Bridget dropped her eyes, fearing both the anger in Magda's eyes and the chance the girl might put a spell on her.

'Foreign eyes. Witches' eyes,' Magda heard her muttering.

She smiled to herself. If being a witch kept Aunt Bridget at a distance, then so be it. She'd be a witch!

Yellow and mauve-headed crocuses bloomed in sheltered spots in the park at the heart of Victoria Square. Even a few brave daffodils were bursting into bloom and birds were chirping in the three solitary trees around which the flowers clustered. Best of all, James Brodie came home from the sea. He so rarely came home, staying away for years at a time, which seemed to suit Aunt Bridget down to the ground. He sent her his wages and that was enough.

'Bridget, my darling wife. I'm home again from the sea. Give us a kiss and hug, girl!'

'James Brodie, you're drunk!'

'So I am,' he responded, wobbling slightly on his muscular legs. 'Celebrating my return from the sea to my happy home and my beautiful wife.'

Magda brightened at the sight of him. Describing Aunt Bridget as beautiful tickled Magda's funny bone.

'Now how about that hug and kiss,' he said, swaying and using his spread arms to keep upright. 'Then tonight we'll go out and paint the town, my dear, dear, Mavourneen. How would that be?'

Aunt Bridget grabbed his sleeve, pulled him into the house and slammed the door.

Magda glanced through the window. The girls across the road had witnessed her uncle's return and were grouped in the door over there, looking over and laughing out loud.

'Magda! Help me get your uncle up the stairs.'

'Darling wife,' he said. 'Darling girl,' he said to Magda then frowned. 'Are you Isabella? You certainly look like Isabella.'

Magda turned her head away from the beery breath.

Even between the two of them, it was no easy feat getting her uncle up the stairs and into bed. Like her father, he was a big man and had to be placed so that his feet stuck out between the iron rungs at the foot of the bed.

'You take them boots off. I'll deal with his clothes,' ordered her aunt.

Magda did as she was told, tugging off each sea boot and knitted sock, expecting the smell of unwashed feet, yet getting the smell of Sunlight Soap instead.

His socks had been washed. She wondered who by.

Every pocket was turned inside out in Bridget Brodie's search for money. Coppers, florins, half crowns, ten shilling notes, pound notes and even one or two fivers, were tipped onto the bed.

'Hah! He didn't manage to drink his way through all his wages,' remarked Aunt Bridget. 'Well! I can certainly use this.' She tucked the fivers down into the front of her dress, and piled the rest on the rickety bedside table.

'That one too I think,' she declared, grabbing a pound note and stuffing it where she'd secreted the rest of the money. 'He'll only spend it on the drink if I leave too much there. Then where shall I be? In the workhouse and I've no intention of ending up there!'

Aunt Bridget – the meanest and cruellest woman Magda had ever come across – pressed a half crown into her hand.

'Say nothing. Tell him he drank it all.'

James Brodie slept the rest of that day and all night. He appeared the following day looking bleary eyed, smelling like a horse and looking around the place as though it were the house that stunk and not him.

Aunt Bridget's rat-like eyes watched him pull up a chair and sit with his head in his hands over the table.

She nodded at Magda. 'Give your uncle a cup of tea. Bit of toast too. Soak up the booze that it will.'

Her uncle groaned. 'I seem to have lost some money.'

Aunt Bridget turned on him.

'Lost it? Lost it? You drank it all away. You always drink it all away and get so blathered that anyone can dip their hand into your pocket and rob you!'

James rubbed at his eyes.

'Then I'll need to get a bit more. Do you care to go to the dog track tonight, wife? I feel me luck's in. I really do.'

'That I do not. I've got things to do here.'

'Your toast, Uncle. And your tea,' said Magda setting both down before him.

He looked up at her as though trying to remember who she was. Once he did, his face softened and a gentle look came to his eyes.

'*Bon journo, signora.*'

The words he uttered made her heart flutter.

'My mother used to say that,' she said.

'Ah, yes. Your darling mother. Has Joseph not been in touch?' he asked his wife.

Aunt Bridget's mouth set into a straight line as though her lips had been pickled in concrete and wouldn't break open.

'No! Expects me to keep the kid on thin air. It's not easy, Jim, not now she's getting to be a woman. Not easy at all. I'll have to get a job if he doesn't send something soon.'

'You'll do no such thing! I'll have no wife of mine turning out to work, and there's a fact! Here!'

Bridget looked at what she held in her hand. 'Not much, but it's hard times. I suppose I'll have to manage.'

'Have the lot. I'll be off to sea again 'afore long, but I've got a shilling or two left for the dog track.' He turned to Magda.

'Seeing as your aunt won't come, would you like to come with me, Maggie darling?'

She didn't like being called Maggie, but did like the way her Aunt Bridget's face dropped like a stone from a ten-storey building.

'I'll get my coat.'

She ran up the uncarpeted stairs to her room and took her shabby grey coat from the peg.

As she put it on, she kept her ear to the gap in the door, laughing quietly to herself as she heard what was said and imagined the resultant look on her aunt's face.

'Will you come with us Bridie – you know – out and about like a family?'

'That I will not, James Brodie! You know I don't approve of gambling. I'll be off to mass like a good woman should be – a man too. I prefer to be there alone with me thoughts and anyway you've been that absent from church, the good Lord isn't likely to recognise who you are.'

'Well, that's a bloody big lie,' Magda murmured. 'The Red Cow more like.'

Being on the verge of adulthood had made her braver than she'd ever been.

'Have you ever thought of divorcing Aunt Bridget?' Magda whispered to her uncle.

'Good Lord, no,' he muttered back. 'She'd damn me to hell for even thinking it.' He grinned suddenly. 'Have sometimes thought about murdering her though. Set her slippers on fire when she's snoring like a pig in front of the fire after a session at the pub.'

'You know she goes to the Red Cow?'

'Of course I do. Know about 'er and the landlord too. The man must be mad. Or blind. Or both.'

Magda laughed, amazed that her uncle knew his wife so well.

'Don't lose all the money,' Bridget Brodie shouted after them.

Her eyes narrowed as she watched her husband and her niece walk off together. She began muttering to herself.

'Lost one Brodie to that foreign slut and now it looks as though I'm losing another to her offspring. Don't seem fair. Ain't fair.'

Her husband was right though. Magda was beginning to resemble her mother, though she couldn't recall Isabella having grey eyes. Dark hair, yes, but not grey eyes.

She stood there pulling at the bristles on her chin and tapping a stained finger against equally stained teeth.

Suddenly she became aware that she herself was being watched from across the street. Winnie One Leg was standing with one arm braced against her doorway.

There was something about that woman that made Bridget nervous. The girls she'd call names at any time, but Winnie was a different matter.

Despite the way she limped, she had handsome features and an imposing presence. For a start she was a good six inches taller than Bridget.

They held each other's challenging gaze. It was Bridget who buckled and asked Winnie how she was.

Winnie said she was fine.

Hatred boiled like a suet pudding in Bridget's mind, a pudding that had boiled since that bastard Joseph Brodie ditched her for a foreigner from Naples.

Wrapping her arms across her pancake breasts, Bridget crossed the road, a devious and potentially lucrative plan forming in her mind.

The fact that Winnie was regarding her with contempt went unnoticed. All that mattered was getting her final revenge on the Italian whore and her daughter. And what better revenge was there than to make the girl a whore?

She adopted all the charm she possessed.

'Winnie. If you would like to come over to my place, there's a little business I'd like to discuss in private.'

Winnie was disinclined to enter the scruffy little house on the other side of the street. Still less was she inclined to discuss business with this disgusting wreck of a woman.

Women that knew Winnie professed that she could read people like books, and as it was with books, she liked some but was unimpressed with others. Bridget Brodie fitted into the latter category.

She nodded. 'Lead on.'

Bridget, that boiling pudding of an idea spurting steam in all directions, almost skipped across the road.

Once Winnie was inside, she closed the door though didn't stray too far from it.

Winnie's gaze swept over the poor furnishings, the smoky fire, the attempts by someone to prettify the place with home-made paper flowers gathered in a plain clay pot.

'It's about Magda,' hissed Bridget, the pupils of her eyes resembling the heart-of-glass marbles. 'She's of an age to go out and make a living and being the daughter of a whore – an Italian whore as a matter of fact – I think the best place for her is with you. For a price. Of course.'

Bridget did not possess the perceptiveness of her neighbour from across the road, so she could neither notice nor evaluate the cold, hard look Winnie was giving her.

'And what does your niece think of the idea, Mrs Brodie?'

'Call me Bridget.'

Winnie decided to do no such thing.

'Is she willing?'

'Oh, I dare say you can beat the willingness into her. What else is a girl like her to do with her life? All she has are her looks and the wantonness passed down from her mother.'

Bridget paused.

The moment she saw that pink tongue lick over those yellow teeth, Winnie knew what she was going to say next.

'As with all apprentices, I take it there will be an indenture to pay. As I'm her next of kin, I would be the one to hold that indenture – in safekeeping you might say.'

In times past when Reuben had controlled her life, Winnie might have agreed to the plan. As it was she had of late been nostalgic and regretful about that time. If only her daughter had lived. If only Reuben hadn't been the man he was. If only the doctor hadn't refused to come – except for an exorbitant fee.

So many 'ifs' she thought. So many things that might have been.

In her dreams she saw the young woman that her daughter would have grown into. Dark haired, flashing eyes – perhaps grey eyes – like her own.

Magda was so like her.

'Mrs Brodie . . .'

'Bridget.'

'Mrs Brodie. I hear what you say, but I find it difficult to understand. You are offering me a member of your family into a life that is – for those of us who take it up – the start of a road to nowhere. It's a hard, cruel life Mrs Brodie, yet you are willing to hand me Magda knowing full well what will happen to her; the softness, the youth hardened with experience into nothing more or less than a cynicism about life.'

Bridget folded her arms and fought to understand what Winnie was saying. She was offering her a sure-fire hit with the men that visited over the road. Why didn't she name what she was prepared to offer?

'So let's cut to the bargain; how much are you willing to pay me for her?'

Winnie shook her head. 'Let's you and me get things straight, Mrs Brodie. I will repeat again in case you're not hearing it straight; women come to the oldest profession in the world, not out of their own choice, but as a last resort. Some are made promises never kept by the men they thought loved them. Once they've fallen into the trap, there's no climbing out – not easily anyway. But Magda has a choice in life. If she comes to me of her own free will, then that's a different matter. Good night, Mrs Brodie,' she said.

Bridget Brodie stumbled as Winnie pushed her roughly aside.

'I beg your pardon,' yelled Bridget.

Winnie cared not a jot for being rude. How could a woman so callously sell off a member of her family? How could she?

She'd disliked the Irishwoman even before she'd entered that gloomy house. She disliked her even more now.

As she re-entered her own establishment, one of the girls asked if she was all right.

'You look as though you've seen a ghost,' the girl remarked.

Winnie mumbled a wordless response. Her feelings and thoughts had turned inwards. If seeing a ghost meant feeling as though the past had come back to haunt her, then indeed she had. Tonight she would toss and turn in her bed with dreams that were memories and memories that turned into dreams. The baby, the daughter she'd lost, would drift through her dreams, though as a young woman on the threshold of life – and that young woman would be Magda Brodie.

Chapter Thirteen

Magda

At the dog track James Brodie took great delight in buying Magda jellied eels and boasting of how he knew a man who knew a man who knew everything there was to know about racing, most particularly dog racing.

'He gave me a formula, he did. That's a way of working out which animal is going to win.'

Seemingly the formula only worked for the friend of a friend, not for her uncle.

'Never mind. Enjoy your jellied eels. Tell me what you're going to do now you're soon to be a young lady and leaving school.'

'I'm not leaving. Not exactly. I've won a scholarship.'

'Well, there's a wondrous thing. So tell me about this school of yours.'

She told him about her one true friend, a girl called Susan Barnes who had ginger hair and a freckled face.

'I wish I could do more for you,' he said once she'd finished. 'Now wouldn't it be a fine thing if I could lay a few pounds on the next race and give the proceeds to you to put towards your future. Trouble is I've got the dreams of a toff and the money of a pauper. In fact I've only got two bob left.'

He eyed the single coin sitting in his sweaty palm.

'How about if I were to place a bet?' Magda suggested.

'You can't. You're too young.'

'But you could put it on for me, couldn't you?'

'Of course I could. A tanner will do if you've got that.'

'I've got a bit more than that.'

She pulled out the half a crown Aunt Bridget had picked from her husband's pocket and given to her.

'Half a crown. Can I choose the name?'

'Well,' he said laughing. 'Why not? You can't be doing any worse than what I've been doing.'

He took her to where the dogs' names for the next race were listed on a chalk board.

Magda looked down the list. 'That one,' she finally said. 'Fruit Fancy.'

'Any particular reason for that?'

She shook her head. 'Not really, except that I do know somebody who runs a greengrocery barrow in the square. Or used to rather. He moved away.'

He patted her cheek, grinned, shook his head and ambled off to place her bet.

Magda tucked into the last of her food.

'Fancy your chances, girl?'

She looked up into the face of Bradley Fitts. He was older than her so naturally taller. He also looked more like a man, his clothes natty and not bought off the Jewish tailor who had a stall in the market where he took orders and showed off his cloth.

He was eyeing her as though seeing her for the very first time – and liking what he was seeing.

'I'm here with my uncle.'

Even to her own ears she sounded nervous. She knew that was not the way to sound with Bradley Fitts. You had to front him out; not easy when he was that much taller, that much broader and flanked by the Sheldon boys.

Bradley flipped two fingers under the brim of his hat, which sent it further back from his face.

'You've certainly grown into a looker, Magdalena. Lovely looking in fact.'

His eyes swept over her before lingering on her face.

Magda felt her face getting hot.

Bradley leaned closer. 'I don't like you being 'ere, Magdalena. And I don't ever want to see you 'ere again. Unless you're with me that is. Got it?'

Bradley Fitts wouldn't know it, but his manner reminded her of Aunt Bridget. From the moment she'd arrived beneath that roof, she'd been bullied, starved, slapped and intimidated. But that was when she was younger.

Her eyes flashed, her temper flared and she stood up close to him, her anger spitting up into his face.

'Just you listen to me, Bradley Fitts. You have no right telling me what I should or should not do, and who I should be with. You do not own me and you never will. Now get out of my way. I want to see who's won the last race.'

Her legs were shaking as she pushed past him to find Uncle Jim, but she felt big and brave.

Behind her the eyes of Bradley Fitts burned with indignation, following Magda Brodie until she disappeared in the crowd.

'One hell of a brush off,' said one of his friends.

Bradley threw him a warning glare. 'Nobody brushes off Bradley Fitts. I'll show her who's boss, just you wait and see. All she needs is a slap or two to show her who's in charge.'

*

'Uncle Jim. Do you know where the twins are?'

'Twins?'

'My sisters. Venetia and Anna Marie. And Michael. My ba . . .' She stopped. Michael wouldn't be a baby any longer. 'My brother too. Do you know where any of them are?'

'Sure. Well, your sisters I do. They're with my parents in Ireland. Did you not know that?'

'Oh!'

Magda could hardly believe she was hearing this.

'Oh!' she said again, her eyes brimming with tears of joy and her hand covering her open mouth.

'How would it be I write the address down for you?' he said.

Magda was aware of her aunt's hard scowl, but she didn't care.

'It would be very well. Very well indeed!'

She fetched him a piece of paper and a pencil.

Uncle Jim licked the end of the pencil. 'Now let's see . . .'

He wrote painfully slow, forming each letter as a child just learning to write might do.

'There,' he said, eyeing his efforts with pride. 'That's the address of my folk – your grandparents in Ireland.'

'And Michael?'

He shook his head sadly. 'Now that I don't know. Only your father knows that.'

'This stew's done. Now get everything off the table.'

Aunt Bridget brushed everything aside, crumbs and bits of screwed-up paper falling to the floor.

Magda managed to grab the piece of paper and for a moment studied the address. Happiness welled up inside her; she now had an address for grandparents she'd been told by her aunt were dead. The twins were there. Uncle Jim assured her they were.

That evening he told her tales of his travels and the adventures he and her father had had as boys.

'Right scrapes we got up to.'

Aunt Bridget had sat there gloomily, pretending to knit a tea cosy. She'd been knitting that same tea cosy for years, brought out to make her look industrious every time Uncle Jim came home.

It was close to midnight by the time he'd finished, talking twenty to the dozen between bottles of brown ale.

Eyes heavy with tiredness, Magda dragged herself up to bed.

Jim Brodie left for sea in the early hours of the morning.

Magda heard the front door slam and the thud of his boots gradually diminishing as he left home and wife behind him.

Seeing as it was so early, she lay dozing for a while, thinking how kind he was and how wonderful that he'd given her the address where her sisters were living.

The piece of paper! Where was it?

She got washed and dressed for school quickly, and then rushed downstairs thinking she was late in lighting the fire. It wouldn't get lit if she didn't do it.

The fire in the grate burned feebly except for one single piece of paper turning black then blue with flame.

Aunt Bridget was eyeing her with a look of triumph in her beady black eyes.

'No need for you to light the fire. I did it.'

Her dark hair flew around her face. She knew what her aunt had done.

'My grandparents' address! You burned it.'

'Oh, did I now!'

'Yes. You did.'

'Well, there's a shame! Now you won't be able to go over there and see them. Just as well, though. You're old enough now to get out and find a job. It's time you brought something into this house.'

'You are a nasty, conniving, jealous old woman,' said Magda, measuring her words in time with the slow, firm steps she was taking towards her aunt. 'Some day you're going to burn in hell for what you've done, Bridget Brodie.'

Her aunt raised a threatening finger and wagged it at her.

'Don't you dare talk to me like that. Don't you dare!'

Her voice petered away. Her finger folded back into her palm and her hand fell to her side.

'I do dare,' said Magda, taking more steps so that her aunt's back was finally against the wall. 'I'm not a child any longer, Aunt Bridget,' she said, now looking down at a woman who had been taller than Magda, bad and wickedly intimidating from her greater height. Now it was Magda who was the taller one.

'You! You! With your dark looks and them witches' eyes. You're just like your mother. The devil's daughter, tempting the sons of men to lie with her, to fornicate like a dog and a bitch on heat . . .'

'Stop that! I will be reunited with my sisters, Aunt Bridget. Their address is up here,' she said, tapping the side of her head. 'And you can't destroy what's up here!'

'You've no money to go there. No money at all.'

'Then I will get some,' Magda shouted back.

With that she swung out of the house, slamming the door so hard that the panes in the windows threatened to fall out.

All the way down the road she held her head high, though her heart was breaking.

On her way to school she cut through Victoria Square. The costermongers were wheeling their carts into position and setting up their stalls.

As she had every time she entered the square, she

looked towards the place where Danny Rossi used to juggle pears and apples, laughing and singing and telling her she could have whatever fruit she managed to grab from his juggling.

He wasn't there of course. He was probably away training to be a policeman. Their days sitting on the bench eating cheese sandwiches seemed a lifetime away. He'd never written, or if he had Aunt Bridget had got to the letters first before she had chance. In all likelihood she would never see Danny again.

Despite what she'd shouted at her aunt she hadn't had enough time to memorise the address and Ireland was a pretty big country.

Chapter Fourteen

Winnie One Leg

Winnie One Leg eyed Bradley Fitts and thought how like his father he was; just as arrogant, just as cruel. Both had also shown weakness for a woman – even if only for a while. Bradley was obsessed with Magda Brodie. Reuben had once loved Winnie – or so it had seemed at the time.

Eyes that had once burned with the passion of youth now regarded Reuben's son with a shrewdness resulting from experience.

She knew men very well, and she knew Reuben Fitts very well indeed. In a short-lived fit of guilt he had given her money and set her up in this place. It was her job to run the business and she had. The lump sum he'd given her following the dreadful labour she'd endured had been gainfully invested. The thing about men was that no matter they be rich or poor, many were at the mercy of their lower regions.

It had always amazed her how many upper crust wives regarded sex within marriage as a duty, not a pleasure for both to enjoy. Sad marriages. Sad men.

On account of this, some very influential men visited her establishment. Thanks to their advice she was a very rich woman, rich enough to plan for imminent retirement.

She'd told Reuben this in writing, in the letter just handed to Reuben's son, Bradley. The envelope was sealed. This was a matter between her and Reuben alone.

. . . I trust you'll have no objection to me retiring . . . in view of our shared experiences . . .

He'd know what she meant. He couldn't voice an objection because she knew too much about him. He could probably guess that she'd held on to some pretty incriminating evidence that he would never, ever wish to be revealed.

She'd already purchased a nice little cottage in Prince Albert Mews, a place in the West End of London where she could live the rest of her life in peace under an assumed name. Alone of course, but that was the sad fact of her life. There had been no more pregnancies after that first child. There couldn't be. Intensely able in her analysis of men, she studied this young cock that was Reuben's son, child of a far younger woman whom Reuben had chosen to marry.

Bradley Fitts had inherited his father's callous disposition. The arrogance had come with being respected since an early age as the son of a frightening man.

His tone was ugly as he counted out the money.

'It had better all be here. Wouldn't want no creaming off the top, would we Winnie?'

Her retaliation was swift and meant to deflate him.

'No. That's why I've numbered and recorded the notes. So that there's no creamin'.'

She noticed the sudden ballooning of his cheeks as he clenched his jaw.

Her sharp little eyes never left his face.

Yes, Bradley Fitts. I'm an old bird and better young cocks than you have tried to outwit me.

Her gaze dropped to his shiny shoes. The rug he was standing on had pink flowers at each corner. At the centre a huge one blossomed. She barely restrained herself from smiling. If only he knew what he was standing on.

It had been with great joy that she'd lined out the aperture in the stone floor. Yes, there was a cashbox locked in a strong cupboard that Reuben had supplied. That was where she kept the dues rightly belonging to Reuben and from which she had fetched the sum she'd handed over to his son.

But the hole in the floor. That was a different matter entirely, known to her and her alone. The money within was her money, earned from her wages by listening to the advice of the clever men who entered this house; bankers, titled gentlemen from both houses of parliament. And that wasn't all. Besides money there was a complete record of all the illicit businesses run by Bradley Fitts. At the threat of any harm, those records would find their way to Scotland Yard.

Neither son nor father knew of her meticulous record keeping of information as well as cash, though she had hinted at it in her letter. She knew so much about Reuben Fitts; of his business dealings, of how much money he had. She also knew that people who had upset him were rarely seen again so she'd made two copies of those records, one of which was with her solicitor. She would be safe because she'd made Reuben aware of this.

Chapter Fifteen

Magda
1935

Magda was on her way to the pictures with her orange-haired friend Susan who had started a job at the brewery.

'I still can't believe it,' Magda was saying. 'I've always wanted to become a nurse or a doctor since my mother died. I knew I had to stay on at school, but didn't think I'd be able to. Can you believe that?'

Susan guffawed with laughter. 'Never mind that, I can't believe you actually WANT to stay on at school. Fourteen, and that was it for me. Love working for a living. Love earning money.'

'I can understand that.'

Susan came from a poor family. It was understandable that she wanted some money at last, at least enough to enjoy herself before she got married and had kids – which was what most girls wanted. But not Magda. Magda burned with a desire for something else entirely. Was it so wrong to lie a little in order to get what she wanted? Winnie had convinced her that it was not.

'The end justifies the means,' Winnie said to her. 'A lot of good will come of this. Thanks to the Great War, more and more women have become doctors, and if the news from Germany is to be believed, there'll be more women doctors in demand before very long.'

Winnie sighed. 'Another war to inspire human progress. Sad as it is.'

Winnie had also informed her how come she had secured an interview and what she was supposed to say when she got there.

'You don't live here in Edward Street. This is the address where you live,' she'd said, handing her what looked like a sheaf of examination papers. 'And your folk are fine people already involved in the medical profession. You're an upper class girl on paper. Behave accordingly. Oh, and tell them you're twenty, not eighteen. Being the right age is important. And having the right background, and that's been arranged.'

It never failed to amaze her that Winnie knew such very influential people and that some of them were not quite as upright and honest as they should be.

'I'd be lying,' she'd said to Winnie.

Winnie had fixed her with a stern expression. 'If you wish to give assistance to a poor woman in labour, then lying is what you have to do. Imagine her dying without you being around to help her. That should make it easier.'

It wasn't easy, but she resolved to live with her reservations. One lie balanced out by one good deed.

The letter had come that morning inviting her for an interview at Queen Mary's Hospital Medical School. Money to live on would be the problem.

Susan offered her home-grown wisdom.

'You've got a bit of time between the interview and starting at the hospital. How about your old man?'

'My father?' Magda grimaced. 'I haven't heard from him in years, and neither has Aunt Bridget if she's to be believed.'

'How about your mother's family?'

Magda shook her head. 'My mother was Italian,' she said, as though that explained everything, especially the fact that the family was too distant to expect money from that quarter.

'Mine was a pushover. That's what my dad said,' said Susan with a grin.

When Magda got back from the pictures, Aunt Bridget was standing at the door. A tall man with greying fair hair and the look of a seaman was standing there looking awkward.

Her aunt was saying something. 'Lost at sea you say? You're sure?'

'I'm sorry, Mrs Brodie.'

'Have you got the pay that's owing?'

The man nodded. 'I have Mrs Brodie. 'Tis here, plus his payment card for his insurance with the Sailors' Benevolent Society. There's a fair bit to come, and what with no burial to . . .'

Suddenly aware what he'd said, he looked embarrassed and apologised again.

Aunt Bridget took the oilskin bundle from him.

'A few Hail Marys will do as well as a coffin for my poor man,' she said, her voice cracking as though she were about to break down.

'A good thought, Mrs Brodie. A good thought indeed.'

Bridget's breasts heaved in a big sigh prior to looking at him and chancing a weak smile.

'Would you care to come in for a cup of tea whilst you're here, or a little of something stronger. I can soon send the girl up to the offie to get us something to drown our sorrows with.'

Bridget's manner couldn't have been clearer. One man was

gone, but here was another she might be able to get her claws into.

The seaman spluttered his apologies but declared he had a ship awaiting his return before setting off to Venezuela.

'Uncle James is dead?'

Magda was saddened; no more jellied eels, no more dog racing when the only sum won had been by virtue of half a crown that Aunt Bridget had stolen from her husband's pocket.

'Ah yes,' murmured Bridget, impatient fingers loosening the ties of the oilskin parcel the man had handed her. 'But he's left me a bit, so I won't be destitute, what with you leaving school and bringing a bit in too. Yes, I shall be fine, though as a widow I can always do with a bit more . . .'

Magda recognised the conniving look that came to her face. Bridget was planning something.

She didn't know quite what until she discovered a brand new writing pad with a couple of pages missing. Her aunt had written to someone, but who?

The most obvious possibility was to James's brother, Joe Brodie, her father. But letters took a while to catch up with a man at sea.

The other possibility was some other relative she knew nothing of. Not grandparents. Aunt Bridget had assured her they were dead.

Asking her would do no good. She would simply deny ever writing anything.

But Aunt Bridget rarely told the truth.

Chapter Sixteen

The Twins
1932

It was the middle of June 1932 when Bridget's letter arrived in Ireland. There were two armchairs set to either side of the kitchen fire at the farm near Dunavon, funny-shaped old things with hoods over the top and stout little buttons holding the upholstery in place.

It was to these chairs that Dermot Brodie and his wife retreated after a hard day's work and mostly after the girls had gone to bed.

Molly Brodie had wept when she'd heard of Isabella's death and had been more than willing to take in the twin girls, Venetia and Anna Marie. She'd also suggested to Dermot that they take in the eldest girl and the boy too, but he'd rejected the idea.

''Tis up to Joe to arrange. They're his responsibility and however they turn out as a result of his actions, is down to him and him alone.'

It was to one of these chairs that Molly went now, sinking into its nest-like comfort, though feeling no comfort at all.

She had read the letter from her daughter-in-law, Bridget,

stating that James had been drowned. The first reading had not been enough, and nor had the second. She read it for a third time.

The letter had been delivered to the village post office. The postmaster, a Welshman, an aloof but dutiful man, had forwarded it on via a boy on a bicycle; hence it had not arrived until they were sitting down to supper.

She'd informed her husband that they'd received a letter. He'd instructed her to place it behind the clock on the mantelpiece until they'd eaten. He did not approve of reading at the table. Neither did he wish an audience whilst he read. He would read it first before passing it to his wife, seeing as it was addressed to the pair of them.

It was now gone nine o'clock. The girls had gone to bed without argument.

Dermot had reached for the letter, opened it and read.

His face had gone white.

He read it a second time before passing it to Molly.

As Molly cried, Dermot sucked on his pipe as though it was lit, when as yet it was not.

His teeth still gripping the pipe, he put his thoughts into words, aiming his voice at the glow of the fire grate.

'Them and their dreams of seeing the world. They should have stayed here, the both of them. On the land where they belonged.'

He drew once more on his pipe then spit into the fire where it sizzled and vanished.

'A disappointment. The pair of them.'

Chapter Seventeen

Magda
1935

Magda bubbled with excitement as she told Winnie all about the interview at Queen Mary's Hospital for the East End.

'I still can't believe I've got this far.'

'And you'll go much further,' said Winnie. 'You're a bright girl and we need more women doctors in this country. Women understand women's ailments better. There's no reason why you shouldn't become one.'

'There is one thing that might stop me, Winnie. It costs money to attend the medical school, money I haven't got.'

'Can you not write to your father?'

Magda shook her head.

'Have you grandparents?'

Magda sighed. 'According to Aunt Bridget, they died years ago.'

Winnie looked intensely at the young woman she'd become so fond of. Was she being silly thinking her own daughter would have looked like her? Possibly, but seeing as it soothed her long-standing heartache, did it really matter?

'Magda, what would you say if there was somebody to

sponsor your studies? How would that be?'

'Wonderful, but I can't see . . .' She paused, hardly daring to hope and overwhelmed by Winnie's generosity. 'I couldn't possibly pay you back. You've done so much for me already.'

'Oh yes you could. In the best way of all. I would sponsor you, Magda. You remind me of the daughter I lost. Like your mother, she might have survived if there'd been a doctor around.'

Magda stroked her heated brow, the room seeming to spin around her. 'I don't know what to say.'

'Nothing. Leave it with me, Magda Brodie, and you'll be a doctor yet.'

All that night, Magda barely slept, her mind reeling at her good fortune and the prospects for the future. It would be two months before she actually entered the hallowed portals of Queen Mary's and she needed to do something in the meantime. Money wouldn't just put food on the table, it would put clothes on her back. She couldn't possibly present herself at Queen Mary's in clothes that had been unpicked, let out and let down; childish clothes, clothes that no longer properly fitted the young woman she had become. And she would not accept any more of Winnie's generosity. She had to do something for herself.

She had the luck to be taken on by Mrs Skinner, a woman of wide proportions and a huge laugh that rippled all the way down to her belly. It was she who had taken over the pitch Danny used to run with his father.

Warm thoughts came to her when she thought of Danny, wondering how tall he was now, how much more of a man than the last time she'd seen him.

Working for Mrs Skinner turned out to be a godsend.

For the first time in her life, Magda had money of her own. She also had more than one young man trying to catch her eye.

'I'm not ready for that,' she'd said to Mrs Skinner who fancied herself as a matchmaker. 'I'm not rushing into anything. Not until I've made my way in the world.'

It turned out the customers in the market liked Magda's dark good looks and friendly smile, the way she could be as bawdy as the worst of them or as politely spoken as the best.

Though Mrs Skinner couldn't pay her too much, she had enough to buy food and a few decent clothes from the second-hand clothes stall.

'*Voila*! I have a nice green jumper here,' said Jean Claude, the Frenchman who ran it. He'd come over after the Great War having fallen in love with an English nurse. 'And a skirt. It is silk. Lovely for the evening. And a jacket. Tweed. Ideal for the winter I think.'

He also found her a slim coat in lovely silver grey astrakhan with a fetching fur collar.

'I can't afford this as well,' Magda had said to him whilst nuzzling her chin and nose into the fur. 'Mothballs,' she said, wrinkling her nose.

'The balls of the moth will vanish,' Jean Claude responded in his inimitable way. 'Talcum powder. Or lemon juice brushed through it; no more balls of moth!'

'But I can't afford . . .'

'You can pay me weekly.'

He leaned into her, his black moustache almost tickling her cheek.

'Most of my customers look like sacks in these beautiful things. You will look beautiful. You must always wear beautiful things.'

Magda accepted his judgement and his generosity.

It was rumoured that Jean Claude had once worked in a top fashion house in Paris, but had given it all up for the love of his nurse. Her name was Irene, a serene woman with pale blonde hair and blue eyes set in a heart-shaped face. They had three children all of whom interspersed their Cockney accent with words that were definitely French.

'Now all you need is somebody to take you up west in that finery,' said Mrs Skinner after Magda had proudly shown her what she'd got. 'Somebody with a few bob to spend. Take my advice, Maggie my girl. It's better to be an old man's darling than a young man's slave.'

Magda laughed. 'You are a one, Mrs Skinner. You definitely are a one.'

The next day she was in the square as usual, joking with the passers-by and accepting their compliments about how nice she looked.

'How about I take you out tonight, sweetheart. We could go dancing. How would that be?' The man offering had a silver tongue and the most successful pitch in the square. He also had a wooden leg and was rumoured to be a bigamist.

'I need to stay home and do some knitting,' Magda responded.

'Can't imagine you knitting.'

'Can't imagine you dancing.'

'Can't imagine you even owning a pair of knitting needles.'

'You're right. I've only got one needle.'

'Can't knit with that.'

'And you can't be much of a dancer with only one leg!'

Loud laughter from a crowd of onlookers followed.

Magda exchanged a wink and a grin with Mrs Skinner.

'You'll be breaking a few hearts with your good looks, Maggie darling,' said Mrs Skinner. 'You'll make as lovely a blushing bride as I was, ain't that right, Jack?'

Her husband Jack smiled and nodded. 'You was indeed, my darling. Slender as a reed at seventeen.'

Magda hid her smile. Mrs Skinner was now as wide as a door, her chins resting one upon the other.

'Well. What have we here? If it isn't the lovely Magdalena.'

The instant she heard him use her full name, Magda knew who it was. Bradley Fitts.

She pretended to concentrate on tipping three pounds of potatoes from the scale scoop and into the canvas bag of a woman with three kids hanging around her skirts.

'Ninepence, love.'

Bradley moved so he stood beside the woman, his hand resting on one of the children's heads.

'Ain't you going to say hello, Magdalena? Ain't you glad to see me?'

The woman handed over the money. Magda turned away, all fingers and thumbs as she placed the coins in the wooden cash box. Hopefully he would be gone when she turned back.

He wasn't. There he was standing between her and the queue of customers that had formed.

'How about you come out with me tonight? We make a pretty pair, we two. You know I've always liked you. Tasty you are. As tasty as they come. How about it?'

The thing she'd learned about the likes of Bradley Fitts was that it didn't do to show fear. Show fear and he would work on it, a mix of charm and intimidation until the object of his bullying was totally in his power.

'I'm not a pie,' she retorted, pushing her hair back from her face.

A puzzled expression came to features that were too coarse to be handsome.

'Did I say you were?'

'You said I was tasty. In which case I don't want to go out with you. You might bite me.'

'Now there's a thing,' chuckled Mrs Skinner.

'There's nothing funny, Missus,' snapped Bradley, not amused by Magda's comment and throwing her a warning look.

Mrs Skinner was about to ask him who he thought he was, when her husband whispered Bradley's surname into her ear.

Bradley's gaze travelled back to Magda, smiling as though he were charm itself.

'I've no time to argue. Business before pleasure. Another time, *Magdalena*.'

He rolled his tongue around her name as though he could taste it or her on his tongue.

'If she don't want to go out with you, she don't have to,' declared Mrs Skinner.

Without warning, his hand shot out, grabbing one of Mrs Skinner's chins.

'Just mind your tongue, Missus.'

Small and skinny as he was, Jack Skinner stepped forward.

'Take your hands off my wife.'

Magda heard the trembling in his voice and saw the threat in Bradley's eyes.

Bradley made a move towards Jack. Magda got in between the pair of them.

'All right. I'll go out with you. Just leave Mr and Mrs Skinner alone. Please.'

Bradley's eyes flashed to her face and for a moment the air was electric with tension. He pushed Mrs Skinner back so that she almost flattened her husband.

His last look was for Magda.

'Be here when I get back.'

'Get off,' hissed Mrs Skinner once he was lost in the crowd. 'Get on home before he comes back.'

'What if . . .?'

'We're off too. We're shutting the stall early.'

Mr and Mrs Skinner began speedily sorting out the stall, throwing everything into a chaotic mess so they could wheel it all away before Bradley Fitts came back.

Magda hurried home feeling more scared than she'd ever felt in her life. It was with great relief that she gained the poor sanctuary offered by the scruffy house in Edward Street, using the key she now had to get in.

Magda locked the door and slid the bolt across. Like a cornered mouse, she cowered down in the dark, waiting for the tell-tale sound of footsteps.

Laying her head on her knees, she waited. It was getting dark outside and feeling frightened had tired her.

She closed her eyes and didn't hear the approaching footsteps or see the gloved hand raised above furtive eyes that scoured the interior of the dark room.

The sound of somebody trying the lock followed by an insistent hammering sound jolted her awake. Her heart flew into her throat. Again a fist hammered on the door.

'Magda! Let me in this minute. I'm catching me death out here. Open this bloody door or I'll lay into you so hard; I'll take the skin off your back!'

Magda leapt to her feet. Her aunt fell into her arms, her breath heavy with the stink of stale beer.

She looked totally dumbstruck when Magda held onto her in the only hug that had ever happened between them.

'What's this all about? What you been up to?'

Magda pushed back from her.

'Nothing, Aunt Bridget. I was dreaming it was the bogeyman hammering at the door, but it wasn't. It was you.'

Chapter Eighteen

Magda

It was the last Saturday before Christmas. The stall had been busy all day and at the end of it, Mrs Skinner made sure that Magda had plenty of food to take home with her.

Mr Skinner, as skinny as the greyhounds she'd seen at the White City, arrived just in time to give his wife a hand wheeling the barrow home.

'Maggie my girl. This is for you.'

A plucked chicken was pulled out of a sack and dangled in front of her face.

'A little bonus from us,' Mrs Skinner laughed on seeing Magda's surprised face.

Magda thanked them. They were kind-hearted people who'd worked hard all their lives and the only people she never corrected when they called her Maggie.

Off she went home, burdened with the lovely things she'd bought from Jean Claude, plus the fruit, vegetables and chicken the Skinners had given her.

A skipping rope was stretched across the pavement.

There's somebody under the bed. I don't know who it is, I feel so jolly nervous . . .

The girls turning the skipping rope laughed when Magda

jumped through it and she laughed with them. Her exuberance vanished on noticing the black car parked outside Winnie's place. Bradley Fitts was the only person she knew who owned a car.

A couple of street urchins who had been climbing over the car were clouted off by Emily.

'Get off you little perishers.'

She chased them round the car and it was difficult to know who was enjoying it more – the kids or Emily.

'It's not your car,' one of the boys shouted.

'It's the doctor's car. Now get off before I tan yer asses!'

Magda breathed a sigh of relief that it wasn't Bradley Fitts, and then worried why the doctor was there.

'Is Winnie well?' she asked Emily.

'Winnie's well enough, though 'er leg keeps playing 'er up. But there. She's over fifty. What else can you expect at that age? Anyway, what's it to you?'

'I just wondered . . .'

'The doctor's for Gertie. She can't bring the baby. It's too big.'

A spine-chilling scream came from inside the house.

Standing as stiff as a statue, Emily folded her arms and flashed her eyes into the house.

'Poor cow. She's 'avin' a pretty bad time of it. Still. That's it. She's a woman. She's expected to give birth in pain. Says so in the Bible.'

More screams.

'Can't he do something? The doctor?'

Emily shrugged. 'How would I know? I'm not a bloody doctor!'

'Isn't there a midwife living close by?'

'Old Mrs Brown? She's birthed every babe in the streets hereabouts and got rid of a few too. She tried to get rid of this one for Gertie, but it didn't work. So she won't be 'round just in case she gets reported. The doctor came though, once he was promised double his due. Help keep his mouth shut. Need it to be over with fast. Can't 'ave our gentlemen faced with that racket. Too late for the hospital though. Silly cow should 'ave gone earlier. Still, won't be long now.'

'I'm sure the doctor will do his best,' said Magda, disturbed at the thought of Mrs Brown being both a midwife and an abortionist.

She'd heard the girls speak of abortion before; of getting drunk and taking strong laxatives, and then sitting in a hot bath before Mrs Brown came round with her water pump, her yard-long piece of rubber piping, and a box of soap flakes.

Feeling sick inside, Magda almost ran across the road. Emily had been so offhand. She never used to be like that. But things had changed between them. For a start she was grown up, had left school and was working.

Once back inside the house, she leaned against the door. The door was thick but nothing could hold back the screams of the woman across the road.

'Something should be done,' she muttered.

'What's that?'

Bridget Brodie was slumped in an armchair, her increased weight forcing the stuffing out through the bottom.

Magda noticed her aunt's flushed face, the flaccid jowls resting on the collar of her cardigan. She was drunk – again.

'It's Gertie. One of the girls over the road. She's in labour. Sounds as though she's having a hard time.'

'Serves the slut right!'

Magda slammed the fistfuls of carrier bags onto the stained and rickety table.

'No woman deserves to be in that much pain!'

Her aunt's droopy eyelids sprang open.

'She's a slut. Sells her body for money so she deserves all she gets.'

'No woman deserves to suffer. There are doctors and midwives and ways of alleviating the pain.'

'Now there's a big word! 'Eviating. Where did you get that from? Off your common mates in the market? Off that French rascal's charming words? Mark my words, hussy, he's not being kind to you out of the goodness of his heart. He's after sliding his hand up yer leg. Men are all the same. Love you and leave you. That's what they do. Love you and leave you.'

As she uttered the last words, her aunt seemed to deflate like a balloon grown soft and used up after Christmas.

'That is not how it is! That is not how it is at all!'

Magda took herself and her purchases upstairs to her bedroom. She'd heard in the market that her aunt's 'fancy man', Tom Hurdon at the Red Cow, had dropped dead of a heart attack. A new landlord was taking over. Rumour had it he had a wife, a hard-nosed type who wouldn't tolerate her old man carrying on with another woman. Having her aunt at home more often was worse than having her down the pub.

There was little furniture in the bedroom, but what there was she'd made more attractive by painting things white and pasting on flowers cut out from old birthday and Christmas cards, salvaged from elsewhere.

Even the cards she now made for Venetia, Anna Marie and Mikey were recycled from old ones that she'd begged off people who'd received them. Some came from another of the market stalls. One or two had actually been given to her. This year, because she was now earning, she'd actually bought two cards – one for the twins, one for Mikey.

For the twins she'd chosen a lovely scene of snow and a

deer, antlers stark against an evening sky. For Mikey she'd chosen a jolly-looking snowman complete with bowler hat, green scarf and a pipe.

Words were so important, she thought. I want to say how much I miss them, but don't want them to know what I might have to do in order to see them again.

Using a new fountain pen she'd been given by Mr Skinner, to the twins she wrote,

Wishing you a Merry Christmas. There's a baby being born across the way. Very much in the spirit of Christmas, don't you think?

Aunt Bridget sends her regards. I hope you are both well. I myself have left school and am hoping to become a doctor. It seems like a dream. I dearly hope it comes true.

In the meantime I'm helping out some nice local people. They have a stall in Victoria Square. If you do ever get to London, Mr and Mrs Skinner will always know where to find me. And Aunt Bridget of course.

If you ever get to London? She covered her eyes with one hand. Who was she kidding? This card would never be posted. It would sit with the others in the shoebox until such time as she found them – if she found them. If only she really could remember the address Uncle Jim had written on the piece of paper her aunt had thrown on the fire.

It was some time before she could bear to write something in Mikey's card, and even then she only got as far as wishing him a Merry Christmas.

Downstairs, her aunt was still sitting where she'd left her, eyes closed, mouth open. She woke up on smelling the meal Magda was cooking.

'What's for dinner?'

Since losing her fancy man, Bridget had been eating almost as much as she drank. Bottles were still coming home from the off licence but the interest she'd once had in lipstick and rouge had transferred to food.

'Roast chicken with carrots, onions, potatoes and cabbage. I've made stuffed apples for afterwards with custard.'

Magda watched her aunt eat. She was being looked after and fed. The old bitch should be grateful.

'Aunt Bridget. It's Christmas and there's no knowing where we might be next year. I want to find my sisters and my little brother. I want the addresses my father left in that Bible.'

Up until now her aunt had concentrated on shovelling food from plate to mouth. The moment Magda spoke, she glared across the table.

'All these years I've looked after you. I'm not long for this world, and I would have hoped you'd look after me the same as I've looked after you,' she bleated as though she were weak as water when a better description of strong as the brown brew from a stout bottle was more the order of the day.

Magda felt a furious rage boiling up inside. This woman who had treated her so badly now wanted looking after in her old age?

'I can't believe . . .' Magda began, her teeth aching with the effort of controlling her anger.

'Your no-good father has sent me next to nothing for your keep. He always was one for fine promises that were never likely to come true. Glad I didn't marry him myself. That's all I can say,' cried Aunt Bridget with a flapping of hands that made her look like a disgruntled chicken.

'Well, he didn't marry you!' Magda yelled. 'He asked my mother to marry him and she said yes.'

'So did I,' shouted her aunt, banging the table so hard it rattled the cutlery and crockery and sent gravy slopping off the plates. 'So did I,' she repeated, her eyes showing severe disappointment, swiftly replaced with a look that Magda could only interpret as hatred.

A sudden realisation flashed through Magda's mind.

'You mean it, don't you?' Magda said, hardly able to breathe as she said it.

'Of course I mean it. That was the way of that father of yours. Joseph Brodie promised me, but didn't keep his promise. Married his Italian fancy piece and left me behind with my bottom drawer filled ready to become a bride. His brother James was second best. Jim was always second best,' she murmured, more to herself than to Magda.

'And besides,' she shouted as Magda headed for the door and out into the street. 'What makes you so sure those brats will still be where he left them? What makes you so sure of that, eh?'

Chapter Nineteen

Magda

Magda ran from the house barely holding back the tears but also determined that she would not spend her life looking after her aunt.

All these years she'd borne the brunt of that woman's vindictiveness. All these years she'd waited for a father who never came. In her heart of hearts she knew he was as much to blame for the deprivation she'd endured as Aunt Bridget.

What are you running away from?

The thought popped into her head from nowhere; unless you have a guardian angel, she thought. What am I running away from? Aunt Bridget? The past? Or am I running away from the thought of failure; that Winnie might not be true to her word, or might die before my dream is fulfilled?

Carrying negative thoughts in her head slowed her speed, as though they were too heavy to bear.

She came to a bend in the river where houses gave way to a view of a black mud bank, except that the mud wasn't just mud but a stew of stinks and substances. The smell was mostly of sulphur from the gasworks and rotting bones from the fertiliser plant. When the wind dropped it wasn't so bad.

From a stone-lined parapet, she watched barges making

their way up and down the river. Some were carrying goods offloaded from Canada Wharf, the East India Docks. Others were en route to St Katharine Dock further up river.

The Thames was crowded with ships, but all she wanted was one particular ship, one particular merchant seaman and he went by the name of Joseph Brodie. Everything began and ended with him.

'Magdalena!'

Bradley Fitts was standing with his hands in the pockets of his overcoat. The brim of his trilby hat cast a shadow over one half of his face. The features of the other half were sharply defined by a gaslight hanging from the wall of a brick warehouse behind them.

'Magdalena,' he said, closer now. 'You and I 'ave got things to talk about.'

He smelled worryingly masculine, mixed with tobacco and sweet cologne.

She stood with her back to the parapet, fingers clawing at the cold stone on either side of her. Although fear had made her mouth dry, she held her head high. Never show a bully that you're scared of him.

'Out and about on your father's business?' she said tartly.

He ignored her question, if indeed it was a question, and kept her as his centre of attention.

'You got goose pimples,' he said running his eyes over her body as intimately as he might his hands. 'Fancy coming out without a coat. Must 'ave 'ad somethin' on your mind. Bit serious was it?'

His voice was as smooth as treacle. He was right about the goose pimples and at mention of them she shivered.

'I had my reasons,' she said, folding her arms. She held his gaze unblinking for the most part.

'This'll keep you warm.'

He pulled his hands out of his pockets then his arms out of his sleeves and swung the coat around her. The warmth of his body was still in the lining and although her first instinct was to fling it back at him, she suddenly realised just how cold she was.

'Thank you.' She shrugged herself deeper into it and hung her head. His action in lending her his coat had taken her by surprise.

'Something's troubling you. Care to tell me what your beef is?'

No. She did not want to tell him anything. Not Bradley Fitts of all people, but somehow it came out. Not all of it. Just the bits that really mattered.

'I want to find my family, but I don't know where they are, and even if I did, I don't have the money to go looking for them. I know where the addresses are written, but my aunt keeps it under lock and key.'

'I could get it for you. She wouldn't dare stand up to me. And then, you could show me how grateful you are. You promised to come out with me. Remember?'

The lending of the coat had all been part of his strategy and she'd fallen for it. Now he was offering her more and wanted more, but she didn't dare; the price for his help would be too high.

She tensed when his arm crept around her shoulders, pulling her ever so slightly closer to him.

'You're right. That takes money. P'raps I can help you there, us bein' old school mates an' all that.'

'We weren't school mates. You were much older than me.'

'Might 'ave been then, but the gap's not so wide now is it? Only about four years between us. Ain't that right?'

She couldn't disagree with him, and anyway what did it matter?

'Now I can loan you some money if you like. I don't need you to pay it back right away. Take yer time. We can step out one night and talk about it.'

Even the warmth of his overcoat couldn't stop her from shivering at his suggestion. She knew how it would work; the girls at Winnie's place had told her that much. She'd owe him money and at some point when she couldn't repay, she'd end up beholden to him and she knew damned well what that meant!

'I'll give you a lift,' he said to her.

'No.' She slid his coat from her shoulders. 'I'm nice and warm now. I'll be fine. A brisk walk and I'll be home in no time.'

'Suit yourself.'

He shrugged his shoulders into the coat but left the arms dangling.

She walked swiftly away without looking back. Bradley Fitts was another reason for getting away from here. There were so many reasons to leave and few to keep her here, except for family ties. Not to Aunt Bridget, but to her link with the past and the family she'd known.

In the absence of a reply to any of her letters seeking information about her sisters and brother, it always came back to her mother's Bible, which was still locked away in the most obstinate cupboard ever made.

She'd tried everything she could to open it whilst her aunt was out. Nothing had worked. The only thing left was to take an axe to it but she doubted that would work either. Still, it was worth making the effort just to see her aunt's face.

'Cow,' she muttered under her breath. 'You bloody, crazy cow!'

Aunt Bridget was standing swaying in the doorway when she got home.

Magda barged past her heading for the coal house out back.

'You pushed me. You strumpet, you, you pushed me!'

Bridget Brodie barely kept herself upright and didn't like it that her niece had ignored her.

'Where do you think you're going?' she shouted when Magda did not respond but shot out into the scullery, flung the back door wide and headed for the coal house.

Bridget Brodie leaned on the wall for support. Befuddled by drink, she looked totally confused.

'What in the Lord's name are you doing out there? Answer me, ungrateful whelp that you are.'

Magda came back in holding the axe handle with both hands, the head of it resting on her shoulders.

'Jesus!' Fearing she was about to be sliced in two, Bridget covered her head with both hands and crumpled at the knees.

Magda stomped upstairs to Bridget's bedroom, a gloomy place of dirty sheets and empty bottles.

She stepped over to the cabinet, lifted the axe high above her head and prepared to swing.

She heard her aunt's footsteps charging up the stairs.

'No! No! That's Jim's cabinet. He made it himself.'

Having second thoughts because she'd been fond of her uncle, Magda held the axe aloft and looked at her aunt.

'Uncle Jim made this cabinet?'

Her aunt nodded. 'He wanted to be a joiner. Liked working with wood, but he wanted to get away from home even more so. Your grandfather was never the easiest person in the world to get on with.'

'My grandfather?'

Resting the heavy head of the axe on the floor, Magda leaned both hands on the handle.

'Your grandfather.'

'You told me that my grandparents were dead.'

'That they are.'

'Sometimes you speak as though they're still alive.'

'My head aches so much nowadays . . . I'm ill. At death's door in fact.'

'You're not ill. It's the booze.'

Magda looked at the cabinet. 'I don't care if Uncle James made this. He's dead and won't care if I bash it open. I want my mother's Bible.'

Aunt Bridget chewed at her lips. 'It's not in there. I sold it.'

'Is that true?'

'I swear by Our Lady, that I did!'

Magda regarded her aunt through narrowed eyes, scrutinising a figure that was going to fat. A blush of broken veins over her face made her nose look like a Victoria plum.

'Who did you sell it to?'

'The pawnbroker. I put it in with some other stuff that I took to the pawnbrokers. I was a bit short, what with your father not sending money on a regular basis.'

'I want it back,' said Magda.

'I promise I'll go along to the pawnbroker tomorrow and find out where it is. How would that be for you?'

'Don't bother. I'll go myself.'

'No need. I swear on the Holy Mother herself. You'll have to give me the money seeing as I don't have enough to redeem it myself.'

'I would if I didn't suspect that you might wander into the Red Cow and spend the money there. Though I suppose seeing as your fancy man is no longer running the place . . .'

A thunderous expression came over her aunt's face before she shrugged.

'You're right, there's no point me promising because I didn't take it to the pawnbrokers. I burned it. Burned it on the fire where it belongs. Just like your mother is now burning in hell. Just like you will burn for your friendliness to the fallen women across the road. Whores and sluts, all of you!'

Magda exploded with anger.

'That is it! I am leaving this place, Aunt Bridget. You can feed yourself or drink yourself to death for all I care.'

She swung out of the room, went into her own and threw everything that was of any value to her into a few brown paper carrier bags and the string bag Danny had given her. On handling that string bag, she paused, regret clutching at her throat. She so wished Danny was here now.

Once everything she owned was in those bags, she rushed down the stairs.

Aunt Bridget followed, shouting abuse and telling her she was on the road to hell and it was no more than she deserved.

She was still shouting when Magda was outside in the street, looking around her, wondering which way to go.

Across the road she saw Winnie come to the door, seeing a client off the premises.

She looked expectantly at Magda.

In the absence of anywhere else to go, Magda met her half-way across the street.

'I need somewhere to stay. I don't know for how long, but I have to tell you this right away. If what you said about helping me get into medical school still holds, then I will do that. But if it's just a sprat to catch a mackerel and you want me to be a whore, then I'll be that if I have to. I have to get to Ireland, Winnie. I have to find my sisters. My brother too if I can. It's just something that I have to do.'

Winnie smiled. 'Never fear, Magda Brodie. There's no need for you to get the wherewithal to find your family by becoming a whore. Making you a doctor is something that is my dream as much as it is yours.'

Whilst her aunt shouted abuse and hurled anything to hand

out into the street, Magda sighed and stepped inside Winnie's domain.

Winnie bade her sit down and poured her tea.

Magda accepted it gratefully, sipped, sighed and expressed her feelings.

'Sometimes at night I dream I'm over there with them. Then when I wake up I wonder if they're dreaming that they're over here with me.'

Chapter Twenty

The Twins
1932

Over in Ireland, Venetia Brodie opened her eyes and smiled into the dawn's grey light. Today was the first day of the rest of their lives – her and Anna Marie. Her sister had been reluctant at first to fall in with her plans, but the prospect of being left alone was worse than going.

Venetia had not fully drawn the curtains the night before. She congratulated herself on her perception that what light there was could filter in and wake them up.

The cold light of dawn was being kept at bay by a pair of tan-coloured velvet curtains given to Grandma Brodie by the woman she used to work for in Cork. That had been in the days when she was single and a second parlour maid, a time she consistently reminisced about, repeating herself with the same old tale.

Though years old, the curtains had been given her as a wedding present and still had plenty of wear in them.

It was Venetia who first opened her eyes and once she was awake, the excitement of what the two of them were about to do prevented her from going back to sleep.

'Anna,' she whispered, her breath turning to steam on the cold, damp air. 'Are you awake?'

'I am now,' her sister grumbled, turning beneath the pile of grey woollen blankets.

'Are you ready?'

Anna Marie sighed. 'Are you sure we should be doing this?'

'Of course we should. I'll not stay here a moment longer. Now come on. We're not children any longer and fit only to be ordered about as though we were.'

Both sisters lay looking at each other, the bedding pulled up to their chins.

'Right,' whispered Anna Marie at last.

Even in the morning gloom of a grey Irish dawn, Anna perceived her sister's wide grin.

'Right then,' whispered Venetia like the seasoned conspirator she was. 'Ready, steady. GO!'

The two sisters threw back the bedclothes in unison and sprang out of bed. Both had gone to bed fully dressed, only their shoes waiting at the side of the bed for their feet to slip into them.

Venetia folded the toe of her stocking, wishing she'd darned the hole the night before.

'Will you look at that,' she sighed.

'No. Not if you want to get going,' returned her sister. 'You should have darned it when Granny told you to.'

'I'll darn it when I want to darn it,' she whispered back with an air of defiance.

The fact was they'd lived with their grandparents since they were seven years old and Venetia could never remember a time when she hadn't resented being ordered around by them. The time before that she remembered as bright and cosy. She refused to listen when Anna Marie suggested their circumstances had been far from cosy.

Venetia had coloured their past with comfort that had never been theirs.

'Of course we'll see them again,' she declared when Anna Marie had spoken of their older sister and their baby brother.

Anna Marie never argued with her twin because Venetia always won. She was stubborn and strong; not that Anna Marie was weak, but what she did have was a dislike of confrontation.

One memory they both shared was the day they went to see the Christmas lights in a place her mother called Oxford Street. They'd taken a bus up west to look at the lights and the bright displays in the shop windows.

They hadn't bought anything of course because everything was priced far above the few shillings their mother had in her purse. All they could do was to press their noses against the windows and make wishes that would never come true.

Both money and news of their father were in short supply then and it was just about the same now.

'I don't think he'll ever come back,' said Anna Marie. 'And we'll never see Magda and Michael ever again.'

'Oh yes we will,' said Venetia. 'If our father doesn't come back and get the family together, then we'll go looking for them. Sooner or later we're bound to find them.'

'Gran and Gramps won't let us.'

'One day they won't be able to stop us. Besides, we can sneak away if we've a mind to.'

'We need money to live. Money to help us find our family. It won't be easy.'

Once they'd left school it was expected that they would work on the farm.

'Not if I can bloody help it,' declared Venetia.

It had been Venetia's idea that they were now old enough to leave this place and seek their fortune in the world, that fortune to be spent on finding Magda and Michael.

'And New York's the place you should be,' Patrick Casey had told her.

Even at fourteen years of age, Venetia was wise to the desire she saw in his eyes, even though he was four years older than her, but then, Venetia considered herself quite a young lady and far more mature than her twin.

It had taken a lot of persuading to get Anna Marie to go along with her plan. Even now she could see her twin shiver as she shoved one arm then the other into her coat. She reckoned that the cold was only part of the reason, but she wouldn't let her opt out of her plan.

'Will you stop being such a nervous ninny,' she hissed, her breath steaming from her mouth in the frosty air.

'I'm not a ninny. It's cold outside.'

'It's cold in here too. What do you expect? It's nearly Christmas.'

Anna Marie had always been less rebellious than her sister. She understood her sister's bitterness about their mother dying and the family being split up, but unlike Venetia she accepted the situation. She even liked the farm – and she loved their grandma. But Venetia was persuasive and determined and Anna Marie just couldn't find the courage to stand up to her.

Venetia lifted the old iron latch on the bedroom door and eased it open inch by careful inch, all the while holding her breath in case it squeaked.

Anna Marie gasped when it did.

Venetia placed a finger in front of her pouting lips to shush her.

Easing the door open, she cocked her head and listened for any sign that her grandparents had heard.

The sound of snoring came from behind the closed door across the landing. How did her grandmother put up with such a racket? An echoing snore sounded, steadily joining with the previous snore. Both were at it.

Venetia turned round and whispered to her sister that they would have to go down the stairs on tiptoe.

Anna Marie nodded nervously and licked her dry lips. At the same time, she tightened her hold on the small battered suitcase that banged against her side. The stairs were winding and narrow, a quarter landing halfway down where the cat frequently slept. He was there now, curled up into a ball, his tabby fur heaving in sleep.

He opened one eye as they stepped over him and languidly stretched out one furry paw so that Anna Marie, following behind her sister, nearly stepped on him.

By the time they'd reached the bottom of the stairs he was up and right behind them.

Anna Maria suggested he wanted milk. Venetia told her to ignore the creature and keep her voice down.

'D'ya want to wake everybody up?' she hissed.

In response Anna Marie stuffed her fingers into her mouth. She certainly did not want to wake everyone up. The consequences of being found out were too terrible.

In her mind she went over how she'd come to this predicament. Venetia had asked for her help. Headstrong and opinionated, her twin had declared herself to be in love and intending to run away with Patrick Casey.

'But I couldn't go on me own and leave you behind,' she'd said. 'I'd be worried about you all the time and I'd be homesick – not so much for this place, but sick with worry about you.'

On reflection, Anna Marie could see that her sister had been appealing to her sympathy as well as almost accusing her that her staying behind would blight her happiness.

The two of them had stuck together since their father had

left them here. Where one went – usually Venetia – the other followed. They were inseparable and neither could contemplate life without the other.

When she'd asked whether Patrick was going with them, Venetia announced airily that he didn't think he was, but she intended working her womanly wiles on him.

'He'll come. He won't be able to resist.'

The downstairs room was cold and grey in the early morning light. Embers glowed from amongst the white ash in the grate; evidence of their grandmother's insistence on using only coal in her fireplace, never the poor smokiness of freshly dug peat.

'Peat,' she'd proclaimed, 'is for the poor who till the fields. There's no room for such stuff in town; sure, isn't the air thick enough with horse droppings and them new-fangled motorcars and suchlike?'

Even if there had been chance to stop and take a bite of breakfast, Venetia knew she couldn't possibly keep it down – she was that excited. The world and Patrick Casey were waiting for her and Anna Marie was coming too.

The cat's tail curled around Anna Marie's leg as it purred for milk.

'Leave it,' Venetia hissed at her. 'We haven't time to bother with that flea-bitten creature.'

Anna Marie frowned. 'Mouser isn't flea bitten.'

'No,' said Venetia with a grimace. 'He's not much of a mouser either.'

Venetia opened the front door, the resulting draught sending the ashes from the fire floating into the air. The cat slipped out of the door before she could shut him in.

'Mouser, you contrary creature, you,' said Venetia in a hushed voice.

The town of Dunavon was not as large as their grandmother made out and all alleys and side streets led onto the high street, where the shops were situated. Once a week the market, where farmers and others roundabout brought their produce and animals, throbbed with sound and liveliness.

'He's not here yet,' whispered Anna Maria on stepping into the high street. She sounded just about as nervous as she looked.

Venetia oozed confidence. 'He said wait at the bus stop and get on it. If he can't make it with the lorry, he'll meet us in Queenstown itself. At the quay. And he'll have the tickets all ready for us. And stop whispering. We're out of the house now.'

'But someone up above one of these shops might hear us,' Anna Marie whispered back. 'And they all know who we are and they'll tell . . . they're bound to.'

Venetia sighed and shook her head. 'Oh, but you're such a silly goose at times, that you are. So what if they do. Once we're in Queenstown, it'll be too late.'

Anna Marie frowned and pouted. 'No I'm not a silly goose.'

Venetia was not one to admit it, but she was feeling a bit nervous herself. Out of sight of her twin, she crossed her fingers behind her back. It would be an hour before the bus to Cork pulled in and there were bound to be a few locals getting on who knew them. If luck was with them, Patrick would be along with his father's lorry.

His uncle had bought the lorry army surplus after the Great War. He was famous all around for the noisy, smoky vehicle, which he'd painted green and hand written his name in gold-coloured lettering along the side: Seamus Casey & Sons Ltd, Haulyer and Transporter – Distanse No Objet.

The fact was that Seamus had only daughters and no sons, but had decided that was how his business was best styled. Neither was he a limited company, though he was of limited education, which accounted for his abysmal spelling.

Not that Venetia cared a jot for any of that. It was Patrick she had an eye for; Patrick who let her clamber up beside him when he was taking peat to Kennedys' General Store, or dead horses to the place where they were made into glue, or bricks and mortar when his father was carrying out the building side of his business. The truth was that Patrick's father did any job that needed doing as long as it paid.

'Phew! That's a terrible smell,' Venetia would say to him when it was dead horses he was hauling.

'Never mind, my darling,' he would say. 'When I'm rich I'll buy you perfume from Paris. How would you like that?'

She'd told him she would like it a lot and had even allowed him to kiss her.

The one big truth that could be said for this part of Ireland was that it was damp. Someone had told her that Ireland was wetter than Wales, but seeing as she'd never been to Wales, she had no opinion to offer. Ireland was damp; of that there was no doubt.

'My feet are freezin',' said Anna Marie, stamping her feet in turn in an effort to keep warm.

'Ah, stop yer moaning,' said Venetia. 'We'll be warm as toast before long. Patrick's got a blanket in his lorry. We'll be snug once we're under that.'

'And how would you know it's so snug?'

'It's a blanket. It's bound to be,' returned Venetia, purposely turning her head so that her sister could not see her guilty expression. She knew for sure it was warm beneath the blanket – especially when she'd been snuggled up to Patrick.

Anna Marie was doing enough worrying for the two of them.

'What if he doesn't come? We've barely enough to live on, and if we do end up paying the bus fare . . .'

'He'll come,' whispered Venetia, mostly to herself. 'I know he'll come.'

Sure enough, the smell of unburned fuel from a leaky exhaust, accompanied by the odd backfire, heralded the arrival of Patrick and his father's ex-army lorry.

'See? Told you so,' said Venetia, her smile wide enough to crack her face, her cheeks pink from pleasure not early morning dew.

The brakes squealed as Patrick brought the dark green vehicle to a juddering halt, then swung open the door. His grin was infectious and his eyes were dancing with vitality despite the early hour.

'Will you hurry up? I haven't got all day.'

Venetia got in first and barely avoided the smacker of a kiss Patrick was aiming for her lips.

'Patrick Casey! We'll be having none of that!'

For some reason she didn't want her sister to see her doing something so personal. It was a different matter when she and Patrick were alone.

'Well? Haven't changed your mind, have you?'

'How about you? Are you coming with us?'

'Oh no. Not me,' he said, shaking his head vehemently. 'I've got a job of work and besides, me father couldn't carry on without me. He's getting too old to be running the business on his own.'

Venetia slumped back in the seat wearing a disappointed expression whilst Patrick helped Anna Marie up into the cab.

'That's up to you, but I have to say I think you're making a mistake.'

The cab only had two seats, so the two girls squeezed on one, Patrick needing the other seeing as he was the one driving.

Venetia eyed him sidelong, desperately wanting to lean over and squeeze his thigh, even get him to pull over so they could have a kiss and cuddle, though not with Anna Marie aboard.

Patrick began whistling as they rumbled along the road. He

liked Venetia a lot, kissed her a lot, but that didn't mean he had to go with her to the ends of the earth. Ireland suited him fine.

'Do you know I've seen little of Ireland, let alone America?'

'America is bigger. A lot bigger. Come on, Patrick. What do you say?' Her tone was demanding.

'What would I get in America that I don't have here?' he said, shrugging his shoulders in that nonchalant manner of his, his brandy brown hair falling across his eyes.

Venetia looked as though she might stab him with her eyes alone.

'Me for a start, Patrick Casey.'

'Then, don't go.'

He took his eyes off the road for a moment to look at her. She was well worth looking at and he could honestly say he'd seen a lot more of Venetia Brodie than most people.

'Are you stupid or something, Patrick, wanting to stay here all your life? I certainly don't want to stay in this dump. What you want to do is up to you, you're a free man for all that, but if you loved me as you say you do, you would come. No question about it!'

She badly wanted him to change his mind and come. Having just her sister for company was not enough. Even now Anna Marie was looking at her goggle eyed having heard Venetia mention the words Patrick and love in the same sentence.

The truth of the matter was that without Patrick coming with her, she was having second thoughts. Getting on a ship going to New York was exciting but also daunting. She'd only been on the sea once before when her father had first brought her and Anna Marie over from England. Neither of them had wanted to come. Neither of them had wanted to leave their sister Magda.

Whilst their mother was ill and even after her death, their older sister had done her best to look after them. Only three years between them, yet it had seemed as though Magda was more like ten years older.

'Your gran and yer granfer are going to give you hell when they find out you've run away,' warned Patrick.

Anna Marie turned visibly pale. 'Perhaps we should go back . . .'

'Nonsense.' Venetia was tidying her hair in the lorry's rear-view mirror, running her fingers through the thick, dark locks. 'They're old fashioned,' she said as she smeared lipstick onto her lips, lipstick she'd kept hidden in the chamber pot beneath the bed during the day and under her pillow at night. Thankfully it was never discovered.

'The thing is that we've left school and should be allowed to do what we want in life. All they want me and Anna Marie to do is help around the farm.'

'I don't mind helping,' said Anna Marie timidly.

Venetia ignored her and carried on with her criticism of the people who'd looked after them for seven years.

'The animals stink. Especially the chickens with all that poo around their backsides. Even the eggs are tarnished with it.'

'Venetia, the animals can't help . . .'

'You're a silly goose, Anna Marie. But it's not just the animals. It's being forced to go to mass three times a week. I mean, what's the point and how do we know God even exists?'

'It's about belief . . .'

'Belief my ass. If there was a God, he wouldn't have taken our mother and split up the family!'

Anna Marie sucked in her breath. 'You shouldn't say that word, Venetia. It's rude.'

'Ass, ass, ass.'

It was obvious from Venetia's expression that she was enjoying teasing her sister.

'Good job Granfer can't hear you,' said her sister whilst Patrick, who was used to cussing, kept his attention on the road. 'You know what happened the last time you remarked that God was dead.'

Venetia nodded. 'Aye. Got me mouth washed out with soap and water for my pains. And confession three times a week. Though I still believe what I said,' she imparted to her sister. 'If God cared that much, he wouldn't have taken our mother or parted us from our sister and brother.'

Anna Marie hissed at her to keep her voice down. 'And you never mention our father in yer prayers,' she added.

'Might already be dead,' snapped Venetia, wishing her sister would stop reminding her of the past and fix her thoughts on the future.

As the lorry bumped and rattled along the road to Queenstown, Venetia tried to remember what her father looked like. It had been at least two years since his last visit. As usual he'd made all the sweet promises about coming back with presents and taking them off to see Magda, and even Michael if they'd a mind to.

He'd charmed his daughters, but not his parents. His mother had looked at him with a mix of love and rebuke. His father had narrowed his eyes, growled and asked, 'What have you come back for?'

Later she'd seen them in the barn together, not looking the way father should look at son or son look at father. They were squared up as though about to exchange blows. In the morning Joseph Brodie was gone.

As usual it had hurt badly when he'd failed to keep his promise. Their father was their only link to the past – not that Anna Marie seemed to care so much for him as Venetia did. Venetia, like her mother before her, could forgive him everything.

The blame, Venetia decided, was with her grandparents for shouting at him the time before that when he'd come home unannounced. They'd called him shiftless, unreliable and self-centred. He'd laughed off their accusations, but she knew, or at least thought she did, that he'd been hurt. He was that kind of man, a bit like Patrick, with his dark hair and blue eyes – Spanish complexion they called it.

All the way, Venetia tried to persuade Patrick to go with them. He'd laughed and been pleasant enough, but wouldn't budge. He was not going and that was that.

'Ah, but you'll change your mind when we get to Queenstown and see the shiny sea,' she told him.

In response he grinned and shook his head. 'You'll make somebody a nagging wife, Venetia Brodie, and that's for sure.'

'Yes,' she said, smiling at him. 'Worth it though, 'cause I'd make up for the nagging in other ways.'

She saw his grin widen and hope that he'd be the one she'd marry surged in her heart.

The sight of Queenstown with its big houses, busy streets and the smell of the sea fair took Venetia's breath away.

Anna Marie was also excited, hanging out of the open window, her pale brown hair blowing in tendrils across her face.

'Will you look at all this now? Have you ever seen such a grand place?'

'Of course I have,' snapped her sister. 'This is grand enough, though not as grand as London.'

'Oh come on, Venetia. You can't remember London. We were only little.'

Anna Marie's laughter was as bright and bubbly as a brook flowing over moss-covered stones and very surprising. Up until now leaving home hadn't sat well with her but the sight of the sea had.

Out of the corner of her eye Venetia caught Patrick eyeing her sister with interest. It hurt.

'Queenstown is grand enough, though I wouldn't mind going to London,' he said to her. 'Though only once I've had my fill of Ireland.'

The lorry grated to a stop outside the dockyard gates.

'There's the dock and all the fine ships. That's where you'll find them,' said Patrick, nodding in the direction of brick buildings and towering cranes. 'Now come on. Get on yer way. I've got a long drive back home and can't be hanging around here.'

His manner was chirpy, his eyes brilliant and Venetia found herself feeling less enthusiastic about leaving to build a new life.

After springing out of the driver's side, Patrick passed across the bull-nosed front of the lorry and opened the passenger side door.

Gripping Anna Marie's trim waist with his huge hands, he swung her down from the cab first.

'Why, yer light as a feather,' he said to her.

Anna Marie blushed when he held her a little too close for a little too long.

'Are you forgetting the girl you said you'd love forever?' Venetia's tone was confident, though underneath she was a little piqued that he hadn't rushed to help her down from the cab.

His wide grin and the twinkle in his eyes was reassuring as he turned back to help her down.

'As if I could ever forget you.'

The kiss he gave her and the way he hugged her close against his body allayed her fears. Patrick Casey was still hers and hers alone. She wound her arms around him and felt the warmth beneath his coat.

There was nothing in his attentions to Anna Marie. No need to get jealous, she told herself. Anna Marie is scared of going on that boat and he's just trying to reassure her.

145

'You've noticed she's a bit nervous about all this,' she whispered into his ear.

'I did,' he murmured back, his arms still enveloping her.

'She read about the *Titanic* and all those people drowning.'

'You'll be fine,' he whispered and kissed her again.

Once their lips parted, she glanced over at her sister, thinking that she would be eyeing her jealously. Instead she saw she wasn't looking their way at all, but stood there, bag clutched with both hands in front of her and staring down at her feet until the two of them had finished.

My, but I'm going to miss him, thought Venetia. She looked up into Patrick's face, feeling desperate for him to change his mind. 'Come with me, Patrick. Please.'

He laughed. 'I couldn't do that. I couldn't leave me old dad without somebody to drive the lorry. I'm the only one who can.'

She knew it wasn't strictly true, that both his father and his younger brother could drive, though his father preferred to drive a horse and his brother was only twelve years old.

Venetia chose to believe him. He was torn between his family and her. She couldn't blame him for that, could she?

'When I make my fortune I'll come back and buy you a bigger and better lorry,' she told him.

'I'll look forward to it.'

Once she knew for certain that they'd finished hugging and kissing, Anna Marie came and stood by her side.

Together they watched Patrick insert the starting handle into the surly beast, turning it again and again before the cranky engine spurted into life.

'Behave yourself, girls,' he shouted, then with a wave he was up into the cab and gone.

Venetia brushed a tear from her eye and stood there watching the spluttering, banging old lorry belch out smoke until there was only smoke left. Both the lorry and Patrick were gone.

'So now what?' asked Anna Marie.

Her sister sniffed, straightened and thrust forward her stalwart chin.

'We get a job on a boat.'

'What if we can't?'

'Then we get on the boat anyway – and hope that nobody sees us.'

Chapter Twenty-one

Magda
1935

Magda followed Winnie into her private rooms. It was not the first time she'd been in here, but it wasn't as it was before. Tea chests overflowed with items that had filled cupboards or sat inside Winnie's glass-fronted cabinet.

'You're leaving?'

'I'm not the woman I was.'

'Your leg's worse?'

Winnie's face sagged, the corners of her eyes and lips down-turned, her flesh seemingly too weary to cling to her bones.

'It's more than that.'

She gestured to one of the chairs on which were a pile of books. 'If you'd like to remove those . . .'

She slumped into a chair, both hands on her walking stick as Magda lifted the books with slim fingers, placing them gently but firmly on top of another pile.

What was it about this girl that made her think of her own dead child? She'd had other girls here as disadvantaged as Magda and not felt so inclined towards them.

'I take it your aunt's been up to her old tricks,' said Winnie.

'If you mean she's been drinking and shouting and yelling all around the house, then yes. She won't let me have my mother's Bible and tells me such lies about it. First she says it's locked away in a cupboard that Uncle James made, and quite honestly I hate to destroy anything he made, the poor man. She led him a terrible life. No wonder he stayed at sea. And now he's dead. Then she tells me she sold the Bible, and then she says she pawned it, and now she says she threw it on the fire.'

Winnie eyed her steadfastly, her grey hair neatly packed into a black net snood, a necklace of mauve beads at her throat.

'And which do you believe?'

Magda tapped the fingers of one hand on top of the other.

'I think it's still there in that cupboard. I think the only way I can get it is if I pay her for it. I don't know how much she wants, but . . .' Her shoulders hunched then fell when she sighed. 'Knowing my aunt it won't be for pennies. She'll take everything I have, that is the little I've saved from my wages.'

'How old are you, child?'

'Eighteen.'

A feeling like the thrust of a knife pierced Winnie's heart. Her daughter would have been Magda's age – had she lived – had Reuben Fitts not insisted she get rid of it and get back to work. On her back. With him taking the biggest cut of the money.

Only the fact that she had nearly died had made him relent and pay her for her troubles – and the fact that his mother had interfered and told him to do the best for her seeing as the experience had left her crippled.

So he'd given her money, set her up to run this place. Not that she'd done too badly, but the time had come to get out.

Whilst she sat there, contemplative and thinking thoughts

she'd never thought to think, Magda's eyes swept over the disruption.

'I'm leaving this place,' Winnie explained. 'I'm too old and too sick to carry on. It's time I retired.'

Magda looked at her in alarm. 'But if you're not here, how can I stay here?'

'You can come with me. I'd like that, but only if you're going to the interview.'

Magda eyed her resolutely. 'If I can.'

'Is it really what you want?'

Magda looked down at the floor whilst she thought about it.

'My mother died because she couldn't afford a doctor. By the time she got to one, it was too late.'

'Your mother. Of course. It's not going to be easy. Most doctors are men, but there are far more women doctors than there used to be. The Great War's mostly to thank for that. First they were not welcome, then they couldn't get enough. And once it was over, there was a big gap where men used to be and they began crying out for doctors no matter whether male or female. That's as I understand it anyways.'

'Women doctors would be better at helping women.' Magda looked into the glowing coals in the fireplace. 'I saw my mother cough up blood. I heard Gertie screaming. Emily said the doctor took a long time coming and then only came when he was paid double the fee. I wouldn't do that. I *couldn't* do that.'

Winnie made herself more comfortable, sitting to favour the less damaged hip. Her thoughts were dashing around like painted horses on a merry-go-round. After all these years she was moving out of this place to a very pretty mews cottage that had once been a stable with the coachman living above. For the first time in years she would be alone with only her books and her memories for company. It had been a difficult decision to arrive at, but she knew her pain was becoming worse and she wasn't likely to make old bones. However, much as she had convinced herself that she would at last have her independence, the thought of being alone had suddenly become less attractive. Alone. Nobody. No friends. No family.

Those old memories aroused by Magda's appearance had refused to fade. Magda, she had decided, was the daughter she'd never had.

'Magda. I meant it about sponsoring you.'

Magda looked at her open mouthed, her fingers falling to play with the string handles of the carrier bags that held all her belongings.

Her hand stilled in its fidgeting. Her eyes were wide and luminous, strikingly beautiful against her creamy complexion and the mass of dark hair falling about her face.

'I don't know . . . what to say . . .'

Winnie sighed. 'I'm going to tell you something, Magda. You know they call me Winnie One Leg. You know I have a painful problem with my hip. This is because the baby I was expecting was pulled from me in pieces. There should have been a doctor called and I should have gone to hospital. But there was no one. You've seen how it can be with Gertie. My dead daughter is long gone. I would like you to be that daughter to me and, in return, you train as a doctor. A fitting memorial I think.'

The young woman sitting opposite her stared in disbelief, her eyes seeming to fill her face.

Winnie sat hardly daring to breathe – not that she breathed that deeply nowadays. Her lungs weren't much better than her hips thanks to the deprivations of a childhood in a northern seaport.

'I'm moving to a little place in Prince Albert Mews. A little cottage where I shall spend the rest of my days. I'd like you to move there with me – if you would like. Even if you don't want to fall in with my plan to make you a doctor, I'd still like your company. But only if you want to. If you want to join the girls here, well that's up to you but that's not your only option. And well, it will be under new management . . .'

She let her voice trail away and did not exhibit a single look or word to influence Magda's decision. It had to be her decision, hers and hers alone. But it had to be done quickly. Reuben or his son would be along to oversee the changeover between her and the new madam.

Winnie looked at the clock, the only thing left on the high ebony mantelpiece.

'The removal van is coming soon. It's not safe for you to stay here tonight. I wouldn't want word getting back to . . .' She paused. 'Certain people.'

'Bradley Fitts.'

'That's right. It's best you leave right away. Go with the van. I'll pay them to keep their mouth shut. Set about sorting things out at Prince Albert Mews. I'll be there as soon as I can. Will you do that?'

Magda was sitting with her hands tightly clasped, her beautiful eyes shining with wonder.

'Do you mean it? About me becoming a doctor?'

Winnie felt a strange tightening in her throat as though she were about to choke or cough up a fish bone. She wasn't choking. And she hadn't been eating fish.

'Yes. I meant it. It would be a tribute to me. It would be a tribute to your mother.'

When Magda nodded and said a quiet yes in agreement to her plan, it felt in her head as though somebody had shouted out three cheers for Winnie One Leg.

One of the girls came banging on the door to let Winnie know the removal van had arrived.

Winnie shouted back that she'd be just a minute.

Then she stood there, ear to the door until she was sure the footsteps had receded into the front parlour where the girls waited for men.

She handed Magda a thick green shawl. 'Quickly. Put this shawl around your head and get out there. Climb up into the back of the van and make it look as though you're something to do with old Tom, the removal man.'

Magda grabbed her carrier bags with one hand whilst holding the scarf tight beneath her chin.

'And you,' Winnie said turning to the van's owner who'd only just stepped into the room, 'take my girl with you. Not a word to anyone.'

'Not a word,' he said, taking the pound note she was offering from her hand. 'Not a bloody word. Who is she anyways?'

'My daughter,' said Winnie. 'She's my daughter.' And in her heart, she was.

Magda got as far into the back of the van as she could whilst tea chests and furniture were loaded in behind her.

Finally the doors were closed and Magda was alone in the darkness. The van smelled of dust and mothballs, but it didn't matter. Thanks to Winnie, her life was about to change and ultimately her wish might at last come true. But she knew better than to hope too much, better than to rush into things without planning everything in advance. Once she had money there were options, and options were what she dearly needed.

Once the van was heading towards the end of the street, Winnie's fear loosened.

For a moment she stood looking up at the outside of the house that she was finally leaving.

'So she's gone.' Emily was the only girl not occupied with a man.

Winnie felt her fear re-emerge. She would have preferred that nobody had seen Magda leave.

'Having her live with you then?'

'That's none of your business.'

'Isn't it? Bradley Fitts has got a soft spot for our Magda. You know that, don't you?'

It wasn't like Winnie to lose her temper, but she could see where this comment was heading.

'It's over, Emily. The girl's father has come home from the sea. She's off to live with him. Tell Fitts that and make sure he bloody well believes it!'

Emily held her head to one side. 'What's it worth?'

'I thought you were her friend.'

'I'd like to escape this game too, Winnie. But you know as well as I do that once you're in it, it's a devil of a job to escape. Best not to enter the game in the first place.'

Winnie pursed her lips whilst eyeing Emily as though seeing her for the first time. The eyes that looked back at her were as hard as her own had once been, but she hadn't always been like that. She'd been kindly once – even to Magda – but there it was, whoring had hardened her. Money was everything.

Resigned to what she had to do, a crisp five pound note found its way out of her purse and into Emily's hand.

'Her father's come home. Just you remember to say that.'

Emily's smile wasn't exactly sincere. 'Of course I will, Winnie. Of course I will.'

The next morning Winnie took a taxi to a bay-windowed building close to Chelsea Bridge. The brass plaque set into the wall outside said 'Cottemore and Brown, Solicitors'.

To set her plan in place, she needed the assistance of those in high places and she'd certainly made the acquaintance of plenty.

Her dear friend, Henry Cottemore, had advised her to buy the pretty little cottage that she was moving into.

'These sweet little places where coachmen used to live will become very fashionable in future. Horses belong to the past. Cars are the future,' he'd told her.

Winnie had heeded his advice and bought one for cash, the one thing she was never short of.

Winnie prided herself on knowing some very influential people. A twinkle came to her deep-set eyes when she thought of the men who paid for the services offered by her establishment. City aldermen, judges, merchants and bankers wearing bowler hats and swinging a rolled-up umbrella. They all had their vices and over the years some of these men had also become friends and useful business advisers.

Henry Cottemore was one of these. In his middle years, married to a wife who preferred life in the country to that of the city, he became a regular patron at Winnie's establishment where he found the companionship and physical satisfaction he so badly missed.

'Jennifer prefers pets,' he'd said to Winnie back then. 'She has three dogs in the house and gundogs out back and she looks after them very well. I only receive the little love she has left, sparse as it is.'

His days of taking comfort in the arms of one of her girls were now only a fleeting fancy, but more often than not he merely entertained the fond memories of how things used to be.

Over the years, out of mutual respect and a shared past, he gave her advice about her investments and knew more of what she was worth than anyone else could possibly know. Winnie was very well off and quite frankly he admired her.

Presuming she wished to make some alteration to her portfolio of stocks, shares and property, he bid her take a seat and asked what he could do for her.

His office smelled of beeswax and was graced with the steady ticking of a wall clock.

Henry rubbed at his hands. 'Rheumatism,' he said. 'Quite frankly, Winifred my dear, I never expected to ever get this old. I thought I would be twenty-one forever.'

'But we were young once,' said Winnie with a smile.

'If only we could turn the clock back,' murmured Henry.

Winnie didn't respond. Henry was speaking from the experience of a privileged youth. In her case she'd been turfed out to work, an under-maid in a house in Bloomsbury.

The work had been hard, the hours long and the wage almost non-existent. She'd hated that place, the only joy one half day per week off and one full day a month.

On those precious days she'd walked Regent's Park and if she had tuppence in her pocket, she'd get the tram up to the West End and stare in windows where rich folks shopped.

Sometimes, just sometimes when she'd had more than a shilling in her pocket, she'd gone to the music hall with Ruby the scullery maid. That was where she'd met Reuben Fitts, the man she'd fallen head over heels for and who had quickly blighted her life.

'Now,' said Henry. 'What is it you want to see me about?'

'You've met my adopted daughter, Magda?'

Henry Cottemore contemplated this woman who was much younger than himself and had once been beautiful. Life had not been kind – certainly not in her early years, but something had happened that had ignited a new light in her dark blue eyes. He wondered what it was.

She began telling him about adopting a daughter and how she felt it was like a memorial to the baby daughter who had died.

'I have plans for her.'

Henry raised a querulous eyebrow.

Winnie saw his questioning look and shook her head.

'No. She will not be going the way of the working girls. I want to give her the opportunity to be something better. That's why I moved here so that we'd be separate from all that. No,' she said, shaking her head. 'I have other plans for Magda, but I need your advice. I want her to be educated. She did very well at school and has been working in the square on a market stall, but she's too good for that. She's bright, really bright. I want her to do more than work in a factory, a shop or even an office slamming her fingers on one of those new-fangled typewriting machines. She's been accepted for an interview at the medical school at Queen Mary's Hospital. She wants to be a doctor.'

Henry looked down at his shoes feeling very privileged to share Winnie's plans. If he'd still been a wild, young stud, he would be curious to see this wonderful girl who had so impressed his old friend. If she was that beautiful, in the past he might have whisked her away and set her up in a nice apartment in Chelsea. But he wasn't young. He was older and wiser and Winnie, bless her heart, trusted his judgement. He was also in no doubt that Magda was very special to her – female doctors were still few and far between and securing a place for this girl would be a challenge.

'Does Magda know of your plans?'

'We've discussed the matter, though I don't think she truly believes me just yet. I suppose I should get her father's consent if I was going to adopt her legally, but nobody's seen him for years.'

'Does she have any other family?'

'Sisters. A brother. Her aunt who lives across the way from me. Hard as a brick she is. Kept the girl short of food and just about everything else. Puts her neglect down to the father. Reckons the bounder's failed to send a sou for her for years. My guess is that the Connemara mare as we call the Irish bitch spent it all on herself.'

157

'So what is it you require me to do?'

'You have medical contacts at Queen Mary's – them that are physicians?'

One finger thoughtfully stroked his lips as he nodded.

'She has an interview there. I want to make sure it goes well. That they overlook her . . . background. I want them to give her a chance. I know it can be done – if you know the right people.'

Henry threw back his head and laughed.

'Winnie, you demand too much.'

'Is it too much? Isn't it true you know just about everyone of importance in London?'

'I wouldn't go so far as to say that . . .'

'Can it be done?'

He met the spark of hope in Winnie's eyes. Her face glowed with intent and also affection.

'I'm going to tell her tonight that everything is in place for her to learn about being a doctor, that she'll pass the interview with flying colours. I want you to make sure she does. Can I tell her that?'

Henry hesitated. Yes, he did indeed know the right people capable of circumventing the normal qualifications needed for a medical student. But Winnie, for all her sordid past, was not a fool. Indeed he regarded her as having an exceptionally bright mind. If she thought Magda was worthy of becoming a doctor, then who was he to argue? He had to take it at face value.

'How old is she?'

'She's eighteen.'

'That's very young.'

'She's very mature.'

'I'm glad to hear it. I'll tell my contacts that she's twenty and has undertaken a foundation course.'

Winnie nodded. 'I would appreciate that.'

Henry Cottemore removed his glasses and smiled at her over the big desk with its elegant ink well, and leather-bound blotting pad; legal files were piled at each end like Palladian pillars.

'I take it our friend Reuben Fitts has no interest in the girl.'

Winnie shook her head a little too abruptly. 'No. He does not.'

Chapter Twenty-two

The Twins
1932

'It's dusty under here. I'm going to sneeze,' whispered Anna Marie Brodie, her hand clamped over her nose.

'Don't you dare!' her sister hissed back.

'I can't help it.'

'Try and concentrate on our future. We've done enough work on the farm. I would never have left school if I'd thought that all I would do was pluck and draw chickens, and salt bacon for the next two years.'

'I'm scared,' said Anna Marie, wishing she hadn't been talked into this hare-brained scheme in the first place. She had been quite content to work on the farm. Venetia, however, was headstrong, wild and persuasive.

'I'm going to sneeze again,' she murmured.

Venetia clamped her hand over her sister's mouth, but the sneeze came out anyway – just as somebody entered the cabin.

First they saw a pair of polished black shoes.

'Out from there, whoever you are,' shouted an angry male voice.

They crawled out to find themselves looking up at the

enormous belly of Chief Steward Kevin McCall. Once they were standing, they found themselves looking over the big belly to the red beard that hid the lower half of his face.

It was his job to accompany Mrs Brennan, the housekeeper, to check cabins and state rooms for cleanliness before passengers for the 'Northern Star' arrived for the trans-Atlantic voyage.

He'd eaten too much liver and onions at lunchtime and could still taste the onions. As a consequence the wind in his stomach was causing him pain, and in consequence of that he wanted to let wind – from either end. As a man of some status on board, he couldn't possibly do that in front of Mrs Brennan. He'd hoped to get the inspection finished in record time. Finding two stowaways served to make his stomach lurch and his temper short.

'Mrs Brennan. Will you please send for the police?'

Mrs Brennan obeyed immediately, out of the door so fast it was as though there were a mutilated corpse in the cabin rather than two young girls robbed of their dream.

Small piggy eyes formed the focus point of a glowering expression.

'Turn out your pockets!'

His voice was like thunder.

Anna Marie obeyed immediately, but not so Venetia. Her dream was in tatters.

'We got nothing in our pockets,' she said defiantly.

The piggy eyes almost vanished above ballooning cheeks as he fought to hold back his wind.

Seeing that the contents of their pockets came to no more than a handkerchief in one and a few pennies in the other, he turned his attention to their suitcases.

'What's in the case?'

'Nothing.'

'Open it.'

Venetia frowned. 'Are you the sort of man who likes to see young women's underwear?'

'Open it!'

Venetia shook her head. 'No,' she declared hotly. 'You're not a policeman. You've no right looking in my case. Anyways, we wanted passage to America. We want a job. We can clean the cabins, look after the guests. Can clean them better than the cleaners you've got now. They've left fluff under the bed. That's why Anna Marie sneezed.'

Kevin McCall growled and sucked on his beard. It felt as though his guts were about to explode.

'I've no time for this,' he snapped.

They were locked in a crew cabin to await the arrival of the police.

Venetia sat on her suitcase, her arms entwined around her knees.

Anna Marie was pacing up and down, her blue eyes looking extra large in her paler than pale face.

'They'll put us in prison.'

'Don't be stupid. All we did was hide in a cabin.'

'That man thought we took something. We might never go home again.'

'We took nothing, you silly goose,' Venetia smiled as a wicked thought occurred to her. 'Mind you, depending whether they still send thieves overseas, we could say that we did. Perhaps we'll get to America that way.'

The crew cabin they'd been locked in, though built for six, was far smaller than the least of the passenger cabins. Two police constables arrived and filled the room.

Venetia stood up and gave them as fierce a look as they gave her.

Anna Marie crumpled onto the lower bunk of a two-bunk arrangement, her knuckles white with tension.

'So we'll be asking you a few questions,' said one of the policemen.

First they were asked their names. Venetia saw no harm in telling them this, so didn't throw her sister any of her more threatening looks.

After that, they went through the same questions as Mr McCall who stood out in the corridor behind them.

What were they doing there?

Had they taken anything?

Did they know it was a criminal offence to board a boat without first buying a ticket?

Venetia explained in no uncertain terms that they wanted to get to America and were willing to work their passage. They were not thieves and had not taken anything not belonging to them.

'Right.' Both of the policemen turned and began talking with Mr McCall where he stood out in the corridor.

The most senior of the policemen, in age if not in rank, suggested to Mr McCall that, seeing as nothing had been taken, the girls be released.

'Unless you happen to want more willing hands for the crossing to New York and want to take them on?'

'Certainly not! I will not give these girls a job on principle. They stole aboard without permission. Besides, I doubt they're old enough. Cabin stewardesses must be at least eighteen years of age, though we prefer them older. It makes for less trouble. Young girls are trouble!'

'The cabin was unoccupied you say.'

'It was.'

'And nothing was missing?'

'Not as far as I can tell, but I know their type. I demand you arrest them.'

'For what?'

'Trespass.'

The senior policeman, a man with a reddish face and greying hair, eyed the two girls over his shoulder.

'Hardly worth bothering. Mr McCall, this is not the first case of its type we've been called out to, and it won't be the last. It's a regular occurrence. The others were let off with a warning. I think the same warning applies here.'

'I suppose it will make no difference if I insist?'

'None whatsoever,' said the first policeman.

'Then that's settled, Mr McCall,' said the second. 'We'll take them with us and make sure they get home safely. Wherever home happens to be.'

The police station had been built to resemble a castle, though it had never been such. It was a mere fifty years old, built of grey stone with small windows, which only served to add to its look of invulnerability.

'So,' said the sergeant who had brought them in and given them cups of tea, 'where exactly are you from?'

Anna Marie opened her mouth to answer, but closed it again when Venetia kicked her ankle.

'Here,' said Venetia resolutely. 'From right here.'

She fixed her eyes on a silver button on his tunic hoping the lie would be believed.

However, the sergeant was a local man and knew a country accent when he heard one.

'No, I don't think so,' he said softly. 'Now just so's we get this right and you don't fall into further trouble, tell me the truth of where you're from and things will go well for you. I might even get you a couple of ginger biscuits to go with that tea. You must be starving.'

'Dunavon!' Anna Marie's eyes were full of tears and neither she nor Venetia had had anything to eat since the night before.

Venetia glared at her sister. 'I told you to say nothing.'

The police sergeant sighed and shook his head. 'What you did was a pretty desperate thing, but you must have had good reason to do it. How about you tell me what that reason was?'

Tears were spilling silently from Anna Marie's eyes and between dabbing at them, she was twisting her handkerchief like she would strangle a rabbit.

'Our mother died, our family was split up and we've left school, but my sister here didn't want to work on the farm. She doesn't like the smell of chickens; she thought it would be a good idea to go to America and seek our fortunes. It was her that persuaded me to go with her.'

'Traitor,' Venetia hissed.

Anna Marie hissed back. 'It's true. You're the one who wanted to leave.'

Sergeant Beverley controlled the urge to smile. He'd been telling the truth about them not being the first girls wanting to stowaway to America. They were young and foolhardy, but he had to admire their pluck.

'I would have gone meself when I was younger. Yes, indeed I would. But my mother was widowed and loved me. You can't just leave those that love you, now can you?'

Anna Marie blew her nose then looked to her sister. Wasn't she always the one with an answer for everything?

Venetia was staring at the floor, both hands cradling a white china cup.

'Your grandparents must be very worried.'

Venetia frowned. 'But we've only been away just over a day. How could they know?'

'Well, somebody told them. Someone who knew where you were.'

The two sisters exchanged a brief glance. Anna Marie's expression was one of puzzlement but also of relief.

Her sister was far from relieved; in fact she was dismayed

and disbelieving. On reflection she accepted that her first suspicion was right. There was only one person who knew where they'd gone. Patrick Casey!

The Garda informed them that arrangements had been made for them to go home.

'In style,' he added. 'In a motor car no less. And guess who you're travelling with? Father Anthony, off to take up his appointment as parish priest in your home town. How lucky for you is that?'

They were told to get themselves ready to travel, use the lavatory and take doorsteps of bread and cheese each, with the police station's compliments.

Father Anthony was waiting for them, sitting in the police station reception area, the green wall behind him almost as dark as his black priest's robe.

He was sitting with his elbows resting on his knees reading what looked like a prayer book.

Shoving his prayer book in the hidden pocket of his robe, his youthful face visibly hardened as he got to his feet.

'Ah. The runaways. Shame on you both. The pair of you need horsewhipping. I dare say your grandfather might very well oblige.'

His words coming as they did after the kinder tones of the police sergeant startled Anna Marie and made Venetia wary.

He towered over them, the top half of his body similar in shape to a wedge of cheese, his hips so shallow that at first glance he seemed to have room for only one leg.

Bony cheekbones half hid his eyes so it seemed he was looking at them from over a window ledge. His hair was black and curly. The black moustache looked as though it had been stuck on as an afterthought and plastered in place with wax.

'I'll make sure they get home safely,' he assured the

constabulary in clipped, superior tones. 'Though it isn't quite the way I intended introducing myself to the community – returning errant young girls to a farmyard!'

The car was a small Ford with spindly wheels and a boxy, compact look about it.

Riding in Patrick's father's old lorry was about the nearest either girl had ever got to riding in a motor car. But a lorry wasn't a motor car. It was like comparing a donkey cart to a carriage.

'Hold still,' the priest ordered.

He sniffed each of them in turn like a dog checking for rats.

At last he seemed satisfied. 'You seem clean enough and don't smell of the farmyard you came from, but wipe your shoes before getting in my car. I don't want you to get it dirty.'

Anna Marie was a picture of submissive humility. Venetia looked as though she wanted to hit him over the head with a large hammer. Her eyes flashed at him.

'We only live on a farm, Father. We live in a house, not with the pigs.'

'I don't care,' barked Father Anthony, his dark eyes glowing like black coals beneath equally black bushy eyebrows. He turned his back on her, brusquely opening the doors, his movements sharp and premeditated.

'Get in!'

Even Venetia jumped at his command. Those eyes stayed with her, like she'd always imagined the devil's eyes would look. Hopefully she would never get to find out.

'Now,' he said once they were all in the car, the two girls in the back seat, huddled over their luggage, the priest behind the wheel of the motor car pulling on a pair of tan kid gloves, 'you will treat this car with the utmost respect. This car belongs to the O'Donnell family, big landowners. They have bought me this vehicle out of the kindness of their hearts and their regard for Mother Church. I promised I would take good care of it. I cannot have it sullied by filthy hands making sweaty marks upon the leather seats. And try not to breathe on the windows. Now I would thank you to stay silent and reflect upon your wickedness.'

Even though they were in dire circumstances, even though it didn't bear to think about the welcome they would get when they got home, Venetia was not submissive like her sister.

'How would you know if we were wicked? You don't know us,' she said, her dark eyes blazing, her hair tossing around her face like a black cloud before a storm.

'Women are wicked. From the time Eve seduced Adam, it has been an incontrovertible fact.'

'We haven't been seducing Adam,' Venetia replied hotly. 'We just wanted to go to America.'

'Well, you're not going to America,' he stated as he turned the steering wheel, his black eyes seeming to dart everywhere in case some errant sinner – or a tinker in a donkey cart – dared to bar his way. 'Has it not occurred to you that your thoughtless actions worried your family?'

Anna Marie, already regretting following her sister's suggestion, hung her head and began to cry.

The priest was unsympathetic. 'Mop up those tears. You do have a handkerchief I suppose.'

Anna Marie got out the screwed-up mess that was her handkerchief and began dabbing at her eyes.

Tight lipped and boiling with rebellion, Venetia sat stiff and upright staring straight at the back of the priest's head. The priest had a pink boil at the base of his neck, which she stared at, willing it to burst and seep pus into his white starched collar.

It could well have been that the priest felt the force of her angry look because suddenly those coal black eyes met hers via the rear-view mirror.

If she'd been wise she would have looked away, perhaps even hung her head and sobbed like her sister, but that wasn't her way. Only the sudden thought that those might indeed be the eyes of the devil in that mirror made her look away.

Trees, cows and dark brown fields behind unkempt hedgerows lurched each time the priest crunched the gearstick. The towns and countryside they were travelling through became more and more familiar.

Venetia thought of her grandfather's anger, her grandmother's relief; she also thought of Patrick. Why had he so easily betrayed her?

Anna Marie sat silently looking at the passing scene but seeing nothing. There was a terrible empty feeling in her stomach as though she'd not eaten for a week. She was dreading getting home and, more importantly, dreading the consequences of their running away.

The closely packed shops of Dunavon High Street passed in a blur of blandness. Even Venetia was beginning to feel nervous. Soon they would be home and facing the music – if it could be called that, though music was far from what they were likely to get. Venetia shivered at the thought of it.

Eventually they turned into the stony lane that led through the fields to the farm.

The lane was uneven and littered with tufts of coarse grass and potholes big enough to bathe a pig in.

The priest muttered under his breath as the car bumped along, tilting from one side to the other depending on the position and depth of the potholes.

Ahead of them a large pool of water had formed across the breadth of the lane.

Father Anthony took one look at it, muttered his disgust at such a barrier being put into his path and stopped the car.

'We'll get out here. You'll have to carry your own luggage.'

'We'll get our feet wet. And we're wearing our best shoes. They'll be ruined,' Venetia stated defiantly.

Father Anthony slammed his hands down on the steering wheel.

'I'll not contaminate the O'Donnells' car with mud and cow shite.'

Having never heard a priest use the same word for manure as their grandfather, the two girls exchanged surprised looks, Venetia only barely managing to stifle a giggle.

Father Anthony sent her a piercing look via the mirror. 'Wipe that stupid grin off your face and get out. And don't forget your luggage.'

Anna Marie retrieved her brown suitcase and Venetia the canvas bag that her father had brought home from the sea.

Bundling his cassock waist high, Father Anthony picked his way around the edge of the puddle then stood waving his arms, ordering them to get a move on.

'Don't dawdle. If I can do it, you can and I haven't got all day.' He pulled back his sleeve. The face of a fine wristwatch flashed into view then was gone again.

Another present from the O'Donnells thought Venetia. And didn't the priest realise that his hands were free so it was easy for him to skirt around the puddle?

Venetia cursed the fact that she was wearing her best Sunday shoes that had two-inch heels and were made of black suede. They were already taking in some of the water that could not be avoided.

'Come on. Hurry up.'

No doubt impatient to deliver them, he began walking backwards. Not all that he was walking through was plain, ordinary mud.

'He's stepped in a cow's pancake,' murmured Anna Marie. 'Do you think we should tell him?'

'No! It won't be us to blame for sullying the O'Donnells' car. Serves him right for holding his head so high as though there were a stench of shit under his nose.'

'Venetia!'

Venetia hissed back. 'He used the word shite and he's a priest and meant to lead by example, so why can't I?'

The girls held back. Their grandfather took off his hat before shaking the priest's hand. Their grandmother seemed to bob a little curtsey.

As though he were a king of Ireland rather than a priest.

Venetia determined that she would never bow and scrape before the likes of Father Anthony, a man who would have her walk through water and ruin her best shoes whilst loaded with luggage.

After apologies were given for troubling him and thanks for his kindness in bringing them home in a fine motor car, their grandfather beckoned them with a dirty, gnarled, wrinkled finger.

'Over here. The pair of ye. You'll thank Father Anthony for bringing you back and apologise for putting him through so much trouble.'

Both girls flinched, Anna Marie more so than her sister.

Dermot Brodie's eyes glinted like particles of ice beneath his shock of snow-white hair. He smelled and looked like a man of the earth, his corduroy trousers tied at the knees to stop the hems being muddied by his boots.

His soulful expression had come about through disappointment as much as from age. Both sons had fled the farm choosing instead the dangers of the sea. He'd loved them greatly and them leaving had scorched a hole in his heart. The hole had been plugged with unspoken sadness for the dead one and contempt for the one who still lived.

He eyed his two granddaughters; twins, though no one

looking at them would guess that. His heart had leapt with joy when Joseph had left them here. Anna Marie looked so much like her grandmother had once looked with her big blue eyes and dark blonde hair. Soft and gentle too. Whereas Venetia . . . Fiery and dark. A girl that could easily be led astray.

He had no doubt as to who had been the instigator of them running away. Venetia. It was always Venetia.

Even though female, he'd thought they'd have knuckled down to the lifestyle he wanted for them – the same one he'd wanted for his sons. But there was still time to mould them to his wishes, and he would mould them yet!

He watched with narrowed eyes, as with bowed heads, they muttered their thanks and their apologies.

In Anna Marie's case the action was one of genuine humility. Not so her twin sister. He knew that beneath that submissive action defiance blazed in her eyes.

Dermot Brodie knew his granddaughter well. Venetia acted the part of the prodigal daughter, but in her heart nothing had changed. One way or another, she would still leave here.

Anna Marie had only one wish above all others and that was for Father Anthony to stay for tea. Dermot Brodie was not a man to be crossed, even by his own family. Even as a child he'd scared her with his big frame, square shoulders and loud voice. The moment Father Anthony left the true reckoning would begin.

Two planks of wood were placed over the puddle so that the priest could regain his motor car without needing to crease his robe.

The lane being narrow, he backed the motor car all the way down, bumping along in an even more disorderly fashion than when he drove forward. Even from this distance the sound of the shrieking engine put their teeth on edge.

The chill blue eyes left the retreating vehicle and turned on the girls.

A whiff of masculine sweat drifted from the armpit of Dermot Brodie's shirt as he raised his arm and pointed his finger.

'Into the house!'

Anna Marie scurried ahead of her sister, suitcase banging against her side. Venetia took her time, her face expressionless and half hidden behind the canvas kit bag.

She knew very well what was to come, but this was just one incident in her life and would soon be over. Things wouldn't always be like this and besides the blame didn't really lie with them.

When she got hold of Patrick Casey he'd get the sharp edge of her tongue. First things first. There was her grandfather to be reckoned with. So how about confessing?

The farmhouse kitchen smelled of cooked food and lately skinned rabbits. Their little bodies were laid out, stripped of skin, which was spread out separately ready for scraping and drying.

Venetia took a deep breath and began her confession.

'Granfer. I'm sorry. It's my fault not Anna Marie's, but you see, I don't like animals and she does. Do you think I might get a job somewhere in town or as a lady's maid at the big house?'

A heavy hand connected with her face.

'Speak when you're spoken to. And that's the way it will be from now on. Not a word from either of you. And no going out of this door into town or anywhere else without my say so or that of your grandmother. Disobey me and you'll get a good thrashing. Is that clear?'

The blow had stung. She felt the heat of it tingling deep into her flesh. She did not move; did not blink and did not answer.

'Answer me. Is it clear?'

The shadow of his hand, raised between her and the light from the window, fell over her face.

She nodded. 'Yes.'

173

Anna Marie began to sob again.

'And you?'

Anna Marie nodded, her hair falling forward to hide her face, her shoulders moving in time with her heaving sobs.

Venetia glanced at her sister, then at her grandmother. Molly Brodie was watchful, her hands tucked behind the bib of her apron. She made no attempt to meet Venetia's wide-eyed plea.

Their grandfather was far from finished. That thick, gnarled finger, the end yellowed by nicotine, the nail black with dirt, was straight as an arrow, pointing into one twin's face then the other.

'You've put everyone through a lot of trouble, and I'll not have it. Not so long as you're members of this family. You'll both stay under this roof and work on this farm until the day you're married.'

He turned to his wife. 'Cane!'

The old oak dresser Molly Brodie was standing next to was adorned on each shelf with her best plates – willow patterns inherited from her mother. There were two drawers beneath those shelves, one holding cutlery for dining use, the other holding carving knives and table linen.

It was neither of these that she opened, but ducked for the porcelain knob of the cupboard nearest her.

Anna Marie gave a little yelp of alarm.

Venetia's mouth hung open as her eyes followed the course of the cane from her grandmother to her grandfather.

'Bend over. The pair of ye!'

Venetia eyed the thin cane, no thicker than a riding whip. Beside her Anna Marie's sobs became noisier and she was shaking with fear as she bent over the big old pine table where they ate their meals.

This was too much to bear. They were sisters, twins, and would always protect each other. Venetia sprang between her sister's backside and the cane.

'No. Don't beat her, Granfer. It's not Anna Marie's fault. It's mine. 'Twas me that persuaded her.'

She saw him jerk the cane to shoulder level, gasped and covered her face.

She heard her grandmother's voice. 'Dermot! Not her face. Please!'

Venetia gradually lowered her hand enough to peer over it, almost wetting herself with fear. The cane would have left a scar if he'd used it. Thank God her grandmother had interfered. It didn't happen often.

Her grandfather pointed at the table. 'Get out of me way and bend over next to your sister. Now!'

Venetia touched her sister's shoulder as she bent over the table beside her.

'I'm sorry,' she whispered.

Again and again he brought the cane down on one sister's rear then the other. The clothes they were wearing did little to soften the blow. It still stung.

Dermot Brodie's voice boomed around the low-ceilinged room.

'Humiliating! That's what it was. Humiliating.'

Each word was uttered on the fall of the cane. Venetia counted six for each of them. She half guessed that her grandfather had laid the cane more heavily on her backside than on her sister's. She hoped for Anna Marie's sake that it was so.

'Let that be a lesson to you both,' he said at last.

Rubbing her backside with both hands, Anna Marie straightened. She was red faced and sobbing fit to burst. Venetia had stuffed her knuckle into her mouth, biting on it to stop from crying out. Once it was over, she stood expressionless and stubbornly refused to show any sign of emotion.

Dermot Brodie noticed.

'My God, look at her. The girl deserves six more.'

He reached out to grab her.

'No!' Molly Brodie stepped between the man she used to love and one of the grandchildren that had made such a difference to her empty life. 'They've both had enough. They're only girls, Dermot. Just silly girls. And that cane's a nasty thing. A relic of the past.'

His heavy brows turned heavier, his expression that of a man who believes he's always in the right. It wasn't often that Molly stood up to him, but she was doing it now, willing him to do as she asked with the most pleading of looks.

He lowered his arm, looking at his wife as though she too needed a beating.

'So, it's a relic is it?' The timbre of his voice had sunk to a growl; there was fierceness in his eyes and a hard set to his jaw. 'Let me tell you, woman, that cane was used on me by my father and his father before him. If I'd given those boys of ours more beatings, perhaps they wouldn't have ended up so useless. Joe is like he is because of you, Molly. You were too soft with him, and you begged me to be the same. And look at him. A foreign wife, a family and him off gallivanting around the world without a care. And we left with the consequences. Spare the rod and spoil the child. Now that's a fine old saying,' he declared, his physical exertion in laying on the cane reflected in his red face and sweaty forehead.

'One of our sons is dead, Dermot. Remember that.'

Whilst Anna Marie continued to sob, Venetia had hung onto every word. She couldn't remember much about her father, the man who had wandered the world leaving his family to their own devices. What she was hearing helped put flesh on the scant memory she had of him. He'd left the farm to travel the world and his younger brother had followed him.

'I must take after him then, wanting to travel the world,' she blurted, her dark eyes luminescent above pink cheeks.

Dermot Brodie's long, hard face seemed to drop to his chest and his voice grew louder.

'Well, would you listen to that! The girl's no shame! No respect for her elders. Well, let me tell you this, my girl,' he shouted, his red, sweaty face only inches from hers, 'any more of yer wild ways and I'll hand you over to the sisters at St Bernadette's. They're the ones who know what to do with wayward girls!'

Venetia gulped at the threat and Anna Marie sobbed from behind a veil of pale brown hair. They'd both heard of the place. Hearsay relating to its reputation was patchy at best and spoken of in whispers – as though to speak of it out loud would bring down a thunderbolt from heaven.

Girls who were wayward went there; the wild, the unruly and those who were so feeble minded that they'd acted brazenly and ended up in the family way.

That night as they lay in the dark in their beds, Anna Marie's small voice trembled.

'I don't want to go to St Bernadette's. I'll be good from now on. Very good and I'll never leave the farm. Not ever.'

Venetia lay silently on her back, arms folded behind her head, staring wide eyed, and seeing pictures in the darkness of foreign lands, blue seas, golden sands and the soaring skyscrapers of New York.

In the short term there was little chance of leaving the farm without permission and mostly in the company of their grandmother. But it couldn't last forever. Surely they wouldn't be kept here until they were married? If so, then they were no more than prisoners. She couldn't believe it would be so. There had to come a time when past behaviour would be forgotten. That is when I shall make new plans, Venetia decided. That is when I shall leave.

Chapter Twenty-three

Magda
1936

Magda had arranged to meet her old friend Susan and was looking smart in a navy-blue costume with a nipped-in waist, black court shoes and handbag.

'You look a bit like the Duchess of York,' said Susan.

'And with your red hair you look like Maureen O'Hara. She's got red hair like yours,' returned Magda and sighed.

'Not schoolgirls any more,' said Susan, 'and three cheers for that.'

'I miss the old place.'

'Goodbye and good riddance,' laughed Susan. 'The brewery pays me a good wage. For the first time in me life I've got a few bob in my pocket – that's after me mam's took 'er share of course.'

'I'm still sad though. Do you remember Miss Cameron and that lovely stew she used to save for us?'

'Mrs Norman! That's what she is now.'

Dear Miss Cameron, their favourite teacher, had left just two months before they'd left school behind to marry her sweetheart, a man who'd returned from the Great War with only one arm, but luckily enough money to get them through.

The rules were that a teacher had to leave once she was married. Magda thought it unfair and she said so. Susan didn't care much one way or the other.

'Who cares about working for a living when you can be married and have a man look after you?'

'I'm not sure about putting my trust in a man. My mother did and he left her to get sick and ill with no money. And then he left me with Aunt Bridget. I've never been too sure whether he sent her any money to keep me with or not. It's possible he did, but she spent it on drink. But he left me there. Left me there and didn't come back.'

Susan sniffed. 'My dad weren't much better. Too many kids and not enough money, and what there was he still had to have for his drop of bitter down the boozer. Still, I'd sooner be married. And the sooner the better. In the meantime I'll go on working at the brewery and enjoying the fifteen shillings a week – well – less me keep. But the rest I spend on me. The pictures, the Palais, a tube of lipstick and a small bottle of Evening in Paris. Lovely!'

Magda laughed. 'You as a mother with babies. Well, that would be something.'

'And you going on to study a bit and try and become a doctor. Well, there's a surprise!'

'I suppose so, though it was always there at the back of my mind. I mean, what with my mum dying without a doctor on hand; not until it was too late.'

'But you won't be earning anything for ages. I couldn't stand that.'

Susan's laughing eyes were full of disbelief. She couldn't quite take it on board that it would be a long time before Magda earned anything as a doctor.

'Lucky your old dad put enough aside to pay for you to go

to medical school,' Susan said to her. 'He couldn't be all bad. Had to be your Aunt Bridget spent all the dosh.'

'Had to be. Glad he managed to keep some back. It came as quite a surprise.'

Magda turned her face away, pretending to study the tired-looking playground where they used to play doctors and nurses as children. She wasn't good at lying and she couldn't bear to tell her friend that it was Winnie One Leg who had paid for her tuition – Mrs Jones as she was presently calling herself since moving into her cosy mews cottage.

As she turned away from the grey stone building, she felt Susan's eyes on her.

Susan folded her arms across her ample chest and closed one eye. 'Go on. Tell me what you're doing 'round 'ere. What's on yer mind?'

'Nothing. There's nothing on my mind.'

'Yes there is. Have you got a sweetheart you're not telling me about? Has he asked you to marry 'im?'

Magda laughed and shook her head, her dark brown hair catching the light as it swung around her shoulders.

'Don't be silly. I'm too young.'

'No you ain't. My mam was only fifteen when she had me.'

'Well, it's no sweetheart,' said Magda feeling her clothes were in marked contrast to those Susan was wearing.

Susan was dressed in everyday clothes; a pale green dress, the colour long washed out, and a beige cardigan that only barely buttoned up over her full breasts.

'I've something more important than a boy on my mind. There is another reason I've come back.'

'There's nothing more important than boys,' returned Susan. 'And getting married. I can't wait to get married and have kids and a place of me own. Wonderful!'

The summer air was warm and Magda almost felt as

though they were girls again, excited to be on the threshold of adulthood.

They stopped outside the corner shop where they used to part company, Magda to walk in the direction of Edward Street and Susan to George Street.

'How about us going out tonight – just a look around the shops,' Susan suggested. 'How about we . . .'

'I'm going your way anyway. There's something I have to do,' Magda said thoughtfully. 'I want my mother's Bible. My aunt keeps it under lock and key. Winnie offered her money on my behalf, but she wouldn't accept it. I think it's the fact that it was from Winnie – the wages of sin and all that. I think if she were to accept money it has to be from me. She'll want a lot, anything to make me pay for the wrong my mother did her – she believes my father would have married her, if my mother hadn't come along,' she explained, in answer to Susan's enquiring look. 'This time I've got a bit more to give her. I've been saving a bit from my allowance.'

Susan nodded in understanding. 'Old cow. She should let you have it. How about you keep her talking out front and I barge past her, nip inside and pinch it?'

'I wish.'

Susan eyed her warily. 'Will she let you have it this time?'

Magda took a deep breath and hunched her shoulders. 'This time I'm giving her everything I have.'

'Want me to come with you?'

Magda shook her head. 'No. This is something I have to do alone.'

'So how about we meet up on Thursday and trot up west and take a look around the shops?'

'Why not?'

Magda avoided looking across at the women in the house that Winnie used to own.

Taking a deep breath, she rapped hard on Bridget Brodie's door.

After a few minutes of no response, she stepped back into the road and looked up to the bedroom windows. A curtain twitched then fell again.

The very thought of seeing Bridget Brodie again sent shivers through her system.

This evening, she was here in person with more money than would keep Bridget Brodie in booze for a year.

The slap of footsteps in floppy slippers sounded from inside. The ill-fitting door, its paintwork peeling and its timbers twisted with age, was yanked roughly open.

Bridget Brodie's face was a reddish blotch against the gloom of the room behind her. The familiar smell of mildew and filth filtered outwards. This evening the smell was laced with cheap sherry bought from the corner off licence and poured straight from the barrel.

In the past Bridget Brodie used to plaster her face with makeup and wear nice clothes; the latter bought with the proceeds of selling Magda's humble belongings. But Bridget Brodie's life had changed when her husband James had been lost at sea, presumed drowned, though he had provided for such an eventuality in the form of a lump sum saved with the Sailors' Benevolent Fund. Not that there was much left of it.

Her hair was dishevelled and grey, her face, devoid of makeup, was now greasy, redder and scarred with pimples. Her clothes, a grubby cardigan, a grey skirt and stockings rolled around her ankles, were dirty and smelled sour. She looked in need of money to fund her bad habits, which was fine as far as Magda was concerned. It was all to her advantage.

Her aunt took on a sideways stance, her eyes swerving warily to look her niece up and down. When she gave her what passed as a smile, but might just as well have been a sneer,

Magda noticed there were fewer teeth in her head since the last time they'd met.

'Back are ya?'

After swallowing hard, Magda said, 'I came here to buy my mother's Bible.'

Aunt Bridget stared at her whilst allowing the words to sink in – as though her niece was speaking in a foreign language.

'Is that so?' she said at last, the glint of greed in her eyes.

'Yes,' said Magda, warming to her subject and wondering why she'd ever been frightened of this woman.

'Well, there's a thing! And I suppose you'll be telling me you have a job. And I suppose I know full well what it is. You're going to be a whore over there – if yer not one already.'

Magda felt her face flare red. 'I am not . . .'

'I really don't care if you are. Now clear off. This here is a respectable house. Go back with your whore friends across the road there!'

Bridget Brodie swayed unsteadily, perhaps with the effort of trying to close the unyielding door, but more likely because she was drunk.

Magda jammed her foot into the opening.

'I've come for my mother's Bible and I'm not leaving until you give it to me.'

'Go away!'

The door scraped the floor on its way to closing.

'In case you didn't hear, I'm willing to buy it off you,' Magda blurted. 'You must need money – for food – and drink.'

The door quivered then became still.

'Buy it you say? A decent amount this time? Not the wages of sin mark you. That Winnie tried that one on. I won't be having her money, that I won't!'

The wicked little eyes grew smaller as though she were counting the change in her hand.

'Plenty of money,' said Magda, though the thought of handing over money for what already belonged to her was sickening.

'Pay me? From a whore's money? No,' she growled shaking her head and pursing her purplish lips, 'I won't be taking any money earned by fornication. That I will not!'

To Magda's dismay, she resumed closing the door, though the door itself, being so dry and neglected, was obstinate, its rotting wood grating over the uneven flagstones.

'Enough money to keep you in sherry for a year. And the good stuff if you like. Not the stuff from the barrel,' shouted Magda.

She could not bring herself to tell her of studying to be a doctor, not without declaring Winnie as her sponsor.

'I'm working for the brewery. In the office. I can even bring you home a nice bottle of stout. You'd like that Aunt Bridget – wouldn't you?'

She was making this up as she went along, working out how she could fulfil her promise. Susan. Susan would get the stout for her.

It wasn't easy being polite to this woman who had been cruel to her as a child, but Magda was determined to get back what was rightfully hers.

When Bridget Brodie smiled, her lips curled back from yellowed teeth and ugly gaps.

'You'll pay me for it?'

Her tone was both vindictive and incredulous, but also grasping. She'd take anything if it came easily.

Magda heaved a huge sigh and told her that was exactly what she would do.

'If you return it to me I'll give you a week's wages. One pound ten shillings and sixpence.'

The money had been carefully saved from the allowance Winnie gave her. She crossed her fingers behind her back, hoping against hope that the amount quoted would be acceptable. She had more if it was not, but it wasn't wise to display all your cards with Aunt Bridget. One pound ten shillings wouldn't be enough. Not for her.

'No.'

Bits of rotten wood crumbled from the bottom of the door as her aunt pushed it.

'Ten pounds,' said Magda. 'I'll give you ten pounds. That'll keep you in sherry for a year won't it?'

Realising she'd offered too much too soon, she bit her lip. If there was one thing her aunt knew how to do it was bargain and hopefully get something for nothing.

'Ten pounds?' Her aunt shook her head, a snakelike smile on her bloated face. 'That Bible is worth everything to you. EVERYTHING! So there is a price I'll be having from you, but not a penny below twenty-five pounds. Twenty-five or I throw it on the fire to warm my aching bones.'

'You mean that?'

'Of course I mean that. Twenty-five will buy me a few sacks of coal then I wouldn't need to burn it, would I?'

Magda felt her breath catch in her throat. To get away with twenty-five would be wonderful.

'Twenty-five. I think I can manage that.'

There was something about the look in her aunt's eyes that turned her blood cold. This was not about money. This was about revenge for being the daughter of the woman who had taken the man she loved. The next thing she said wasn't exactly unexpected.

'Fifty pounds. Fifty pounds I want. It's only fair. I took you in when you had nowhere else to go. I looked after you and it's about time you paid me back for my trouble. Come on now. That Bible is worth it – to you. And me? All I can do with it is put it on the fire to warm my bones.'

It was useless to argue that she'd been neglected as a child. All Magda could do was agree.

She did a quick calculation. It was a lot of money. She'd saved a little, but fifty pounds was a fortune. Would Winnie lend her that sum? She had to hope that she would.

'I haven't got it with me. I'll be back with it on Friday night if you can have the Bible ready for me. Is it a deal?'

A triumphant sneer flickered like a weevil over her aunt's mouth.

'That seems fine enough. Friday night it is. I'll have it ready here. Sure I will.'

'Fifty pounds. Is there any chance I can take it now? I'll still bring the money on Friday.'

Spindly wrinkles erupted around her aunt's narrowed eyes and spittle oozed from the corner of her mouth when she smiled.

'Do you think I'm a bloody fool? Oh no, Magda my girl, I'll not hand it over until you pay me. Then you can have it.'

'On Friday. All of the fifty pounds?'

'Are you deaf, girl?'

She nodded, could barely speak, and it was hard not to look elated. But she knew she mustn't look mightily pleased. If her aunt thought there was any chance of getting more money, she would demand more.

It didn't occur to Magda that she'd been holding her breath until the door shuddered shut. The rancid smell of old drains lingered in the air, but even that was better than the filthy smell coming from her aunt's crumbling home. At least when she'd been there she'd cleaned it round a bit.

The fact is that the house her aunt lived in was as ill-used as she was. Edward Street was far from being handsome. The big old houses on one side of the street had been built for merchants' families some two hundred years earlier. On the opposite side the houses were mean and cramped, small places built of red brick with two rooms downstairs, and two upstairs.

Her Aunt Bridget's house was squeezed in between its neighbours, both of which were boarded up due to timber problems in the roof.

Despite its age, Winnie's old place was well looked after both by Winnie and by whoever owned it now. Its stonework was as clean as it could be, the door newly painted and the brass knocker so brightly polished it gleamed in the sunlight.

A dark girl wearing a glittering blue headband sat in the window, her head held proudly. Magda held up a hand meaning to wave, and then let it fall. Winnie had ordered her never to acknowledge anyone in that house again and never to linger anywhere around Edward Street after dark. It was summer, but evening was setting in.

'The alley cats are dangerous,' Winnie had told her. 'And not all of them have got four legs.'

Heading back to Prince Albert Mews, her footsteps were lighter than they'd been in a long while. The Bible might soon be in her possession. She would finally be able to search for her family, even if it meant opting out of medical school.

Winnie and the delicious aroma of the evening meal were waiting for her when she got back to the cottage.

'Something smells nice,' said Magda as she lay down her bag and took off her jacket.

'A little lamb with fresh vegetables for tonight,' Winnie said to her.

Winnie set her plate in front of her.

Magda, feeling somewhat pleased with herself, breathed in the appetising aroma. The pleasure did not last. Winnie was bound to be upset if she mentioned putting off her start at medical school and leaving Prince Albert Mews – even if it was only for a little while.

Picking up her knife and fork, she flashed her benefactor a heart-warming smile.

Winnie sat herself down, rubbing her bad hip as she did so. Magda knew it was getting worse, but then Winnie was getting old.

'You were late coming in.'

Magda guessed that Winnie had been watching out of the window for her, as she had every day since they'd moved here.

'I went to see Aunt Bridget. I asked her again for my mother's Bible.'

Winnie's head seemed to jerk in surprise.

'And?'

She tapped a bony finger against the side of her face, elbow resting on the table. Her eyes were strangely piercing, almost as though she feared what she was about to hear or could read the words in Magda's mind.

'She's going to let me have it but at a price. I've been careful with my wages from the market. I've managed to save enough to buy it from her. Fifty pounds in fact. I didn't tell her I was going to medical school. I told her I've got a job in the office at the brewery and that's how I managed to save so much.'

'I can help. You know I can and she's not to know,' said Winnie.

Magda chewed methodically on a portion of lamb chop. Telling Winnie that bit had been easy. Telling her the rest wouldn't be so easy. Laying her cutlery carefully on her plate, she swallowed and prepared herself for what had to be said.

'Once I have the Bible, I'll have to opt out of medical school whilst I search for my family. I don't think they'll mind if I do. I hope you don't either. You see the moment I have that Bible back, I can find my sisters and brother. Their addresses are in that Bible. Once I have it, I can seek them out.'

All the while she spoke, her eyes stayed fixed on those of Winnie's.

'Ah yes. You would,' Winnie said slowly, as if she understood completely and approved of Magda's actions. Inside her heart was breaking. She couldn't bear to be parted from her. It was almost as though her baby had not died but they'd merely been separated for many years. And now she was talking about leaving again – even though only for a short while. She had one other suggestion to make.

Sighing resignedly, she raised her eyes to meet those of her benefactor, hating to tell it as it was, but not able to stop herself.

'I'm not your daughter, Winnie. She died. I have my own family. Even my father is out there somewhere.'

Winnie suddenly froze.

Magda met the twinkling blue eyes briefly before dropping her gaze back to her plate.

'It's gone cold. Anyway, it's only the fatty bits left.'

'Throw it on the fire. Here. Take mine too,' said Winnie.

After scraping the leavings onto one plate, Magda threw the lot onto the fire, for a moment regarding the fat sizzling on the hot coals.

'It used to spark and sizzle like that when Aunt Bridget was cooking it. She used to cook it on the fire in the grate seeing as it was just for herself. One day she caught the rug on fire. I threw a kettle of water on it, but the place was filled with smoke. She used to smoke in front of the fire too, and then fall asleep drunk. I suppose I'm lucky that the Bible didn't go up in flames long ago. She says she'll throw it on the fire anyway if I don't pay her the money.'

Winnie watched as Magda closed and latched the door of the range. In her heart of hearts she believed that if Magda left now, she would never come back. She couldn't bear it if that happened. She just couldn't bear it.

'But never mind,' Magda said brightly, determined that nothing, not even unhappy memories, would ruin her day. 'As long as she hands over that Bible, I don't care what she does.'

Winnie forced herself to match the girl's happy mood, though inside she felt only despair. She did not want Magda to leave her. She wanted her to stay, but if Bridget Brodie kept her word, then the one person she loved above all others would most definitely leave – unless she could persuade her to stay; unless she could do something to alter things and put the Bible beyond her reach.

Those are wicked thoughts, Winifred Sykes. Terrible wicked thoughts. What would your mother have thought of you to sink so low?

Poor old Mother, always so law abiding, with nothing much to show for her honesty except a drunken lout of a husband, a house full of half-starved children, the only reward an early grave.

Winnie stared into the dying flames of the fire after Magda had gone to bed counting some blessings and envying her poor worn-out mother for the children she'd had in plenty and had never asked for.

Chapter Twenty-four

The Twins
1934

On the farm in rural Ireland, spring turned into summer, summer into autumn and the mists rolling in from the Atlantic Ocean sucked at the gaps between buildings and trees. Damp as they were, the mists were nothing to the rain that leaked incessantly from the overcast sky, the clouds dark grey like the inside of a kettle.

Venetia looked out from the open barn door. It seemed that Patrick had abandoned her. It must have been beaten out of him, she told herself. He wouldn't have told where they'd gone unless he was forced to. Would he?

She sighed.

'Ireland has to be the wettest country on earth.'

'Never mind. It'll soon be Christmas,' said Anna Marie who had just finished collecting eggs from the few hens left who were still laying eggs.

A sudden fall of rainwater from an overflowing gutter dropped in a curtain between Venetia and the soaking yard.

'That's right. It'll soon be Christmas and all those parties to go to.'

'You're being sarcastic.'

Anna Marie sounded hurt.

'Of course I'm being bloody sarcastic. What a life! What a bloody life!'

'And you shouldn't swear.'

Venetia gritted her teeth to stop herself from saying something even more hurtful. They had not been allowed out either alone or together since returning from Queenstown. Three times a week attending mass was the height of their social life. Venetia couldn't believe that their grandfather had really meant what he said. Neither of them could leave until they were married.

'How are we going to get married if we're not allowed out to meet any fellahs?' said Venetia after deciding to ignore her sister's remark about swearing.

'There's Mr Duffy. I think he quite took a shine to you.'

Venetia pulled a face. 'He's a widower and has hairs growing down his nose and out of his ears. Besides that he's forty if he's a day. I don't want to share an old man's bed. I want a young man who smells good and looks good. Mr Duffy smells of oil.'

Joe Duffy owned the garage in the High Street. At first he'd only had one shed attached to the side of his house, but as more and more farmers bought tractors, his business had grown along with the size of his shed.

The trouble was that even though he employed two young mechanics, he enjoyed getting involved with the work himself. Even when dressed in his best for Sunday mass, he still smelled of oil.

'Do you remember that last Christmas we were all together?'

Venetia stopped trying to wring the water from her hair. Her jaw visibly relaxed. 'Yes.'

'Do you think our Magda is married? I mean, she might be seeing as she's a year older than us – or is it two years?'

'Three,' murmured Venetia, her thoughts suddenly twisting away from the present into a past only dimly remembered.

'I've often wondered if she'll come looking for us. Wouldn't it be nice to see her come walking up the lane? Do you think we'll recognise her?'

'Perhaps.'

Venetia didn't remind her twin that Magda and she were supposed to look very much alike.

'I would have thought she might have come by now,' said Anna Marie thoughtfully. 'If she wanted to find us that is. I expect she's doing very well for herself in London. She's probably married or at least got herself a nice young man and everything that goes with it.'

Venetia made no comment. The past was such a murky place, part dream and part reality.

Having not received a response from her twin, Anna Marie went on wondering.

'I wonder whether Father will be home for Christmas. I hope he is. I can't remember the last time I saw him . . .'

'Of course he won't be back! Who can blame him? Who'd want to come back to this dreary old place when there's a world out there to be travelled? I wish I were a man, and then I could run away and work where I pleased. I'd jump on a ship – just like he did.'

Anna Marie eyed her sister warily.

'I'm not coming this time. Do you hear me Neesh? I'm not coming this time.'

'I wouldn't want you to,' said Venetia, flouncing out of the barn regardless of the rain. 'Next time I'll go alone. I'll do better that way.'

Scraggy brown hens clucked and screeched as she barged through them. She wasn't seeing them.

After taking off her boots outside, she sauntered into the

house, carefully avoiding the kitchen and running up the stairs.

Once in the bedroom she shared with her sister, she shut the door quietly but firmly behind her.

The old kitbag her father had left behind hung on the back of the door. Anna Marie had been told never to touch it.

'It contains private things,' Venetia had told her.

Anna Marie had looked hurt, which had made Venetia feel quite guilty. Her sister wouldn't dream of prying into private things. She just wasn't like that. She obeyed the rules. She always would.

Unhooking the bag from the back of the door, Venetia rooted deep inside, removing a few precious mementoes of her time with Patrick; dried flowers; her last school report that her grandmother had wanted to frame.

Loved singing and acting in the nativity play.

Her grandfather had threatened to throw it in the fire if she did.

'To my mind it's not at all proper for a girl to be doing things like that and for us to keep a record of it. Not if she wants to find herself a decent man to keep her for the rest of her life,' he'd declared in a loud voice.

It was no good trying to reason with him that things were changing for women, though her grandmother did try, reminding him that women had won the right to vote years ago.

'No wonder this country is like it is,' he'd yelled. 'Women! What do they know about anything except housework and having babies?'

Her grandmother had saved the report, given it to her granddaughter and Venetia had squirrelled it away.

At the very bottom of the bag her fingers finally touched what she was looking for. A game of snakes and ladders. It was a little battered, but the colours were still bright. The game had been a Christmas present long ago when the whole family had been together in the workhouse. The address of the workhouse was stamped on the back.

She caressed the battered cardboard and thought of Magda and her little brother. She remembered them both, but suspected that Anna Marie barely recalled Michael, their baby brother.

Where were they, she wondered?

The one thing she did know was that it was only wishful thinking to depend on Magda to come and rescue her. She would have to do that for herself.

Chapter Twenty-five

The Twins
1935

Spring of the following year followed a pattern of rain and sunshine and a westerly wind that was mild one day and raucous the next.

Anna Marie did her best to be cheerful thinking it the best way to keep her sister's spirits up.

'Springtime is the most wonderful time of year. Breathe that lovely fresh air. And look at all this new life.'

Venetia looked glumly at the things that made her sister so joyful. Fluffy yellow chicks just out of their eggs were a delight to the eye as were new-born lambs playing in the field.

'Soon be slaughtered. Once they're old enough,' Venetia remarked glumly. 'And we're getting older. Turning into old maids. That's what we are.'

Life on the farm did not suit the dark-haired twin with the flashing eyes, especially now when she couldn't get away to see Patrick, and not just to kiss him again – though that thought was never far from her mind. She wanted to scold him for his wicked betrayal.

The smell of May blossom drifted with the petals tossed by the wind.

Anna Marie couldn't think of anything else to say as they trudged into the barn where a sack of bran mash and a pile of potato peelings were waiting for them, to be mixed together for the chickens. She was finding her sister harder and harder to deal with. It sometimes occurred to her that she might even be happier by herself – not that she'd tell Venetia that!

One poured in bran mash, the other the potato peelings then together they added water. Venetia lit the fire in the small range beneath the old copper containing the mixture. As it warmed they would take it in turns to stir the heavy load, the steam clamping their hair to their heads and filling the barn with a sweetly appetising smell.

'Your turn,' said Venetia handing her sister the wooden paddle used for stirring, the wood bleached white from being immersed in so much boiling water.

She rubbed her back as she straightened, and then smoothed her hair back from her face.

'I feel like a damp rag. And I look like a rag doll.'

'That's not true,' said Anna Marie, leaning into the job of stirring, her face now as damp as that of her sister. 'You're eye-catching, Venetia. You always will be.'

Venetia shot her a look. It wasn't often her sister called her by her full name. It was usually Neesh and always had been since they were small and neither could pronounce the name of the other.

'You're so happy here, Anna Marie. I can't understand it, really I can't. All these smelly animals.'

'They're all God's creatures.'

'That may be, but they still smell.'

One of the double doors of the barn was open. Venetia folded her arms and leaned against the door post, her eyes surveying the rough stone walls surrounding the yard, the hens and their chicks, the pigs snorting up roots in the sty. She wrinkled her nose.

'Now me, I'd prefer powder, paint and some perfume from Paris. And nice clothes.' She sniffed. 'Not likely to get that here though.'

Anna Marie made no comment. She was bending to her task, her hair falling forward around her face.

'Hey! Did you hear that on the wireless? There's going to be something called television in England. It's like having a picture house in the corner of your living room. That's what it said on the wireless. Now wouldn't that be grand!'

'I heard. Grandma said it would never take the place of the wireless though.'

'They'll have plays and things on – like at the pictures. God, but it's such a long time since we went to the pictures. I'd like to see that John Wayne again. Do you remember him? And Tallulah Bankhead. And Marlene Dietrich. Oh, but aren't they beautiful? That's what I'd like to be you know. A film star!'

Anna Marie laughed but stopped abruptly when Venetia threw her an angry frown.

'You don't mean it, do you Neesh? I mean, ordinary people like us don't get to be film stars.'

'They do if they get to Hollywood. That's where I'm going to go. I'm going to Hollywood to become a film star.'

Anna Marie wiped the sweat from her brow. 'Your turn to stir.'

Venetia took hold of the paddle and began to stir, the water slopping around and her thoughts miles away. Why hadn't she thought that before? If there was a fortune to be made in America, it had to be in Hollywood.

Anna Marie was wiping the wetness from her hands, which had become red and wrinkled after being subjected to the steam.

'Granfer said neither of us can leave here unless it's to get married.'

'I have to get away,' Venetia declared. Her sulky lips stretched over her perfect white teeth. 'If it means getting married first, then I'll do it. Then I'll run away from my husband.'

'You wouldn't!' Anna Marie went quite pale.

Venetia tossed her head. 'I might have to run away to England first. That's not so far.'

Anna Marie stopped adding more bran into the potato rinds, a feast the flock of brown hens were gathering for out in the yard. She had never been naturally disobedient; most of the scrapes she'd got into had been orchestrated by her sister. Feeling quite worried about disobeying again, she made the only suggestion she could think of.

'We could ask for permission to go.'

Venetia stopped stirring, handed the paddle to her sister and sat down on a bale of hay.

'Are you mad? Why would we ask permission to run away?'

Anna Marie felt her cheeks burning. She hated it when Venetia snubbed her like that. It made her feel stupid.

'What if there was a good reason for us to leave? What if we said that we wanted to find Magda and Michael?'

For once Venetia, normally with an answer for everything and the out and out ringleader and organiser, didn't know what to say. The truth was that she too had often wondered about their older sister and baby brother. They'd asked their grandparents how Magda was, but had met a frightened silence on their grandmother's part, and outright anger from their grandfather.

'You're never to mention your sister's name again. Is that clear?'

Venetia reminded her sister of that fact.

'We're not to mention her. Remember?'

Anna Maria sighed. 'I wonder why. I wonder what she's done.'

Anna Marie recalled that visit, one of the rare ones their father had bothered to make and just after their Uncle James had been lost at sea.

'She's with your Aunt Bridget and doing fine,' he'd told them.

Believing him was a matter of faith. Despite the years he was as fickle in his dealings with his family as he'd always been.

Their grandparents' attitude towards Magda had changed some time after that.

'I expect she got into some kind of trouble. You know what Granfer is like about girls getting too friendly with boys – and the like.'

Whilst the girls stirred in the barn, their grandmother took a break from curing hams.

She rubbed her back, a normal occurrence nowadays after hours of bending and lifting, mixing and rubbing in the salt and herbs that would give the ham its unique taste.

Now she had a few minutes to herself, to sit and muse and write in her diary, a secret book that not even her husband knew about.

Pressed flowers served as bookmarks for those entries she was particularly prone to looking at. There was a bluebell marking the day she'd received the news of James's death, a cowslip for the last time when Joseph had come home. She'd asked her eldest son if Bridget, James's widow, would be able to cope with just Magda for company, and wouldn't it be a grand idea if she came back to Ireland and the pair of them live with the rest of the family.

Joseph Brodie replied that, indeed, he couldn't think of

any reason why the pair of them, Magda and James's widow, wouldn't jump at the chance. What he failed to convey to them was that he hadn't been back to Bridget's grubby house since leaving Magda there all those years ago. Not only did Joseph believe what he wanted to believe, he chose what truths he would tell and what ones he would hold back.

A tiny spray of speedwell, the blue flower as bright as the day she'd picked it, marked the day she'd received a response from Bridget Brodie after asking that she and Magda come to live with them at the farm.

After Joseph had gone back to sea, Molly had written in response to the telegram Bridget had sent advising them of the death of her younger son.

The words didn't come easily, especially as she needed to dab at her tears whilst writing heartfelt words of condolence and sadness.

I want to throw my arms around you and my granddaughter, she wrote.

Their grandfather was less moved to emotion.

'You never liked Bridget. Why would you want to throw your arms around her now? Besides, Joseph had her before James. Did you not know that? She's a woman of dubious character. Aye, that's what she is.'

'Whatever she is, she's still my daughter-in-law.'

Despite her husband's misgivings, Molly had gone ahead and written her letter.

The response she received was unexpected and a terrible shock. Basically Bridget told her not to meddle in her life and that she had no intention of ever returning to Ireland. She preferred England thank you very much.

And as for that ungrateful little tramp, Magda, she's run away from home and become a prostitute. Living with a woman who runs a bordello. Blood will out as they say . . .

Molly Brodie had collapsed into a chair, her hand flat on her chest as though her heart would jump out through her ribs if she moved it. Even now she felt a terrible pang of anguish; were all her family doomed to be scattered far and wide, never for her to see them again?

Dermot had fallen to instant silence at the news, his snow white brows beetling over those fine blue eyes that both sons had inherited from him.

'Is that so?' he'd said at last, and left the room.

From that day forth he'd forbidden anyone to speak Magda's name ever again. There'd been anger in his eyes, but also sadness.

'It's what comes of marrying outside yer own,' he'd muttered, shoulders hunched and head bowed as he slopped through the yard in his big boots, his baggy trousers tied at the knees.

Molly shook her head, closed the diary and reached for her cup of tea, which was fast turning cold.

Although she'd never admitted it to her husband, she'd liked the lovely Italian girl her eldest son had married.

Chapter Twenty-six

Magda
1936

Thursday night. This was to be a celebration of Magda being accepted into medical school.

As planned she met Susan on the corner of George Street, which turned out to be something of a shock when Susan came trotting along looking like a grown-up Shirley Temple.

'Crikey!' Magda exclaimed. 'What have you done to your hair?'

Susan's wild, frizzy red hair was a mass of permed curls.

'Me sister Doris did it,' said Susan. 'Stinks a bit, but don't look bad does it? Reckon I look even more like that Maureen O'Hara?'

'It looks . . .' Magda pretended she needed to clear her throat as she searched for the right comment, '. . . different. I hardly recognised you.'

The truth was that Susan's frizzy hair wasn't easily tamed into curls, straightness or even shortness. It was wild and had a mind of its own. Back in her schooldays wearing it in plaits kept it under some kind of control, but Susan wasn't a child any longer.

The sleek look they'd both admired on mannequins in shop window displays up west needed hair that was sleek and wavy. Susan's was far from being sleek and a lot more than curly.

Susan patted her hair with both hands. 'Me mam had a fit. Said that when me father finds out he'll give me what for. I look like a wandering haystack, she said. Never seen a wandering haystack. Never seen a haystack for that matter.'

'Your dress looks nice.'

Susan's dress was home-made and looked as though it had been run up from a faded curtain that might once have been red. As it was the colour had faded to a dull pink. Pink wasn't exactly ideal but red with ginger hair would have been awful.

Susan beamed. 'Me mam made it. The beads I borrowed from our Doris. She's not going out anywhere tonight and Derek is working the late shift at the docks.'

'Right,' said Magda. 'How about a trip up to the West End? It's on me. I've got some celebrating to do.'

Susan's freckled face broke into laughter. 'Lead me to the nearest bus!'

Magda giggled too. Their heels clattered in unison on the pavement as they dodged the detritus left by the street market and swayed their way to the bus stop.

They gathered admirers en route. Magda didn't look round to see where the wolf whistles were coming from, but Susan couldn't resist.

'Cor! He's nice.'

Magda hustled her along. 'Come on. We're celebrating, remember?'

'Him that's whistling at us . . . he's got a car. Can you believe that?'

Magda dragged at her friend's arm.

'Come on.'

'No. Look. Take a look. He's handsome. Real handsome

and he's not a docker. Not with a car like that. That's Bradley Fitts! Bet your life he can show a girl a good time. I don't know why you don't go out with a big shot like that. He's sweet on you and . . .'

'No!'

Magda quickened her step and wished she hadn't come here. Winnie had told her not to come back to George Street, but she'd determined that she would. She dragged on Susan's arm.

'He went to the same school as us. Remember? Can't we just say . . .?'

'No! He's trouble, Susan. He was a bully at school, remember?'

'Yes, but he's not the school bully boy now.'

Magda grimaced. 'Nowadays he's a professional bully.'

Once they were out of sight of the car and the wolf whistles had stopped Susan was again engaged with the idea of getting one of those bright red trolley buses and going up west. For now at least the admiring wolf whistles were forgotten.

One hundred paces further and there was the bus stop.

The evening was pleasant and although powder puff clouds were piling up behind the chimney pots, the sun was still shining.

Magda felt a huge sense of relief. Bradley couldn't have seen them. She hoped not.

Just as they were about to cross the road to the tram stop a horn sounded. A car rolled to a stop in front of them.

'Going somewhere nice, girls?'

Magda dared to turn.

Bradley Fitts was leaning out of the car window, his gaze fixed on her and a Woodbine hanging from the corner of his mouth.

Panicking, she looked up the street hoping to see the bus

coming. Not one in sight. Typical. Just when you needed one badly. Any other time there'd be three in a row.

'I asked you where you were going, Magdalena. Didn't you hear me?'

It was Susan that answered, dimples appearing at the corners of her mouth and a blush on each cheek. 'Up west. We're celebrating. My name's Susan. I went to the same school as you, though you were a few years ahead of me, mind. You were there the same time as my brother, Ralph.'

'Is that so?'

His eyes never left Magda's face.

'It's Magdalena that's a friend of mine,' he said, savouring her name long and slow as he always did. 'We're old friends in fact, old friends that are likely to get to be close friends. Very close. Isn't that right, Magdalena?'

Magda looked anywhere except at him; the window of the tobacconists shop, the alleyway dividing it from the second-hand furniture shop next door where weeds grew out of the crumbling brickwork.

His eyes seared through her clothes like hot shears. Self-consciously, she wrapped her arms around her handbag, holding it tightly to her body, wanting to run, but knowing there was nothing for it but to face him.

'Look,' she said, sounding far more emboldened than she felt. 'My friend Susan and I are going up west to look at the shops. That's all.'

'It's a celebration,' blurted out Susan.

Magda shot her a sharp look. Not that Susan was taking any notice. She couldn't take her eyes off Bradley Fitts, flattered that a young man who owned a car could be interested in them.

Bradley got out of the car. Resting his elbow on the roof, he stood there smiling, his eyes narrowed against the smoke

206

from his cigarette. His friend got out too, leaning on the car bonnet where he proceeded to pick his teeth with an unlit match.

'So what are you celebrating?' asked Bradley Fitts.

Giving Susan a nudge with her toe, Magda answered. 'Old friends meeting up.'

Thankfully Susan got the message and didn't go boasting of her friend Magda passing the interview to medical school.

'Sounds nice. So how about making it a foursome?'

Susan nudged Magda's arm. 'Why not? We're just two girls alone, and these two young men are by themselves.'

Bradley Fitts smiled his sly smile, recognising that Susan was pliable.

'Very sensible of you, my dear,' he said, directing his winning smile and flattery at Susan. 'Makes sense for us to paint the town together. My treat of course.'

'I don't think . . .' began Magda.

'Oh, come on,' Susan whined.

Magda took a few steps away, but Susan hung on.

Bradley concentrated his charm on Susan.

'So where do you work, Susan?'

'At the brewery. I'm doing all right for meself too. Nice to 'ave a bit of money.'

He nodded as though he were genuinely interested, whilst his eyes slid sidelong to Magda.

'Good pay is it?'

A gold tooth flashed at the side of his mouth.

'Of course. I work in the office doing all that typing and stuff.'

'Is that so?'

Susan actually worked stripping the hops from the bines, the bits the machinery couldn't get at.

'This is Eddie Shellard,' Bradley said, nodding at the man leaning over the bonnet. 'Eddie is my driver. He works for me. Say hello to Susan and Magdalena.'

The car driver was familiar too; Edward Shellard, the boy who had begged Winnie for food all those years ago, and she'd given him the leavings of a loaf.

Susan flushed with pleasure.

Magda tugged at Susan's sleeve.

'We'd better be going . . .'

Bradley stepped in front of them, Eddie just a little behind him so that the pair of them blocked the pavement.

'I'll give you a lift. We'll make a night of it. How would that be?'

His tone was smooth, his movements swift and purposeful. He swung the car door open, an extra hindrance across their path.

'Hop in. Only the best for girls like you.' His look was as slippery as his tone of voice.

'Girls like us?' Magda snapped.

'Pretty girls,' he said, reaching out and chucking her under her chin.

She took a step back. His touch filled her with alarm. If Susan hadn't been so impressed . . .

She reminded herself that Susan didn't know him as well as she knew him. Smiling he might be, acting the gentleman he might be, but first as last, he was Bradley Fitts and was far from being a gentleman.

'Well. We ain't got all night. Come on, get in.'

He took hold of Susan's arm as though he were helping her in, when in fact he was being insistent.

'Come on, Magda. You're coming too,' Susan called from the back seat of the car.

Magda hesitated, torn between her instinct that to get into

the car was asking for trouble, and not getting in was leaving Susan alone. She had to get her out of there.

Magda bent into the car. 'I don't want to go with them.'

'Come on. In or out. We haven't got all night.'

A pair of hands landed on her back and pushed her in. The car door slammed shut behind her.

Eddie Shellard swung in behind the steering wheel, Bradley swiftly getting into the front passenger seat.

'Drive, Eddie. Let's give these girls a good time.'

Magda grabbed the door handle. 'No! I want to get out.'

Susan grabbed her arm. 'Oh, come on, Magda. It'll be all right. We'll have a great time, won't we Bradley?'

Bradley Fitts turned round in his seat.

'Hey,' he said in an oily voice. 'Now where's the harm in having a little drink with us at the Railway Hotel before going home? Celebrate the two of you meeting up again. Nothing wrong with that is there, Magdalena? Such a beautiful name, Magdalena. Beautiful girl too.'

Magda hit away the hand that attempted to caress her cheek.

'Anyway, you haven't told me where you work, Magdalena. Maybe I'll meet you outside where you work at some time. Maybe we'll go for a drink after work, p'raps go for a meal in some fancy restaurant. How would that be?'

Magda swallowed the chalky feeling in her throat.

'We weren't going up west to go into a pub. We don't go into pubs. Besides, we're too young for you. You're in your twenties and we're not.'

Bradley Fitts eyed her over his shoulder. A smirk spread like a cold sore over his lips, twisting one corner upwards.

'I like 'em fresh,' he said thoughtfully, more to himself than to her. 'Don't you, Eddie,' he added. 'Don't you like a fresh young thing that's more grown up than she thinks she is and just needs a bit of experience to set her up just right?'

Eddie had been silent up until now, and when he had spoken it was only to say yes or no to whatever Bradley suggested.

On this occasion he burst out laughing. 'Untouched and ripe to be plucked,' he said.

Magda's memory was jogged by his remark. The men who'd visited the place Winnie used to own had made remarks like that. Their laughs had been like that too. She used to hear them from across the road. She'd hated them for those remarks.

Bradley turned halfway round in his seat. She hit away the hand that landed on her knee. 'I don't want to go with you. I want to get out.'

The smile on Bradley Fitts's face turned to a sneer. 'Let's get this straight, sweetheart. Nobody turns down Bradley Fitts. Nobody. Get it? You've done it too many times before, but not this time. Right?'

Magda heard the threat in his voice and shuddered at the coldness of his eyes. The strong intimidating the weak – just like her aunt.

She had to stay calm. She had to get through this.

'Is that so, Mr Fitts?' she said. 'Let us out and I won't go to the police.'

His eyebrows shot up to his hairline.

'Police? Now why would you want to do that? I've done no wrong. You accepted my invitation to get into my car. Ain't that right, Eddie?'

'That's right, boss.'

Up until now Susan had been keen to take Bradley up on his offer. Hearing what he was saying and the way he was saying it changed her mind.

Magda felt Susan's fingers digging into her arm. Her friend's bravado had disappeared. She was scared.

'It'll be all right – won't it?' Susan whispered.

Susan, usually the bubbly bright one afraid of nothing, had

lost her sparkle. The freckled face had lost its pinkness. Her eyes were round and frightened.

Magda controlled her own fear. If they were to escape this situation unscathed, she had to keep a cool head. Panic and they were lost.

'You're abducting us,' she said resolutely. 'That's how the police would view what you're doing. They'll throw away the key. You'll spend years in jail. There! Do you want that?'

She couldn't believe how calmly she was dealing with this, but then, what choice did she have? There was no guarantee it would do any good.

For a moment he stared at her with that cold, codfish look of his.

She prayed he was thinking it over. He wasn't saying anything. Just looking.

Suddenly he snatched at her face, pinching in her cheeks with horribly strong fingers. She knew then that her threat had made no impression. Bradley Fitts would have it his way.

'I'm taking you out on the town. And you'll be grateful. Get it? You'll be grateful!'

He flung her backwards so hard that the back of her head bounced against the top edge of the seat.

Susan huddled closer, shaking from top to toe.

'What's going to happen to us?' Susan whispered.

Magda swallowed hard. 'Nothing – not if I've anything to do with it.'

She sounded far braver than she actually felt. She knew without needing to see her reflection in a mirror that his fingers had left red marks on her cheeks. Threatening this man with the police had done no good whatsoever – like water off a duck's back, as Winnie would say.

Her thoughts raced this way and that, searching in her mind for some way out of this.

Inevitably she thought of one or two of the girls across the road. For the men they appeared compliant. When alone they voiced their contempt. All that had mattered was getting paid for what they did.

She had to follow their example. In the case of Bradley Fitts, they had to pretend to enjoy this night out. They had to buy time and trust, enough so they could make their escape.

She gave Susan's hand a reassuring squeeze before catching sight of Bradley's eyes in the rear-view mirror and saying, 'You win. We'll come for a drink with you.'

Bradley Fitts took his gaze away from the road ahead and the busy traffic of a London night, and turned a smiling face to her.

'That's more like it. Never refuse Bradley Fitts. You have to learn that. Now I'm telling you, girls, you'll enjoy yourself. You just see if you don't. First a couple of drinks in the pub. Then I might even take you to my old man's club for a bit of dancing. How would that be?'

'Dancing?' Magda nodded, her brain working overtime. 'Yes. I . . . we . . . like dancing, don't we Susan? Though I'm not sure we're quite dressed for it. My hair for a start . . .' She made a big show of smoothing back her hair and flicking at the corners of her mouth to dislodge excess lipstick. 'Still, if you won't take no for an answer, we might as well enjoy ourselves.'

Magda crossed one leg over the other and clasped her hands around her knee. She saw Bradley's eyes follow the action. He would interpret it that she was feeling more relaxed. More pliable. More submissive.

'That's my girl,' he said, bringing his gaze back up to her face. 'You and me are going places, girl. You know how I feel about you. How I've always felt about you.'

He squeezed her clasped hands before turning back to face the front.

Out of the corner of her eye, she saw Susan looking at her wide eyed. The girl who had been so keen to go out with these men now looked like the little girl she still was – despite the new hairstyle.

Magda raised a finger to her lips in an action that begged Susan to say nothing.

Susan blinked. Then she gave a little jerk of her chin as a sign that she understood. Say nothing. Keep calm. Wait for the chance.

Magda stared out of the window. Shops, houses, blank walls and dark alleys tumbled past in quick succession.

After taking a few turnings off the main road, the car came to a stop at the kerb. The pub was situated on a corner. An old gaslight hanging from a wall bracket hissed above.

The moment the car came to a standstill, a swarm of small boys wearing ragged pullovers and hand-me-down short grey flannels crowded around.

'That your car, Mister?' The kid who spoke had a pudding basin haircut and a heavily freckled face.

'It belongs to Mr Fitts here,' said Eddie who had got out first and was holding the door open for his boss. 'You've heard of Mr Fitts, haven't you boys? So you know not to touch it and not to let any other bugger touch it. Right?'

Bradley Fitts nodded at Eddie. 'A farthing each to guard it.'

Eddie fished in his pockets and found enough farthings and ha'pennies to go round.

Bradley opened one of the rear doors of the car.

'One at a time, girls.'

Magda stepped out first, wincing at the fierceness of his grip on her upper arm. A warning.

Susan remained in the car until Eddie had finished paying the kids. Her face was paler than Magda could ever remember it.

213

Bradley Fitts swung Magda to one side of him and addressed Susan.

'Right. Get out.'

Susan did as ordered. Eddie grabbed her as tightly as Bradley was holding Magda.

'Hold onto her, Eddie. Want to appear the gentlemanly escort, don't we now.'

Eddie laughed.

Bradley slipped his arm through Magda's, holding her tight against his body.

One of the kids pushed open the pub door and earned himself another coin.

Bradley hustled Magda through, closely followed by Eddie holding onto Susan.

A fog of cigarette smoke and stale beer covered them like a blanket, killing the fresh air that had dared to enter with them.

The night outside was warm; the public bar of the Kings Arms hot and humid, a thick soup of tobacco, beer slops and stale sweat.

'Lounge bar, Eddie,' Bradley ordered. 'We have ladies with us and standards to keep up.'

His hand firmly cupping Magda's elbow, he steered her through a door and deposited her at a small round table.

'Port and lemon for you I think, Magdalena. In fact, I insist,' he murmured, his moist breath falling into her ear as his hand ran down her back.

'Why do you always call me Magdalena?'

Smiling, he shook his head and shucked his hat back further on his reddish-blonde hair.

'It's your name, isn't it?'

She nodded.

'But nobody calls me by my full name – except you.'

His smile widened. 'I'm not just a nobody. I'm different.'

The lounge bar had wooden floors, small round tables on iron legs and bentwood chairs. Supposedly better equipped than the public bar, the people in here were tidily dressed – no grimy work clothes smeared with coal dust from the gas works or blood from Smithfield or Billingsgate.

The barman, far older than the young thug who'd just entered, touched his forelock and addressed Bradley as Mister Fitts, his voice oozing humility.

Once released from Eddie's grasp, Susan clamped herself to Magda's side.

'What are we going to do?' she whispered.

'We're going to walk out of here,' Magda whispered back. 'They think we've fallen in with their plans, but we haven't.' She looked at Susan. 'Have we?'

Susan shook her head. 'They're scary.'

Seemingly convinced that they were now compliant, Bradley and Eddie were up at the bar. Other people up at the bar stepped aside to make space for them.

Compared to the other men, these two were dressed like lords, both wearing smart suits.

Never mind dancing; it was obvious that at the end of the evening there would be a price to pay.

She asked a woman sipping sherry the whereabouts of the lavatory.

The woman pointed to a door in the far corner at the end of the bar. 'Down there ducks.'

Bradley saw where they were going and told them not to be long.

'Got your drinks.' He held up the two dark drinks and jerked his chin in the direction of a table.

'That's very generous of you. We'll be right back,' Magda threw him a reassuring smile.

'There might be a door along here,' Magda murmured to Susan. 'If there is, I'm going to open it and dash out – even if we end up behind the bins at the back of Battersea Dogs' Home.'

The corridor was narrow and dark and had no door to the outside.

'No wonder he didn't mind us coming out here,' Magda said with a sigh. 'Oh well.'

She slapped open the door of the ladies' lavatory, wrinkling her nose as the smell of urine and drains came out to greet them. 'Keep your fingers crossed, Susan.'

Besides being a bit smelly, the toilets were cold and dark. There were three cubicles on one side and three sinks on the other. A chipped mirror hung above one of them and a towel for those who actually did wash their hands was draped over a couple of empty beer crates.

'No door,' remarked Susan, peering from behind Magda.

'There doesn't need to be,' Magda murmured back, her eyes falling on a small sash window at the far end.

Her heels clattered over the concrete floor to the window. It took both hands to heave it open. She looked out.

The window overlooked the yard at the rear of the pub, a small area squeezed between the backyards of crowded housing.

Barrels and empty beer crates were piled each side of a pair of double wooden gates. She reasoned that even if they were locked, it would only be a matter of sliding back a bolt.

'Right,' she said hitching up her skirt. 'The one thing Bradley Fitts forgot about girls like us is that we're not too ladylike to climb out of windows.'

'I can climb as well as my brothers,' chirped Susan who seemed to have returned to her old self.

Once the towel was placed elsewhere, the wooden beer

216

crates, stained with stale beer and old soap, were placed one on top of the other.

'I'll go first, shall I?'

'If you like. I'm right behind you,' said Susan.

'Take off your shoes. Heels are no good for climbing either up or down.'

Magda went first, swinging her legs out first even though her skirt rode up to her backside, then dropping to the ground.

'Do it like I did,' she hissed at Susan.

'No. I'm good at this,' Susan hissed back.

She sat sideways on the window ledge, one leg over before the other.

'You'll get stuck that way.'

Susan was adamant. 'I told you. I'm good at this. Better than my brothers.'

She threw down her bag. Magda caught it.

A light went on in an upstairs window flooding the yard with sudden light.

'Quick,' urged Magda.

Susan tried to swing her other leg over but stopped halfway.

'Ooops.'

'What's ooops supposed to mean?'

'My knicker leg's got caught on the catch.'

The sound of raised voices came from the front of the pub. Magda peered round the corner to the back door. So far, nothing. But Bradley and Eddie were bound to come searching for them shortly – or ask the landlord whether there was a window in the ladies' toilets and, if so, what did it look out on. Once they knew, they'd be out here in the yard and that would be it.

'Come on. Do something,' hissed Magda.

The sound of something ripping indicated that Susan had indeed done something.

'Well, that's them finished with,' she declared. 'That's my elastic gone.'

'Susan!'

This time, Susan followed Magda's advice and swung both legs over the window ledge. Unfortunately, her knickers fell to the ground first, a patch of white cotton amongst the dirt.

Susan picked them up. 'They're a bit ripped,' she said, squinting at them in the semi-gloom. 'But they are repairable. Can't throw away a good pair of knickers now, can I?'

She shoved them into her handbag and clipped the catch shut.

Just as Magda had suspected, the double wooden gate to the yard was held shut by two bolts, one at the top and one at the bottom.

Luckily both were fairly well oiled, no doubt due to the fact that the draymen came on a regular basis to make deliveries and liked things to run smoothly. It was a well-known fact that they were rewarded for their diligence with a pint of beer at each pub. Goodness knows their condition by the time they finished their round.

They slid out through the gate, pulling it to as best they could behind them.

A bus ride or two and they were back where they'd set off, both breathless.

Susan was apologetic.

'Sorry. That was my fault.'

Magda shrugged. 'Well, it was certainly some celebration. Nothing ventured, nothing gained. Nothing lost either.' She grinned. 'Only your knickers.'

Susan burst out laughing. 'A stitch in time saves knickers!'

The joking continued. 'Lucy Lastic is your middle name.'

'Well, what a bloomer that was!'

'A pair of bloomers,' Magda corrected.

Magda couldn't help feeling elated, and not just because they'd escaped the clutches of Bradley Fitts. Tomorrow she would pay her aunt for that big old Bible. First off she would write to her grandparents in Ireland. Then, once the basic introductions had been made, she would travel over there.

Her heart leapt at the prospect of seeing them. In her mind's eye she could visualise the meeting; the tears, the laughter, the swapping of stories.

She told Susan of her intentions and of her concerns.

'I think Winnie is worrying about me going, but I told her I'll be back.'

'Why? She's not related, is she? And family is family.'

Susan's comment was like a knife in her ribs, stabbing into something soft at her centre, something she'd been keeping securely locked away.

'Look at it from her point of view. She's old and without you she's all alone.'

The laughter was gone. Magda hadn't wanted it confirmed to her that once she found her family, nobody else mattered. She didn't want it to be that way, but Susan had made a point.

'If it were me that was old and alone, I'd want to keep you close,' said Susan.

Magda shook her head. 'I think she'll be fine. I think *we'll* be fine.'

Susan stopped walking and raised a solitary finger. 'Listen.'

The mad jangling of bells announced the approach of a fire engine.

Magda sniffed the air.

'I can smell burning.'

She saw a thick pall of smoke and sparks spiralling into an ink-black sky.

'Not my house,' cried Susan. 'Please God, not mine.'

She ran towards the fire. Magda ran after her.

'Not our street,' said Susan coming to a halt. 'It's from Edward Street!'

Magda cursed under her breath, then burst into a run, her pulse racing, her court shoes clattering over the uneven pavements.

Even at a distance she could taste the iron dryness of scorched air as sparks and smoke seared the sky. The flames crackled, snapped and popped.

They stood together, the pair of them, their upturned faces lit by the flames.

A policeman pushed them back as the fire engine rattled into the street and men dived off, hauling hoses that had come too late; too late to save the house, Aunt Bridget, or the one thing that Magda held dear.

'Everything burnt to a cinder,' said one of the girls from the whore house.

'So's your Aunt Bridget,' said Susan. 'Probably burning in hell.'

Despite the flames, Magda felt as though her blood had turned to ice. There was no love lost between her and Bridget Brodie; it was sad to admit it, but she really didn't care whether her aunt was alive or dead.

What she did care about was her mother's Bible. Tears stung her eyes. The Bible was the key to finding her family. It was gone.

Chapter Twenty-seven

The Twins
1935

Anna Marie was forking hay when Venetia raced up to her, apron flapping and her boots thudding into the muddy ground.

'Guess what? The Caseys are coming out to fix the stone wall that fell down in the gale. Isn't that marvellous, Annie? Isn't that just plain marvellous?'

Anna Marie looked at her sister's excited expression and felt that perhaps she didn't know her sister's mind at all.

'He let you down. He wouldn't go to America with you. And he told on us. I didn't think you were ever going to forgive him.'

It was true. Her sister had declared again and again that she would have words with him when she could. However, the chance to have words with him had never quite come about. There had been no chance to meet alone; their grandparents saw to that. The only time either of them had seen Patrick Casey was from a discreet distance. Either he was with his father doing a building job in the town, or on the rare occasions that Patrick attended mass. The Caseys were known to be a bit lax in their churchgoing, keeping their attendance to a Sunday, the day they considered was the Lord's and his alone.

'He'll never leave here,' Anna Marie stated. 'Surely you should know that by now.'

Venetia's eyes flashed and she adopted a coquettish pose to her body, looking at her sister sideways, hair held with one hand and piled on top of her head.

'He won't be able to resist. All I need is a little time alone with him and we will be leaving – together!'

'Are you going to get him to marry you?' Anna Marie looked shocked and incredulous.

'Why not? He's who I want anyway, and let's face it he's about the only good-looking fellah around here.'

Anna Marie looked away. She rarely disagreed with her sister, mainly because it was easier to go along with everything she said. What she was certain of was that Patrick Casey would never leave his father's employ. If he had been willing to leave and loved her enough, wouldn't he have boarded the ship with them at Queenstown?

Her views on her sister's relationship with Patrick were not new. She'd had this opinion for a while, but had never dared point it out to Venetia who was as head-over-heels in love with Patrick as he was with her. Or was he? Anna Marie blushed at the memory of the way he'd looked at her in Queenstown. There'd been something in his eyes that had caught her breath.

Venetia caught sight of her dreamy look. 'What are you going sheep eyed for?'

Anna Marie thought quickly. 'I was thinking, what about us not mentioning Magda but saying that we'd like to go to England to find Michael?'

Venetia shook her head. 'Michael's been adopted. Da told us that didn't he? You can't go looking for kids that have been adopted.'

'But Magda . . .'

'Oh for heaven's sake! Our sister's a whore. Do you really think we'd be allowed to cross the water to look for her? I heard Gran and Granfer talking about it. Apparently the letter came some time ago, just after Uncle James got himself drowned. Gran asked Aunt Bridget if she'd like to come over here to live and to bring our sister with her. She turned Gran down and at the same time told her that our sister had become a whore selling her body to any man who'd have her. That's what she said. Gran wasn't sure it was true, but you know what Granfer's like once he thinks bad of someone.'

Anna Marie went very quiet, her mouth shifting from side to side as she considered what to say – if anything.

Venetia cocked her head inquisitively. 'Well. Go on, moon eyes. Tell me whatever else it is that Gran's told you. I know you two talk together when nobody else is around. What's she told you about our sister?'

Anna Marie chewed her lip. The fact was that she was closer to Gran than Venetia was. They were very alike and Gran was lonely and told her things.

'Go on,' urged Venetia, sucking a corn stalk whilst leaning against bales of straw piled six deep.

Anna Marie fiddled with her hair. 'Gran says that it wasn't a good choice to leave our sister with Aunt Bridget seeing as our father jilted her in favour of our mother. She reckons she might have taken out her bitterness on Magda.'

'Is that so?' Venetia was astounded that her sister knew so much.

Anna Marie nodded. 'That's what she says. I pray for her every night you know. And for Michael. It might help, don't you think?'

Venetia was no longer listening. She had turned in the

direction of the track leading down to the farm and the unmistakable sound of a lorry. 'It's him,' she said, her eyes shining.

Anna Marie had no need to be told who she meant. The Caseys were coming to repair the stone wall that had come down in the gale. Patrick would be driving.

Venetia tore off her overall and brushed at the straw that had fixed to her dress.

'How do I look?'

Anna Marie told her that she looked fine.

Their conversation was at an end. Venetia's eyes were bright with interest and her thoughts were with Patrick Casey.

She was about to dash out from the barn when she saw her grandfather standing with his hands through his braces, chewing the fat with Patrick's father. His presence brought her to an abrupt stop.

'You can't go over there,' Anna Marie whispered over her shoulder.

'No matter. There's a lot of wall came down in the gale. There's a lot of work to be done on it and I'll get the chance to talk to him direct. Be sure that I will.'

'I don't know why you're bothering,' said Anna Marie shaking her head. 'He told where we'd gone, yet you're still sweet on him.'

Venetia tossed her head. 'Perhaps the truth was beaten out of him. If so, you can hardly blame him for speaking out in order to avoid the pain.'

Anna Marie was not convinced. 'You may not have noticed it, but Patrick is broader and taller than his father. I would think beating him was an uphill struggle.'

Venetia glowered at her sister. It wasn't often that Anna Marie spoke so boldly or hit the nail on the head. For a moment Venetia was thrown off balance, but she couldn't get

Patrick out of her head. There was only one conclusion she could reach.

'And what's going on might I ask? You're jealous! That's what it is, isn't it?'

'No! No! Not at all!'

'Well, you seem to be noticing a lot of things about him of late. I'll thank you to mind your own business. Stick to your hens and your pigs. You suit them well with your fluffy ways and your feet in the mud!'

A pink flush travelled up her sister's neck and onto her pale cheeks.

'I'm not jealous,' pleaded Anna Marie.

'It wouldn't do any good if you were. He likes a lively girl, does Patrick. Not a meek little mouse with chicken feathers in her hair and muck on her boots.'

'That's not fair!'

Anna Marie looked as though she were about to burst into tears.

'Oh shut up,' snapped Venetia, turning away, her attention fixed on Patrick.

He was helping his father unload the mortar, sand and tools from the back of the lorry.

There was no need to worry about whether he was still in love with her or not, she told herself. She'd heard no rumours that he was sweet on anyone else. Not that much gossip reached them on the farm, but plenty went on before and after mass. Before was best because at least you could go in and confess you were a gossip afterwards.

If her sister was sweet on Patrick, well, what did it matter? Patrick loved her, Venetia. He'd often commented on her raven hair, ravishing figure and flashing eyes. Anna Marie was her exact opposite; pale faced, light brown hair bordering on mousey. Pale blonde her grandmother called it, but at this moment in time Venetia preferred to call it mousey.

She sank back into the gloom of the barn, hoping her grandfather hadn't seen her. Patrick was setting his cap more firmly onto his head. Following that he took his coat off, throwing it over the tailboard.

His shirt was taut across his back as he bent and lifted more items from the rear of the lorry whose paintwork was not as bright as it had been. At the sight of those more defined muscles her breath caught in her throat. Before Queenstown he'd been less muscular than he was now. If only she was closer. She felt a great urge to reach out and touch him, even to smell him. My, but there was something delicious about a man's fresh sweat.

So why hadn't he been willing to go with her to America? Back then she had been fully convinced that he loved her enough to miss her if she left. Getting to Queenstown and seeing the big ships berthed there should have been enough to send his pulse racing; it had certainly got hers racing.

Despite what he'd done, she still wanted him. At night she dreamed of him and that moment in Queenstown when he'd thrown his arms around her and declared that he would miss her. Immediately following that he'd got in the lorry and headed home. She hadn't expected him to. She really hadn't.

But you still soldiered on, she thought to herself; whilst he betrayed you.

Her dislike for being dumped back with her grandparents in the hated countryside was undiminished. She didn't like doing the things country girls were expected to do; feeding pigs, storing hay, driving cows and like she was doing now with her sister, plucking and drawing the chickens after their grandfather had slit the poor birds' throats.

And the weather. Surely America had better weather than this? Even England did, or so she'd heard.

Today was as wet as only Ireland could be, the sky overcast and a cold wet wind blowing in from the south west.

'I hate Ireland,' she grumbled, one hand holding the warm breast of a chicken, the other up its rear end groping for entrails.

'It won't last forever. And anyway it's nearly the weekend and we'll have a good lunch after mass. Granfer's always in a good mood after a good roast. And it'll be a fine day on Sunday; I'm sure of it. Everyone will be happy.'

'Except for these chickens,' muttered Venetia.

'I wonder what Magda and Michael are doing now,' Anna Marie whispered as they prepared the birds for the table.

'Not doing what we're doing, that much is for sure,' Venetia said glumly.

She felt Anna Marie's eyes regarding her. 'You're not going over there to speak to him are you? Granfer will be fair mad with you if you do.'

'No. Of course not!' Venetia snapped.

'You mustn't.'

Venetia looked over at her sister who seemed so content with her lot in life, while she was anything but.

'I've hardly said a word to him these past two years except for a brief *'Hello', 'Nice to see you', 'Wasn't that a good sermon Father Anthony gave us'*. That's all! It's not enough for me, Anna Marie. Not enough at all.'

'If our grandfather . . .'

'I know,' she responded, kicking the invasion of chickens back out of the door. 'I know.'

The following day turned out a bit drier. The sun dared show its face between the flock of clouds the wind was chasing across the sky.

Best of all, the stone wall was still in the process of being rebuilt and Dermot Brodie had hitched a caged trailer onto the back of the tractor. Today was the day he was taking three sows over to the Morans' place to mate with their boar.

'Now's my chance,' whispered Venetia to her sister.

Alarm lit up Anna Marie's face like a light bulb.

'What if he comes back whilst you're over there?'

Venetia was adamant. 'I'll deal with that particular problem when it happens. But look! How can I go over there looking like this? You'll have to help me tidy myself up.'

They were still in the process of plucking the last of the chickens.

Anna Marie eyed the fluffy feathers that had floated up from the birds being plucked and settled in her sister's hair. Her hands too were bloodied and her chin smeared with it.

After she'd washed the blood from her face and hands and Anna Marie had picked the feathers from her hair, Venetia took off the sack apron.

On hearing the cranking of an engine, both girls turned round in alarm.

'No. They can't be going already.'

Venetia was beside herself. She edged towards the door. Patrick's father was cursing the starting handle, which had jerked in his hand hard enough to break his arm.

'He's going.'

Venetia's voice and face were united in dismay. The effort of tidying herself up had come to nothing.

'He's going,' she said sadly. 'And he didn't even see me.'

'Never mind.'

'I do mind,' she snapped. 'I mind a bloody lot!'

All day she kept looking out, fully expecting him to come bumping back down the lane to continue with the wall. She guessed her grandfather had sent them away on account of he wouldn't be there himself. He was going to great pains to keep her from Patrick Casey; great pains not to leave either of them alone with any man.

The feeling of being ill-treated by her grandfather festered in Venetia's mind all day and half the night. The rest of the night she dreamed of Patrick coming to her, climbing into bed beside her as a husband might do.

Imagining how it would be was a bit like writing a story or play, steering the characters to do what you wanted them to do. And she was centre stage of course, the most beautiful woman in the world married to the most handsome man.

Sometimes she dreamed it was daytime, the sun shining and she would run into his arms. Leaving the job of repairing the stone wall, he would declare his undying love for her on bended knees. Unable to curb their desire, they would throw themselves into the straw.

'Blow the old stone wall,' she would breathe into his ear. 'I've missed you, Paddy.'

He would be lost for words, his hands fumbling beneath her blouse, clasping her breasts, fondling her nipples and raining kisses and excuses onto her face as to why he'd betrayed her and why he couldn't go to America.

'My dear old dad hasn't got long to live.'

She told herself it was all right to say this because Mr Casey was in vital health, but this was her dream and in her dream she could do exactly as she pleased.

'Besides which,' he said to her once the run of the mill excuses were brushed aside with Venetia's hungry lips, 'your granddad would make mincemeat of my wedding tackle if he sees us together.'

This particular statement was unwelcome, but in her dream she placed a hand over his mouth and smiled into his face.

'Now that would be a shame. P'raps I'd better check that everything is still in working order, don't you think?'

On waking she recalled that they really had said that and
blushed with pleasure on remembering what followed.

They'd been lying in the long grass in Two Acre field. He'd
gasped when she had the temerity to grope between his legs
and had looked at her with a stunned expression and hardly
able to catch his breath.

'No girl's ever done that before.'

'Well. There's always a first time.' She paused. 'Patrick
Casey, I'm going to marry you,' she finally said to him. 'And
then we'll go to America.'

Laughing at her suggestion, he'd thrown himself back into
the sweet grass of Two Acre field.

She'd groped him often; the field again, the hay barn or even
the seat of his lorry; anywhere they happened at that moment
to be 'canoodling' as her grandmother would say.

His laughing had annoyed her.

'You're not the only fish in the sea, Patrick Casey,' she'd
told him. 'And I'm going to find the one that's got the ambition
and the nerve to cross the ocean with me. That I am!'

There'd been no turning back after that. Patrick was
the one for her and she was the one for him – or so she'd
thought. That was until she saw him yet again looking at Anna
Marie in that special way she'd seen him look at her down at
Queenstown.

Anna Marie Brodie kept telling herself that she had no
interest in Patrick Casey, yet every time he looked at her she
felt herself blushing.

He'd smiled at her when she'd gone shopping with her
grandmother for flour and the other things the farm did not
produce. He'd also helped her get aboard the pony and trap,
holding one of the big canvas shopping bags whilst she
climbed aboard.

Her grandmother hadn't heard him tell her what a pretty

girl she was becoming and wouldn't it be nice to meet up some time.

She'd felt more and more foolish as her face turned to flame. Why did she have to blush so much?

Anyway, she kept the encounter to herself and tried to convince herself that she felt nothing for him. But at night he came to her, smiling through her dreams. My, but Venetia was right about one thing; he was the best-looking lad around. Nobody could deny that.

'The Caseys' work on the wall is almost complete. They deserve a bit of cake and tea before they leave. And it's a hot day today. A little time in the shade will do them good.'

The news that they were to have a little tea party to celebrate the imminent rebuilding of the wall came as a surprise.

'You don't have much of a social life. Not the way things are.'

Their grandmother's eyes had twinkled when she said it. Anna Marie thought she detected a sudden dropping of one eyelid in a secretive wink. Had she heard Patrick's comment that day outside Flynns' grocery store?

Venetia bubbled with excitement as she set out the crockery whilst her grandmother made the tea. First Anna Marie placed a paper doyley on a glass cake stand. She'd made the cake herself and set it down proudly, looking like a mother with a new-born infant.

Determined to hide her enthusiasm, Venetia darted about, setting out one set of tea plates, deciding they weren't quite good enough, and then returning them to the dresser to be replaced by another set.

'One set will do,' her grandmother proclaimed. 'Keep going as you are, something is bound to get smashed.'

Venetia avoided meeting the look of distrust in her

grandmother's eyes. It was pretty obvious a close watch was going to be kept on her, more so than Anna Marie.

'What will I say to him?' she whispered to Anna Marie.

'You might not get to say anything,' her sister whispered back.

Leaving clods of mud on the cast-iron scraper outside the door, father and son entered the kitchen along with Mr Smiley, a strange, silent man who trimmed the hedgerows and never said much, and Barry Gallagher, the butcher from Dunavon who'd arrived to take away a delivery of plucked chickens and cured hams.

They brought the smell of earth, blood and dusty hedgerows with them, shook the dust from their caps and remarked how good it was of Mrs Brodie to make them tea, and wasn't that a wonderful cake on the table.

'Looks too good to put a knife into it,' said Mr Gallagher, the butcher.

'Nonetheless, it will be cut,' said Molly Brodie. 'Anna Marie made it. Anna Marie must cut it.'

Anna Marie was already blushing with pleasure at both the compliment and the fact that Patrick had smiled at her when he thought Venetia wasn't looking. Even her grandfather was urging her to go ahead, pride shining in his eyes.

Venetia was occupied with handing out cups of tea, smiling at everyone, the widest smile reserved for her darling Patrick.

Their eyes locked for a moment, both wearing secretive smiles because indeed there were secrets they shared.

'Fetch more milk, Venetia. There's plenty in the pantry.' Her grandmother handed her a jug.

By the time she came back out with a copper jug containing milk freshly squeezed from a cow, Patrick had polished off a slice of cake and Anna Marie was handing him another. He was also showering her with compliments.

'You're a great cake maker, Anna Marie. I'd be eating cake all day if you were making it.'

Anna Marie headed off to hand out more cake to those for whom a single slice was not enough.

Venetia began handing out more tea poured from a heavy metal teapot that could hold a whole gallon.

She smiled up into Patrick's face. 'More tea to go with your cake?'

He said yes, his smile and his eyes for her sister as much as for her, only this time she noticed it and stepped on his toe.

'Ouch.' The hot tea slopped onto his hand.

Her grandmother shouted at her to be careful. Her grandfather merely shook his head and raised his eyes to heaven.

The fact that Patrick seemed to be paying as much attention to her sister as to Venetia cut deep. She had a plan, one she was sure would regain Patrick's affection.

Whilst emptying the tea strainer into the sink, Molly Brodie happened to glance out of the window.

'Will you just look at that!' she exclaimed. 'It looks as though somebody's left the gate open to the vegetable garden. Anna Marie, will you chase those chickens off before there's nothing left? They're pecking it bare.'

Her granddaughter was about to say that she was sure it was shut, but didn't bother. A bit of cool air would be welcome after the heat of the kitchen, and she also wouldn't mind a moment to think. Was it her imagination or had Patrick Casey's fingers brushed against hers purposely when she'd handed him his third slice of cake?

Half a dozen chickens were scratching in the dirt and pecking at the green shoots of late-flowering broccoli.

'Here. I'll give you a hand.'

She looked up to see Patrick Casey coming through the gate.

233

'Close it behind you then they can't get back in,' she shouted to him as she tossed one of the hens over the fence.

For the moment she didn't question why Patrick Casey had suddenly appeared. She was perfectly capable of dealing with the hens herself.

The last hen, a dark red one that was almost the size of a cockerel, played an elusive game around the gooseberry bushes at the far end of the garden.

Patrick bent low to one side of the bushes. 'We'll do what the army calls a pincer movement. You go that way. I'll go this.'

Anna Marie laughed at his description, but did it anyway.

The hen tried to crash her way forward away from both sets of grabbing hands. Unfortunately for the hen she was far too big to pass through the prickly canes. Wings flapped and she squawked defiance as Patrick grabbed her, brought her up over the gooseberry bushes and threw her over the fence.

'She's a bit of a rebel is that old girl.'

'She'll be a bit of a roasted rebel if she doesn't start laying again,' remarked Anna Marie.

'Your cheeks are stunningly pink,' said Patrick.

'I'm hot. Chasing those chickens.'

She was speaking the truth. Just for once her face wasn't flushed because of her shyness but because of exertion.

'Stunning,' said Patrick with a wry smile. 'I meant what I said. And what I said to you outside Flynns' the other day.' He looked towards the house. 'I suppose we should go back in now before someone's told to fetch us.'

She nodded as her natural bashfulness returned. She was out here, alone with the man her sister was in love with. And she was feeling an emotion she had no business feeling at all.

*

234

Molly Brodie washed dishes whilst Venetia wiped. Usually it was the other way round, but today Molly had insisted. Standing in front of the sink she could see all that was going on outside.

She had a feeling about Patrick Casey and had decided he was not the man for her dark-haired granddaughter with the flashing eyes. No matter what her husband Dermot thought, she knew the girl would never settle down to farm life or even to life in the local town. There was restlessness there, no doubt inherited from her son, Joseph, and like him she would leave.

But Anna Marie! Her heart sang at the thought of Anna Marie marrying and staying here, company for Molly in her old age. And grandchildren. Well, that too would be wonderful.

Chapter Twenty-eight

The Twins

It was a fine August, the sun scorching the fields to gold and the brook at the end of Two Acre field reduced to barely a spit.

Dermot Brodie had fallen on rough ground and hurt some bones in his foot. The doctor in Dunavon had told him they were broken and there was not much he could do about it.

'They don't mend. Not those silly little bones that God placed there to join up with your toes.'

Dermot had muttered that if they were that silly then why have them in the first place. But that was that and there was nothing for it but to employ another labourer besides Mr Smiley.

Johnnie Devlin was a big man with a strong voice. Dermot considered that a definite advantage when dealing with the cows who were rebellious at the best of times. It also meant that there was less work for the two girls to do.

'One of them might have to earn a bit of a living in town,' he'd said to his wife. 'The devil makes work for idle hands to do.'

Venetia was in the pantry, patting butter with wooden paddles. The pantry, a cool place of stone shelves and meat safes, was adjacent to the kitchen.

She'd listened to most of their conversation wearing a glum expression and lamenting the fact that life had treated her so unfairly. At least in London she'd have a proper job and be free to do as she pleased. The picture houses; that's where she'd spend most of her time. Perhaps also a pub or two. Anything but be isolated with nothing but pigs and chickens for company.

Her ears pricked up at the possibility of her or Anna Marie obtaining a job in town.

The plan that had been festering in her mind suddenly seemed accessible. She had to be the one who took a job in town. Any job! And anyway, wasn't Anna Marie the one who enjoyed working on the farm?

All the same, she had to tread carefully and appear nonchalant about the prospect.

The cows were bellowing out in the yard as they were steered in for milking. Johnnie Devlin's booming voice was audible above it all.

'Listen to that,' said Venetia. 'He's got a louder voice than the cows. They respect him. They never respected me. I bet he won't get half the kicks that I got. But then, I was never that good at driving cows. Our Anna Marie was better at it. The animals like her. I'm sure of it.'

Her grandmother raised her head from lathering a leg of pork with ground sage and breadcrumbs.

'The loud voice is on account of his deafness. He was with the artillery during the Great War. Stood too near to the guns so he did.'

Venetia had heard this before, but it didn't hurt to hear it all again.

'Is there anything for me to do here? I've finished peeling the potatoes and I've mixed the mash and peelings.'

'You can weed around the pea sticks. There's bindweed growing up with the plants.'

'I did that this morning.'

No one had noticed that Venetia had got up earlier than anyone this morning and gone through both routine and other tasks in double quick time. The quicker I work, the less there seems to do she'd decided and was pleased with herself for thinking out such a plan.

'Best ask your granfer if he's got a job for you then. Unless you'd care to dust and polish upstairs.'

'I've done that.'

Molly Brodie eyed her querulously. Venetia had never been the most willing of the twins around either the farm or the house. Her head was always in a dream, that one; just like her father.

'Are you up to anything?' she asked.

'No. Of course not,' said Venetia. 'It's just that there isn't enough to do around here – not girls' work anyway. As for the cooking, well, Anna Marie is best at that.'

Her grandmother jerked her chin in acknowledgement. Anna Marie did indeed like cooking and baking. Nobody could deny it.

With a sigh of finality, Molly Brodie patted the leg of ham, the skin and flesh now totally encased in her special mixture.

'There's enough to do around here for now what with Christmas coming up, but after that . . . well.'

She eyed her granddaughter as though making up her mind whether to tell her what she and Dermot had already decided.

'Your grandfather and I think it might be a good idea to find you a little job in town. Something to keep you occupied and out of trouble until you get married.'

'Is that so? Are you sure?'

'Sure we can manage without you, or sure we can trust you?'

'Well. Both I should think,' Venetia gasped.

It was hard not to sound enthusiastic, but getting a job in town fell in nicely with her plan.

The fact was that Patrick spent a lot of time at his father's place of business in town, mostly alone in the workshop doing bits of carpentry or mending something that had gone wrong with the lorry.

All she had to do was be in town by herself, impossible most of the time, but if she could only get a placement – perhaps in a shop; perhaps doing a bit of cleaning in one of the grand houses on the hill behind the high street.

She helped her grandmother wrap the ham in a large piece of muslin, tie it at one end and hang it from a hook in the pantry.

'There's enough for you to do until Christmas what with the butcher wanting chickens and ham, but after that . . . well . . . let's see what comes along, shall we?'

Anna Marie held open the gate to the field as Johnnie Devlin, the cowherd, drove the cows away from the milking parlour and back out into their field.

Just for a change in soggy, wet Ireland, the night was fine and clear. There was a threat from frost but as far as Anna Marie was concerned, it was a small price to pay for an inky sky sparkling with stars.

She mentioned that the cows were noisy tonight. Johnnie remarked in his loud voice that they must know it was Christmas.

'The night when our Lord was born,' he added. 'I bet you loved Christmas when you were a bairn.'

She was about to agree with him, when a thought suddenly struck her. She couldn't remember how it had been when she was small, at least not before that last Christmas when they'd all been together; Magda and Michael, besides her and Venetia.

Try as she might, she just couldn't recall anything before that. Everything had ended and begun with that last family Christmas.

Tilting her head back, she looked up at the stars. They were so clear, so bright it felt as though if she reached up she could grab one and bring it down to earth; put it in her pocket; wish upon it.

The last option was by far her favourite and she knew exactly what she would wish for. She would wish to see her sister and little brother again. It didn't matter that Magda might have sinned in the sight of God and her grandparents. They were still sisters; they would forgive and forget and still love each other; she was sure of it.

Venetia too had made a wish. Although she had prayed for Magda and Michael – silently of course in case her grandparents might be listening – she had her own Christmas wish and all to do with Patrick Casey.

She'd closed her eyes and crossed her fingers in the time-honoured way of making a wish – Christmas or otherwise.

'A job. I want a job to get me out of this bloody place.'

There was a warm glow around the fire in the farmhouse kitchen, but there was also work to be done before its heat could be fully enjoyed.

Cows still needed to be milked, hens fed and eggs collected over the Christmas period. The weather was cold but re-entering the warmth of the old farmhouse was pleasurable. A crisp winter and a warm hearth. What could be better?

My Christmas wish, she thought to herself, though I have to wait for the result until the New Year.

The first sign that Venetia's wish was likely to come true happened on the first Sunday of the New Year.

As they were filing out of church it was mentioned that

Father Anthony, the young priest who had collected them from Queenstown, was in need of someone to clean for him two days a week.

Mrs Moran, grandmother of the same Moran who had a boar named Boris, had been housekeeper at the parish house for as long as anyone could remember. Close to eighty years of age, she'd declared that she was getting too old to do the heavier work. Someone was needed to help out for two days a week. It was her daughter who mentioned it to Molly Brodie.

Molly voiced the offer to her husband. 'Like a blessing from heaven. I wouldn't think she'll get up to anything sinful in Father Anthony's house.'

For a moment Dermot Brodie's doughty eyebrows dropped enough to obliterate his ice-blue eyes. 'If she does she won't be coming back here. Mark my words on that.'

Christmas came and went and January saw heavy falls of sleet that were trying hard to be snow.

The weather was of no concern to Venetia Brodie. Her chance of freedom in sight, she began counting the days to when Mrs Moran gave up her two days a week and she took them over. A date was fixed. All she had to do now was to let Patrick in on her plan.

Days on the farm passed more slowly than ever, the brightest day being when Patrick and his father came to build a new stone wall, which would enlarge the yard outside the milking parlour.

Anna Marie tried not to notice that Patrick had arrived, or at least give no sign that she was taken with him. He belonged to her sister. That's what she kept reminding herself.

Venetia connived to spend most of her time out of the house and in the barn, sometimes scratching for things to do. All the time she waited for the opportunity to get closer to him, to speak, even to touch him if she could.

Grandparents as watchful as ever when Patrick was around, she sat frustrated on a bale of straw, kicking her heels and feeling badly treated by them that should love her and therefore let her have her own way.

Anna Marie was pitch forking fresh bedding out for Merrylegs, the pony that pulled the gig. Once that was done she filled the feed bucket with corn for the hens.

She was thinking deep thoughts. 'Have you ever wondered why our father never writes to us?'

'He can't be bothered?'

'Or he can't write. I mean, even a little note would have been lovely. Just a line or two says it all, don't you think?'

She looked up from what she was doing to see her sister staring at her as though she'd said something terribly profound.

'I'll feed the chickens today.' She grabbed the bucket of corn from her sister.

Anna Marie looked at her in amazement.

'I thought the chickens made you sneeze.'

'That depends.'

Anna Marie saw her sister look to where Patrick and his father were taking down the stone wall. The lorry was parked between the wall and the barn where she and Venetia were sorting out animal feed. For a moment her sister disappeared and seemed to take a while reappearing.

Anna Marie sucked in her breath. Her sister could be wild at times, but in this instance she really should be careful.

Her attention switched to the house. Her grandmother, barely five feet tall and as round as a turnip, was feeding wet laundry through a mangle, the water splashing over her black stockings and her working boots.

The mangle turned more slowly then stopped altogether as Molly Brodie's blue eyes followed the provocative sway of Venetia's hips.

When Venetia veered away from the pigsty, the turning of the mangle resumed, Molly Brodie assured that her grand-daughter was not heading for Patrick Casey.

Aware that she was being watched, Venetia had purposely headed between the barn and the lorry where the hens were pecking in the earth.

Anna Marie watched with her heart in her mouth. For a moment her sister disappeared behind the lorry, which was now between her and the pigsty. There was no chance of her having a private conversation with Patrick. He was too far away.

She was up to something; Anna Marie was sure of it.

Venetia scattered the corn too quickly so it fell in great heaps. The chickens fell onto it in great heaps too, fighting and clucking with indignation.

'Done!' Venetia exclaimed.

There was a jaunty air to the way she sauntered back, head high, shoulders back and a definite spring to her step.

Anna Marie's blonde eyebrows almost met when she frowned. Her blue eyes were full of puzzlement. Something was going on here. She hadn't had time to scatter a whole bucket of corn, yet it appeared she had and was heading back and looking mighty pleased with herself.

'Here,' said a smiling Venetia swinging the bucket at her so she had no choice but to grab it. She strode off with her hands in her pockets and whistling a saucy song.

Bucket bumping against her side, Anna Marie ran after her.

'What have you been up to?'

'I've fed the hens, of course,' smirked Venetia with a toss of her head.

Just for once, Anna Marie bridled at her sister's dismissal.

'Don't treat me as though I'm a fool. You didn't go out there just to feed the hens. And anyway, judging by how fast you came back, you left the corn in a mountain, you didn't scatter it as you should have done.'

'They won't mind. It's corn. What should I do, hand it to them on a silver plate?'

Anna Marie persisted.

'Gran was watching. If she thinks you've been talking to him . . .'

Venetia's huge dark eyes were like candles glowing in the dark. Her complexion, usually so creamy and unblemished with the kind of blushing Anna Marie was plagued with, had a rosy hue.

'I couldn't talk to him could I, you silly goose. He was with his father on the other side of the truck. I couldn't *talk* to him.'

Her sister eyed her warily, not sure whether she was being duped or not. From where she was standing it seemed indeed that she couldn't possibly speak to Patrick.

'You did something . . .'

She said it slowly, her eyes scrutinising her sister's face for some kind of explanation.

Venetia lifted herself onto a pile of straw and giggled. 'Promise you won't tell on me?'

'On the Blessed Virgin . . .'

Venetia's expression turned taut.

'No. On our mother's grave. I know you'd swear on the Blessed Virgin and then likely confess your sin to Father Anthony. Swearing on our mother's grave is a different matter.'

Anna Marie bit her bottom lip as she always did when she was undecided or nervous. She felt both at the moment, weighing up whether she should swear, a thing the church said they should never do under any circumstances, and nervous because she wasn't sure she wanted to share her sister's confidence; doing so might well get her into trouble. She'd gone through enough beatings thanks to her twin.

244

'I'm not sure I want to know.'

'Yes you do. I'll take it that you have sworn and tell you. It's simple. I nodded at Patrick before going behind the truck, and then I flipped a note into the back of it. He saw me do it.' She frowned. 'At least I think he did.'

Anna Marie sank down onto the hay bale beside her, fearful of a future without Venetia, without her twin.

'Are you going to run away with him?'

Venetia laughed and looked at her derisively. 'Don't be such a daft duck! Well, that is, not first off. I'm going to meet up with him, use my charms and get him to go with me to America. And before you say, what about me, it's up to you whether you come with us or not. But this time he has to marry me first.'

Anna Marie bit her bottom lip again, wishing she hadn't asked and wishing she could make up her mind whether she wanted to go to America at all. She quite liked the farm and loved her grandmother. Her grandfather wasn't worthy of love but he was due some respect and certainly she feared him. There was also the matter of being attracted to Patrick. If he ran away with her sister, then that would be the end of it. The funny thing was she didn't know whether to be glad or sad about it.

Venetia's expression turned from happy to devious.

'I've got another secret for you. I'm not spending all Monday and Friday cleaning the rectory. It might have taken Mrs Moran all day to clean it, but I can speed through it in half the time. The rest of the time I'll be with Patrick. That's what I've told him.'

Chapter Twenty-nine

The Twins

Although the priest's house had many rooms, only a few were used, occupied as it was by just one man. Father Anthony only used the ground floor front-of-house rooms, the kitchen and scullery left to Mrs Moran and now Venetia. He slept in a front bedroom and had the luxury of a bathroom just across the landing. The other rooms were cold and filled with unused furniture, some covered in dust sheets and the less attractive pieces shoved into one corner.

'A priest should live in an impressive house,' stated Mrs Moran when Venetia had suggested he should live in something smaller. 'He's the most important man hereabouts so should have the biggest and the best.'

Mrs Moran followed her around on that first day, her voice a drone of information. Chief amongst it seemed to be remembering to water the huge aspidistra that sat in a pot at the bottom of the stairs.

'And be careful with that pot. It's Delft. Worth a fortune that pot is.'

'It's chipped,' said Venetia, fingering the rough edge that had been hidden by a dark green leaf.

'What? Well, that wasn't there before,' declared Mrs Moran with a loud snort of indignation.

Venetia wasn't fooled. She saw spots of red flare in the old woman's cheeks and knew where the guilt lay.

Just as she'd supposed, Mrs Moran was painfully slow, rubbing her bowed legs and rolling from side to side because her hips were as bad as her legs.

She was careful that first Monday to take things easy and make the work last all day. The same on the Friday of that week.

The following Monday, after she'd convinced Mrs Moran that she could polish, sweep and dust to her own high standard, she was all alone.

The old lady's last warning was that she should never clean the study when Father Anthony was in there.

'That's where he writes his sermons and deals with parish business. You'll not go in there when he's busy. The good father has to concentrate. He'll ask for you to give it a clean when it's needed.'

That was fine with Venetia. The sooner she could get the work done, the better.

She raced round the house like a whirlwind, doing what had to be done. Father Anthony kept to his study except when she prepared him some lunch. Mrs Moran hadn't mentioned preparing the priest's lunch was one of her duties, but he disappeared into his study afterwards or went out to visit a sick parishioner or the well-to-do family that sponsored him.

Mid-afternoon, once she was sure the coast was clear, she set off to see Patrick. Checking her reflection in the bathroom mirror, she brushed her hair, took off her apron and pinched her cheeks to make them a little pinker. She'd brought with her a stub of red lipstick she'd had forever, just enough to slither along her lips.

Her blue dress was far from her best, but she'd ironed it

before leaving this morning and the whiff of beeswax wasn't too obvious. It would have to do.

It was no more than a hundred yards along the back lane to the builders' yard and workshop where Patrick dabbled in carpentry.

The smell of new wood pared by a hand-driven lathe floated out as particles of sawdust on the air.

Patrick was bent over the lathe, intent on forming a chair leg from a piece of virgin wood.

'Patrick?'

He spun round immediately, the chair leg spinning along the workbench like a stone from a catapult.

At first he looked at her as though seeing a ghost.

She smiled whilst inhaling the scent of him, taking in the broadness of his shoulders, his need of a shave and the scent of fresh sweat.

She lingered by the door, her voice as seductive as her demeanour – a bit like that Maureen O'Hara, the American actress she'd seen at the pictures. My, but those film stars could be so enticing!

'Patrick. It's been nearly two years and more since Queenstown. Did you know that?'

He nodded. 'Ahuh.'

'And then you drove back here and told my granfer that me and Anna Marie had run away and were in Queenstown.'

'Ahuh.' He nodded again. 'I'm sorry. That I am. Truly sorry.'

She shook her head at him as she might at a small child.

'You have to make up for what you did, Patrick Casey. So! What are you going to do?'

He looked at her as though he were groping for the words to say when all she wanted was for him to reach out, to grope her for God's sake!

'Venetia.'

He took a step towards her.

'Patrick,' she said, barely able to control her amusement. This was lovely, but at the same time so funny.

She took a step towards him, he did the same and then they both did a couple more.

The crashing together was inevitable. The warmth of his body seemed to draw hers in until it felt as though they were melded together.

Like drowning, Venetia thought, feeling as though she were sinking into a blue-black void as they kissed and sucked on each other, groped, fondled, stroked and caressed.

It was as though there had been no intermission between their meetings before he'd taken her and her sister to Queenstown and the period of purgatory that had passed since.

'I might just as well have been a nun,' she said to him as they clung to each other in the lorry cab.

'You? Never!'

She couldn't exactly recall climbing up there because how they got there was not that important. It was the bit before and the bit they were now experiencing.

So they were lovers again – only more so because they were both that much older.

The haunts in which they'd canoodled were restricted by the fact that they had little time to spare and this was where the old lorry came in handy. It was their very own love nest, the little place where they could hide from the world and nobody knew they were there.

The windows got steamed up but that was fine with Venetia because it meant they wouldn't get cold when they took off their clothes.

She didn't protest when one thing led to another and his hot kisses swallowed any protest she might make – if indeed she wanted to protest – which she didn't.

'Do you love me, Patrick? Do you love me more than all the tea in China?' she asked him, her long tanned arms entwined around his neck.

'More than all the wood in me old man's shed,' he said breathlessly, and tried to kiss her.

She jerked her head away. 'What's that supposed to mean?'

'I love the smell of wood; the feel of it too. Just like a woman's body. Like your body. Soft, silky and shapely.'

For a moment she looked at him as though he were slightly mad in comparing a woman to a piece of wood; then she laughed.

'Go away with you. You're a fool and that's for sure,' she said, though she could hardly control her giggles.

He pretended it hurt when she slapped his shoulder.

'I can hardly go away dressed like this,' he answered with a wicked grin.

'That's true.'

He was lying on top of her, his loins between hers and his legs and backside bare. Every so often she caught a peek of him in the rear-view mirror above his ass. It made her grin, but she daren't burst out laughing. The last thing she wanted was to make fun of him. It was imperative that he loved her. It was imperative that he couldn't possibly do without her.

She asked him if he was happy. He said that he was.

'Are you?'

She nodded. 'Oh yes, Patrick Casey. I'm very, very happy.'

Pressing her hand against the back of his head, she brought his lips down to meet hers.

Just before their lips pressed together, Patrick said, 'You're a very clever girl, Venetia, throwing that note into the back of the truck.'

'I know.'

*

It was Monday afternoon and Anna Marie was helping to hang out washing that her grandmother had beaten and bashed into whiteness.

The sheets cracked in the breeze and those items that should have shown some colour were almost white. Grandma Brodie prided herself on the whiteness of her washing even if it did mean boiling out the colour in the big old copper that sat above a brazier in the outhouse.

Anna Marie found the smell of fresh laundry enticing and buried her face into a sheet. The sheets fluttered like clouds that might float away in the sky if they weren't fixed with pegs.

'Lovely smell,' she murmured.

'Will you stop wiping your nose in my washing,' said her grandmother whilst wrestling with a patchwork quilt that she had high hopes of drying on a breezy day such as this.

'It's a lovely day,' she said on coming out from behind the sheet.

Her grandmother responded that indeed it was. Enough to bring a smile to any face.

Anna Marie's smile froze on noticing that her grandfather was harnessing the grey pony to the small cart that he'd made himself and dared to call a gig.

She recalled Venetia saying that gig was short for giggle. 'That's what it makes you do – giggle,' she'd remarked – out of earshot of course.

'Where's Grandfather off to so early in the afternoon?'

She asked the question casually as though merely curious as to his destination. The truth was that she knew that her sister darted off early from cleaning the priest's house.

Still determined to control his granddaughters' lives, Dermot Brodie collected Venetia from the rectory on the days she was cleaning there.

Anna Marie was privy to the truth.

Molly Brodie, three wooden pegs hanging like teeth from the front of her mouth, went back to hanging out her laundry.

'Into town. He's off to pay Roger Casey for the wall he built for us. By the time he's finished there, it'll be time for him to fetch your sister. She'll be finished by then and even if she's not, he can doze while he waits in the gig. It won't hurt him at his age.'

Anna Marie stood frozen to the spot. The more positive side of her character advised her not to worry. The more instinctive side was curling around inside her like a cat that's backed into a corner.

Both the positive and negative slugged it out until she found herself breathing deeply as she reassured herself that all would be well.

There's no reason why it shouldn't be, she told herself. By the time he meets Roger Casey, joins him in a pot of tea or even something a little stronger, Venetia will be where she should be, waiting for him where she should be waiting.

Besides, he and Mr Casey could talk the hind leg off a donkey whilst slugging back a whiskey. Only after that would he get round to picking Venetia up from the leafy lane a hundred yards along from the entrance to the rectory.

She was reassured, but only for a moment. Everything depended on where Venetia and Patrick happened to be parked. The lorry, her sister had told her, was their little love nest. She'd also told her their favourite place.

All she hoped was that her grandfather wouldn't see the lorry pulled into a leafy glade just off the road into town. Best if they were parked on the other side of town out of the way. That's where she hoped they would be; that's what Venetia had told her.

She bit her lip and felt hugely worried. Venetia didn't always tell the truth.

Chapter Thirty

Venetia
1935

'Kiss me again before I put me knickers back on,' said Venetia through over-kissed lips. 'Then I'll tell you all about what we'll do when we get to America.'

Patrick's passion abated at mention of leaving home and he tried his best not to pull a face. Venetia's charms were the stuff of dreams and although he had a soft spot for her sister, Anna Marie, he gave in easily to temptation. And Venetia was extremely tempting.

Venetia was his downfall. He'd do anything she wanted him to do – especially on the physical front. But this dream she had of going to America – well – that was a different matter.

Suddenly she noticed that he was finding it difficult to meet her eyes.

'Well? Are you coming with me this time, or not?'

He scratched his head. He always scratched his head when he had a big load of thinking to do.

'That's a big decision – going to America. I'm not sure it would suit me. I've me father to think about. I'm all he's got since me mother passed over.'

'You can't stay with him forever. You're not a boy any longer, now are you? You're a man. The man I want beside me for the rest of my days. And nights.' She uttered the last two words whilst smiling and tracing circles over his bare chest. 'Just think of those nights,' she added seductively.

He was thinking of them. She could tell he was. His lower lip hung loose and his eyes were fixed on her bare breasts rather than on her face. Despite his loose lips he couldn't say a word.

Venetia cupped his face in her hands and jerked him round to face her.

'Look into my eyes and promise me we'll go to America together or I'll cover myself up right now!'

Leaving go of his face she flipped the edges of her open blouse over her breasts.

'Oh, don't do that . . .'

His fingers barely had chance to brush her bare breasts before the door of the lorry was hauled open and all hell let loose.

Venetia screamed as Patrick was pulled away from her. A pair of strong hands had hooked into his shoulders and pulled him out head first, his shirt hiked up to his chest, his unbuttoned trousers falling down to his ankles as his ass hit the hard road with a thud that made him cry out.

'Jesus!'

'Never mind Jesus! 'Tis me, boy, that you're answering to!' shouted Dermot Brodie as he yanked the boy to his feet.

Grandfather!

Venetia fought to cover herself up, but the buttons seemed to have acquired a life of their own, the buttonholes not seeming to be in the same places they had been.

Fumbling at her buttons, she thought ominous thoughts; someone must have told him, she decided. Someone must have told her grandfather where she would be at this time of the afternoon – certainly not cleaning the house of that pompous priest! To her mind there was only one person who could have told on her, who knew one of the places she was likely to be. Anna Marie. It had to be.

Dermot Brodie's voice was as big as his hands and his movements were swift. Holding fast onto Patrick's collar, he flung him round then slammed him against the side of the lorry.

'Ya scum,' he shouted, slapping the boy on both sides of his face.

Patrick looked as scared as a rabbit facing a gun, clinging on grimly to his trousers, which he'd managed to pull up. Even when Dermot did let go of him, he was too scared to move.

Venetia cowered in the lorry, fighting to make the buttonholes work with the buttons, but her fingers had turned to sausages and the buttons were still at odds with the holes. It was as though they'd had a quarrel and one had no wish to know the other.

'Sir. I'm sorry. But the devil made me do it. I was tempted and couldn't resist. Just like Adam I was, sir. Just like Adam when Eve offered him that apple!'

With a sinking feeling, Venetia covered her face with both hands. She murmured Patrick's name over and over again. How could he deny her like that? How cruel! A startling truth that she'd tried ignoring suddenly came to her; this wasn't the first time he'd betrayed her.

'And as for you . . .'

Her grandfather's big square shoulders filled the open door. Feeling totally helpless, she cringed beneath his thunderous countenance. There was pure disgust and outright anger, both hinting at a promise of the thrashing to come.

'Look at you! Half naked and acting the part of the whore. Harlot!'

Venetia's glossy hair swung around her face as she shook her head emphatically.

'No! I'm not a harlot! We're going to get married. We love each other and then, once we're married, we're leaving this miserable place and we're off to America. That's for sure!'

From what Patrick had just told her grandfather, it didn't sound that way at all, but she had to hope. She had to dream.

'Is that so?' Dermot Brodie growled the words. At the same time his white brows dipped together like a pair of broken crows' wings. 'Well, until that happens you're living under my roof, you'll stay under my roof and you'll not go out unless it's with my say so. And that's for sure on my part!'

She gasped when he pulled her out by the hair. Her hands flew away from her blouse and to her head in an effort to assuage the pain.

On sight of her breasts, her grandfather swore. 'Holy Mother, forgive me.'

Suddenly she remembered her knickers. God forbid that he found out she was wearing none.

Neither God nor fate was on her side. Her knickers fell to the ground behind her; her grandfather's eyes widened when he saw them. For a moment he seemed to curl into himself, like a volcano that's about to explode.

The slap that landed on her cheek sent her hurtling backwards against the bull-nosed bonnet of the ex-army lorry, her legs buckling beneath her.

With a heavy thud that bruised her bare buttocks, she ended up splayed on the running board, her head spinning and stars dancing in front of her eyes.

A warning finger, stained with the dirt of Ireland and the nicotine of cheap cigarettes, waved in front of her face.

'I promise that this is the last time you'll play the Jezebel. Wait till I get you home, my girl. You'll rue the day you were born.'

Chapter Thirty-one

Venetia

Feeling numb and frightened – not that she'd ever admit to the latter, Venetia sat on the side of the bed, which was nearest the window. From here she had a good view of the yard, the stone barns with their slate roofs, the hens scratching in the weeds and the green fields beyond the wooden fences.

The far side of the first field was bordered with stunted thorn trees that provided shelter for birds and the small creatures living around their roots.

The sun was doing its best to peek out from behind a bank of grey cloud. When it did break through, pennies of sunlight dappled the trees, the buildings and the pastures.

Not that Venetia was quite taking it in. Neither did she quite believe that she wouldn't be seeing the same tired old scene for some time. Not that she was really seeing it or thinking much about it. She had other things on her mind. Her world was about to change and she was scared.

She'd heard her grandfather tell her grandmother that it was sure to rain later. In response her grandmother told Anna Marie to go out and get the washing in.

Anna Marie had told him about the secret place in the wood. Her sister had protested that she'd done no such thing, but it was too much to believe that it had happened by pure chance.

'Oh, Neesh, why do you have to be so?'

'You're jealous,' Venetia had muttered from beneath the bedclothes and refused to speak to her ever again.

The sound of her grandfather's voice boomed from the kitchen, loud enough to break eardrums if she'd been close by. But she wasn't close by. She was up in her room waiting for the moment she dreaded and, anyway, even when her grandfather was close at hand, he never spoke to her. The taciturn man who spoke sparingly had not said a word to her since the day he'd found her with Patrick Casey. It was as if she didn't exist.

She turned her gaze slowly from the window to the battered brown suitcase sitting on the floor at the end of the bed. That same suitcase had been packed with her belongings for the trip to America. But she wasn't going to America now. Far from it.

Her eyes filled with tears and she swallowed hard. The prospect of leaving the Loskeran Bridge Farm was harder than she'd ever thought possible.

Last night Anna Marie had tried to make it up with her.

'It wasn't me. Honest it wasn't. Granfer just happened by. That's all.'

Venetia had remained silent, her hands behind her head, staring at the ceiling. She thought she heard snuffles that might have been sobs from the direction of her sister's bed.

'I can't believe you're going,' Anna Marie said at last as the old house creaked around them. 'I'll miss you. Honestly I will.'

Venetia was unforgiving. 'Is that so? I thought that was what you wanted. Me out of the way so you could have Patrick to yourself.'

'That's not true!'

Venetia could not bring herself to believe her. She was

hurting and somebody had to bear the blame. Her sister was first in line for that.

'I said nothing.'

Venetia turned on her side, pulled the bedclothes up to her chin and didn't answer. The future scared her. She was going away. She'd said brave words in front of the family.

'Well, it's time I found my own way in the world. St Bernadette's is as good a place to start as anywhere, I suppose.'

She wasn't feeling brave. On the contrary she was frightened.

There was no sisterly conversation, conducted in whispers in a darkened room. Only an echoing silence and the knowledge that neither of them was asleep.

Anna Marie had been instructed to stay out of the way today, the most terrible of days.

Venetia had not shown any reaction when told she'd been declared out of control and enrolled with the sisters at St Bernadette's.

'There you will learn general housewifery and domestic science with a view to a placement in service with a suitable family in Dublin or Cork – even in London. Distance matters,' Father Anthony declared, the man responsible for making the suggestion.

Their grandparents regarded him with great respect and remarked how wise he was for one so young. They were also apologetic about Venetia's behaviour. To think that she'd left the priest's house to fornicate – for they were sure she had.

Father Anthony had condemned Venetia for her behaviour, but accepted Molly and Dermot's apologies and their plea for his advice.

The priest prided himself on his social connections, dropping names here and there that sounded grand, though the

Brodies wouldn't know them at all. They merely accepted their place in life and that he knew better than them.

'Should all go well and Venetia mends her ways, there's a chance I can place her with Dublin relatives of my bene-factors, the O'Donnells. The Findley-Adams family live in Queenstown.'

Venetia didn't give a hoot about the status of the Findley-Adams family, but her heart had lifted at the mention of Queenstown, the gateway to the Atlantic crossing.

She'd learned long ago that the trans-Atlantic liners sailing from England and Europe to America called in at Queenstown. That was indeed the reason why she'd had Patrick take her there in the first place.

She often wondered how things would have been if only she and Anna Marie hadn't been discovered, though with hind-sight she should have known her sister would probably back out of the plan.

But if there was a chance of getting to Queenstown, by her-self if she had to, then she would play along with the plan to go to St Bernadette's.

Patrick Casey had denied any promise to marry her, though her grandfather had warned him that if he'd left her in the fam-ily way, then he'd have no choice in the matter.

'I'll stick a pitchfork up yer ass all the way to the altar,' Dermot Brodie had declared.

To Dermot's surprise, Patrick's father had disagreed with his old friend's statement and said that the choice of bride should be down to his son alone.

'I'll not force him into marrying the girl simply because she was free and easy with her charms.'

Dermot Brodie had considered his old friend's attitude as a slur on the family's honour and an end – at least temporarily – to their friendship.

Venetia had heard it all whilst sitting like stone in the gig outside the ramshackle barn the Caseys used as builders' store and garage for the lorry.

The two older men had stood glowering at each other, hands clenched as though about to throw a fist at each other besides the odd insult.

'Then I have no more to say to you,' said Dermot Brodie.

'Nor I to you,' replied Roger Casey.

They'd been friends all their lives and now they weren't speaking.

But it's not my fault, Venetia told herself. It's Patrick's fault. And perhaps Anna Marie's.

Once she knew that Patrick had dismissed the idea of them marrying, the prospect of going to St Bernadette's wasn't so bad – not if it eventually got her to Queenstown.

And she would not say goodbye to her sister, of that she was sure.

A soft knocking sounded at the bedroom door before it opened. She assumed it was Anna Marie.

'I've no wish to speak to you.'

She looked up surprised to see her grandmother's sad eyes regarding her with nothing but love and affection. Her blue eyes, the same blue eyes that her sons had inherited, were kindly.

'I wanted to say goodbye and say how nice you look.'

Venetia murmured her thanks. The blue spotted dress was the best she owned, though in all honesty she'd worn it many times before.

'I've got my coat,' she added, nodding at her coat lying beside her on the bed, its deep rust colour warmed by a sudden splash of sunlight.

'Are you sure you wouldn't like something to eat before you go? It's a long journey.'

Venetia shook her head. The very thought of eating anything made her feel sick.

'I couldn't.'

Her grandmother nodded and seemed to be eyeing the dull
brown pattern of the floor rug. 'Understandable that you're
nervous . . . under the circumstances . . .'

At the sound of a motor car they both turned to face the
window.

Father Anthony had been gifted the Ford motor car in perpe-
tuity by his wealthy sponsors and made full use of it, gadding
about all over the countryside. He could also be seen outside
the parish house washing it at least twice a week.

Molly Brodie shook her head. 'That car! I've heard those
people who gave him it are very rich indeed.'

She watched thoughtfully as she eyed the motor car winding its way up the track to the farmyard, preferring to face that
than the dismay in her granddaughter's eyes.

At last she turned from the window and addressed Venetia.
'This is all very unfortunate, but do your best and you might
gain something out of the whole sorry affair.'

Venetia tried to stop her chin from trembling. She had
meant to appear disdainful of this parting to the bitter end, but
now it came to it she was less so.

Courage having flown, she flung her arms around her grandmother's neck. 'I'll miss you.'

Her grandmother winced and then returned the unfamiliar
hug. Hugging and showing affection didn't come naturally to
the Brodie family; more's the pity, she thought.

A work-worn hand patted Venetia's back.

'I'll miss you too, my darling. I'll miss you too.'

On the instructions of her grandfather, nobody stood outside the house to wave her goodbye; her punishment for being
so wayward, wild and disobedient. Obey the family, you stay

with the family. Disobey and there's no place for you.

Then I won't look back and I won't be coming back. I'll look straight ahead to the fine time I'm going to have once I get that liner to America. That was her decision.

Of course there was the little matter of being interned in St Bernadette's where she would be trained in domestic service for up to a year, perhaps more, but she chose to gloss over that. It wouldn't last for too long and if she kept focused on her intentions, the time would pass quickly.

However, she couldn't help being curious as to what this place would be like. Father Anthony would know.

She stole a glance at him long enough to notice that his brow was furrowed, his shoulders hunched over the wheel and his hands gripping it as though the car would fly off into space if he dared let go.

She decided to be contrite. That way she might find out something.

'I expect they're a bit strict at this place, but it's for my own good I suppose. And I am regretful of my behaviour, Father. Honestly I am.'

My, she thought. I sound like my sister.

Father Anthony pressed his thin lips firmly together before bestowing her with a response.

'And how are we to know whether you're sincerely repentant, Venetia Brodie? How are we to know?'

'Oh, but I truly am, Father. And I hope that Patrick Casey is too. That I do.'

His response was angry.

'That's enough of laying the blame at his door, Venetia. 'Tis you who was the temptress; you the harlot who bared her body and led him astray. You should be ashamed of yourself and rightly so. In time I trust the nuns will beat the lust out of you. And I would thank you here and now not to attempt your wicked wiles on me. In that regard I'd rather you kept silent until I deliver you into the good grace of the nuns. And the sooner the better. A quiet life where you can reflect on your sins. No outside influences. No radios or nights watching American films with those half-dressed film stars and their swearing, drinking men!'

Venetia opened her mouth to say that the last thing she'd had in mind was to tempt him. He was a priest. She would never do anything so wicked. As for American films . . . how did he know what American film stars wore? How did he know that the characters in those films swore and drank?

She took a longer glance at his profile: handsome maybe – as a marble statue is handsome, but just as cold. His close proximity had become distasteful.

She turned her head, more to hide her frightened countenance than to watch the fields and woodlands they were passing.

The interior of the car, the priest and even the passing landscape, seemed to be closing in on her. Her stomach heaved. Her head began to ache. Her head flopped against the cool glass of the car window.

'I think I'm going to be sick.'

'Not in my car!'

He swerved the car quickly to the side of the road, almost driving up onto a bank of wildflowers, waving in colourful splendour.

He pushed her out so fiercely, that she landed on all fours, snagging her stockings in the process.

Not caring about stockings, priest or anything else, she heaved the contents of her stomach into the long grass, thinking as she did so that the flowers didn't deserve to be blighted so. It turned out to be such a little amount, hardly likely to be noticed yet it had felt much more.

She closed her eyes and wished she didn't feel so bad. Fancy being frightened enough to be sick. She'd prided herself on never being afraid of anything. But you've never been sent away from home before, she told herself. And you've never been sent to St Bernadette's. No wonder you're feeling sick.

Father Anthony ushered her back into the car, pushing her into the front seat, slamming the door behind her though not before winding the windows down.

'You stink. I don't care if you freeze to death; I'm having the windows open.'

Just the presence of Father Anthony sitting next to her was suffocating enough, so the open windows were welcome. She turned her head to face the rushing air, not caring how cold it was. It was only July and although the weather was not that warm, it certainly wasn't likely to freeze her to death.

The rest of the journey passed in silence. Not once did she attempt to speak to him, make any comment about his car or the passing scenery, or ask questions about the place they were going to. She didn't care what it was like. All she wanted was to endure this ordeal and pass through unscathed on the other side.

The fresh air helped clear the fuzziness in her head and her stomach seemed to have settled down though she didn't think she would ever be hungry again.

Even when the high stone walls and the iron gates of St Bernadette's loomed up before them, Father Anthony made no comment that they had arrived at their destination. He got out of the car and pulled at a length of ornate cast iron hanging to one side of the gate, then got back in. Somewhere far off there was a jangling sound and beside her the rasping of day-old stubble as the priest stroked his chin.

A black-robed nun appeared, a circlet of iron keys hanging

from one hand. She nodded at the priest before thrusting a key in the lock and pulling in the gate.

'Get out.'

The sudden instruction startled her.

'Well, go on. Get out. You can untie your suitcase yourself. You're not helpless,' snapped the priest.

She'd expected Father Anthony to come in with her, though she hardly relished his company. A miserable man, she wondered whether his celibacy might have something to do with it. Not natural, she thought, for a man not to have relations with a woman.

Without his help, she took her suitcase from the back seat. Her attention went to the nun; like the priest, celibate. But at least she might be happier, she thought, and threw the nun a smile.

'Hello. I'm Venetia Brodie. I think I'm expected.'

The returned smile was tight, if it was indeed a smile at all.

'Good afternoon, Venetia Brodie. I am Sister Consuela. Come in and don't dawdle. I've no time for dawdlers.' The nun's tone was brisk though not unfriendly.

'I've no intention of dawdling,' Venetia replied. 'I'm glad to be here.'

'Well, that will be a first,' said the nun looking surprised.

The gate shuddered and rattled in its iron frame as it was slammed shut. On the other side of it, Father Anthony backed his car onto the road, swung it round and drove off. He didn't wave. He didn't look back, but Venetia didn't care about that. In her mind she was both geographically and effectively half-way to Queenstown. She was here and the sooner she was out of here again the better, though she wouldn't go back to the farm. Never. Not ever.

Chapter Thirty-two

Anna Marie

Anna Marie took over the job of cleaning the priest's house, polishing the brasses, doing the laundry and even pressing the young priest's clothes.

It was a bright October day and she was singing 'The Flower of Killarney' as she cut bread and cheese for the priest's lunch. The sun was warm on her hair, the sky was blue and dried leaves driven by a brisk wind rattled against the window panes.

She got to the line, *not so fair as she,* when suddenly she realised she was not alone.

Father Anthony was standing in the doorway wearing an expression of rapt attention.

For a moment it seemed her tongue was wrapped round her teeth, but at last she found her voice.

'Are you ready for your food now, Father?'

'Yes,' he said, seeming to come out of a daze, his abrupt manner returned. 'I'll just go and wash my hands.'

By the time he came back, his food was ready and waiting.

Anna Marie poured him his tea from a large brown pot and as usual left him to help himself to sugar.

'Two sugars, please Anna Marie. It's as well you get to know what I like. I intend inviting people to tea here to discuss parochial matters. I'll need you to help me with that, so we might as well get to know one another better. To start with, you can pour a cup of tea for yourself. Keep me company and help yourself to some bread and cheese.'

Normally she would have busied herself somewhere else in the house whilst he ate and take her lunch once he'd left the kitchen.

She stood there feeling flustered, unsure what to do.

He gestured at the table. 'Well, come on, girl. Get yourself a sandwich and keep me company.'

Recognising that his manner had made her nervous, he shook his head and indicated the teapot with an ink-stained finger.

'A pot of tea is for sharing; don't you think Anna Marie?'

Father Anthony made her nervous. He was arrogant, abrupt and had a habit of talking down to people. Even if he hadn't been a priest, she didn't think he would have had many friends.

'I heard you singing,' he said once she was sipping her tea and eating her sandwich, trying not to chew too loudly or swallow too quickly. 'You have a fine voice,' he said to her. 'Will you sing to me again?'

'Here?' The very suggestion of singing in front of him made her knees shake.

'Well, of course,' he said, sitting back in his chair as though her singing to him was the most natural thing in the world. 'Your fine voice is a gift of God. So why not sing to his representative here in this parish? Your voice could be your fortune, Anna Marie. Take my word for it. But eat your bread and cheese first. There's no point singing on an empty stomach.'

She did as he told her, the food as tasteless as chalk in her mouth at the prospect of having to sing afterwards. The tea also was doing nothing to ease the dryness in her throat.

As she ate she became aware of his eyes on her.

'You're nothing like your sister. Not so talkative. But I can talk for Ireland you know, though only when in the right company. Now take the O'Donnells. Finbar O'Donnell is a man of learning and recognises the same in others. We have grand conversations, Finbar and I. Grand conversations!'

His face positively shone with pretentious pride that he knew such people and regarded himself as being their equal.

It could well be true; after all they were the family who had bequeathed him a motor car.

Anna Marie swallowed the last of her tea, though goodness knows she'd taken long enough about it. The moment could be put off no longer; she had to sing.

'Well, stand up, girl, so I can hear you properly.'

The chair scraped back as she stood on shaky legs. Keeping her gaze fixed on the pot shelf just behind his head, she began to sing 'Ave Maria'.

'No. Not that. I've heard enough of that to make me wish Schubert had never been born. Sing "The Flower of Killarney" again.'

She swallowed first, folded her hands in front of her, and began to sing. As she sang she kept her eyes on a big cast-iron pot immediately above his head.

The notes finally fell away and still she stared at that pot.

'That was fine. Very fine indeed,' said Father Anthony.

When she looked at him, he was smiling up at her, hands clasped together.

Every workday after that the priest insisted she take her midday meal with him and sing to him afterwards.

The study where he wrote his sermons was still off limits for cleaning without his say so. Weeks passed and not once did he condescend to let her in there.

'It must need a good dusting by now,' she told Leah, a

friend who had gone some way to filling the void left by her sister.

'Wait till he's out. Go in and give it a good do then,' Leah advised. 'Who knows what he's hiding in there,' she said with a mischievous grin.

Patrick also advised the same and this after he'd asked her grandfather's permission to court her.

Dermot Brodie had seen the shy glances they gave each other and placed no obstacle in their way. His opinion was that this granddaughter was totally different to her twin sister and could be trusted to behave herself.

'I'd like this one to get married before long. That'll be one off our hands and no reason to worry,' he said to his wife.

Molly was not so certain it was a good idea, but conceded that he was right about Anna Marie's character. She was no rebel, that much was for sure.

In the meantime Anna Marie continued her job at the rectory. It came as something of a surprise when Father Anthony asked how would she like to extend the two half days to two whole days?

'With your grandparents' consent of course,' he counselled her. 'I wouldn't want Dermot to think he didn't have a say in this. I'll give you a note confirming as such so he knows you're not following your sister's lying ways. Now how would that be?'

His proposal filled Anna Marie with alarm.

'I'd prefer not to do it,' she told her grandmother. 'I'd prefer not to work there at all. I prefer to work here on the farm every day.'

'Well, you're the funny one,' exclaimed her grandmother. 'Most girls would jump at the chance. It's an honour, almost. And what's more, Father Anthony says that you do a good job. In fact he told me that you're the best domestic help he's ever had there.'

The fact that he valued her so came as something of a surprise – at least on the housework front.

'And I have to sing to him,' she exclaimed as though it were somewhat improper.

'Oh my! I knew you had the voice of an angel, but to be asked to sing in the presence of a priest. I presume he has you sing "Ave Maria"?'

Anna Marie shook her head. 'No. Popular tunes.'

'Well,' said her grandmother, looking somewhat surprised. 'Some popular tunes are very pleasing. And very proper.'

Anna Marie resigned herself that her protests had fallen on deaf ears. On the contrary, the fact that the priest actually *requested* her to sing pleased them no end.

It felt uncomfortable to be sitting across the table from him. Her respect for a priest, ingrained from an early age, was too deep-rooted for conversation, at least on her side, to flow easily.

As for Father Anthony, he was kind enough, quite attentive at times and that in itself was discomforting. He asked her a lot of questions about how she might be missing her sister, was she courting a lad, and was it anyone he knew. Blushing profusely, she denied that she had a sweetheart and didn't know of anyone who might be interested in her. The fact that Patrick was sweet on her, she wanted kept from him. After all, he was the one who had driven her sister to St Bernadette's.

'Look at me,' he said to her.

She'd done as ordered, raising her calm blue eyes to his face.

Reaching across he'd taken her chin between forefinger and thumb.

'Just as I thought. Anna Marie Brodie, I'll warrant those eyes of yours have the lads round here gasping to get closer to you. Mark my words; you're the prettiest girl in the neighbourhood.'

He'd let go her chin though it felt as if the imprints of his thumb and finger had left it burning, as though touched by hot cinders.

She continued to make him tea and a sandwich at lunchtime and afterwards she would sing to him.

The conversation kept returning to sweethearts.

'I do hear that young Patrick Casey is interested. Has he attempted physical contact as he did with your sister?'

Anna Marie felt as though her face had burst into flame.

'No,' she muttered, and wished she could go home – right now – and never come back.

'Ah! Such a pretty girl like you. I don't believe it.'

In her mind she thought about Patrick Casey, a calmer young man without her sister's fiery influence.

Her grandfather and Patrick's father had made up their differences. Venetia's wild ways were blamed for leading Patrick astray, but as no harm appeared to have been done on his part, and Venetia was in a place where she must mend her ways, the old relationships were easily patched up.

Patrick sought her out and they talked a lot, mostly of what was happening locally and how about she go with him to the pictures.

Venetia was rarely mentioned and only by Anna Marie. Patrick did his best to skirt round the subject and when asked outright whether he missed her, he admitted that Anna Marie herself was the one he had in his sights.

'Give it time. Give it till you're eighteen or so and we can think about marrying.'

'Two months' time.'

'Is that a fact?'

He'd looked taken aback at her birthday being so near.

Anna Marie thrilled at the thought of Patrick being in love with her – for surely he was as was she with him. On the other hand she also felt guilty. Wasn't she stealing her sister's man?

She put this to Father Anthony after they had eaten and she'd sung yet another popular air. At his request she'd also sung 'Falling In Love Again'.

'I do like a husky voice on a woman. Have you seen the film?'

She replied that, no, she hadn't been allowed to see *The Blue Angel,* and she was surprised that he had. Rumour had it that the star had been scantily clad. Venetia, who had a thing about film stars, had told her so.

For a moment the classic lines of his face seemed to stiffen, though the look in his eyes leaped like the flames of a fire.

'Do you love him? Do you want him? Do you really want to marry him and do you really know what marriage means? Have you considered the physical side and your duty to your husband?'

There were too many questions for her liking and, blushing profusely as she always did when his conversation went in that direction, she shook her head, her gaze dropping into her teacup.

He got to his feet and stood behind her, his hands resting on her shoulders.

'Anna Marie. You are so young. So innocent, but your body is ripe for a man. That it is.'

She felt his breath brushing her hair as he sighed deeply, his palms hot and moist through the thin material of her blouse. She closed her eyes and nervously bit her lip. His fingers opened and closed over her shoulders. It felt good yet she knew it was wrong, especially when his fingers began to slide down towards her young breasts.

She got up so quickly, the back of the chair nudged the priest backwards.

'I'd better get on or I'll never get everything done,' she stammered, her face on fire. She backed away from him and grabbed a broom, not exactly a weapon, but she could fetch him a hefty whack if she had to.

She had to get away from him, not just his closeness, but this kitchen, this house. Her grandparents would never believe her if she told them. There was only one person she could confide in who would believe her.

Patrick listened to her as she related what had happened.

'You have to tell someone,' he said.

She shook her head. 'He's a priest. He can do no wrong. Nobody will believe me and, remember, he's got the backing of rich people – those O'Donnells he's always on about.'

Some days later she broached the subject of going back to two half days per week. 'There's not enough for me to do,' she said to him.

'Ah! But there is. Mr and Mrs Malone will be calling on me regularly for afternoon tea. They're visiting once a month. They're great people, the Malone family. They believe in using their wealth for the greater good, supporting the Catholic Church in its good deeds. I suggested we meet up once a month with other members of the local parochial council to discuss the progress of their favourite projects. I shall require you to make sandwiches, bake a cake and serve tea. I presume you can do all these things, Anna Marie? After that we'll look again at whether there's enough for you to do here. How would that be?'

She found herself unable to argue.

The day of Mr and Mrs Malone's visit was only a week away. She told herself that she could survive until then.

He summoned her to his study the week before, the first time she'd ever been invited to enter.

She entered nervously, half afraid of its dark woods, dark colours and shelves filled with gilt-edged tomes on religion, missions and Catholic lessons.

'Shut the door behind you, and let's begin,' he said as he sat behind a desk the size of her single bed at home. 'Now I know you can make tea and sandwiches. Though cut them thinly for these people, Anna Marie. None of your generous slices of bread cut as thick as doorsteps. These are gentlefolk. They're refined and like refined things. And on that note . . .'

His hooded eyes looked her up and down. The colour rushed to her cheeks. She dropped her gaze to the toes of her black leather shoes – sensible shoes – the heavy kind she wore for working in.

'You can't possibly serve Mr and Mrs Malone in that get-up. Do you have something more suitable you could wear?'

In her mind's eye Anna Marie fingered the few clothes she happened to own, finally settling on the only dress she thought suitable.

'I do have a black dress, Father. It has a white lace collar and cuffs. It's my church dress so I'd have to wear an apron over it so I wouldn't get it dirty – greasy and all that.'

Father Anthony looked thoughtful. 'I wouldn't want you to do that. Your church dress should be kept for Sundays and mass, not waiting on me and my friends.'

He pronounced the words, 'my friends', with something approaching the same deference with which her grandmother spoke of the Pope.

'I tell you what,' he said, looking her over again as though he had every right to be measuring her up that way. 'Father Joseph's old housekeeper kept her maid's uniform upstairs in the closet. I should think it were your size. I believe it was only worn when the archbishop was paying a visit. How about you take a run upstairs and try it on. It might be a bit big for you, but I'm sure a girl like you is handy with a needle and could put it to rights in no time.'

'Yes,' said Anna Marie, blushing more furiously than ever. All she really wanted was to go back to the original arrangement. The truth was that Father Anthony, with his thick dark hair and his hazel eyes, made her feel uncomfortable. He'd actually said to her that if he were not a priest, but a young man of the parish, he would be her sweetheart in no time at all! No priest had ever said anything like that to her before.

However, there was nothing she could do but fall in with his plans.

She brushed against the aspidistra as she climbed the stairs, the feathery touch of its leaves making her shiver. Or was it something else? A feeling of apprehension and a general dislike for this big old house with its dark wallpaper and heavily curtained windows.

A window of coloured glass depicting the Virgin Mary cast colours over her face and the landing in front of her.

She looked up at the gently lowered eyes, the enigmatic smile, and heaved a huge sigh. This house felt so enclosed, like a prison, and the priest and even the Virgin Mary, like a jailer.

The room once occupied by a housekeeper held a single cast-iron bed, a chest of drawers with bun feet and a washstand with spindly legs and a blue and white jug and basin.

The wardrobe was of heavy oak, but plainly made in country style and very early Victorian. Prepared for the smell of mothballs and faded clothes, she opened the wardrobe door.

To her relief there was no such smell and the single black dress looked far more up to date than she'd expected it to be – in fact it looked almost new.

The dress was black and along with it were a starched white linen apron and a small cap with black ribbons to tie it on with.

Anna Marie laid the items out on the dark pink eiderdown covering the bed and sniffed again. The outfit didn't smell of anything; not mothballs or that musty smell when something is left forgotten. Her first impression had been correct; in fact it smelled quite fresh.

She smiled at the thought of wearing it and how smart she would look and Father Anthony had advised her to try it on, so try it on she would.

Carefully unbuttoning the back of the dress, she laid it out on the bed ready to put on. Her own dress, once she'd taken it off and laid it out too, looked shabby in comparison.

She was wearing little beneath her woollen dress, a warm affair and fit for the job she was doing.

Underneath she wore just a pair of cotton drawers that she'd trimmed with lace herself, and a thin vest that drooped at the front so her breasts kept popping out.

The vest was scruffy, she decided, too scruffy to wear under something as crisply clean as the maid's outfit.

Pulling the vest off over her head, she flung it onto the bed. As she stretched to pull the dress over her head, she caught sight of herself in the mirror attached to the inside of the wardrobe door.

She'd once envied Venetia her more developed figure and had considered her own puny and almost boyish. But no more. Her breasts were round and firm, at least the size of oranges and just as good a shape. She smiled at her reflection; she hadn't exactly caught up with her sister, but what she had was attractive and pleased her.

The buttons were at the back of the dress and not that easy to do up, but she managed. After the dress came the apron. Sliding the wide ties around her waist she tied them a bountiful bow in the small of her back.

Her reflection was pleasing. Now for the cap.

Scraping her hair back behind her ears, she finally crowned herself with the pretty little cap.

Her eyes sparkled at the sight of her own reflection. Father Anthony would be pleased with how she looked. She was sure of it. His visitors too would be impressed.

Father Anthony gave her a few minutes to go into the room and find the clothes.

Still sitting where she had left him, he now looked up at the ceiling hardly able to contain his excitement.

She was so pretty, so innocent, like a spring flower, or an unblemished Madonna.

He patted his chest as he counted to ten, aware of the thudding of his heartbeat.

Barely audible, but he heard the discernible squeak of the wardrobe door. The room was directly above the kitchen. She'd finally opened it.

Rising slowly and carefully, he pulled the chair out from beneath him and headed for the stairs, the landing and the room next door to that once occupied by the housekeeper.

The room was dusty, the door well oiled. No squeak from this one. The dust was another matter.

Father Anthony held his breath. Wasn't it typical he thought that a tickle in the throat arises at the most inconvenient time?

In an effort to stop the threatening cough, he placed a hand around his throat, fingering his windpipe as though such movements might dissipate the problem.

To his great relief it seemed to work. Now he could concentrate on what he was doing, drink in the delectable scene in all its glory. Nobody would know; certainly not the girl.

He'd discovered the hole in the plaster purely by chance when trying to hang a picture of some obscure Irish saint on a rusty nail already hammered there. Either the nail had been too rusty or too weakly secured, or the picture had been too heavy. Whatever the reason, the picture had crashed to the floor and the nail had fallen out of the wall.

What was left was a small hole; certainly not enough to poke a hand through or even a finger, but certainly enough of a peephole to see into the next room.

That was exactly what he was doing now, his eye against the hole, his face turned slightly to one side so that his cheek lay against the faded wallpaper.

Chapter Thirty-three

Magda
1936

It was most people's opinion that 1936 was a year to go down in history. King Edward VIII had abdicated in order to marry his American divorcee, and King George VI had taken his place.

People were still arguing about the rights and wrongs of the whole scandal, but other people had more important things to think about. Important to them that is.

Magda Brodie, now a second-year medical student, hugged her lecture notes against her chest as she descended the slippery steps from the annexe that was presently serving as a lecture room. The building was old and had served its purpose for some time, but the heating was almost non-existent. The students joked about leeches used in past ages for blood-letting still being stored in the dusty cellars. A few more months and she would be leaving the lecture rooms for *real* medicine on the wards of Queen Mary's Hospital for the East End.

'Merry Christmas and a Happy New Year!'

On raising her head to see who had called her, her foot slipped and she landed with a bump.

'Magda. Are you all right?'

The young man standing over her had glossy brown hair and kind blue eyes behind the horn-rimmed glasses he wore.

Magda laughed. 'Just give me a hand up. If we hear a cracking sound, we'll know I've broken something.'

'That may not be enough. I can always give you a thorough examination if there's any doubt,' the young man replied. His eyes twinkled mischievously.

'You're a cheeky monkey, Andy Paddock,' she said as he helped her to her feet.

'Doctor Andy Paddock, if you don't mind.'

Feeling slightly privileged that someone like Andy who had been studying for five years was interested in her, Magda smiled at him. 'At long last. I bet it feels good.'

'To be a real doctor at last after all those gruelling lectures and grovelling to senior house doctors? You bet it does! Now. I know you're going home for Christmas and so am I, but what about celebrating New Year together? I'm on duty. You're on duty, but we could possibly squeeze an hour or two together – perhaps around midnight.'

'Nineteen thirty-seven. I'm so looking forward to it.'

'So you should. You've done wonders in your first year and second year. Now for your third – out there in the thick of things.'

'That's what I want.'

Alongside training on the wards full time, she'd opted for assisting a charity working in the East End with impoverished families. A lot of the work would be with children and attending women in labour.

'You're a brick,' he said to her, his eyes shining with admiration. 'Can I give you a lift home in the orange box?' Andy was one of the few doctors who happened to own a motor car – nothing grand, just a little black Ford that he fondly called the orange box. That was in fact what it looked like; an orange box on wheels!

Magda looked down at her hand, which was still in his. Not that she could feel much through the thick mitten, but it still made her feel good.

'No, but thank you. The underground is close by and if I don't hurry I'll miss my train.'

'You know I like you a lot, Magda.'

It came out in a rush as though he'd been building up the courage to say it.

She nodded, her head slightly bent forward so she could feel the weight of her hair on the nape of her neck. It was still long, though captured in a snood nowadays away from her face. She was a doctor in training. Compromises had to be made.

'I have to go now. Have a Merry Christmas Andy. See you soon.'

He looked a little dejected that she didn't go even halfway to making a reciprocal comment. The truth was that she couldn't say that she felt the same way, because she really didn't know whether she did. She was fond of Andy Paddock, newly qualified doctor from a well-to-do family. But did she love him? Time will tell, she said to herself. Give it time; besides you want to be a doctor before you're anybody's sweetheart or wife.

With a look of regret, he let her hand go.

'I'll be seeing you then.'

He waved and she waved back, only stopping when it seemed she was making no forward progress.

The pavements were slippery and she was careful where she stepped. It was gone ten o'clock when she finally got down onto the platform for the eastbound train.

The cavernous tunnels echoed to the sound of footsteps and

for a moment she thought she was hearing more than just her own.

Refusing to bow to her nerves and look behind her, she kept going until she gained the station itself.

The underground stations were nearly empty, the main army of people commuting to the new suburbs already sitting in their living rooms, drinking Ovaltine and listening to the radio. Just a few stragglers remained, men in bowler hats likely to travel only one stop, a merchant seaman, kit bag slung over one shoulder.

A prim-looking woman wearing a shabby coat and scuffed shoes, probably a domestic servant on her way home to the East End, got in behind her. For one moment she turned anxious eyes in Magda's direction but then seemed to change her mind.

Alms for Christmas, thought Magda. So many people with families needed money for Christmas. If the woman had asked, she would have given her a shilling, maybe even half a crown.

A drunk huddled in one corner suddenly blinked open his eyes and began singing 'Hark the Herald Angels Sing', in a pretty decent baritone despite the drink.

Magda smiled to herself. So what if he was drunk? He was harming nobody, just enjoying himself.

The only other occupant drew her attention and once drawn she couldn't look away. He wore a trench coat over a navy blue suit; his shirt was crisply white, his tie a moderate shade.

At first she couldn't see his face, hidden as it was beneath the brim of a tan-coloured trilby hat that matched his trench coat.

Becoming aware that he was being scrutinised, he looked up.

His deep-set eyes were a compelling blue beneath dark eyebrows; his features strong and even.

At first he looked surprised to see her, almost as though they knew each other.

Magda searched her memory. No. If they had met before, she would have remembered him.

His mouth opened as though to acknowledge her; then he smiled, shook his head as though mistaken and turned away.

He got off at the next stop, though not before tipping the brim of his hat in her direction, his smile just as controlled as before, just as enigmatic.

She turned her attention back to her notes on that day's lecture. The lecture had occurred after an early-morning start on the women's ward where she'd been required along with a number of other students to accompany a senior around the wards. They'd lingered over one particular woman patient who had been in labour for three days.

'One day more and I'll operate,' the surgeon had said loftily before moving onto other patients.

Magda had frowned and looked back at the woman, feeling for her pain. By her judgement, three days seemed too long.

The surgeon noted her expression.

'She's a charity patient, Miss Brodie. Surgery costs money. Please remember that.'

A hand touched her sleeve, disturbing her thoughts.

'Excuse me.'

She jerked her head back from her notes. The face of the woman looking at her so intently was thin with a long nose and jet black eyes. Magda recognised the woman she'd taken earlier to be a domestic servant.

'Are you Doctor Brodie?' she asked in a hushed voice.

Magda racked her brains. This was certainly a night for coming across people she might or might not know.

'I'm not a doctor. Not yet anyway. Just a medical student. How do you know my name?'

The woman looked sheepish. She was wearing a shabby coat, shiny with wear, the seams coming undone. Her knitted hat and mittens had a wrinkled look, made from a variety of unpicked garments if the mix of colour was anything to go by.

The woman's eyes were round and unblinking.

'I made enquiries at the hospital and somebody pointed you out to me. I was going to make meself known outside the hospital, but then I saw you talking to that young man. I didn't like to intrude, so I followed you, waiting for the chance to get you alone. Susan sent me.'

'Susan! How is she?' asked Magda, relieved that this woman was not dangerous and knew her old school-friend.

'That's why I've been waiting for you. She needs to see you.'

Magda glanced at the wristwatch Winnie had bought her for her birthday.

'Can this wait for tomorrow? It's late and my aunt will be worried.'

She called Winnie her aunt even though they were unrelated but it saved having to explain anything.

'Please. It's very urgent.'

The jet black eyes pleaded and the woman's pinched face pinched itself in further.

'Is she ill?' Magda asked.

The woman nodded.

Magda settled back in her seat, resigned to going with this woman.

'All right,' she said.

Absorbed as she was in her studies, it had been a while since Magda had seen her old friend. Susan had married the first man to ask her.

The woman's thin body, so rigidly held up until now, suddenly deflated like a balloon with a slow leak.

What's Winnie going to think, Magda worried to herself

as the train pulled into her stop and within minutes pulled out again?

Winnie would assume that she'd been asked to stay on and assist. It wouldn't be the first time. Even junior doctors were put upon to deliver more hours; medical students were no exception. Whilst studying they doubled as cheap labour; it was hard, but that was the way it was.

Her reflection looked back at her as they rattled through the dark tunnels of the underground. In her mind she was with her friend Susan again and the thought of that chirpy face and wild red hair made her smile.

They hadn't seen much of each other since leaving school. It was only when she'd bumped into her out shopping in Clapham High Street with two kids piled onto a pram that she knew what had happened.

'I married Billy Sellers. You might remember 'im. Two yards wide with hands like shovels. Not the sort for getting down on bended knee an' all that,' Susan had said to her, nodding at the eldest child who looked to be no more than two or three years.

Their paths had divided. With the help of a friend of Winnie, Magda had got into medical school with the barest of qualifications. Any protests about it being cheating had fallen on deaf ears.

'It's not what you know, it's who you know. And besides I'm owed favours.' Winnie's eyes had twinkled with untold secrets and vivid memories.

The train rattled to a stop.

The pinched-faced woman ground the stub of a Woodbine underfoot and jerked her head, indicating that Magda should follow.

'What's Susan suffering from, Mrs . . .?'

'Ruby. Call me Ruby. Women's trouble.'

286

Magda didn't press her for more information. She had an inkling of what that might be and was on her guard.

The dark streets of an area close to the docks and far meaner than Edward Street echoed to their footsteps. The flickering of gaslights made their shadows seem longer and almost monstrous, falling like giants up the fronts of flat-faced houses.

Life was all around. The sound of voices raised in violent quarrel fell from a bedroom window. Somewhere a baby cried and ahead of them cats yowled in close combat with each other.

'In 'ere,' whispered Ruby, the woman with the pinched face.

She pushed open a paint-scabbed door, strips of it hanging in ribbons. The smell of overcooked food and gangrenous walls greeted them.

'Susan's got the upstairs rooms. I got the downstairs,' explained Ruby.

Just as they reached the stairs, something scuttled across the floor.

'Mouse,' said Ruby. 'Place is bloody running with the little bleeders.'

She began to climb the stairs. Magda followed on behind.

The landing at the top of the stairs was tiny. There was a door on both sides and no floor covering – just bare boards.

Ruby tapped on one of the doors and called out, 'It's me, Susan. I've brought your doctor friend with me.'

Magda was about to remind Ruby that she was far from being a doctor, but didn't bother. She certainly wouldn't be doing any doctoring tonight; she hadn't brought anything with her. All she could do was give advice.

The room was dominated by a double brass bed and lit by a single gaslight. The curtains wavered in front of the draught blowing in from around the ill-fitting window. The wallpaper was dark, the wall-mounted gaslight fighting bravely against the gloom.

Besides the big bed, there was little other furniture in the room, all of it well used and dating from the last century.

'Magda. Nice of you to come,' said Susan.

She was lying to one side of the bed, bedclothes up to her chin. Even by the frail light, Magda could see that her old colour was sadly lacking.

She grinned, just like the girl she used to be. 'Sorry about the place. Not exactly a palace but we do what we can, don't we Rube? We do what we can.'

Susan's ginger hair was like a squashed pumpkin behind her head. Her eyes were as lively as ever, though there were dark lines below them and blood at the corner of her mouth.

Magda felt her worst fears coming true. She knew how things were amongst the desperately poor, what lengths they would go to in order to improve their lot.

After placing her lecture notes onto a chest of drawers that she noticed had one drawer missing, she pulled up a stick-thin chair to the side of the bed and sat down.

Ruby, she noticed, had lit up another cigarette and stood on the window side of the bed. The draught whirled the smoke up into a thin spiral that circled around her head.

Magda stroked Susan's hair back from her forehead. 'I'm sorry I haven't visited you before.'

'You're a busy woman. My word. Fancy a girl who grew up across the street from a whore house becoming a doctor.'

'Susan, Ruby said you were ill. Women's problems. What exactly is the matter?'

Susan's merry eyes travelled to Ruby and stayed fixed as though sharing a secret. Still with her eyes on Ruby, she began pushing the bedclothes down.

'I've got two kids asleep in the other room there. Billy comes home from the sea, knocks me up and goes again. I 'ardly know where the next loaf of bread is coming from. I can't face having another kid.'

Raising herself up on her elbows, she turned imploring eyes onto Magda's face.

'Help me, Magda. For old times' sake, please help me. I'm all ready. Ruby's got everything you need to get rid of it.'

Magda stared at the turned-down bedclothes, the shabby cotton nightdress pulled up over meaty thighs. She was being asked to do exactly what she'd feared.

'Susan, I can't!'

'It's easy. Ruby's seen it done, but it takes a proper doctor to do it properly. And you're my friend, Magda. Come on. For old times' sake. If Billy finds out . . .'

She stopped abruptly and Magda guessed she hadn't meant to go this far.

'You're saying it's not Billy's?'

Susan shrugged and tossed her head, her pert nose sniffing.

'I gets lonely. He's away, and I gets lonely.'

It was as though an awful chill had descended on her shoulders.

'Whose is it?'

Even to her own ears, her voice sounded small and scared. Somehow she had an idea of what the answer would be.

'Eddie. Eddie Shellard.'

Magda closed her eyes and turned her head away.

'Oh come on, Magda. You're my oldest and best friend. I need you to get rid of this kid. I don't want it, and Billy certainly won't.'

Magda looked at her, hardly able to believe that Susan had indeed been her best friend. In the past she would never have made demands on her like this.

But that was when we were girls, she reminded herself. Susan has other priorities now.

Magda shook her head. 'I'm sorry. I can't help you. My career . . .'

Susan swung her legs out of the bed. 'Well, that's bloody typical. Forgotten where you came from, Magda? Forgotten where the money came from to pay for you to become a doctor?'

Magda bridled and felt the heat coming to her cheeks.

'My father paid for my education . . .'

Susan laughed. 'Believe that if you like girl, but it ain't the truth. I hear tell your old dad came looking for you some time back and a right state he was in. Not a penny in his pocket. I bet he had a pound or two though once he left your place. Old Winnie paid 'im off. Told 'im to scarper and leave her to look after you. That's what I 'eard!'

'That's not true!'

'Don't you look down your nose at me, Magda Brodie,' shouted Susan, pushing Ruby aside as she came round from the other side of the bed. 'You're the pet of a brothel madam. Old Winnie earned a bit of immoral herself. Reuben Fitts paid her off. She was his bit on the side, but when she got crippled, he took pity on her and gave her a little pot to set herself up in a living. I mean, no bloke was going to pay for the services of a crippled whore. So she became a madam. A whore managing whores. And that's the truth of it!'

Being assailed with all this information, blasting at her like the heat from a furnace, was too much for Magda to bear.

A child began to cry. The smoke from Ruby's cigarette seemed more noxious mixing with the stale, sweetish stench of decay. Small specks on the grimy wallpaper moved; bugs – lots of them.

Feeling sick to her stomach, she took off, her feet hammering down the stairs, hurling herself at the door and leaving it swinging on its hinges. The sound of children crying followed.

Was Susan telling the truth? Why hadn't Winnie told her that her father had been back?

The flash of moving lights and the sound of an engine came from somewhere behind her. The car came to a halt. The door flew open blocking her path.

'Out a bit late, darling. Fancy a lift 'ome, Magdalena?'

The flame from a lit match touched to the tip of a cigarette illuminated the face of Bradley Fitts.

Her heart skipped a beat. Perhaps he would have grabbed her as he'd done before, but suddenly somebody shouted.

'Hey! Doctor! You've left your papers behind.'

It was Ruby, waving the folder in which she kept her lecture papers.

She hurried back to Ruby, thinking of how to escape Bradley Fitts yet again. There was no lavatory window this time.

'You got too carried away,' said Ruby, a fresh cigarette jiggling at the corner of her mouth.

'I'm sorry. I was confused. Upset too.' She took the folder. 'You will look after Susan?' she said hesitantly, her attention alternating between Ruby and the stationary car. 'I would have helped if I could – if I was more qualified . . .'

She saw Ruby's eyes stray to where the car was parked. She chanced a glance, hoping it was pulling away; it was not. It was still there under the streetlight, its black bodywork gleaming.

'My, but look at that! A motor car around here. If it had been daytime the whole street would have been out to take a look. Know 'im do you?'

'No.'

A slow smile spread across Ruby's narrow face. In this light her eyes looked non-existent, just black holes above that narrow smile.

'Your fancy man is it?'

'No.'

Ruby's smile spread wider. 'That's Bradley Fitts's car. Is it like father like son? Old Reuben had Winnie, and now the son's 'aving you?'

Magda licked the nervous sweat from her upper lip.

'No! But he frightens me. Can I come back inside until he's gone?'

Ruby drew back.

'Not bloody likely! The Fitts family rule the roost around 'ere in case you didn't know. And I ain't one to upset the apple cart.'

The crying of a child came from a downstairs room.

'Gotta go,' said Ruby.

The door slammed shut in her face. She was alone – and scared.

She turned, her heart pounding, her blood racing.

If she could leave the street another way . . .

There was a wall. From the other side came a cloud of steam and a clanking of goods trucks, the grating of metal wheels on iron rails.

There was no way she could get past Bradley Fitts without him dragging her into that car – and she knew that was exactly what he had planned for her.

She had no option but to face him.

Trembling with fear but ready to run, she began walking in his direction.

He'd got out of the car and was leaning against the street-lamp, the tip of a cigarette glowing red as he held it to his lips.

His eyes locked with hers and a triumphant smile twitched around his mouth. Since leaving the area, she'd made a point of not straying too near Edward Street and the scruffy streets beyond where Susan now lived. One reason was that her life had taken a different direction; her friends had changed and she had aspirations she'd never had before. The other reason was to avoid the likes of Bradley Fitts.

Her breath steamed white and rapid from her mouth and although her legs were like jelly, she strode purposefully – just like her father had done when he'd dumped her at Aunt Bridget's.

Her father. Could it really be that he'd come looking for her?

The question would keep. Concentrating her mind on appearing brave, even if she didn't feel it, was what mattered at this moment.

The narrow street they stood in came off a larger one. Together they formed a 'T' shape, the houses on the major road as blank and dark as the terraced houses to either side of her.

Accompanied by the sound of slow footsteps, a giant shadow fell against the row of houses on the main road.

Bradley Fitts's attention flipped from the shadow and sound to her and back again.

Magda stopped. Hopefully she was saved. Surely it had to be a policeman, a copper in uniform patrolling his beat.

Hugging her folder against her chest, she watched Fitts and watched also for the figure that was sure to turn the corner.

She crossed her fingers. It had to be a copper.

It seemed that Bradley Fitts was thinking the same. He got into his car, closed the door and proceeded to do a 'U' turn in the middle of the street.

The street was narrow; the car hard to turn. Fitts had kept the engine running whilst waiting to accost her, but now, suddenly, it cut out.

Although it was too dark to discern clearly, she could

imagine him slapping the wheel and cursing as he reached for the starting handle. He had no choice.

He got out of the car, went swiftly round to the bonnet, bent down and inserted the handle. It started on the third turn and once the engine sounded, he threw the handle back into the car and got in himself.

A tall dark figure had appeared on the left-hand corner of the street. The car appeared to be going left, but at the last moment turned right and drove off.

She reached an astounding conclusion; whoever the man was, Bradley Fitts had decided to veer away from him. And fast!

Chapter Thirty-four

Venetia

Four weeks before Christmas; the weather was wet and slate-grey clouds were tumbling across the sky as if they were in a hurry to go somewhere.

Venetia was on her knees scrubbing the black and white tiles running the length of the corridor outside the nuns' quarters. All the inmates were there to learn self-discipline and domestic skills; this included the frequent scrubbing of the floors.

The swishing of heavy skirts announced the arrival of Sister Conceptua.

'Your visitor is here,' said the nun, her clasped hands white as marble against the dull black of her habit.

Elated by the news, Venetia struggled to her feet, rubbing her aching back as she did so.

Her back had been aching a lot of late; early, the nuns told her, for someone who was only some six months pregnant. 'Wait until you're nearer your time. Your back will be really aching then.' This was usually said with a hint of glee, as though every discomfort was well deserved.

The sharp retort that a celibate nun wouldn't know how it felt to be pregnant stayed locked inside. She wasn't quite as flighty of speech as she had been. Finding herself pregnant had affected her plans for the future. She had so badly wanted that domestic position in a big city – wherever that city might be, though her heart had always been set on Queenstown.

The joy she felt that her grandparents had at last agreed to visit swept away all the bitterness she'd experienced at them placing her in St Bernadette's. Her letter had got there.

'Take off your apron and smarten yourself up,' said Sister Conceptua. 'And don't run,' she added when Venetia broke into a brisk trot.

Venetia felt a mix of trepidation and excitement. Her grandparents had come to visit her; had Anna Marie come too?

The visitors' room was beyond a locked door to which only the duty sister and the Mother Superior had the key.

Once she'd tidied herself up, she headed to where Sister Conceptua waited for her, her body as wide as the door that opened into the visitors' room. A bunch of keys hung from her chill white fingers.

'Are you ready, Venetia?'

Venetia nodded, her mouth as dry as the rough bread she'd eaten at lunch time.

Listening to the key jarring in the lock was nail biting. What had their reaction been to her letter and the covering one from the Mother Superior telling them that she was expecting a baby? Not that Mother Superior had used such innocent words as that.

'I know you have written to them, but it was also my duty to write to them, given the situation that only came to light once you arrived here. I have told them that you are bearing the consequences of sin. They will be shocked and hurt. No doubt it will take them some time to come to terms with what you have done. You cannot expect them to respond straightaway.'

'I thought they might want to visit,' Venetia had responded hopefully.

A look of disbelief and outright accusation had peered back at her from within the stark white wimple.

'In my experience that is the last thing relatives of shameless girls wish to do.'

You were wrong, she wanted to shout now she knew they were here. It had taken some months for them to come, but they were here at last.

Somehow she'd expected the whole family, but only a lone figure waited for her in the visitors' room.

The room was painted a pale blue; a plaster Madonna stood in one corner, a 'sacred heart' picture hung from the wall in front of her above a black cross in a cheap brass base.

Her grandmother, seeming smaller than when Venetia had last seen her, arose from the chair in the corner of the room as she entered. She was wearing her best rust-coloured coat, the one set aside for mass on Sundays.

Venetia held out her arms to embrace her.

'Don't!'

Her grandmother held up both hands, palms outwards as though she would push her away.

Disappointed, Venetia let her arms fall and swallowed the hurt. The pleas for forgiveness and declarations that she missed her family died on her lips.

Her grandmother's eyes were shaded by the brim of the hat she wore that went some way to hiding her face.

And her shame, thought Venetia, remembering the Mother Superior's words.

All the humility she had meant to display died.

I will be the way I was.

'You came alone. Well, I suppose you had to. Busy at the

farm I suppose what with Christmas coming up. I'm surprised you bothered.'

The work-worn face stiffened as though she'd slapped it.

'You haven't changed a bit, have you? Always thinking of yourself regardless of the upset you might cause. And now this!'

Molly Brodie waved her wrinkled hand at Venetia's growing bump.

'I thought Granfer might have come with you – seeing as I'm carrying his first grandchild. I thought he'd be over the moon if I give birth to a boy.'

Her grandmother took a deep breath as though she were gathering in all the words she needed to say.

'Dermot – your grandfather – doesn't know about the baby. It was a hard decision, but I decided to keep it secret from the family. I think it's best that way. I told him I was visiting you because it's close to Christmas.'

There was something about the way her eyes shifted around, looking at anything rather than at her granddaughter.

'So you've not told Patrick's family.'

'That I have not!'

The statement was delivered with an air of finalisation.

Venetia felt sick inside. So! Patrick did not know. His family did not know. There was only one other person her grandmother might have let in on the secret.

'Does Anna Marie know?' she asked slowly.

Her grandmother shook her head. 'No. I've told nobody, and for good reason.'

Venetia waited for her to deliver the reason, but her grandmother was taking her time getting round to it.

'The thing is, Venetia, that once you've had your child, there's nothing to stop you going away to work in a big house as planned.' She looked away as she spoke, the brim of the hat hiding most of her face. 'There are plenty of childless couples seeking adoption.'

Venetia looked at her in disbelief.

'You're telling me to give my baby away. But I won't. What would Patrick think of me if I did that? Once he knows, he'll marry me. I know he will.'

One look from her grandmother's striking eyes and she knew that Patrick would not be marrying her.

There were many reasons why he couldn't. The worst of all entered her mind. She'd heard that an epidemic of influenza had taken off a high number of young people. Or an accident? TB? A whole host of reasons.

'Is he dead?'

Molly Brodie took hold of all her courage and said it quickly.

'He can't marry you. He's already married.'

'Married?'

Venetia sank down onto a hard wooden chair as though her legs had turned to jelly. He'd betrayed her! He'd betrayed her again!

'Married? Are you sure?'

Her grandmother nodded and bent her head.

'He's married your sister. He's married Anna Marie. That's why you must never come home. That's why neither of them must ever know about the baby. We have to give their marriage a chance. The nuns will see that things are done properly. You can count on it.'

Venetia sat silently, staring at the black cross without actually seeing it and feeling a great urge to smash the plaster Madonna into a hundred pieces.

'I've brought you some new underwear for Christmas. I thought you could probably do with it, especially once the baby is born. I'll leave it here.'

She placed a brown paper parcel on the table next to the black cross.

A black cross. New underwear.

Molly Brodie got to her feet.

'I'll be going now. Take care of yourself.'

A beam of light caught her grandmother's gold wedding band as she raised her hand and rang the bell that would summon a sister to open the door that led into the outside world.

Neither attempted to approach the other; Molly Brodie out of remorse, Venetia out of shock.

A black-robed figure stood on the other side of the open door.

Molly Brodie paused before leaving.

'Merry Christmas,' she said, and was gone.

Venetia sat numbly as the Mother Superior confirmed what her grandmother had said; arrangements had been made for the baby to be adopted.

'I don't want that.'

She kept her eyes fixed on the floor as she said it, as though emblazoning her wish on the only carpet in the whole of St Bernadette's.

'I'm afraid you have no choice in the matter. You're under twenty-one and your grandmother has expressly stated that she feels it's for the best. As we do, Venetia, for both you and for your baby.'

The nun studied the young woman sitting in front of her and thought how forlorn she looked, yet what a firebrand she had been on arrival.

She prided herself on being a good judge of those characters that had passed through St Bernadette's. Some 'wayward and wild girls' fell to pieces the moment they entered the double iron gates at the end of the drive. Others hardened, but few bubbled with hope as Venetia had done – until she found out that she was having a baby that is.

'Seeing as you're in the last two months of your term, you'll be moved from here into the maternity wing. It's cosier, quieter and more suited to expectant mothers. Perhaps whilst you're there, you'd like to help out with the other unwed mothers and their babies. I'm sure it will help occupy your mind until you give birth.'

The nun took Venetia's silence as an affirmative and shrugged her narrow shoulders. 'So be it. It doesn't much matter. Your family doesn't want you so you have no choice.'

The rain diminished halfway through December to be replaced by a biting cold that froze the pipes and numbed the bones of the older nuns. They could be seen rolling from side to side, favouring one hip or knee over the other as they made their way to chapel.

Now sharing a room with four other unwed and expectant mothers, Venetia had changed too. In awe of the newborn babies, she found herself looking forward to giving birth.

Unlike some other establishments that catered for unmarried mothers, those that had given birth were not separated from those who had not. According to Sister Theresa, the sister in charge of the maternity wing, hearing of painful experiences would likely double the fear of giving birth, and didn't the girls deserve it? According to her philosophy, doubling the fear would likely put them off fornicating out of wedlock in future. It hadn't yet occurred to her that it might put them off even if and when they did marry.

'I didn't think they were so small,' Venetia said to one new mother as the babe's tiny fingers clung to just one of hers. 'Like a little china doll.'

Rosa, the mother, a slightly plump girl with curly hair and pink cheeks, merely grunted in response.

Venetia ignored the girl's negative reaction; she couldn't take her eyes off the tiny human being.

'Makes you wonder at the size they grow into doesn't it?' Venetia persisted. 'You can't help wondering if your baby boy will grow to six feet or more, or your little girl gets to be curvy or skinny.'

'Who cares? I won't be around to see it.'

Rosa continued turning the pages of the book she was reading and sounded as though she meant it.

'Don't you care?' Venetia asked her.

Rosa shook her head and continued thumbing through the book as though she were reading the pages at breakneck speed.

'I've done all I can for her. I've given birth to her, I've given the first milk that cleans out her innards, and from now on she's somebody else's responsibility, somebody else's child.'

'Seems a shame, her being given away so near Christmas. How about the father? Does he know?'

Rosa's eyes slid sidelong from beneath her greasy curls.

Their eyes locked. Rosa's expression said it all. She didn't need to explain.

'I take it he doesn't care,' said Venetia.

'All he wanted was a bit of fun. That's what he told me. A bit of fun. I didn't even know what he was doing. Can you believe that?'

Venetia knew she was telling the truth. So many girls knew nothing about sex. Having grown up on a farm where sows were taken to boars and a domineering cockerel kept a flock of chickens laying eggs, she knew what was what.

'So who was he?'

'He was the master of the house I worked in. I was the

302

scullery maid. I was kept scrubbing pots late at night. He came down to enquire after my welfare and commiserate that there were so many to clean. That's what he told me. Said I should be having some fun and he'd show me some fun and said I would like it. I did like it. Beat scrubbing pots that's for sure. Next thing, I'm expecting a baby.'

Rosa's baby was collected by a childless couple from Liverpool. Rosa left just after.

Two other babies were born in the cold weeks before Christmas. Venetia was fascinated by all of them, but saddened that they would be given away. It didn't seem right at this time of year.

At night as she lay in bed, she patted her swollen belly and began talking to the baby growing inside her. Even if she only held her for a few days, she would give that baby lots and lots of love. Ideally she desperately wanted to find some way of keeping the child. But how? She had no husband, no money.

What if I married the first man to have me, she thought to herself. Old, crippled, young or mad, I don't care. Just so long as I can keep my baby.

If she did find someone to marry her, it certainly wouldn't be for love, but just to give the baby a father and respectability. One of the other mothers had told her that one of the girls had done exactly that; married a total stranger for the sake of her child.

The more she thought about it, the more she loved her baby and wanted to keep her. She kept thinking of the baby as 'her'. She'd convinced herself she was expecting a girl.

The pain she'd felt at hearing that Patrick had married her sister was still hard to bear, but getting better. It was the baby that mattered and somehow she would contrive to keep it.

Despite being heavily pregnant, she was still expected to help out around St Bernadette's.

When the snow came she was handed a broom and with two others told to sweep the snow from around the front door.

Muffled up to the nose in scarves, hat pulled tightly down over her ears, she heaved the brush into the snow, sweeping great swathes of it to either side.

'Not so fast. We don't want to go back in just yet,' hissed one of her colleagues, a girl more heavily pregnant than she was.

The girl's name was Phyllis and she'd been sent over by her parents in Liverpool to escape gossip.

Venetia had to admit that she was right about not rushing to go back into the sprawling building. The snow was blindingly white and the sky sharply blue. Despite the cold, the sun made everything seem warmer and melting ice dripped from the overhead guttering.

The milkman's cart was coming out from round the side of the house, his pony's hooves struggling to get a grip on the icy surface.

As it followed the curve of the drive, the pony's front legs slid. The milk ladles rattled against the churns as the cart slewed to one side.

The milkman yelled at the animal, raised his whip and fetched it a nip across the back.

Venetia saw what he did and was livid. 'Hey! There's no need to do that.'

He shouted out to her that the likes of her sort should mind their own business.

'Sluts the lot of ya,' he added.

Venetia and Phyllis looked at each other, both seeing the twinkle in the other's eyes, and both slinging down their brooms to scoop up handfuls of snow.

The milkman covered his head as snowball after snowball rained down on him.

Where Venetia and Phyllis led, the other girls followed. The milkman was pelted unmercifully.

'And one more for luck,' Venetia shouted.

This snowball was the biggest yet. She put all her effort behind it, stepped forward and let go.

As the snow left her hand she slid on the step, toppled forward, half regained her balance, toppled again, only this time failed to regain her balance. Arms flailing to either side, she landed heavily on her back and slid down three of the icy steps. A pain shot through her when she tried to move.

Phyllis and the other two girls came down to help her up.

'Are you all right?'

Thinking that initial twinge was only temporary, Venetia placed her hands to either side of her and tried to get up. The pain again.

She winced. 'Something hurts.'

'Get one of the sisters,' whispered Phyllis. She sounded scared.

'What are you whispering for?' said Venetia, trying again to at least sit up. 'Come on. I can't lay around here forever. Get me up.'

'No. Lie still. Don't move. Whatever you do, don't move.'

Phyllis pressed on her shoulder preventing her from rising.

'What is it?' Venetia asked her.

Her gaze followed Phyllis's pointing finger to where the white snow was slowly turning pink.

'Your baby was stillborn.'

The news was imparted in an abrupt manner; too abrupt for it to be true, like when somebody wants to spit it out quickly before laughing and telling you it was all a joke. Only it wasn't a joke.

'All that pain? For nothing? You've given her away already before I had chance to see her. That's the truth, isn't it?'

Sister Mary Elizabeth shook her head, sending her starched white headdress rustling like a huge dead leaf.

'No. I'm afraid not. It was the fall, you see. You slipping on the snow brought the birth on early – too early. A few more weeks perhaps . . .'

Venetia looked up at the ceiling wondering why she couldn't cry. It was as if the shock was too much or perhaps there just were not enough tears in the entire world to shed for that unborn baby.

'Where is she?'

Sister Mary Elizabeth looked surprised. 'How did you know it was a girl? I don't believe I said it was.'

'I just knew,' said Venetia.

She didn't know how she'd known; perhaps it was just wishful thinking. A little girl to dress up in pretty clothes – if she could ever afford pretty clothes.

'Where is she? I'd like to hold her. Just once.'

The nursing staff – nuns for the most part except for a doctor when needed – had been instructed not to show compassion in instances such as this. Losing a child born into such circumstances could sometimes be a blessing in disguise. It was as well to harden the mother to the fact so she could put it behind her and get on with her life.

'She's in the mortuary. If you're feeling strong enough, I see no reason why I can't take you there.'

Venetia nodded. It was something she had to do.

The nun helped her into her dressing gown and slippers provided by a wealthy benefactor of St Bernadette's. They were a dull shade of brown. Somebody reckoned they were ex-army from the Great War. If they were then they had lasted a long time.

The nun was only a few years older than Venetia herself and had a gentle manner. She offered for Venetia to take her arm but Venetia said she could manage.

'Then that's fine. It's down three flights of stairs in the cellar. You'll probably manage going down, but you might find coming back up a little difficult. But we'll go slowly, and perhaps we'll call into the chapel on the way. Would you like that?'

Venetia said that she would.

'We'll take an oil lamp with us. There's no lighting down there. Not even gas. Must admit this electricity we have up here is quite wonderful. Almost a miracle.'

'Let there be light,' murmured Venetia.

'Yes indeed,' replied Sister Mary Elizabeth.

The steps leading down to the mortuary changed from being lino covered on the first two flights to bare concrete on the third.

Cold from the cellar drifted up to meet them. The flame in the oil lamp flickered in the draught.

Venetia shivered. The coldness of the concrete permeated the soles of her slippers. The cold air travelled up beneath her clothes.

At the bottom of the stairs, the nun lifted the oil lamp then set it down on a table. On the same table lay a small white bundle.

Venetia stared at it, unable to move. This was not how she'd envisaged her baby. In her imagination she'd seen a sweet little face and a bonny smile, not something vaguely resembling a parcel. And so small. So very small.

'Would you still like to hold her?' The nun's voice was soft.

She nodded, all words having deserted her.

Sister Mary Elizabeth gently picked up the small bundle and told Venetia to hold out her arms, which she did.

Venetia gasped and looked at the nun in surprise. 'She's light as a feather.'

Sister Mary Elizabeth smiled sadly and folded the white cloth back from the baby's face.

At sight of the little face, the rosebud lips, the tiny nose, Venetia felt a terrible tightening in her chest. For the first time since the birth and totally unstoppable, tears squeezed from the corners of her eyes.

'Why?' she asked. 'Why did she have to die?'

'God's will,' said the nun and made the sign of the cross on her chest. 'Would you like to pray?'

Venetia shook her head. 'Not here. I'll pray for her in the chapel. I'm sure my family will pay for a coffin and a proper burial and my grandmother will come too. I'm sure she will.'

She wasn't sure. Not really. Her grandmother had said that nobody in the family would be told. They had Anna Marie's marriage to consider.

Lost in grief, she didn't notice Sister Mary Elizabeth looking at her with unashamed pity.

The nun thought about telling her how it was; that there would be no burial in consecrated ground and no heaven. The child would go to neither heaven nor hell, but for all eternity would exist – if exist was the right word – in purgatory.

Sister Mary Elizabeth placed the child reverently back on the table then picked up the lamp.

She held out her other arm, noting that Venetia's attention was still focused on the small white bundle.

'Come along, Venetia. You'll catch your death.'

After saying prayers in the chapel, the kind-hearted Sister took Venetia to one side and told her as gently as she could about the lot of stillborn children.

'I'm sorry, Venetia. But there won't be a service for your baby.'

Venetia's eyes were big and tear filled. She looked at the nun with a mix of trust and incomprehension, unsure she had heard correctly.

'I can pay. My family will pay. I'm sure they will.'

Sister Elizabeth shook her head.

'Your baby was stillborn and therefore not baptised. She cannot be buried in hallowed ground.'

Venetia felt an enormous wave of anguish. 'But she'll go to heaven – won't she?'

The nun shook her head sorrowfully. 'According to Mother Church, she'll exist in purgatory for eternity – in limbo – between worlds.'

Venetia shook her head. 'But she's just a baby!'

The nun looked down at her clasped hands, wishing she could do more to comfort this troubled soul.

'It's best that you leave here and leave the matter with us.'

'Can't she be baptised now?' Venetia asked.

The nun shook her head. 'No. It wouldn't matter anyway.' She paused. 'Did you have a name for her?'

This was a question Venetia had mulled over many times when talking to her baby while she lay in bed. She'd told the child about her family, her Italian grandmother and the aunt that was left behind in England.

'Magdalena,' she said. 'Her name is Magdalena.'

At first Sister Mary Elizabeth made no comment. The rules of the order specifically forbade her from going against the edicts of the church, but in her heart she was first and foremost a nurse. The wellbeing of her patients was paramount, and this young lady was a patient and needed her help. On top of that she had been seriously considering leaving the order and getting work as a nurse in a general hospital, even if it meant going to England or America to do so. Seeing what Venetia had gone through with the birth and was going through now had finally made up her mind.

So, what do I have to lose, she thought.

'Venetia,' she whispered. 'I can take you and your baby to a place where you can bury her. We'd have to be careful, but . . .'

She bit her lip, unable to believe she was really doing this.

'Could we?'

The look on Venetia's face said it all. Sister Mary Elizabeth made her decision. First she would help this girl; following that – within the next month – she would leave the order.

'It means leaving here with the baby in dead of night. The ground is soft against the wall in the chapel churchyard. It's consecrated ground and very sheltered; even at this time of year there are the first shoots of wild flowers poking through the earth. A nice foxglove perhaps. After that we can say a prayer. You'd have to leave here afterwards. And not go back home,' advised the nun who was also considering her own plan of action. She wanted to save the living, not make arrangements for the dead.

Venetia was adamant. 'I have no intention of going home. None at all. When I leave here I'm going to America to make my fortune, and then I shall go to England. I want to find the other Magdalena, the sister I named my baby after.'

Chapter Thirty-five

Magda
1936

Magda barely controlled her trembling knees, but determined to face whatever or whoever was crossing the street towards her. He was not wearing a uniform; he was not a bobby walking his beat, yet on sighting him, Bradley Fitts had left pretty sharply.

'A little late to be out, Miss.'

He wore a trilby and a trench coat over a dark suit. His face was familiar. And then it came to her.

'You were on the underground earlier.'

A smile lit up his face.

'That's right.'

She half closed her eyes. 'Thank goodness you came along.'

'Thank goodness I did. I'm presuming you no longer live around here. Or around Edward Street.'

She shook her head. 'I was visiting an old friend who got taken poorly.'

It was all she intended saying. Even to seek out someone to do what Susan had asked her to do – carry out an abortion – was illegal.

He didn't question her excuse, but then why should he?

'Goodness,' she said, pulling back her sleeve and glancing at the face of her watch. 'I must get home. My aunt will be worried.'

'It's too late at night for a young girl to travel on the underground alone. Come on. I'll escort you.'

'Oh, no, there's no need . . .'

He took hold of her arm. 'I insist. That man in the car. I know him. He's dangerous.'

'Yes. Bradley Fitts.'

He raised his eyebrows. 'Not a boyfriend, I hope.'

'No, but he wants to be. I can't seem to shake him off. My aunt and I used to live around here, but no longer. We live in Prince Albert Mews,' she said, just in case he didn't believe her.

'Then I'll make sure you get there.' He noticed her nervousness. 'Don't worry. I'm not at all like Bradley Fitts; quite the opposite in fact. Trust me.'

When he smiled she noticed the whiteness of his teeth.

How do I know whether I can trust him? She decided that she did. His voice as much as his face calmed her nerves, plus his undoubted strength. Not the bully boy strength of Bradley Fitts who depended on intimidation to gain respect. This man's strength wasn't just physical; it was something he was, deep down inside.

She stopped suddenly, recalling that he had mentioned Edward Street – as though he'd known she used to live there. Again she thought how familiar he looked.

He noticed her puzzled expression. 'Think vegetables and pigs' tails,' he said, his mouth curling upwards in a seductive smile.

Her jaw dropped.

'Daniel Rossi. Remember?'

Danny! Daniel the adolescent market boy who had taken

pity on a small starving girl and had read detective books!

'Do you still read Bob Barton, police detective?' she asked him.

He laughed. 'Sometimes. It takes me out of myself and away from how things really are. I'm a real detective, Magda. I'm a real policeman.'

Magda was so surprised, she just gazed at him, saying, 'Well, well,' over and over again.

Daniel regarded her with a mix of affection and sadness. He remembered so much about her. 'Did you ever find your family?'

Magda shook her head sadly. 'I followed all your advice. I've heard nothing so far, but some day when I've earned a lot of money, I'm going to employ a private detective to find them. I've heard you can do that.'

'Yes. You can. But you have to understand that some people don't want to be found – for whatever reason.'

She nodded sadly. 'I know what you're saying; I should get on with my life. But it isn't easy.'

They began to walk, his hand still cupping her elbow.

'I can't believe it,' she said breathlessly, gazing up at him. 'I should have recognised you.'

'Have I altered that much?'

The more she studied the handsome face of this man, the more she remembered about the boy who'd been kind to her.

'No. Not really. Have I?'

He looked down at her from his greater height and grinned.

'You're certainly not so skinny.'

'I was skinny. Hungry too.'

'So what happened to the wicked witch?'

'Aunt Bridget's house burned down with her inside.'

'Are you sorry?'

She nodded. 'Yes. Not for her. The whereabouts of my

family was also burned to ashes. I'll never find them now. Not easily anyway.'

The underground station was emptier than it had been earlier. The last train home would run soon.

In the dim light she noticed how blue his eyes were and how sooty black his lashes and brows. Strange that she hadn't really noticed that before. His chin was strong and although his lips seemed slightly crooked, they hinted at determination. She deduced that, like Bradley Fitts, he was not a man to be trifled with.

On the journey home, she told him that she was studying to be a doctor. His eyes lit up with admiration that made her spirits soar.

In return he spoke casually in a way that put her at ease. He talked about London, the mix of people from all over the world, the history of the river itself, how upmarket Chelsea had once been far down river outside the city, how wave after wave of immigrants had settled in the East End, the place where ships of many flags called in to discharge cargoes of cotton, chocolate, tea, coffee and sugar.

'And people,' he said. 'Always they brought more people.'

'My father was always away at sea,' she said to him, and then looked away when she saw how intensely he was regarding her.

'Is he still away at sea?'

She shrugged. 'I don't know. I haven't seen him for years. So I still have no family.'

'Seems old Bob Barton wasn't infallible. That's where I copied my advice from. It seemed a good idea at the time. That bloke just seemed so bloody clever.'

He was leaning forward, hands clasped together on his knees. They rattled on through the dark tunnels, talking warmly in the way they used to, his gaze fixed on her face.

'This is amazing,' he said to her. 'I can't believe I've found you again. I've often thought of you, scrabbling around beneath our pitch. Didn't begrudge you a thing, though.'

'Did your father?'

'No. He thought you would be a beauty when you grew up. My father was usually right about things.'

He smiled and Magda blushed.

'I'm glad I found you again too,' said Magda.

He covered her hand with his and squeezed.

'You never know. Stranger things happen at sea, so they say. And miracles happen.'

He tossed his head and laughed. 'What a load of baloney! All those clichés!'

'Oft spoken phrases; quoted so often perhaps because they're true.'

When they arrived at her station and his hand left hers, she immediately found herself missing its warmth and the sense of security it had given her. Once the doors were open, they alighted from the train. Gently and out of courtesy, his palm still cupped her elbow.

'I'm glad we met up again,' he said to her.

'So am I.'

Her response was sincere. At least talking had made her forget her fear of Bradley Fitts.

'I'm fine from here,' she told him when he suggested he walk her home.

'That wasn't a suggestion. I insist.'

He also insisted on waiting outside until the door of the mews cottage was locked and bolted behind her.

Once inside, Magda leaned against the locked door, closed her eyes and made an effort to compose herself. She'd never believed in love at first sight, but surely that was no guarantee that it didn't exist? Anyway, she knew him from way back.

315

You're being silly, she told herself, opening her eyes and fanning her hand in front of her face. He's just being kind to you, like he always was.

In all honesty, she had considered that being friends with dear Doctor Andy was about as close as most people get. She liked him and had entertained the thought that liking alone might be enough to base a relationship on – even a marriage.

But Daniel Rossi made her tingle all over, besides feeling very protected.

A wall-mounted light bloomed as Winnie appeared and turned up the gas. Her head was an explosion of tightly tied rags; taken out in the morning they would be a mass of curls. At present she looked like the Gorgon of Greek mythology.

She was wearing a shawl over a voluminous nightgown and leaning on her stick.

At sight of Magda, her face beamed brighter than any light could ever do.

'Home at last! I was getting worried, my dear. Working late again?'

Still smarting from what Susan had told her, Magda hedged her response and couldn't even smile.

'Winnie, I need to talk to you. Now. Before we go to bed.'

Winnie looked alarmed, her lined face creasing like the crazing on an old plate.

'Has something bad happened?'

'I don't know,' snapped Magda as she put down her folder and removed her hat and coat, unable to communicate with Winnie in the affectionate way she had always done. 'You tell me.'

On hanging up her hat, a pretty lilac one that Winnie had bought her for her birthday, she immediately regretted her tone. The felt hat was soft beneath her fingers when she stroked it – just as Winnie had always been soft with her.

Be gentle, she told herself. There has to be a good reason why Winnie never told you about your father visiting.

Those, she decided, were the best words to use.

'I presume there's a good reason you didn't tell me that my father turned up a while back.'

Winnie looked shocked at first, then gradually her face saddened and she sighed. Bracing both hands over her walking stick, she said, 'I've made a pot of tea. Let's talk over that.'

They sat either side of the small table in a kitchen that wasn't large but was cosy and smelled of the plum pudding Winnie had made for Christmas. Neither touched the tea Winnie had poured and the silence between them was awkward.

'I should have told you. I should have!'

'What did he want?'

What she really meant was had he come to see her, take her with him, leave the address where she could contact her family. But she had to give Winnie a chance.

'He came for money.' Winnie looked at the daughter she'd always wanted, the one that should have been. 'Your father's a wastrel. He was dirty and smelled of drink and he had no money. He came here demanding to see you, but when I gave him money he changed his mind and left. That was it.'

'You should have told me.'

'I didn't want to upset you.'

'He could have told me where my sisters and brother are. Didn't you think . . .?'

Magda paused. Winnie didn't want her to leave. She thought of the fire and Aunt Bridget dying in the flames. Now her father had come looking for her – after all these years.

'Magda, I doubt he would have remembered where he took them all those years ago. He was in a state. Full of the drink and aching to get his hands on more.'

'I would have liked the option of meeting him.'

'I did suggest he wait, but the moment I gave him some money he was gone.'

Magda turned and stood looking out of the window without really seeing anything at all. Her thoughts were in turmoil.

Firstly it hurt that her father had come looking for her and then left without leaving even a note. Secondly she knew very well that Aunt Winnie didn't want her to leave.

She turned to face the woman who had been kind to her, the woman who had replaced her own mother. But she wasn't her mother and the question had to be asked.

'He wouldn't stay?'

Winnie shook her head.

'Aunt Winnie, I'm not sure I entirely believe you. I know you don't want me to leave. What I'm unsure of is what lengths you will go to in order that I stay.'

Winnie's crooked hands tightened over the walking stick she now used all the time.

Her brows knitted above clear eyes that burned with purpose.

'You still want to be a doctor, don't you?'

'Of course. The reason is too strong to ignore.'

'I'm glad of that.'

'I'll always be grateful for what you've done for me, Winnie, but I have to remind both you and myself that I do have a family. I don't belong to you.'

'I regret that you don't.'

She winced as she straightened; the arthritis that now invaded her whole body had almost bent her double and the pain was excruciating. 'I've already told you why I am committed to you becoming a doctor.'

Magda nodded. 'You did.'

'I know you'll be a good one and a fitting memorial to the daughter I lost.'

Magda sat mutely studying her hands, thinking through her future plans.

Daniel had given her good advice about staying away from the East End.

She'd been offered two training positions, one at the London Free Hospital and one at Queen Mary's. The latter was in the heart of the East End, while the London Free was in Holborn.

The promise was that her training at Queen Mary's would involve visiting those who couldn't get to the hospital; those who needed a doctor to visit.

Despite Bradley Fitts, despite her promise to Daniel Rossi, Queen Mary's beckoned.

The tragedy of her own mother having needed a doctor and Winnie's baby dying at birth was reason enough to become a doctor, but it was more than that. There were other young women in Winnie's predicament. It was only right that she paid them back in the only way she could. They needed her. And the East End was also the place where she'd last had contact with her family. What if they came looking for her?

She had to be there. She just had to. Her father might come back, and this time Winnie would know better than to send him away.

Daniel Rossi stood outside the mews cottage; his eyebrows beetled into a worried frown. He'd set out purposely to corner Bradley Fitts about a particularly nasty attack on a dancer at an East End club. The dancer was pretty, or at least she used to be before she'd rejected Fitts's advances.

From the little Magda had told him so far, she'd done pretty much the same to him.

'He's always been a bully and he's never forgotten that I gave him the brush off – if you can describe climbing out of a lavatory window as a brush off,' she'd said to him with a wicked grin. 'That's why I keep away from that area.'

'Best thing you can do is to stay away,' he'd replied, as taken with her light laugh as he was with the looks of her, and his amazement that such a scrawny girl had turned into a beautiful woman.

The advice was sound and he felt assured that she would stay away from the wrong side of London. The trouble was, would Bradley Fitts stay away from her?

Chapter Thirty-six

Magda

Magda paused and looked up at the brick and white stone archway.

Queen Mary's Hospital for the East End

Her lips moved silently as she read it once and read it again. This old hospital had stood here since the middle of the last century, though it was called something else back then. At present her excitement was such that she just couldn't think what it was. But never mind. She was here and even though it felt as though her feet were floating some few inches above the ground, her mind was made up. She was going to become a doctor and for a moment felt quite elated; that was until a hospital clerk with inky fingers and busy eyes issued her with a map of the hospital. One glance and she was convinced the building had as many corridors as it did wards.

'Don't lose it,' said the officious little man. 'They don't grow on trees and I haven't got time to draw up new ones.'

As he'd already turned to another pile of paper and another task, she didn't think he would notice if she didn't thank him.

'A "Thank you Mr Meeks" would be in order, young woman!'

Not that busy. She gave him her sweetest smile and thanked him anyway.

She was late arriving outside the first ward on today's itinerary to meet a senior houseman, a Doctor Friesman, according to the information handed to her.

Standing head and shoulders above everyone else, he peered over both his spectacles and the surrounding sea of student heads to fix on her.

'We are late,' he said scathingly. 'Do we have a name?'

'Magdalena. Magdalena Brodie . . . Sir.'

'Brodie! We will not be going over the introduction already given. We will keep our ears open as we go along. Are we clear?'

Magda joined everyone else in mumbling a nervous 'Yes, sir,' though had no time to study her colleagues.

A pair of hard eyes landed on each of them in turn.

'We will proceed,' he said.

Doctor Friesman walked with a limp, presumably acquired during the Great War, which would go some way to explaining the sharp orders.

They followed him like a flock of ducklings, white coats flapping.

The smell of carbolic soap dominated the ward and the brown lino that covered the floor looked shiny enough to slide on.

There were six beds on either side of the ward containing patients who looked too scared to move. Strict orders from matron, thought Magda on noticing that each patient's arms had been placed in identical positions over crisply turned-down sheets.

Matron would undoubtedly have known which wards would be visited today, pre-warning the ward sister.

Magda briefly wondered whether the amount of sheet turned

down had been measured with a ruler. It certainly looked that way.

Nurses in starched headdresses, previously fluttering between beds, tactfully withdrew the moment Doctor Friesman strode into the ward. The exception to this was the ward sister who, like all nurses, approached the saintly man with an air of humility.

The small, grey-haired woman wore a tight expression and kept her distance as though he might bite if she got too near.

Or as if she were greeting the Pope, thought Magda.

'Good morning, Doctor Friesman.'

'Good morning, Sister Goodenough.'

'Do you wish me to attend, Doctor Friesman?'

'Of course.'

'When you're ready, Doctor Friesman.' The sister sounded and looked servile, like a handmaiden ready and willing to do whatever he wished.

'Now would be as good a time as any, Sister.'

The woman bent from the neck, a little bow to a respected superior. In response the already tall doctor seemed to grow that much more, as though a show of humility contributed to his own self-esteem.

They stopped at the first patient, the sister awaiting instructions at the head of the bed.

Her head spinning with information, Magda concentrated on what Doctor Friesman was saying. Determined to capture every word, she paid little attention to the other young doctors in the group.

'Symptoms!' exclaimed Doctor Friesman. He was standing at the head of the bed pointing to the patient as though he were a lamb chop.

The student doctors snapped to attention and looked suitably serious. This was the moment when they were expected to assess the patient's condition by referring to the notes and carrying out a perfunctory examination.

'Liverish,' said Magda.

Doctor Friesman raised his eyebrows. 'Our newest recruit says liverish. Well, really. And what brings you to that conclusion might I ask?'

Once she realised that her colleagues were looking at her, Magda wished she hadn't jumped in quite so quickly.

'Well?'

All eyes stayed fixed on her. She gulped and said what she thought.

'His complexion is very yellow. Even his eyes.' She braved the deep frown of Doctor Friesman and the others and dared to move to the head of the bed and pull down the man's lower eyelids.

'As you can see . . .'

In her mind she was reading the medical text that she'd pored over night after night in order to pass the first of the examinations that would make her a doctor. She'd done so with flying colours. Now she surprised herself with just how well she remembered it, concluding that revision was worthwhile after all. She couldn't help feeling smug.

Doctor Friesman's voice snapped her back to reality.

'Stop smiling like a lovesick ninny and remember where you are, young lady. This is not a tea dance. This is a place where the sick shall be healed – even by women!'

Magda clenched her jaw. She so wanted to retort that she was a serious student and certainly not a lovesick ninny. She would also have liked to tell him that his breath was bad and, as a senior physician, he really should set a better example and attend to his diet. However, she would be depending on this man to get her through her training and final exams. Just smile prettily, blush demurely and keep your mouth shut. Sucking the tip of her pencil helped with the latter. Blushing didn't come naturally and she was of too dramatic an appearance to ever incline to demure.

The smell of antiseptics, oil of cloves and tincture of violet coupled with carbolic set her teeth on edge. Perhaps that was why the others of her group were just as silent; either that or afraid to say the wrong thing.

She had eyed her colleagues only fleetingly, catching a glimpse of red hair, brown hair, casually aloof expressions and those so studious it seemed unlikely they were aware of anyone else in the world.

There was also a woman; a very foreign-looking woman.

She'd determined not to interact with any of them; they were of a different class and as likely as not had never experienced the hardships she had endured.

Yes, she was living in isolation, not making new friends. Daniel was the only person she allowed to touch her emotions and he was becoming far more than a friend.

Training to be a doctor wasn't about making friends with your own class or gender. Whether she was right or wrong, Magda felt that, as a woman, she needed to prove herself better than a man. She needed to gain respect from the nursing staff as well as the other doctors. To this end she must be better than anyone else. Day and night must be devoted to study and carrying out the practical side of her vocation, hence not getting involved with Andrew. But it wasn't him on her mind. It was Daniel Rossi.

Walking the wards ended at lunchtime when Doctor Friesman gathered them round, his eyelids flickering like Venetian blinds, fold upon fold.

'Gentlemen. We resume at three. This evening we are entertaining in our club; not far from here. Seven. Sharp.' His omission of mentioning the two female doctors was deliberate.

It was a well-known fact that he didn't think them worthy of the calling, even though women had been admitted to the profession for many years.

As they filtered away from the wards and Doctor Friesman, their footsteps clattered along the corridor that led to the canteen. One of the students, a sharp-faced young man with oiled-back hair and a hooked nose, drew level with her. She vaguely recalled that his name was Paul Swann; 'Double n,' he'd stated with a lofty toss of his head, as though to only spell his name with a singular n was something of a disgrace.

'Amazing what a pair of flashing eyes can do. No doubt you'll pass your finals with flying colours.'

'I *will* pass my finals, *Mr* Swann with two n's, but I can assure you it will be on merit and not because my *people* happen to know Sir Reginald Cliff!'

It surprised her just how much of his boasting she had overheard. Her head had been bowed over her medical notes and the map of unending passages and wards. But there it was; she'd always had the ability to concentrate on more than one thing at a time. Winnie had told her it was a female thing. 'Men can only concentrate on one thing at a time. Women tend to concentrate on many things at once.'

Magda smiled at the thought of Winnie and what she would make of this young man striding beside her who'd boasted of his connections.

'Hmm! And there you were, pretending not to be listening. Well, that's typical of young women like you: make contacts on the social ladder with a view to finding yourself a wealthy husband. Isn't that really why you're here?'

'No.'

Magda grinned. Winnie had also known Sir Reginald Cliff, but in an entirely different capacity. At the thought of it, Magda's smile widened.

Swann saw her smile and immediately assumed that she was laughing at him. Despite his outer air of uptight arrogance, Paul Swann had issues with his nose, his glasses and anyone who appeared unimpressed by his cut-glass voice and air of good breeding. Women had never exactly fallen at his feet, certainly not the pretty ones.

Increasing her stride, he gradually fell behind. She heard him imparting to someone else that once he had qualified and established himself, he would open consulting rooms in Knightsbridge.

'I'll make much more money that way. Wouldn't want to be a *panel* doctor,' he drawled. 'I'll leave the unwashed and lazy to the idealists amongst us! Why work with patients who can only pay pennies when others are willing and able to pay in guineas?'

There were titters of amusement from some of their number, though certainly not from Magda. She clenched her jaw at their ignorance. She wanted to trumpet that the East End poor would prefer not to be poor and even those in Winnie's brothel had not planned to end up there. Careers and jobs for ill-educated women were confined mostly to domestic servitude, shop and factory.

And rich men took full advantage of this. How would it be, she wondered, if Swann knew that Sir Reginald Cliff had specific sexual tastes, which included using the services of the lower women of society? Not that she would tell him: after all, she reminded herself, she was here to fulfil a wish for Winnie and also for herself.

Nobody needed a map of the hospital in order to find their way to lunch; it was just a case of following the smell of overcooked food – mostly cabbage and potatoes.

The corridor had been built as an afterthought onto the main building in a conservatory style so that staff could get to the canteen without getting wet. The consequence was that the nearer the canteen, the more the panes of glass ran with condensation.

Each area of the canteen was segregated; blue for doctors, green for nurses, red for ancillary medical staff.

Magda headed for the tables set with blue table linen and administered by waitresses.

Male students of a similar background to Paul Swann followed him to the table he would no doubt come to consider as his own. Like Bradley Fitts, he was territorial – what was his was his; he also needed lesser men to defer to him.

As she sought a place for herself, she heard them tittering between speaking in loud voices. She caught a few comments, mostly about the suitability of women as doctors.

'Nurses, yes. I can quite see that,' said Paul Swann. 'The most ideal people for cleaning up vomit. And delivering babies I suppose, in which case let them be midwives.'

Fuming at their ignorance, she sat alone with a plateful of bangers and mash, a portion of jam roly poly and a cup of tea.

'So! I am not the only woman mad enough to want to be a doctor.'

Magda looked up. The doe-eyed woman who addressed her had a wide smile and was wearing a long skirt of dark blue silk beneath her white coat.

'Apparently not,' said Magda feeling somewhat relieved.

The new arrival sat down opposite her, chatting merrily as a plateful of mash without sausages, rice pudding and a cup of tea were set in front of her by a chill-eyed waitress.

'My name is Indira Pashan. Like you I am training to become a doctor. Also like you, Doctor Friesman did not invite me to his club. At seven. Sharp!'

Magda laughed at her impersonation, but added, 'Please

don't take it personally. He's not being exclusive just because we're women. It's a gentlemen's club. We wouldn't be allowed in.'

'I am quite used to not being allowed into British institutions. As an Indian living in India, I am not permitted to enter British country clubs in India unless by personal invitation. Luckily this hospital does not differentiate between race and gender.'

'I'm sorry I didn't notice you, but I was so preoccupied. I really feel I need to do twice as well as everyone else.'

Indira's plush lips curled over the edge of her teacup, her kohl-lined eyes deep set and sparking intelligence.

'You are absolutely right. We have to be more singular about what we are doing. There is no room for flippancy.' Loud laughter batted across from Paul Swann's table. 'Like those ill-mannered young men,' she said, sliding her glance in that direction.

Magda found herself fascinated by Indira's looks coupled with her forthright manner.

'I must admit I'm somewhat surprised to meet you here. Being a woman and . . .' She had been about to say being a woman and from a foreign background, but checked herself. Indira made the obvious assumption.

'Ah! A woman and not English! I am hardly the first. Doctor Rukhmabai qualified in 1895. Now that is a long time ago. Doctor Jensha Jhirad, the first Indian woman with a degree in obstetrics and gynaecology, qualified in 1920. We have quite a history here, I can assure you.'

Magda's mouth hung open in surprise. 'I didn't know any of that.' Though she had known that the London Royal Free Hospital had established a hostel to deal with the rush of women wanting to study medicine after the Great War. Even though Winnie and her contacts had fabricated a far more illustrious background than that to which she was entitled, Magda did sometimes feel that she was a fraud. It was bad enough being a woman, but coming from her background she'd sometimes entertained the conviction that she had no business being here at all. She should know her place and had no rights. One conversation with Indira and her mind was made up.

'They want us to feel inferior to them,' said Magda, jerking her head sideways to Mr Swann and friends.

Indira sipped daintily at her tea and shook her head. 'Of course they do. We are mere women daring to venture into a male stronghold, though I am afraid the door has long been open. The horse has fled. Too late to bolt the stable door.'

Magda laughed. Indira was easy to talk to. 'I never thought I'd ever get to be a medical student. My father was a seagoing man, so it's not as though . . .'

'Look. It doesn't matter who you are or where you're from. The world is opening up for women. You can be whatever you want to be.'

'You have vision.'

Indira laughed. 'I have intellect. And instinct. Oh, and my father did drop a word or two with a friend. Good friends are useful in such situations.'

Magda laughed. She would have liked to have declared that she had friends too – or at least Winnie did. Some things were best left unsaid.

'I think we have a battle on our hands. We are really going to have to prove ourselves in order to gain the respect of our male colleagues – if that's ever possible.'

'Male doctors will try to intimidate us, but I find that our resolve to learn and overcome prejudices is far too strong for them to do us much harm, don't you think?'

Magda sighed and sat back in her seat. 'Indira, I think you

and I are going to pass our exams with flying colours. We have to. We both have a point to prove.'

'Purely based on gender?'

Laughter again from Paul Swann's table.

'Not purely based on gender,' said Magda. 'But because we're more intelligent than they are.'

She raised her teacup. 'Here's to us.'

Indira Pashan clinked her cup with Magda's and, when she smiled, her soft brown complexion grew glossy as though it had just been polished.

'We are very lucky you know. This is a very famous hospital. I started out at the London Free, which has a history of teaching women doctors way back into Victorian times, but I wanted to come here to Queen Mary's Hospital for the East End to broaden my experience. And then of course there is the opportunity to go out into the community – like a panel doctor. I will be going back to India where going out into the community will be commonplace. Have you ever been to India?'

Magda shook her head.

Indira went on to explain about the situation in India. 'There are many poor in the countryside who never get to see a doctor. I will do my best to treat those too.'

Winnie was waiting for her that night with a hot meal and a whole list of questions.

'How was it . . .?'

'Did you make an impression?'

'Do you think you will like it?'

'What are the doctors like? What are the nurses like?'

Magda laughed. 'Aunt Winnie, do you think I might get my coat off first before I answer?'

'Of course,' said Winnie, beaming because Magda was happy. She had been worrying that their relationship might have changed following the disclosure of Magda's father's visit.

'Sausage and mash tonight. Best pork sausages. With gravy.'

'Lovely,' Magda responded, despite the fact that she'd had the same meal at lunchtime.

'There,' said Winnie after Magda had taken off her coat and put down the brand new Gladstone style bag that Winnie had bought her on passing her exams. 'You sit there and eat while I drink my tea. Then you can tell me all about it.'

Magda was amazed at how hungry she was. The plate was cleared, and it was only after she'd drunk the last drop of tea that she wondered why Winnie hadn't dined with her, as was her usual habit.

'I had mine earlier,' Winnie replied when she asked.

Magda didn't question whether she was lying because there was no reason why she should. Her old eyes were glittering with interest and nothing but an in-depth dissertation on the day's events would do.

She told her everything, including her interlude with Paul Swann and his reference to Sir Reginald Cliff.

Winnie threw her head back and laughed uproariously.

'That old goat! Smooth as silk on top and coarse as a potato sack beneath. Liked fat girls. Fatter the better, and him as lank and rangy as a starved giraffe!'

As her laughter died, Magda began fingering the embroidered flowers on the corner of the tablecloth.

'I'm applying for a spell with a charity clinic in the East End. It's something I feel I need to do. I went there that night I got home late. Susan, that old school friend of mine, sent a message that I should come.'

She felt Winnie's sharp eyes on her and knew she was half afraid of what she was about to hear.

'Susan's married now. She's in the family way again.'

'She asked you to get rid of it. That's what she asked you to do.'

Magda was amazed at Winnie's accuracy.

She nodded. 'Yes. But I couldn't do it.'

'You'd end up in prison if you did. Anyways, there are women 'round who can do that. It's not any special skill.'

They fell into a pregnant pause, Magda knowing that Winnie was expecting her to say something else; that there was something else to be said.

'Bradley Fitts was outside where Susan lives waiting for me.'

She heard the sharp intake of breath. On raising her eyes she was surprised at the paleness of Winnie's face except for a bright red ball on each cheek – as though something red had hit each one and left behind its stain.

'He's dangerous. As dangerous as that damned father of his. Curse the day I ever met him. Curse the whole damned family,' she cried, throwing back her head so that the sinews of her neck looked like twigs. 'What happened?'

She stared unblinking, her face petrified with fear.

'He challenged me. I rejected him once some time ago, and I don't think he liked it.'

'He wouldn't. Indeed he wouldn't.'

'A knight in shining armour happened to be passing by. I'd met him on the underground just moments before but knew him years ago when I was a kid diving beneath the vegetable stalls in the market. He was kind then. He's kind now. You ought to have seen that Bradley Fitts. He was back in his car and out of there quick as you like. Then after that, my knight in shining armour walked me home.'

Winnie was eyeing her warily. 'What did he want, this knight of yours?'

'Aunt Winnie, you haven't been listening. He really was my knight in shining armour. He took nothing from me, but gave me advice to stay away from Bradley Fitts. And then he brought me home. No demands were made, not even for a kiss,' she added, unable to stop smiling and blushing just at the very thought of it.

'He's a policeman,' Magda said.

Winnie scratched her chin and the depth of her frown almost buried her eyes in folds of loose flesh.

'No uniform?'

'Good gracious, no. Well-dressed, but no uniform. His name is Daniel Rossi.'

Winnie's saggy eyelids disappeared as her eyes popped wide open.

'Rossi? A policeman you say?'

'What is it, Winnie? What's the matter?'

Winnie attempted to answer, but trembled, one side of her face sliding downwards and one side of her mouth falling open.

She gave a convulsive movement, throwing her head back as though she were trying to shake it from her shoulders.

'Winnie!'

A long thin finger pointed at the satinwood cabinet that Winnie had brought with her from the old house.

Magda leapt up, throwing one arm around Winnie's back, checking her pulse with her free hand.

'Hang on, Winnie. Please. Hang on.'

Chapter Thirty-seven

Joseph Brodie
1937

The road into the village of Long Ashton was pleasant enough, winding as it did between green meadows. Cattle grazed on the higher ground and sheep on the low-lying salt marshes where tough grass exploded in tufts between shallow pools.

Joseph Brodie staggered his way along the road, leaving a trail of whisky breath behind him. The skipper of the ship he'd worked on from Lisbon to Bristol had paid him off handsomely, though only half of what he'd been paid remained in his pocket. If it hadn't been for the fact that he'd stolen and supped a bottle of port from the cargo, there could have been half as much again.

Ahead of him was a church spire, which looked not to be too far off the main road.

He rubbed at the ache in his side; the result of too much to drink and having walked too far on an empty stomach. A little rest is in order, he said to himself, and you'll get that soon enough once you make the acquaintance of your boy again.

His breath curled from his mouth like wisps of hair on an old lady's head. Resting his hands on bent knees, he leaned forward to better catch his breath. Once he was sure he was hale and hearty again – as hale and hearty as he was ever likely to be – he straightened himself and thrust his hands into his pockets.

Dust was mostly what his dirty fingers found except for the one thing he was looking for, folded and creased with age, and tucked in a corner.

The paper he pulled out looked unfamiliar and for a moment he thought it was not the piece he was looking for. Surely that had been whiter and smoother than this piece, which was as wrinkled as a turkey's gizzard.

Spreading it out on top of an old milestone that said six miles to Bristol, he smoothed it as best he could and yet again read the address.

Church Lane Cottage, Church Lane, Long Ashton, Somerset.

'Church Lane. Has to be close to the church,' he said, his words drifting away with the whiteness of his breath. 'Of course it does,' he said to himself. 'Now where else would it be?'

'Back in you go,' he muttered, shoving the folded-up paper back into his pocket. 'You'll be safe there my boy.'

In his mind he was imagining how grateful his son Michael, now grown, would be to see him. Of course he couldn't possibly visualise how he would look now. The fact was he could barely remember what the boy had looked like as a baby.

Had he had fair hair, dark hair? Blue eyes, brown eyes?

No matter how hard he tried, no picture popped into his mind. Neither was he realistic about the welcome he was likely to get. As he stumbled along, he considered how lucky he had been that the woman from the workhouse – Miss Burton wasn't it – had forwarded on the address where his son had gone to live.

'I know they're adopting, but I'm not sure they're going about it the right way. They promised to look after the boy for you indefinitely, not take him over.'

That's was the gist of the note she'd sent. That had been back in 1928 after the workhouse had closed down and after he'd already settled his other children elsewhere; Magda with Bridget Brodie, his brother's wife, and the twins back in Ireland with his parents.

He'd been meaning to get round to see his family more frequently, but Joseph Brodie had always been able to find excuses not to do what he should do, but always to favour what he wanted to do – which was mostly get drunk, fornicate and spend every last penny he'd earned.

The fact was that he'd always worked hard, but in order to balance the scales so to speak, he'd also played hard – which meant no money left to meet his responsibilities.

For the first time in his life, Joseph felt emotional about one of his children. He felt as though the boy had been stolen from him without a by your leave.

'Fifty guineas,' he muttered to himself as he stumbled and shuffled along the road, the long strides restricted by stiff knee joints. 'My boy's worth that. He has to be worth that, not the paltry sum they left at the Seamen's Mission.'

He kept muttering the same sum over and over as though doing so made the amount he wanted for his boy more acceptable to them that now called him theirs.

The village pub was shut and in darkness, courtesy of licensing hours brought in for the duration of the Great War and never relinquished.

He'd heard rumours there might be another war shortly, which to his mind was a great shame if it meant the pubs would remain shut and barred against a man wanting a drink.

The long walk had proved tiring and the fresh air was setting his lungs tingling. Wiping the sweat from his brow with the back of his hand, he leaned against an ivy-covered wall. To his right was the neglected corner of the churchyard, a place of moss-covered tombstones and unkempt grass. The sound of a choir singing the wavering notes of *Adeste Fideles* – 'Oh Come All Ye Faithful', drifted out to warm the winter's cold.

The smell of rich earth, newly turned, hung heavily on the damp air as it always did at this time of year when the sun had gone south and the land had been turned by the plough and lay barren, waiting for the first signs of spring.

'Not much further, not much further,' he muttered as he waited for the pumping of his lungs and the gripe in his knees to settle down.

Daylight was beginning to ebb and, although not ideal, he thanked his lucky stars he'd managed to get a lift in a coal lorry heading out to some grand house between the city of Bristol and the village of Long Ashton. If he hadn't he would have arrived in Long Ashton in the dark.

The cottage to which his feet dragged was made of stone, had small windows and no more than a foot wide of planting between the wall of the house and the narrow lane. Even from here he heard somebody singing a Christmas carol in a sweetly feminine voice: 'Once in Royal David's City'.

One of the windows showed light and the smell of home cooking made his stomach lurch with desire.

'Steak and kidney pudding,' he murmured to himself. 'Or shepherd's pie. Or mutton stew.'

The thought of his son feeding him a hearty meal, after first giving him a hearty welcome, warmed him no end.

'Now for a tidy up,' he said to himself. In response to his own advice, he lifted his hat with one hand and smoothed his hair with the other. 'You'll want your son to be proud of you, won't you now.'

Though his clothes were dirty and in need of repair, and his whole demeanour was not much better to behold than a tramp travelling the roads all year round, Joseph Brodie had decided that he was presentable enough, and in that knowledge, which was sure only to himself, he lifted the cast-iron knocker and gave the door a damned good clout.

The singing stopped abruptly and a murmur of voices seemed to rise and then fall, then rise again, as though the folk within were arguing as to who should answer the door.

'If it's her or him – Mr and Mrs Darby that is – then I'll say I've come to claim my boy. If it is Michael, then I shall say . . .'

The door opened before he had chance to finish rehearsing what he would say and how he would say it.

The boy looking out at him was nothing like the baby he'd fostered out. For a start he didn't seem too shy of manhood; what had he been expecting? Of course he was close to being a man!

'Can I help you, my good man?'

The voice crackled between high and low as it does when a boy is crossing over from childhood to manhood. Not that he could remember what the boy had sounded like as a baby let alone a child.

'Michael. My, but you've grown. I hardly recognised you, my boy. Though I dare say, you won't be recognising me. 'Tis your father, Joseph Brodie. Your father who's been away at sea all these years.'

Joseph spread his arms assuming the boy would feel an explosion of joy and run into them, lamenting how much he'd missed his father and how everything would be made up in time.

Michael Darby stared aghast at the dirty, dishevelled man with the prickly beard, the sunken eyes and the hunched shoulders. On sniffing, he caught the stink of whisky or some other such strong drink that neither he nor his parents would ever countenance consuming.

As for the claim that this man was his father . . . Michael recoiled at the very thought of it. His face clouded. He had not the patience of his adoptive father who sermonised on the giving of charity all year round, not just at Christmas.

'Here,' said Michael taking half a crown from his pocket, a small amount from a sum he'd earned writing music for Mrs Anderson who taught music and gave concerts. 'Take this. Don't spend it all at once and don't drink it away. Now be off with you. And Merry Christmas.'

The door was slammed so forcefully, that the shock wave blasted into his face causing him to take a step back to steady himself.

He stared at the door, not quite able to comprehend why he hadn't been given the welcome deserving of a long-lost father.

Coming to no obvious conclusion, he turned his attention to the half crown, closing his fist over it whilst hoping that the pub he'd passed had now reopened its doors.

Inside Church Cottage, Aubrey Darby, who had just finished writing his Christmas Day sermon, enquired of his son why the angry expression.

'Some tramp at the door,' said Michael, slumping down in front of the piano then picking up a fountain pen, seemingly intent on the piece of music set before him. 'I gave him half a crown and told him to clear off.'

Aubrey Darby sighed as he got to his feet. It wasn't easy being a vicar with a headstrong son who wasn't entirely convinced that God really did live in his heaven. But he's at that age, Aubrey told himself. Sixteen and thinks he knows everything. He'll come back to it.

He got up, stood behind Michael and laid his hand on his shoulder.

'My boy, your charity is commendable, but telling him to clear off afterwards was not the Christian thing to do. Whatever did he say to you to deserve that?'

Michael huffed into his music sheets. 'He said he was my

father. Can you believe that? That dirty, foul-smelling man said he was my father.'

The moment the words were out, Michael felt the hand that had lain softly on his shoulder tense. When he looked up into his father's face, he saw a sweaty upper lip and fear in a face where he had never seen fear before.

'Did he give you a name?' His father's voice was tremulous as though the question was reluctantly asked and that the answer would be reluctantly received.

'Brodie. Joseph Brodie.'

The vicar of St Anne's church visibly paled above the whiteness of his dog collar.

'Did he say where he was going?' he asked Michael, already half a dozen steps towards the door and reaching for his hat.

Michael felt his face warming as he lifted his eyes from the music sheet. He stared at the Reverend Aubrey Darby not wishing to confront the sudden oddness of his behaviour, though conceding that it chilled him to the bone.

He was still staring and feeling numb and confused after his father went out of the vicarage leaving only empty space.

The landlord of the Angel shouted at the man rattling the doors to go away.

'We're not open, pal.'

'I need a drink.'

'Well, you ain't gettin' one 'ere. Anyways, looks as though the vicar wants a word.'

The upstairs window he'd been leaning out of fell shut.

'Mr Brodie.'

Joe Brodie turned round to face the man to whom he'd given his son all those years ago.

The Reverend Darby had a high forehead and forlorn features. Nature had bestowed him his sad expression. Even when he was happy he looked sad, but today his sadness was real and intense.

'Mr Brodie. You promised you would never approach us. We paid you not to. For the love of God . . .'

'For the love of my son,' replied Joe Brodie. He shook his head vehemently. 'I did wrong. A terrible wrong. I shirked my responsibilities and went off to live the life I've always lived. May God forgive me . . .'

The two men stood alone and apart, yet both knew there were turbulent feelings here. Aubrey Darby loved his adopted son. Joe felt that though he'd given him away, there was a strange tugging somewhere deep inside.

'If God would grant me one wish, I would wish for the clock to be turned back and my family to be back together.' He hung his head, shaking it just as forlornly as he had before. 'I realise now that it's too late. The boy didn't know me. What's more, he doesn't want to know me.'

Aubrey Darby knew from the words alone that he'd won the battle. Michael was his, but he still felt for the boy's natural father.

'We all have regrets. Nobody can live a life without having some regrets. Please, just be assured that Michael has a good life and is loved.'

Joe Brodie nodded, his dark hair now turning grey at the temples, falling forward over his face. He raised one hand and swept it back.

'I suppose that's the best any of us can hope for.'

Feeling awkward now, Aubrey asked where Joe would go now.

'To visit my eldest daughter and pray that she'll forgive me.'

In a flurry of lavender water and natural concern, Michael's mother came in from the drawing room.

'Has your father gone out? I thought I heard the door slam.'

Michael looked at the trim figure with her short blonde hair, tweedy clothes and single-strand pearl necklace. She looked every inch the vicar's wife, as indeed she was. Daughter of a missionary couple who'd done good works in China and then amongst the poor in the East End of London, she was suited to the life.

A suspicious thought entered Michael's lively mind. His mother was wholesome and blonde, her eyes as blue as the sky. Not at all like his own dark brooding eyes and the lush hair, black as night and flopping over his eyes.

When people remarked to his parents how unlike them he was, they always referred back to a Spanish grandfather on his father's side, though haltingly, as if they didn't want to admit to foreign blood at all.

'Michael. I'm speaking to you. Tell me what the slammed door was about and where your father's got to.'

The adolescent she regarded as her son snapped out of worrying thoughts and turned to face her. As he did so, he caught the smell of the talcum powder she'd used after taking a bath. It would only ever be something as innocuous as talcum powder, not perfume.

Pushing aside unfamiliar feelings of apprehension, he forced himself to sound unconcerned, even slightly offhand.

'He's gone after a man who came begging at the door. I think he must know him.'

'Really?' Eleanor Darby's silky fair eyebrows arched in surprise. The fingers of one hand played with the rope of small, perfectly shaped pearls at her throat. 'Did the man give a name?'

Michael nodded. Determined for reasons he could not quite understand, he kept his eyes fixed on her face.

'Yes. He did. He said his name was Joseph Brodie. He also said he was my father.'

Chapter Thirty-eight

Magda
1938

The smell of dirt, sweat and the sea entered the crisp cleanliness of Queen Mary's Hospital along with three men, two of them holding the third man between them.

'Got buried in the hold of a vessel carrying grain. He needs a doctor. Please! He needs a doctor.'

'Bring him in here,' ordered Magda.

The men did as ordered, sliding the injured man onto an examination couch in a curtained cubicle.

After taking off his cap, one of the men eyed her suspiciously as he addressed her.

'Excuse me, sister, but I reckon this man will need a doctor.'

Magda exchanged a knowing look with Indira. This was not the first time they'd been mistaken for nurses.

'Although this is our first year on the wards, we are able to help.'

'Are you doctors?'

'Almost. We are in training and under supervision.'

Indira was inspecting the leg wound.

'This needs suturing,' she said brusquely.

'Cleaning first,' said Magda.

Since Winnie's death she had thrown herself into her work, accepting extra hours without protest and hardly speaking to anyone unless she had to.

Even Winnie's belongings had been left untouched. She'd told Daniel that it was too early to go through them. Anyway, Henry Cottemore still had to probate the Will, though so far it looked pretty straightforward; everything was left to Magda including the cottage.

She'd tried to explain her inaction to him. 'I can't touch anything until I know it's mine. It's like waiting for Winnie to give me permission.'

She thought she knew what Daniel was getting at; there could be something amongst her papers incriminating Reuben Fitts and his son for their various crimes over the years.

'Henry Cottemore will confirm things shortly,' Magda had told him. Becoming a doctor seemed even more important since Winnie's death, her determination intensified by her feeling of helplessness as Winnie had slipped away.

Daniel had initially been irritated by her stubbornness, and then relented – just as she knew he would. She would have her own way. She was independent now and reliant on no one. She'd even turned down his offer of marriage.

'Not yet. Not until I'm sure I can survive by myself.'

The comment must have hurt him. She hadn't seen him for a few days, but she couldn't find it in her heart to change her mind.

In the meantime, she threw herself into her work.

She worked quickly, clearing the man's throat so he could breathe; calling for his wound to be cleansed before suturing could begin.

'He's lucky to be alive,' Magda told the men who had

brought him in. 'Just the dust from the grain could have killed him.'

'A very lucky man,' said Indira.

The two women worked well together, each instinctively supporting the other.

A student nurse slid through the opening in the curtain surrounding the patient.

'Excuse me, doctor, but there's a policeman outside who says the man was fighting and was pushed into the hold of the ship. He wants to question the patient to find out if it's true.'

Magda looked round. The two men who had brought the patient in had disappeared.

'He can't do that just yet. Not until we're finished.'

'He said he would appreciate knowing when the patient will be available.'

'Tell him . . .'

The nurse cut across her reply. 'I did tell him, doctor, but he said it had to be from the doctor who was treating him.'

No nurse would purposely interrupt an instruction from a senior doctor, but medical students, doctors in name that had not yet passed their finals, were shown less respect – even by student nurses.

Magda's eyes met those of Indira's. 'You or me?'

Indira bowed her head and lowered her eyes back to the neat row of stitching. 'I'm in the middle of some embroidery work. You might put me off my daisy chain if I stop now.'

She threw Magda a sideways slide of her eyes and a bewitching smile.

Magda glanced at her watch noting that she had less than an hour to go before her shift was over. Not that it was really ever over; it all depended on how busy they were.

The greyish-blue eyes settled on her and a ready smile tripped the corners of his mouth.

'Daniel!' Magda declared.

'This incident gave me an excuse to mix business with pleasure. The man in there.' He pointed at the closed curtain with a pencil he pulled from his pocket. 'His name's John Smith – or so I'm told. He wasn't saying much before he was brought here, and I doubt he'll say much now. But I can try. I always have to try.'

Magda frowned. 'Has he done something wrong?'

Daniel sighed. 'I'm not sure. When can I speak to him?'

'He'll be better by the morning. We've cleared out his lungs and a colleague is sewing up the leg wound. There's no reason you can't speak to him in an hour or two.'

Daniel nodded his thanks.

Magda glanced at her watch. 'Look, I have to go now.'

'In case you're wondering – which being a woman – and a very attractive one, you most definitely are, I hear you helped bring the seventh child into the world for one Mrs Gilda Payne.'

'Well! News certainly gets around,' exclaimed Magda, feeling somehow special that this man had taken note of the regard in which she was held.

Daniel's expression turned to one of concern. 'Payne works for Fitts. So did that man in there – until he did something to upset our friend Mr Fitts. That's why he got pushed into the ship's hold. I don't suppose I need to tell you that there's a lot of crime attached to valuable cargoes. As you may have noticed he's a big, muscled man. The word is that when he's not working on the docks, he's doing a bit of heavy work for Mr Fitts.'

Magda had lived with Winnie long enough to know what Daniel was talking about.

'He roughs people up?'

Daniel nodded. 'Pretty badly. But John Smith is also a drinker. He's been bragging about what he's done for Fitts. Our Mr Fitts doesn't like that. When people start blabbing after they've had more than a few pints of bitter, then that's one step too many. Fitts gets rid of them – though in John Smith's case it didn't work out. He's a big man. Not easy to knock a big man down. You didn't happen to notice the two men who brought him in?'

She shook her head. 'No.'

Of late she'd found it easy to forget Bradley Fitts, mostly because she was far too busy studying and working the wards to give him any mind. By the law of averages though, she was bound to bump into Bradley Fitts at some point.

'Has he been hanging round again?'

The question and the fact that Daniel seemed tuned in with her own thoughts surprised her.

She shook her head. 'No.'

'You can add the words, thank goodness, if you wish.'

'Thank goodness,' she said with a smile and he smiled back.

His smile died just before his gaze left her face. He was looking towards the double doors and the people passing in and out of the hospital.

'Well, well. It seems our Mr Fitts is getting downright brazen.'

Alarmed, Magda looked over her shoulder. Her blood froze. There he was, Bradley Fitts waltzing in as though he owned the place. And, as Daniel had remarked, downright brazen.

His eyes checked her and for a moment it seemed that he held his breath. Not for long.

'Mr Rossi,' he said. 'How nice of you to visit. I presume you're visiting my friend Mr Smith.'

His smile was as oily as a spilt pot of Brylcreem. By the looks of it he used the same embrocation to slick his hair back tight to his head and away from those snake-like eyes.

'He's still alive, Fitts, if that's what you've come to check up on.'

Daniel's base baritone wasn't loud, and yet Magda perceived it as strong, something dependable that would never fade, never become an insignificant croak.

Fitts seemed to think so too or at least he gave no audible reply, just a sharp nod of his head. His attention turned to Magda. His eyes raked her up and down, taking in the white coat, the stethoscope dangling around her neck.

Despite Daniel standing next to her, Fitts's presence still scared her. He had a way of looking at a woman that was entirely different to the look he gave a man.

He said nothing to her, but then he didn't need to. His look said it all. There would come a day when they would meet and Daniel Rossi would not be around. The thought of it scared her.

Fitts nodded a farewell to Rossi. 'No doubt I'll catch up with my dear friend John again.'

'No doubt you will,' said Daniel. 'Though not until I've had a word with him.'

Fitts touched the brim of his hat then pulled the collar of his overcoat up around his neck and departed.

He hadn't been obvious about looking at her, yet all the same Magda knew he had taken in every detail.

Daniel's voice broke into her thoughts. 'That clinic where you work. The Bethnal Green Clinic. It's in his territory.'

'Yes,' she snapped. 'But I can't let that fact stand in my way. There are too many people depending on me being there.'

'It would be wise. Surely you could arrange it for just a short time – enough time for me to build up evidence and get him locked up?'

She shook her head. 'Daniel, I have a job to do. I will not stop doing it because of him. The clinic is short staffed as it is. I have to attend. It's part of my training.'

'I won't always be there to protect you.'

Her eyes met his. 'I know that, Daniel. If the worst happens I have to deal with it myself.'

She couldn't help sounding angry even though she knew he was talking sense.

'Excuse me,' she said curtly. 'I have patients to attend to.'

When she left the hospital that evening, her eyelids were heavy as pennies and even when the fresh air hit her, she still had to stifle a yawn.

Due to her tiredness, she didn't at first notice the man standing to one side of the archway, not until he called her name.

'Magdalena?'

She turned. At first she didn't recognise the scruffy individual in dark clothes, a cap pulled low over his face, and then suddenly she knew. He was one of the men who had brought in the injured John Smith. But how had he known her name? She presumed he'd checked with somebody on the way out, wanting to know how the patient was doing. Unless . . . another more dangerous thought came to her. Perhaps he worked for Bradley Fitts. Perhaps he was here on Fitts's behalf.

She had to brave it out. He couldn't hurt her. Not here with people around.

She adopted an air of aloof disdain, strong enough to send the pennies in her eyelids packing.

'Yes. Can I help you?'

'You're Magda Brodie?' He said it in a hushed voice, as if overwhelmed by the very sound of her name and certainly by the look of her. 'I couldn't believe it when I saw you in there.' He jerked his thumb towards the hospital. 'You look just like your mother.'

'My mother?'

'Magda. Are you all right?'

Unable to hear what she was hearing, Daniel came striding to her side, intent on protecting her.

Taller and stronger than the older man and determined to defend her, he grabbed the collar of the scruffy, greasy seaman's coat with both hands. 'Who are you? What do you want with her?'

Magda stepped back.

Presuming the man did work for Fitts, Daniel snarled a warning into the haggard face.

'Take a message back to your boss, Fitts, that if he continues to harass Magdalena Brodie, he'll have me to deal with.'

'Fitts has been threatening you?' The man didn't sound afraid and his gaze never shifted from Magda's face. 'When I saw you, I checked your name. I couldn't believe it. You're going to be a doctor? My, but I'm proud of you.'

Magda felt a strange churning in her stomach and in her mind a memory surfaced from childhood.

'I came looking for you, Magda. I came to ask you to forgive me for leaving you with your Aunt Bridget. I did wrong. I did very wrong.'

Magda gasped. 'Daniel. It's my father.'

Daniel shook his head, his hands only barely loosening his grip on Joseph Brodie's collar.

Joseph Brodie seemed unaware of the hands crunching his coat lapels, his eyes still fixed on his daughter.

'Will you forgive me?'

Although the look in his eyes was pleading, Magda couldn't answer. Not just because her throat had gone dry, but because she wasn't sure of the answer to that. There were too many things she wanted to say, too many nights spent under the roof of a woman who hated her.

'You must have known what Aunt Bridget was like, and yet you left me there. Not only was she a cruel, selfish woman, but I came into contact with people even worse than her; including Bradley Fitts, a man who won't take no for an answer.'

She saw him wince as though surprised at how bitter she sounded. But she couldn't help it. Forgiveness was impossible – at least for now.

'I'm sorry,' he murmured.

Daniel loosened his grip and looked to Magda for confirmation.

'My father,' she said. 'The one who ripped apart his own family!'

'Magda, what can I do to make it up to you?' Her father looked helpless and sounded as though he was about to sob or even fall to his knees in an effort to acquire forgiveness.

Magda was too angry. Too hurt.

Her eyes, her blood, her face – everything seemed as though it were on fire with anger.

'Nothing. You can do nothing to make it up to me. The family seems to be scattered to the winds. I don't know where any of them are.'

'I do!'

She'd half turned away meaning to leave him behind, just as he'd left her. There were no words to describe how much she despised him for what he'd done.

'Where are they?' she asked, her voice sounding small and fragile.

'Your sisters are in Ireland. I left them with my parents, and Michael . . .' He stopped and looked down. 'Michael is all set up where he is. There's no need to interfere with his life. He's no need of any of us . . . or, at least, of me.'

Magda took a deep breath. 'Can you give me their last known address?'

He nodded. 'Sure. Wasn't it the place I grew up in? My parents are dead, but I think the twins are there – one of them at least.'

There were no words. She couldn't speak any words at all. They *were* in Ireland. She only nodded.

Her father began rummaging in his pockets, those outside and those on the inside too.

'I've got this letter . . .'

Finally he handed her the only letter that had ever caught him up on his far-ranging travels. It was crumpled and obviously many years old, but to Magda's eyes it was more precious than gold.

She took it but didn't thank him.

For what seemed like minutes but must only have been seconds, all three of them stood there, waiting for whoever was going to make the first move. It turned out to be Joseph Brodie.

'Then I'll be leaving, Magda my darlin'. Our time is done. All I can wish is that you have a good life.'

Joseph Brodie didn't seem so tall or as broad in the shoulders as he'd once done. It was as though living life to the full had worn him down.

'Where will you go?'

He shrugged, his fists clenching and unclenching as though they needed to do something physical.

'Oh, don't you worry about me, my girl. Back to sea. The only home I've ever loved.'

Magda felt the warmth of Daniel's body close behind her. Together they watched Joseph Brodie's shadow falling up a wall, then over a road before disappearing altogether.

'So do you think you'll ever forgive him?'

She shook her head. 'I feel that I should, but I can't. I just can't. It's been too long.'

Joseph Brodie strode as upright as he could, willing his shoulders not to shake and his eyes not to cry, but they did so anyway.

Her words had wounded him deeply, not that he blamed her for uttering them. He'd done her wrong. He'd done his whole family wrong including his beautiful wife, Isabella. Magda looked like her mother when he'd first seen her in Italy; his lovely Isabella.

Never had his heart ached so much as it did now, and yet he couldn't blame Magda for her bitterness, even her hatred of him. He deserved it but there had to be some way of making things up to her. First as last he had to keep her safe from Bradley Fitts. He'd seen what Fitts and his bully boys got up to on the docks. He had to save her from him – whatever it took.

Chapter Thirty-nine

Anna Marie
1940

Anna Marie breathed a deep sigh, closed her eyes and hunched her shoulders.

'I won't leave here, Patrick. I love the farm. I've always loved it.'

She was finding it hard to understand why Patrick, who had resisted her sister's urgings to sail to America, was now all in favour of leaving Ireland to fight in a war.

'You have to see it my way, Anna, it's my last chance to get a bit of adventure. It makes sense for us to sell up and buy something in England. Bombs are dropping there, and sure it won't be long before they're dropping here too. I want to put up a fight and think it's as much Ireland's battle as it is England's.'

'Ireland is . . .'

'Neutral. But I'm not. People are saying Hitler won't be satisfied until he's got a bigger chunk of Europe and that's my opinion too. He took plenty up till now, but there's more that he's wanting. Before we're halfway through this year he'll have taken more – so I'm hearing. By the end of this year I need to be in England if I'm not to miss the action.'

She shook her head in disbelief. 'But you're Irish. Ireland is a republic. You'd be fighting for England.'

He grinned in the mischievous way he used to when he was a boy.

'That doesn't mean I should miss the chance to go abroad to France or suchlike and have a pop with a rifle at those German blokes. Have you seen the way they strut about? They deserve to be shot at.'

'What am I going to do if you're away fighting?'

Patrick bowed his head, bit his lip and looked up at her from behind a tawny red fringe.

'You could try finding your sister.'

Anna Marie turned her eyes from her husband and fixed them on the view beyond the window. She reckoned she'd done a good job since her grandparents had died. In fact the old place looked better cared for than it ever had. This was in part due to her taking on the right people at the right price. Patrick, whose own father had departed for pastures new having met a widow woman from Sligo and moved in with her, had taken over his father's business. His first move, thanks to Anna Marie's urging, had been to decorate the inside of the house, fix the roof and install a proper bathroom in the smallest bedroom.

The bathroom had been a famous success, neighbours and folk from the town making sounds of approval at the modern bath, the WC and even a washbasin with hot and cold water.

'The hot water is heated by a boiler,' he'd boasted to everyone that would listen.

Some people who could afford such a luxury were so impressed they engaged him to do the same for them.

Working purely for reward had never much suited Patrick;

he'd never shirked hard work, but inside he sometimes wished he had gone to America with Venetia. How would it have been, he wondered, and where was she now?

They'd heard nothing from Anna Marie's twin since she'd been put into St Bernadette's, and perhaps that was what was making him restless. Yes, they were comfortably off, but being comfortable, he'd chided Anna Marie, was not what living was all about.

'You have to *feel* alive, not just *be* alive. Besides, what is there to keep us here – just the farm? We've no kin here about now.'

The last comment was the one that hit Anna Marie the hardest. No matter how much they truckled together in that big bed upstairs, the patter of tiny feet had never occurred. There were no children, though it certainly wasn't for the want of trying.

Feeling Anna Marie's big sad eyes on him and guessing she was brooding on the same old problem, he sat up straight and gave her a direct look.

'You've always said you'd like to look up your sister, Magda. So how about it? Isn't now as good a time as any? I mean, you've still got that letter from her. Nice paper. Nicely written. She can't be a whore like 'twas told to you. She just can't be.'

Anna Marie placed the butter dish on the table next to the slices of bread she'd just cut from the loaf. The letter had been a complete surprise. Magda had not mentioned anything about her life except that she wanted to get in touch, but only if she was in agreement. After all, their lives had separated when they were children.

Her grandfather had forbidden contact before, and she certainly didn't want to meet her if indeed she was a common prostitute.

She tried another tack to dissuade him.

'What if Venetia comes back and finds us gone?'

He barely paused in the act of buttering the thick doorstep of bread he'd placed on his plate.

'She won't be back. She didn't come back for the funeral of your grandparents, so why should she come back now?' he said, his mouth full of bread and butter.

Anna Marie pulled out a chair and sat on the opposite side of the table to her husband. As her eyes passed over the gingham curtains, the enamel stove, the deep sink and the painted dresser that Patrick had built himself, she asked herself whether she could willingly leave all this behind her. It all seemed such a waste of effort. She put her thoughts into words.

'All this work you put in, Patrick. I'm thinking you did all this for nothing.'

He swallowed the mouthful of bread and butter, his eyes shifting to hers then shifting away again. She'd often wondered why she'd never noticed his shiftiness before, the fact that he would wangle his own way at any price, initially without her noticing. Like his constantly moving eyes, Patrick Casey was restless. He couldn't settle. He would never settle – not really.

She'd also heard rumours about him and a woman in Dunavon but had decided to ignore them. It will pass, she'd told herself.

They'd been married a few years now so she noticed more, but accepted her lot. After all, hadn't Patrick been Venetia's man in the first place? There were times she felt guilty about marrying Patrick, but there, Venetia had not been around to protest. They'd heard nothing from her except that she'd run away from St Bernadette's.

It was from her grandmother's diary after her death that Anna Marie had learned that Venetia had given birth to a still-born daughter. Patrick's daughter. The shock couldn't have been worse and the pain still gnawed deep inside. She had told Patrick about a letter she'd found in her grandmother's things from the aunt where Magda had lodged. She had not told him about the diary; in fact she'd thrown it on the fire, her blood freezing as she watched it burn.

Share of her sister's shame had nothing to do with why she'd burned it. The diary would have laid bare the fact that it was her fault that they'd not had children, that he had already fathered a child on her sister. As yet she'd heard no rumours of him having fathered a child with anyone else. She wondered about the woman in Dunavon. Perhaps it might not be such a bad idea if they did sell up and leave.

Patrick was not giving up. 'Look. I don't mean to rub it in or anything, but 'twas me who purchased the freehold of this place. Your family only rented so although it was your family's place, they never owned it. And I do.'

She put down her cup and played with the piece of bread on her plate; she didn't feel like eating.

'If you want to sell it, there's nothing I can do. It's in your name.'

'Aye,' he said, shoving more bread into his mouth as he nodded. 'It's my name on the deeds, not yours. I'm your husband and what I say goes.'

Chapter Forty

Venetia
1938

Never in her wildest dreams had Venetia Brodie ever expected to end up spending weekends in a lovely house with a wrought iron balcony overlooking the promenade at Clevedon, a West Country coastal town. Her plan had always been to get enough money together for the trip to America. Keen to leave Ireland but not having enough money for the passage to America, she had settled for going to England.

The boat from Cork had taken her to Bristol, a city she knew nothing about except that a direct service ran between it and southern Ireland.

The first thing she did on alighting from the boat was to seek cheap overnight accommodation before looking for a job. The only job she was really qualified for was as a domestic servant thanks to the solicitous endeavours of the nuns at St Bernadette's.

Thanks to her London origins and Italian mother, her accent was not as thick and broad as some Irish who came over seeking work. She'd heard there were landladies who refused to let rooms to Irish people, so she made a point of refining her speech even more. In order to aid her quest, firstly for accommodation and then a job, she also adopted a version of her mother's name, calling herself Miss Venetia Bella. Venetia decided it sounded quite exotic and the landlady who rented her a room seemed to think so too.

'You must be on the stage with a name like that,' said Mrs Flugal, a small, stout woman with glossy black hair held back from her face in a severe bun.

'I would prefer that you don't give my secret away,' Venetia whispered in a conspiratorial manner. 'You know how people gossip.'

Mrs Flugal beamed at the prospect of being in on a secret. The wrinkles around her eyes almost collided when she winked and giggled like a girl.

''Tis our secret,' she giggled back, tapping the side of her nose. 'I take it, me dear, that you've a part in that play at the 'ippodrome.'

Venetia assured her that her part was better than being the back half of a horse.

'Could you tell me exactly where it is situated? I need to attend there first thing in the morning.'

'Well, my dear, you must 'ave passed it. Out of 'ere, turn right, and then left down over Park Street. The 'ippodrome is just along on your left hand side. Can't miss it. Grand it is. Really grand. Lovely red plush seats inside and gold and 'lectric lights all around.'

The room was basic but clean; a single bed, a chest of drawers with bun feet, a chair and a washstand with a bowl and pitcher on top of it. A mirror with a frame stained from dried-out mildew hung over a cast-iron fireplace. A gas fire of reasonable vintage sat in the grate and there was a gas ring on top of a three-legged table set before the window.

Venetia saw the light switch on the wall and patted it. The room had electricity; how wonderful was that?

After hanging her hat and coat up on the hook behind the door, she made herself a cup of tea from the few supplies she'd had the foresight to buy en route. There was no milk, but the sugar would give her the energy she needed.

After taking a sip, she smiled to herself.

'Venetia Bella.'

She laughed silently. It sounded quite wonderful. Mrs Flugal had thought so too.

'So perhaps you are an actress,' she said to herself and with sudden nostalgia remembered those childish nativity plays back in Ireland, a country she had no wish to ever return to.

The idea of being an actress took root; better an actress than a skivvy scrubbing floors.

The evening was closing in and lights were coming on across the city. Her room was at the top of the house and the house was situated high up behind the city centre.

A feeling of excitement flooded over her. The whole city swept downhill and her gaze went with it. Rooftops fell like slabs of tilted cake towards the heart of the city and the Hippodrome. Tomorrow she would present herself at the theatre as Venetia Bella, just returned from Italy.

In between now and then she would practise her vowels and eat the pork pie she'd bought at the same shop where she'd bought the tea. Tomorrow she would be up early, washed and dressed in the smart black dress and checked coat given her by the woman she'd worked for in Cork.

The woman, a widow, had owned a ladies' outfitters specialising in funeral suits and formal dresses. Venetia had suggested she diversify into smart outfits seeing as nobody else around seemed to be so disposed.

Her suggestion had worked and she'd ended up being given

some of the items that hadn't sold, including the black dress and the checked coat. She even wore a black velvet hat, which was little more than a huge bow perched on the head.

'Yes,' she said on seeing her reflection in the mirror. 'You are definitely Miss Venetia Bella.'

Her looks had got her all the way to the rehearsal about to take place.

'Italy you say? Well, Venetia Bella, it's a pleasure to have you on board.'

Nobody had questioned her about her acting credentials. Her dark good looks had drawn admiring glances from the men involved with the pantomime, and more envious looks from the women already given parts.

'If you could do something for us,' mumbled the director, the only man who seemed unconvinced that she would suit his high standards.

Venetia was panic stricken. Besides the nativity plays, the only other parts had been for real; the motherless child, the jilted lover, the wild girl interned inside high walls who'd found herself pregnant . . .

The shamed girl! It had to be the shamed girl appealing to her father – or grandfather. Well, she could certainly do that.

She fell to her knees before Henry Steadman-Jones, the director.

'Please! Grandfather. You can't send me to that terrible place. I love him. I know he'll want to marry me, especially when he hears about the baby. We love each other. You have to believe that. We love each other. Please! Please don't send me away . . .'

She began to cry, big loud, convulsive cries, her head thrown back and her hands clenched tightly together. Her whole body collapsed into itself as though suffering great pain. One final sob, and her performance was done.

The single sound of clapping sounded from the auditorium. Others joined in.

On hearing the applause, Venetia unfurled her body and gazed with shining eyes at those sitting in the audience. This, she decided, was the life she was destined for. She was no longer Venetia Brodie; she really was Venetia Bella.

Her eyes met those of the man who appeared to have led the applause. He was older than the others and had the look of money about him.

Venetia got to her feet, met his gaze head on, bowed and bowed again.

Ten minutes later, following an intensive discussion with the man who had led the applause, the director offered her a part.

His thin lips squeezed into a petulant pout, he outlined what he'd been told to offer.

'We can use you in our current production, just an infill part, and then we start rehearsing for the Christmas panto. We're doing Cinderella this year. Being fair and having already been offered the part anyway, Lula there is playing Cinderella. How would you like the part of principal boy? Two guineas a week to start with seeing as you're not known in this country. But we'll bill you as famed actress, Venetia Bella from Italy. How would that be? Once we get you established, we might use you again in other productions and if the public like you – well, your salary could double, even quadruple. Mr Anderson, our sponsor, insists I take you on.'

Venetia had no doubt as to Mr Anderson's identity; he'd been the one who had clapped first and clapped the loudest and longest.

In the months that followed, she refined her speaking voice even more. A strident speaking voice was required for the part of Prince Charming, the principal boy, and she had no problem delivering this.

The only fly in the ointment was Henry Steadman-Jones, the director.

'He wanted Emerald Canterbury for the part,' explained Cinderella in the privacy of their shared dressing room. 'She's his boyfriend's sister.'

'His girlfriend's sister,' said Venetia thinking Cinderella had made a mistake.

'No,' replied Lula. 'His boyfriend's sister.'

She went on to explain that Henry didn't care that much for women. He preferred boys and the prettier the better.

'You must have come across it in Italy,' Lula went on.

'Of course,' said Venetia. 'Though you have to bear in mind that Italy is a very Catholic country. Things like that are not so open.'

Lula accepted her explanation without question.

The fact was that Venetia had never come into contact with men who loved men, but this was what was so exciting. Theatre was a new world to her and she was grateful for the fresh start it had given her. There were characters in the theatre as well as on the stage.

The production was going well and, from the first night, the theatre was packed with jolly people, all enjoying the same old story, the songs, the jokes and the principal boy being a girl, and the ugly sisters being men dressed up as women.

There was also a comic horse. Just looking at the brightly coloured costume set Venetia laughing. Mrs Flugal had been very concerned that she might end up being its back half.

Mr George Anderson came regularly to watch her strut her stuff on stage. On Christmas Eve a vast bunch of flowers was delivered.

Venetia could hardly believe her eyes.

'My word,' she said to Lula. 'Where would anyone get flowers so lovely at this time of year?'

Lula stopped wiping off her stage makeup, turned round and smiled.

'Darling. Don't you know? Our Mr Anderson is a very wealthy man. He owns a huge house outside Bristol surrounded by acres of grass and trees. As I understand it, it also boasts greenhouses where the most exotic of flowers are grown all year round.'

'And he picked a bunch and sent them to me. Nobody's ever sent me . . .' she paused. As an actress she would have been sent flowers. 'Nobody's ever sent me such beautiful flowers as these.'

'Exotic flowers for an exotic flower,' said Lula. 'I think you've impressed him greatly. Be prepared, my darling girl. Be prepared for offers he won't want you to refuse.'

'I don't think I'm ready for marriage,' laughed Venetia.

Lula burst into peals of laughter. 'Neither is he, darling. He's married, but a charmer for all that. Play the field, darling. Play the field, that's my philosophy. Be an actress on stage and off. It makes sense in the long run. After all, we won't be beautiful for ever.'

Lula had given Venetia friendly advice since the first day she'd arrived. Venetia heeded that advice; after all Lula had the experience. It made sense to listen to what she said.

At times she felt terribly sad and alone. Playing a part on stage would help fill the gap, but once she left playing she would become herself again.

Lula was privy to her moods. 'Have you got any family?'

'Some dead. Some lost.'

'Italy's a long way away,' remarked Lula.

'A long way,' said Venetia, unwilling to expand on her circumstances.

Lula patted her shoulder. 'Travel is expensive. What you need is a benefactor to foot the bills. The richer the better and quite frankly, my dear, I think you've already found him. See you tomorrow. Take care.'

She gave her one final pat before leaving.

Venetia sat silently after Lula had gone, thinking about her father, her mother and Anna Marie. She wondered whether her twin sister and Patrick were happy and whether they'd started a family yet.

Thinking of that took her mind back to that dark night when she and a wayward nun had said prayers over the body of her stillborn child. They'd buried it just within consecrated ground so that her daughter's soul would go to heaven and not hang around at the halfway house.

At the sound of somebody knocking, she knuckled the tears from her eyes.

When she reopened them George Anderson was standing there clutching a bottle of champagne and two glasses in one hand. In the other he carried a silver-topped cane.

Venetia looked at him and smiled. Although over twice her age, he was a good-looking man, well dressed and oozing class and distinction.

'I came to ask you if you liked the flowers.'

'They're beautiful.' Her voice sounded squeaky. Through misted eyes she studied this man who had opened up a new world for her.

He wore a dark fedora and evening dress beneath a cashmere overcoat plus white kid gloves. He frowned on seeing that she'd been crying.

'My dear.'

He closed the door behind him, set the champagne and glasses down, then shrugged off his coat and took off his hat.

'My dear,' he said again. 'Is something wrong?'

She smiled at him through her tears. 'I was thinking about my family and missing them. What with all this talk of war and everything . . .'

When he put his arms around her, she didn't resist but sank into them, sobbing against his chest. She felt his heartbeat increase.

'You're bound to be worried about them, seeing as the Italians are batting for the other side.' He held her away from him, took out his pocket handkerchief and advised her to give her nose a good blow.

The sound of her blowing her nose was accompanied by the popping of the champagne cork being pulled from the bottle. He filled both glasses and handed one to her.

'I think you could do with this. Now. Take a good sip.'

She did as ordered, the bubbles pleasantly bursting beneath her nose.

'Drain the glass.'

Eyeing him from over the rim, she again obeyed his instructions.

'Now I will ask you again. Did you like the flowers?'

She shook her head.

'You didn't?' He sounded surprised. 'I thought they were beautiful.'

'Yes, I mean no. They were beyond liking. That's what I meant.'

He nodded at the glass, which was once again brimming with bubbles. 'Drink it all.'

George Anderson took the glass from her hand, set it down on the table and drew her into his arms.

'There, there,' he said, patting her back before his hand caressed her chin and lifted her face to look up at him.

She studied the gaunt though handsome face, the deep-set

eyes that were gazing into hers, the warmth of his body, and the beat of his heart.

It came as no surprise when his lips met hers. He kissed her gently, held her lightly as though she might break if he pushed for more.

Yet he wanted more. George Anderson had fallen for the girl he knew as Venetia Bella the moment he'd set eyes on her. In time she would be his, but her trust in him must be cultivated. There would be no forceful seduction, no demands on her time or her body.

This relationship, he'd decided, should be based on mutual trust and respect if it were to last. And he wanted it to last.

Chapter Forty-one

Anna Marie
1939

'I can't believe I'm doing this,' Anna Marie Casey muttered.

Her eyes followed the last of the furniture being loaded into the back of a van. The new owners of the farm were absentee landlords living in England and had purchased the basic things; bed, cooker, etc., but not the newer items that she and Patrick had bought themselves.

A manager and his family were being installed to run the farm so the furnishings were being kept simple, which suited Anna Marie fine. She had not wanted to sell all her lovely things and had hoped to keep some, but Patrick had insisted.

'The cost of shipping that stuff, it isn't worth bothering.'

Behind her back he'd written to a cousin in London who owned a grand house – his words – where they could have rooms until they got on their feet.

Anna Marie visited Father Anthony at the outset, telling him of her concerns for Patrick's plans.

'I love everything about the farm. I don't want to go, Father, but my husband won't listen.'

To her surprise, Father Anthony had taken hold of both her

370

hands and his face had come so close that for a moment she'd thought he was going to kiss her.

'Anna Marie. Lovely, lovely, Anna Marie,' he said, his eyes burning into hers. 'I must admit I will truly miss you, but it is your duty to be with your husband. You promised to love, honour and obey him. I would stress the last. If it is his wish that you live in England, then that is where you must live. Obey your husband. It is what a woman should do.'

She had felt her eyes filling up with tears. Her little chin trembled when she nodded.

'I shall miss your singing,' he said to her. 'But there you are. All good things must come to an end.'

On showing her to the door, he patted her buttocks. She pretended she hadn't noticed. After all, he was a priest and couldn't possibly mean anything by it, but somehow she wasn't feeling so accommodating as she'd once been. Perhaps the move to London had something to do with it.

How would Venetia handle this, she asked herself.

'Lay his hands on me? And him a man of the cloth who's supposed to be celibate.' She'd have likely slapped his face too.

The thought of the priest's expression cheered her up no end. Yes, Venetia would do that. But *she* wouldn't. Even though she knew his behaviour was dishonourable, she hadn't the courage.

Outside she looked up at the leaden sky and sighed. Her priest had spoken. Her duty was to be with her husband.

Her only consolation was the address in an old Peek Frean biscuit tin she'd found in a dusty cupboard that Patrick chopped up for firewood. The tin had once belonged to her grandmother and held a number of letters and even a few Christmas cards and a postcard sent from Belgium by her grandfather in 1915.

Her grandmother had also kept a letter and a telegram from James's wife, Bridget.

Anna Marie had fallen silent at the sight of it. Magda had

gone to live with Aunt Bridget – somewhere in London. And here was her aunt's address and the news that Magda had entered a house of ill repute where she sold her body for money.

At first she upheld the attitude of her grandfather and felt shocked and ashamed on seeing such a statement. Her sister deserved to be an outcast. On reading it again she thought of Venetia and what she would do on reading this. In her head she could hear her pronouncing that Magda was still their sister.

'Blood is thicker than water.'

But Venetia wasn't here. She had to make up her own mind.

Tucking the letter in with the other bits and bobs that had once belonged to her grandparents, Anna Maria resigned herself to moving to London. After all, she could at least call in on Aunt Bridget and get it confirmed from her how her sister had sunk so low.

Sister Betty Flanagan was a midwife and nurse, aged around thirty with hazel eyes, broad shoulders and an aura of determined efficiency.

Tasks that others would rush at, Betty approached methodically, even slowly. And yet she still finished her tasks more quickly than anyone else. She spoke with an Irish lilt to her voice and was calmly efficient, her strength coming from her manner and some unspoken faith either in herself or something higher. The latter belief held sway. Rumour had it that she used to be a nun. Magda wasn't sure whether it was true or not.

'Doctor Brodie. Your young man is waiting for you.'

There was a sparkle in Sister Betty's eyes when she said it and her statement was accompanied by a knowing smile.

Magda laid the back of her hand onto her cheek. It was warm. She had to concede that.

'Are you as cheeky with the male doctors, Sister Betty?'

'I speak my mind. None of this toadying up that most

nurses do. I'm not here to nursemaid them, thank you very much. Anyway, I like women doctors. They let you know what they're thinking and treat a nurse almost as an equal. They want you to understand what they understand. Men doctors don't do that. To them we're women before we're professionals and most of the time they don't let us forget it. Only here to wash bedpans and clear up vomit; that's what they think. The very idea of it . . .'

The pair of them, the handsome young policeman and the vibrant, dark-haired doctor, were going to the pictures. *Anna Karenina.* Greta Garbo. They were making the most of their time together; who knew where any of them would be this time next year, now the country was at war, the capital in darkness and everyone who could fit into a uniform was wearing one.

Sister Flanagan's mind raced with possibilities as she busied herself carrying out her duties. The first time she'd clapped eyes on Doctor Brodie, her thoughts went back to the other Brodie girl, the one who had given birth to a stillborn baby. Even before helping the girl bury her baby in sanctified ground, she'd been having doubts about her calling as a nun. She'd seen too much hurt caused by those who had never known either passion or childbirth. How cruel the Catholic Church was to tell a mother that her child was doomed to exist forever between heaven and hell.

Her decision to help expectant mothers as a nurse rather than a nun had come shortly after that. To date she'd never regretted it.

For some time she'd been agonising whether to bring the matter of Venetia Brodie up with Magda. She was in no doubt that the two girls were related. On asking around as to the doctor's background, she'd been told she had lived with a wealthy benefactress, now deceased, and was well provided for, unlike Venetia Brodie who had been left to flounder.

Chapter Forty-two

Magda
1939

'Will you join up?'

Magda and Daniel were walking arm in arm on their way home after the pictures. The newsreel had presented a confident picture of Britain's chances against the formidable foe, altering the defeat of Dunkirk into a victory that never was. Sandbags had been hastily piled up against buildings, barrage balloons were floating like fairy elephants in the sky and rationing was beginning to bite hard.

Daniel was taking his time answering.

Magda nudged his elbow. 'Well?'

He shook his head. 'Police officers are in a reserved occupation. They are not required to join up, although arrangements are afoot to bring in retired officers to fill the gaps if need be. But . . .'

'But?'

She could tell by his demeanour that he wanted to say more.

'You know my family's Italian? People of Italian descent are being categorised as aliens. Their movements could be restricted.'

'You think you will be? You think I might be?'

He shook his head. 'No. But my father and mother might be. They still hold Italian passports.'

She looked up at him. 'You'd go wouldn't you? Given the chance. You'd join up.'

'I don't know. It depends. I wouldn't want to let anyone down and as long as they brought in someone retired to take my place . . . Anyway,' he said, turning to her and smiling, 'why would I want to leave you?'

'You might not be leaving me. It might be the other way round. I'm a doctor, Danny, though I'm presuming male doctors will be called up first.'

He hugged her tight. 'I don't think I could stand that. I might have to marry you. The military don't take married doctors – not female ones anyway. At least I could make sure you stayed in England if nothing else.'

She laughed and rested her head on his shoulder. He felt so good to be with and even though she often thought of her family, Danny's presence had filled a big gap in her life.

'All the way home?' he said to her.

She nodded. 'All the way home. But I have to get up early. So you can't stay.'

'I was afraid you'd say that.'

They stopped and kissed passionately, Magda thinking that she might not last the night without Daniel lying next to her.

They broke breathlessly. 'Are you sure?' His voice was warm and moist against her hair. He breathed it in, smelling the hint of lavender – shampoo perhaps. Never mind. She always smelled good.

'Duty calls,' she said to him, patting his chest with both hands. 'Take me halfway. Just as far as the arches. I'll be fine from there.'

*

A Christmas Wish

Neither of them noticed the envious eyes glaring at them from the car on the other side of the road.

Bradley Fitts stepped out of the passenger side of the car. His driver got out of the other.

'What do we do, boss?' asked the driver.

'Follow her.'

'And then?'

'You heard what he said. They're going their separate ways. Now ain't that just fine and dandy! I'm going to follow her. I want you to follow him.'

'But what do I . . .'

'Just warn me if he turns back in her direction. I want her to myself. Have you got that?'

For a while they walked together, their steps in time and soft. They stayed well back, not chancing for either their footsteps to be heard or their shadows to fall too far ahead of them.

Magda and Daniel hugged and kissed before parting company at the railway arches.

'I don't like leaving you to go home alone.'

'It's only a matter of yards,' she laughed. 'This isn't Whitechapel, or the nineteenth century, and Jack the Ripper – whoever he was – is long dead.'

They kissed one last time before breaking apart and going their separate ways.

Bradley Fitts and his driver hung back, Bradley clenching his jaw at the wanton hussy's behaviour with that bastard policeman. The copper was getting what didn't belong to him. Magda belonged to him and him alone, and Bradley Fitts wasn't keen on sharing.

'You follow the copper. Make sure he don't head back this way.'

'What do I do if he changes direction?'

376

'Deal with it. A bit of assault won't hurt. Then leg it. Right?'

Bradley Fitts felt an almighty surge of empowerment. He'd been trying to get close to Magdalena Brodie for as long as he could remember. There had always been willing women in his life, but none of them were as intelligent or as exotic as her. She was the flame and he was the moth but he damned well wasn't going to get burnt. On the contrary, he'd prefer it the other way round. And once she'd received the pleasure of his passion, well . . . anyone could have her . . . and he'd make sure they did.

It wasn't easy to explain why he wanted to destroy her, even to himself. The fact was she'd set herself up above the crummy circumstances of her beginnings. She'd become something good and clean, like a pretty piece of china. He'd always enjoyed smashing china, desecrating something beautiful. And that, mate, is what you want to do to her. Break her into pieces.

In his mind he imagined her naked and unable to stop him doing whatever he wanted to do. She would scream, not realising that would only spur him on to hurt her more, to possess her more.

His pulse quickened at the thought of it. He couldn't wait to have her, and once he had done . . .? Well, that copper wouldn't want her then. No respectable man would want her then.

At one point he thought he heard footsteps following behind him. Sidestepping into a shop doorway, he looked back along the pavement.

Some light fell from shop windows and overhead lamps onto the street. A group of cats snarled and lashed out over something that had fallen out of a dustbin.

He decided that was what he had heard.

The turning into Prince Albert Mews went beneath a pretty arch that connected one rank of shops to the other.

The tarmac road gave way to cobbles and the lighting was minimal.

To the right of the arch was a small opening where one of the old rivers of London swirled between sewers before joining the Thames. Recent heavy rain had swollen the flow of water to a raging torrent and the noise was thunderous as it crashed through the narrow channel.

He slid his tie from around his neck, winding the ends around each hand. Soon it would be around hers. Not that he was going to kill her. The plan was that he'd loop it around her neck at the moment she put her key in the door. Then he'd push her inside. They'd have privacy then; just the two of them together all night and if he worked things right – in fact ending her life – someone else would get the blame – that copper with a bit of luck.

Just as he judged the time was right he was yanked backwards.

'Fitts! I want a word with you.'

Thinking Daniel Rossi had caught up with him, Bradley cursed his driver. On seeing that it wasn't Rossi, he looked puzzled, then angry.

'Leave go of me or it'll be the worse for you.'

'Is that so?'

The man's tone was mocking. His accent was Irish, his breath stank of booze but his grip was like iron.

Bradley attempted intimidation by impressing on him who he was and the likely repercussions.

'Do you know who I am?'

He said it threateningly, which was exactly what he intended. The Fitts family were famous on the manor, gangsters, thugs and dealers in everything illegal. This man, whoever he was, had to be impressed.

'Oh yes. I know exactly who you are. You're a thug and I don't like what you're doing.'

That mocking tone still, and that grip. If the man had been closer to his own height, perhaps he could have head-butted him before landing a punch in his guts. But the man holding onto him was over six feet tall. No matter his age or general health, whatever job he did for a living had kept him fit. He smelled of the sea. A docker. Perhaps a merchant seaman.

'It's none of your business,' Bradley snarled, his own hands gripping the other man's wrists, trying in vain to unwrap the strong fingers from his coat lapels.

'That's where you're wrong. It is my business.'

'She's just a tart,' Bradley snarled, then suddenly leered as a thought occurred to him. This man had also been following Magdalena Brodie, perhaps with the same thought in mind.

'Tell you what. You can have her after me. But I get first go. Right?'

Suddenly he was yanked three feet off the ground, his legs dangling, his feet thrashing in a bid to kick the man's legs from under him.

Struggling did no good. Bradley could smell the man's sweat, drowned in the stink of his booze-laden breath.

The man was telling him something, crying as he did so, like somebody confessing their sin to a bloody priest.

I'm no priest, he wanted to shout, but not a sound came from his throttled throat.

'I neglected my daughter. I've been looking for a way of making it up to her. You're it, Fitts. I'm removing you from her life.'

Joe Brodie's words tripped a light in Bradley's brain.

'You can have everything I've got in my wallet. Everything,' he shouted.

His voice was drowned in the sound of the racing water.

He was closer to the water now, the spray flying upwards into his face.

Fear that other people had felt for him was now his. This man didn't care about his violent reputation and the power of his family and friends.

Panic set in.

'Put me down! Put me down!'

His shouts went unheard. He cried out as one hip was dragged across the top of the stone wall, a jagged upstanding stone tearing through his top-quality trousers and grazing the skin from his flesh.

For a moment he was suspended over the raging torrent, held by the collar of his coat and the seat of his pants. Below him the water thundered into a narrow culvert, a culvert that would no doubt get ever narrower with no room for air, filled only with an icy torrent.

Nobody saw him go in and nobody heard his cry of anguish and the splash as his body hit the thundering water.

Joseph Brodie stood looking down into that dark water for what seemed like an hour, wondering whether he should follow the body he'd sent down to hell. He deserved to go to hell himself. He'd not done the best for either his wife or his children. Too late now. There was nothing he could do about the past and their future was their own.

At one point he'd thought he could make amends for his shameful neglect and reacquaint himself with the family he'd left behind. Meeting his son Michael was the foretaste of realising it was not possible. The boy had eyed him with outright contempt. Other people, good people, had given him the love and affection that he had failed to give.

As for Magda . . . well . . . he'd heard bitterness, even hatred in her voice, but at least he'd done something to make amends. Bradley Fitts would not trouble her again.

He looked up as a light came on in a window of the house where his daughter lived. She'd done well, and he was proud of that.

Pulling his collar up against the cold, he turned his back on his daughter and his past. There was nothing else for it but to keep walking back to the only life he'd ever known, the one he'd chosen for himself.

The sound of a ship's horn came from the direction of the docks. It sounded twice – moving to port – out onto the river and from there out into the world. A lonely sound, but one he was used to.

Chapter Forty-three

Magda

Daniel Rossi looked through the contents of the box Magda had given him.

Her heart fluttered when he raised his eyes to meet hers. She saw jubilation and guessed it was linked to potential justice.

'I'm guessing you know what this contains?' he said to her.

'Sort of. Winnie knew Reuben Fitts for a long time. I'm guessing she knew enough to put him behind bars.'

She placed a tray of tea on the piecrust table in front of their chairs.

'Digestives,' she said. 'No custard creams.'

'Darn.' He grinned. She'd got to know his tastes and he'd learned that he mustn't crowd her; that her upbringing had made her wary of depending on others. In time he hoped she would rely on him. He wanted that badly.

Daniel closed the lid of the box. 'I've got enough here to put Reuben Fitts away for years. Not Bradley of course. We fished his body out of the Thames. He'd been drowned, but there were contusions – suggesting someone had forced him into the water. We've no idea who. All we can surmise is that he upset the wrong person.'

'I'm glad. I shouldn't be saying that should I? He's dead. Gone from my life.'

Daniel turned his cup around in its saucer. 'You haven't heard anything from your father?'

'No. But I do have hopes that his guilt might stir things. I had no reply to my letter to Ireland, but even after all this time, he's more likely to know people there who can help trace my sisters. My brother too come to that.'

Magda noticed Daniel's fingers nervously tapping the lid of the box whilst looking down into the glowing coals of the fire. Something was wrong.

'There's something else in that box, isn't there?'

He heaved a big sigh. Although for a moment it seemed like he was going to deny that there was, she could tell just by looking at him.

'I know it's not custard creams,' she said playfully. 'Come on. Give it to me.'

'I found something. I've left it on top,' he said as she took the box from him.

She turned the small key in the brass lock and lifted the lid. The two notebooks looked expensive and had red silk linings. 'Harrods' was printed inside the front covers in gold leaf.

The letter was lying on top of the books. She frowned at him. 'I didn't see this when I opened it.'

'I found it hidden inside the silk lining of one of the notebooks whilst you were making the tea.'

Magda frowned at the postmark. 'London?'

He knew she'd been expecting an Irish postmark.

She took out the contents, which consisted of a note attached to a letter.

Mrs Patience Armitage,
Compound 54,
Lee Cheong, Peking, China
7th of February, 1938

Dear Miss Brodie,
   I am the sister of Miss Elizabeth Burton, lately of the
Sycamore Lane Workhouse and now with our Lord in
Heaven.
   Time being of the essence when I last left England to
rejoin my husband, a missionary in China, I first had to
sort out my sister's effects. Being in something of a rush,
I bundled both mine and my sister's correspondence
together.
   Having established where your sisters were placed,
my sister was in the process of forwarding your cards
and letters to them under the enclosed covering letter. As
you can see, the letter remained unfinished.
   It was only on my arrival in China that I found the
enclosed items amongst her things and posted them
immediately to you via a British mail ship.
   Best wishes.

'My sisters were in Ireland! These letters and cards I wrote
when I was a child didn't get to them.'

'And your brother?'

She bent her head and read the rest of the report sent to
Miss Burton from a place called Fair Mount House.

'He was adopted. They're not allowed to tell me who by. It
was a term of the adoption.'

'That's usual.'

Magda slumped back in her chair and shook her head. 'Why
didn't Winnie give this to me?'

'She didn't want you hurt?'

Magda shook her head again. 'She didn't want me to go off searching for them. The silly woman. I would have come back.'

'Would you?'

'I think so. She did such a lot for me.'

'Do you hate her for not giving you this?'

She shook her head. 'I should, but I can't. Thanks to my father, my life was a mess. I could have ended up in Winnie's place with the other girls. Easily! I have to thank her for saving me from that. I suppose I almost forgive my father. He couldn't help being the way he was. Neither could Winnie. She loved ruthlessly. Very much so,' she said whilst thoughtfully fingering the letter Daniel had found.

Daniel knew her well enough to recognise that something was laying heavy on her mind.

She took out the records of the Fitts' criminal empire, fingering the lining of each cover. The first one held no secrets, but the second one did.

'A photo.' With trembling fingers she slid it free and brought it up to face level.

The girl in the photo had pale skin and big eyes. She was wearing a maid's uniform and holding a large teapot whilst smiling shyly at the camera. A priest with devilish dark looks was standing next to her.

'She doesn't look anything like you,' Daniel said after studying the photograph.

'No. That's Anna Marie. She looks more like our father I think. Venetia looked like me. Very much like me. We took after our mother.'

Daniel suggested she'd been working too hard and took the items from her hands. 'Leave this to me. I can make enquiries. Bob Barton can go where Doctor Magdalena Brodie cannot.'

'And in the meantime?'

'I'm taking you out on the town. A show and a meal. No arguments.'

His insistence amused her.

'You're breaking my arm and I like it.'

He cupped her face in his hands.

'I prefer kissing you.'

'Don't let it stop there.'

He paused, a little unsure of what she was saying or if he was interpreting it right. The right answer to the question he'd already asked her.

She felt an urge to explain. 'I feel as though a chapter of my life has finally closed and another one is about to open.'

He smiled. Kissed her forehead, kissed her nose and finally kissed her mouth.

'If we were to get married, could you learn to love me?'

'Physically or emotionally?'

She thought she saw him blush.

'Both.'

'We can learn before we get married – if you really want to.'

Magda's bed was warmer than it had ever been in her life. Their clothes were scattered over the floor. Normally the ceiling would be spangled with the efforts of the gas-lit street lamps, but not tonight. A full blackout was in force.

A shrill sound erupted outside just after midnight.

'A siren. Only a practice though.' Danny's voice was calm, reassuring.

Even though the siren wasn't for real, they made love for a second time, lost in the intensity of feeling for each other as though they had to confirm they were still alive and the world hadn't yet blown itself to pieces.

He left her bed sometime after one with a promise that he'd

be back before the end of the week once the shifts worked out. Hopefully he would have news for her.

'Though we could do with a miracle.'

'Well, it is Christmas.'

She didn't add that this would be their first Christmas at war.

Chapter Forty-four

Venetia
1939

Venetia could not believe what was happening to her. Since coming to Bristol just over a year before, and meeting George Anderson, her life had become like a fairy story. She was grateful to him; she loved him, though there was a part of her she failed to share with him.

She knew where her twin sister was and accepted the fact that Anna Marie had married Patrick. It no longer hurt, certainly not since George had come on the scene. But Magda. Where was Magda?

She hadn't told George that whilst supposedly shopping on their last trip to London, she had taken a taxi to her sister's last known address with the aunt in Edward Street. There was nothing but rubble and burned timbers to see. She'd stood and stared. It seemed as though she'd reached the end of her search.

'This ain't no place for a lady,' said the taxi driver as she slid into the back seat.

She wasn't really listening and didn't hear him ask where he was to go next. Her eyes took in the two women watching them from the doorway of the house immediately opposite the burned-out wreck. Instinctively, she knew what they were and although it made sense to speak to them, to ask them whether they knew her sister's whereabouts, she couldn't bring herself to do it. Not because she was afraid of tackling them, but more so because she was afraid that what she'd been told was the truth.

The time when they'd been children together seemed a lifetime away. Her thoughts went back to that far-off time, the last time they'd been together. Sycamore Lane Workhouse.

She said it out loud. 'Sycamore Lane Workhouse.'

'Not there anymore, miss,' said the taxi driver, presuming she'd been telling him where to go next. 'Everything got transferred to Fair Mount far as I know.'

'Fair Mount? Would they have records there?' she'd asked feeling a sudden frisson of excitement.

'Could do.'

'Take me there.'

A Miss Spangler, a plump woman with thick fingers, looked through their records whilst Venetia sat rigidly, taking in the institutional surroundings of brown walls, brown floors and pale glass lampshades hanging from a high ceiling. The smell of mashed potato and beef stew fought bravely with that of beeswax and carbolic soap.

'Ah,' said Miss Spangler. 'I do have an address for your sister.'

Venetia leapt to her feet. 'You do? That's marvellous.'

'Unfortunately I can't give it to you. Not without the person's permission. The correct procedure is that I contact your sister first and inform her that you're looking for her and I can give her your address.'

'Gladly! And my telephone number – my agent's telephone number and my own. Please. If you could pass it on quickly, I would much appreciate it.'

*

Miss Spangler watched the tall young woman with the striking good looks coming towards her. She could hardly believe that this same young woman had spent some time in Sycamore Lane Workhouse. Who would have thought she could rise so far and so quickly? But there, it helped that she'd acquired a wealthy benefactor who had taken her on as a paid companion; at least, that was the story Doctor Brodie had told her when she'd come making enquiries after finding a letter from Miss Burton, a much respected past warden at Sycamore Lane.

Doctor Brodie extended her hand. 'Miss Spangler. How nice to see you. Aren't you a little early for your quarterly check-up?'

Miss Spangler suffered from diabetes and visited the hospital regularly.

'I have something for you. A lady came to see me who claims to be your sister. I have to say I can well believe it – you look so alike . . .'

'My sister?'

Miss Spangler nodded.

'Did she leave an address where I can reach her?'

'Yes. That and a phone number.'

'It's yours,' said George Anderson. 'All yours.'

He watched Venetia with glowing affection as she ran from room to room, her pale and pretty floral dress floating behind her. After the Christmas season was over, they were off to London and a West End theatre. She was doing well, and he was proud of her.

To outside eyes they must appear like May and September, and Venetia as a gold digger, only a mistress and with him purely for the money.

Those who observed might be surprised to know that their relationship was not purely sexual. She knew about his wife and George knew about her family. He even knew about Patrick Casey and what had happened in Ireland. That was what was so great about their relationship. They'd been totally open from the very start, a fact that had surprised both of them.

'I suppose you could call it our love nest,' said George, his face beaming with amusement. 'It's just for the two of us.'

Venetia was equally amused.

'Well, you can hardly move me into the house now can you?'

She looked out of the French doors that opened onto a pretty balcony with wrought-iron balustrade. The sea shone silver beneath banks of clouds all laced with various shades of the same silver.

'This is so wonderful,' she breathed, hardly able to believe her eyes.

George came up to stand behind her, his hands on her shoulders. He kissed her ear whilst his thumbs stroked the nape of her neck.

'This is somewhere to come back to after the production finishes. I can't imagine the war reaching Clevedon. The old ladies who live here won't allow it,' he added with a grin.

Venetia laughed, her long cool fingers stroking his.

'It's lovely. You know, I remember my sister telling us stories about living in a place by the sea when our father came to fetch us. It never happened of course, though it has for me.'

She sensed George's tension and his sudden silence. George wasn't usually silent for long.

'I have a surprise for you.'

As an older man, George Anderson was apprehensive of what her reaction might be. He knew what his own reaction would be if her family didn't approve of her being involved with a married man. Yes, his wife was in a mental hospital, but some people still wheeled out the old chestnut, *in sickness and in health.* As though his wife even noticed he was around.

'You've received a phone call from your sister. She's left her number. I phoned it myself. It's a hospital. Queen Mary's Hospital.'

Her grey eyes seemed to grow lustrous with wonder, as though a great miracle had occurred, but then swiftly clouded with concern.

'Is she ill? Is she sick?'

He shrugged. 'I don't know. She didn't say so and quite frankly I didn't ask. Foolish I know. What do you want to do?'

'She's my sister. I have to see her.'

'Your understudy could take over your part for a few days. Three hours and we could be in London. If you want to be.'

She nodded, her throat feeling too tight to talk. At last she managed to speak. 'I want to. I have to. After all these years I just have to.'

Patrick Casey had taken great pride hiring a taxi to take them to Magda Brodie's last known address. It had not escaped his wife's notice that he enjoyed spending cash. At present they had a nice little nest egg thanks to the sale of the farm, but as she kept pointing out to him, it wasn't going to last forever.

The sight that met them as they got out of the taxi was not at all what they were expecting.

'Jesus! Will you look at that?' Patrick exclaimed, stabbing the brim of his hat with two fingers so that it sat further back on his head.

Anna Marie eyed the blackened timbers and boarded-up windows with dismay.

The arrival of a black taxi cab had not gone unnoticed by the girls across the way.

One of them, a tall girl with pale blonde hair, waltzed in behind them.

'Burned to a cinder. Not a chance of getting out of that fire alive. The police reckoned it was deliberate, though nothing was proved. Related were you?'

'She was my aunt.'

'Oh! Never mind. If there was ever a woman who deserved to go to hell, then she was it.'

The girl's tone was far from respectful and Anna Marie couldn't help responding harshly.

'I never met my aunt, but I do think the dead deserve some respect.'

Patrick eyed his wife with surprise. It wasn't often she lashed out with her tongue.

'Sorry I spoke out of turn,' said the girl, 'but that poor girl that lived there – Bridget Brodie was a right cow to her.'

'Are you talking about Magda Brodie? Would that be her name?' Anna Marie demanded.

'That's right. Luckily she got out before the place caught fire thanks to Winnie One Leg. Winnie used to run this place,' she said, thumbing the house behind her.

'What?'

Anna Marie was in no doubt what she meant. Her mind was racing, trying to keep up with the information she was receiving.

'Do you know where my sister is now?'

'Oh yeah! She's easy enough to find. Lives in a nice place up west – Prince Albert Mews. Winnie left her a bloody fortune. Wish I'd had luck like that. Might not have ended up here if I had. Still,' she added, her eyes meeting Patrick's, 'there are things I might have missed.'

Anna Marie hit Patrick's elbow with her handbag. His eyes were out on stalks.

'Has she got a fancy man or is she . . .? What I mean to say is, what kind of trade . . . I mean. Is she like you?'

Patrick interjected. 'Oh, for goodness' sake, my wife wants to know if her sister is a prostitute.'

The woman stared at her. 'I suppose you won't want to make her acquaintance if she is. I know your sort. You'll only want to speak to her if she ain't fallen on hard times and had to sell herself. Well you'll get no joy from me. Go and find out for your bloody self!'

Longing to get away from the place and this rude woman, Anna Marie dragged at Patrick's arm. 'We're going there. Right now.'

'Prince Albert Mews,' Anna Marie barked at the cab driver.

'We don't know what number,' said Patrick. His feet were aching and he was beginning to get short tempered. Although searching for Magda had been his bait to get his wife to move to London, he hadn't really expected her to take it so seriously.

'We can ask,' muttered Anna Marie feeling more purposeful and useful than she'd felt for years. 'We haven't come all this way to be put off now. We can ask.'

Having had no luck in Edward Street, Anna Marie and Patrick arrived at the local police station hoping they might know the number of the house in Prince Albert Mews where her sister lived – if she lived there at all.

They bustled in, Patrick huffing and puffing impatiently because he'd much rather be in the pub with his cousins and relatives. It was said that if anyone poked their head round the door of this particular London pub and shouted, 'Is there any-one named Casey in here?', twenty-five voices would answer in unison. Police stations were not a place the likes of him felt comfortable in.

Since moving to England, Anna Marie was not quite the

timid little person she used to be. She marched into the police station as though she were a duchess and the lower orders were only there to do her bidding.

'I'm looking for my sister. She lives in Prince Albert Mews but I'm unsure of the number. Her name's Magdalena Brodie.'

The police officer behind the sliding shutters looked at her over the top of his glasses. He had silver hair and his uniform barely stretched across his belly.

'I need to know who you are before giving out such information. And even then, I have to get permission I think . . .'

'Rubbish. Magda Brodie is my sister. I've been told she lives at Prince Albert Mews but have no number and no matter what door I knock on round there, nobody seems to be at home.'

'Of course not. They are gentlemen of means with jobs in Whitehall, and professional people who keep long hours and arrive late home.'

Anna Marie heaved an impatient sigh. 'Now look. If I wanted a report about how people live their lives around there, I would have asked you for one. All I want is my sister's full address. And I don't care what she's done. No matter if she's broken the law, she's still my sister!'

The police sergeant looked confused.

Behind her, Patrick muttered an expletive under his breath. His wife could be downright embarrassing nowadays.

'I hardly think she's done that,' said the sergeant. 'Seeing as she's engaged to a very well-respected police officer. And her being a doctor and all.'

'A doctor?'

Anna Marie was astounded. She'd been led to believe that her sister was a scarlet woman. It seemed this was miles from the truth.

'So. The address?'

*

Queen Mary's Hospital for the East End sported a barrier of sandbags around the main entrance and crosses of sticking plaster over the window panes in case of bomb blast.

Apart from that everything was pretty much the same; it was still busy, still smelled of carbolic and antiseptic.

Sister Betty Flanagan sent a ward maid to go and fetch Doctor Brodie.

'Tell her it's an emergency.'

The woman brought in by ambulance had bright red hair. At one time it might have been exuberant, but damp with sweat it now resembled a close-fitting hat around her head.

'She's been screaming all the way here. Her neighbour said she's been in labour for days,' said the ambulance man.

Sister Flanagan pushed him out of the way so she could better inspect the newly arrived patient.

The woman's face was pale and she was delirious. Best thing to be, thought Sister Betty if you're in that much pain.

She looked up to see Doctor Brodie fast approaching. She looked like a girl, though she insisted she was twenty-eight. Somehow Sister Flanagan couldn't quite believe that. She looked so young it made her wonder whether she'd lied about her age, like the soldiers during the Great War. She wouldn't be the first.

'Apparently she's been in labour for days,' Sister Betty explained.

'Oh Lord.'

Magda saw the red hair before she'd seen the face. The woman lying in agony was her old friend Susan.

At first Magda thought the very worst. 'Susan,' she said, bending low so that only her old friend could hear her. 'Did you try to get rid of it?'

Susan's face contorted with pain before she answered. 'No. I want this baby. I want it, Magda.'

Magda heard the urgency in her friend's voice and believed her. She did not question why this one was so important. She had an awful feeling she might know the reason. A diphtheria epidemic had taken many children from East End homes. She wasn't going to ask Susan if her children had succumbed to the devastating disease; but guessed she already knew the answer.

Magda felt Susan's stomach and followed it up with an internal inspection.

'Can you tell whether me hat's on straight,' Susan quipped, wincing even as she made the joke.

'Just lie quiet, old friend. I can feel the baby's feet. Both engaged.'

'Whoops!'

Susan grimaced again.

Magda did her best to reassure her. 'It won't be the first baby to present feet first.'

The truth was that it wouldn't be easy, but as luck would have it by the time they got to the delivery room, the child had finally positioned itself half decently. They were in with a chance.

'Presenting bottom first,' she said to Susan. 'But I think I can turn it round.'

To Sister Betty, she said, 'Forceps I think. Let's get this baby born then we can all get home in time for Christmas dinner.'

Chapter Forty-five

Venetia

The woman wearing a fur coat marched determinedly through the reception area of Queen Mary's Hospital. She was escorted by a middle-aged man who had the look of wealth about him. His hair was grey, his bearing distinguished. Every so often he encircled the woman's waist with a protective arm, almost as though he were signalling that he would protect her against all comers.

A few of the medical staff thought that face, the glossy hair, the dark grey eyes were familiar.

The building was far from immaculate, dark brown walls swallowing the meagre light from the conical shades hanging from long brown wires.

Someone had made the effort of putting up a few paper chains and a cut-out sign saying Merry Christmas.

The sound of carols being sung could be heard from the side wards where medical staff, from cleaners to doctors, were doing their best to spread some seasonal cheer.

'Excuse me.'

The big man in the handsome clothes had taken off his hat and was addressing one of the nursing staff.

'Do you know where we can find Magdalena Brodie?

Excuse us, but we're not sure whether she's a patient or a nurse. We think possibly the former.'

The nurse looked from the handsome man to the glamorous woman. 'I think you mean Doctor Brodie.'

Venetia shook her head. 'That can't be her,' she murmured. 'Doctors are men – mostly – aren't they?'

George looked amused. 'In Ireland there might not be too many women doctors, but I think you'll find they're a growing strength around here.'

Venetia's jaw dropped. To think that her sister was a doctor. Certainly not the scarlet woman her grandparents had forbidden her to mention.

'Is she here?'

The nurse frowned. 'I'm not sure if she's still here. She was supposed to go off duty at six. But I'll check for you if you like.'

Venetia said she would be most grateful.

She stood waiting, shifting from one foot to the other. What if her sister didn't want to see her? What if Anna Marie had been in touch and told her the shameful episode of her going to St Bernadette's. She might also know about the baby.

Suddenly she got cold feet.

'George. I think I should go.'

He looked taken aback, but being a sensitive man and desperately in love with the vivacious Venetia Bella, he gave in to her every whim.

'Whatever you want to do, sweetheart. Whatever you want to do.'

By the time Magda came out from the delivery room, having helped Susan bring a fine baby boy into the world, her visitors had left.

'Did they give a name?'

The nurse who told her she'd had visitors shook her head. 'No, but . . .' She paused as something crossed her mind.

'Yes?'

'Nothing,' she said, deciding that the doctor looked too tired to bother with her impression that the woman had similar looks to the doctor.

'I'm off now,' said Magda, her coat draped around her shoulders and her Gladstone bag hanging heavy from one hand. 'Even though it's Christmas Eve, ring me if you need me. I do have a telephone now so don't hesitate to use it.'

The nurse said she would ring if any emergency arose.

'Merry Christmas, Doctor Brodie.'

'Merry Christmas,' Magda responded.

Outside she took a breath of fresh air and paused for a moment, looking up at a navy blue sky that sparkled with stars. It was hard to believe that the country was at war on such a beautiful night as this. So quiet. So peaceful.

Daniel was outside waiting for her. She smiled at him. 'I've just delivered an old friend of a new baby. Very apt, don't you think?'

He kissed her then helped her into her coat. 'Come on. It's cold, but once you've got your coat on we can go carol singing if you like. Which carol shall we sing?'

Her smile widened. 'I've just delivered a baby boy. It has to be "Silent Night, Holy Night".'

It took some effort for George to persuade Venetia to return to the hospital.

'I'm scared,' she whispered, then gave a little nervous laugh. 'And to think I can stand up in front of an audience and not feel the slightest bit nervous. But meeting my sister after all this time . . .'

He took hold of her elbow. 'Come on. I'll be with you in case you fluff your lines.'

The lighting in the impressive hallway of Queen Mary's

400

was more subdued than it had been earlier. Venetia walked slowly forward, the tapping of her high heels echoing off the painted walls.

A nurse, her winged headdress fluttering slightly in the breeze, looked up. Instead of asking what she wanted, instead of referring back to the notes she was perusing, their eyes met and locked.

'I know you,' said Venetia, suddenly feeling far less nervous.

'I always knew,' said the nursing sister, her silver buckle defining her status. 'You two look so alike. Doctor Brodie and you.'

'Sister Elizabeth,' breathed Venetia.

'I left the order. I'm now Sister Betty.'

Even once she had all the information, the nerves refused to quieten. 'What will I say? What should I do?'

'You have to face her. You can't stay here,' he said, defining the hotel room they were staying in with a wave of his hand.

She nodded.

'Can I make a suggestion?' he said.

'Anything that might help, suggest away,' she responded.

'The leading lady at the Ilchester has dropped out with a touch of flu. It's only a small venue off Covent Garden, but if you took over the part and we sent tickets to your family . . .'

Magda put down the phone, her hands tightening over it as though disinclined to let go.

Daniel was eyeing her with a pained expression. 'Don't tell me. There's an emergency and you have to go in.'

Magda looked at him with the most disbelieving expression imaginable.

'It wasn't Sister Betty?' He looked extremely hopeful.

She nodded. 'Yes. It was. It seems my family have found

me. Venetia has been to the hospital. She didn't say when she was coming, but she's sure to arrive at some point.'

Daniel wrapped his arms around her.

Magda pressed an ice-cool hand onto her forehead. 'Every Christmas since we parted I've wished for us all to be reunited. I thought I'd feel terribly happy when we were together again. But that's not what I'm feeling at all.'

'Tell me,' he said, rubbing her back as though trying to soothe an imagined pain.

'I feel scared. I don't feel as though they're going to be like family at all. They . . . we . . . are grown up. We're not children any more. We're strangers.'

He shook his head and pressed her against him.

'You will be strangers. For a while. But you never used to be before you were separated, and it stands to reason that you won't be from now on. And what about the letters and cards you wrote them? If they read them they'll know everything about the child that used to be you.'

'I forgot about the letters. That's what studying to be a doctor does for you.'

At the sound of a car rolling over the cobbles they looked out of the window.

Magda's breath caught in her throat. 'It has to be them,' she said breathlessly. 'I hope they won't be disappointed.'

'Of course they won't.'

They made their way down the stairs to the garage that had once been a stable. Daniel turned off the lights before opening the double doors. The cold air, suffused with a hint of London fog, rushed in. The car, its headlights dimmed to wartime diffusion, rolled over the cobbles and came to a stop.

Magda stood there, hands clasped together, wanting to see the people inside the car, but seeing nothing in the all-encompassing darkness.

'I feel as though I'm on the stage,' she whispered.

'You are. It's the performance you've always longed for. The grand reunion.'

The figure she saw was drowned in darkness. There was a man with her.

Magda and Danny stood aside to let them in.

'You must be freezing,' said Magda.

'Yes. Doctor Brodie.'

Our voices sound hollow and unreal, thought Magda, as though we are strangers, not family at all.

Anna Marie came round from the other side of the car. She too stood and stared.

Once safely behind closed doors and drawn curtains, Danny turned on the light.

The two girls stared at each other.

'You look like our mother,' Anna Marie blurted, then burst into tears. The two young women hugged each other. 'And you look like Venetia,' Anna Marie added through her tears.

So where was Venetia, Magda wondered. She was the sister who had turned up at the hospital. Had she changed her mind about seeing her? Surely, if she was going to make herself known, she would have done so by now?

Two tickets for a play at the Ilchester arrived by taxi the next morning.

'For a Doctor Brodie and friend,' said the taxi driver who brought them.

'I didn't order them,' Daniel said.

'The leading lady is Venetia Bella.'

'Ah!'

They were escorted to a private box of plush red upholstery. Rumour had it that the old roué King Edward VII had entertained numerous of his ladies there.

Magda and Daniel had it to themselves. A bottle of champagne was brought.

'Compliments of Mr Anderson.'

Magda and Daniel decided that neither of them knew a Mr Anderson, so presumed he was something to do with Venetia.

The play might have been more enjoyable if Magda had been able to concentrate. As it was, the moment Venetia came on stage, she couldn't take her eyes off her. She was so different from her twin, Anna Marie, and yet so familiar, almost a mirror image of Magda herself.

On occasion their eyes met, Venetia from the floodlit stage, and Magda, her older sister, looking down at her from the semi-gloom of the private box.

Her heart racing, Magda held onto Daniel's hand, unaware she was gripping so tightly until he gently loosened her fingers.

The play was girl meets boy, boy leaves girl, girl as woman catches up with man who now feels differently than he once had.

When finally the lead role was gazing into her man's eyes, telling him that she still loved him, the words she spoke might just as well have been spoken for the two of them.

'. . . even whilst we were apart, I never stopped thinking of you and how it would be when we were reunited, sure in my heart that we would never be parted again . . .'

To Magda it really did seem as though her sister was speaking directly to her. Daniel confirmed it.

'She's speaking to you,' he whispered.

He was right and in that moment Magda knew that her sister had been as nervous as she was to meet again. It had been so many years since they'd last seen each other. They'd been children, frightened little girls torn from each other to proceed in the world as best they could.

The stage was Venetia's medium, the place where she could best express her true feelings. She really was telling her sister that her heart was full to overflowing with joy – just as Magda's was.

Sometimes Magda would dream that somebody was knocking at the door of the house in Prince Albert Mews and, when she opened it, her little brother Michael was standing there. She knew her father had told him about Edward Street. It wasn't impossible to trace her through that infamous address. However, Michael only appeared at the door in her dream, never when she was awake.

'I'm presuming he's happy with his lot,' Magda said to Danny. 'I suppose that's all that matters. And I do have most of my family back.'

Michael was the missing one; there was nobody else, or at least she didn't think there was until a windy March day when the clouds were scudding across the sky like frightened sheep.

A child patient was brought into the hospital by his doting father, a man of late middle age with a carefree look about him and wearing the much patched and darned jacket of a seaman.

'There doesn't appear to be anything wrong with this child,' the man was told by a harassed Sister Betty.

'There isn't. I just wanted to reacquaint myself with the famous Doctor Brodie.'

Sister Betty tucked in her chin and threw him a forbidding look. On spotting Doctor Brodie herself, the middle-aged man swept past her.

'Magda!'

Magda spun round and almost fainted – as though she'd seen a ghost – which in a manner it seemed she had.

'Uncle James!'

'Somebody down at the docks said they'd been fixed up by

a woman doctor by the name of Brodie. I had to see if it was you.'

Magda stood shaking her head in disbelief, looking from the man to the boy and back again. 'Uncle Jim. We were told you'd drowned.'

He flushed bright red and shook his head. 'No. Not exactly. Years ago, I met a girl called Sally and we got on just fine. I got a friend to come round and tell your Aunt Bridget that I'd drowned at sea. It was worth giving up the money saved with the Sailors' Benevolent Society just for a bit of happiness. Now, if what I hear is true and the old mare – pardon me – is burning in hell, I'd like to make Sally and my offspring legitimate.'

Magda shook her head in disbelief and couldn't stop giggling like a silly girl. 'I should have known when I smelled the Sunlight soap.'

Uncle James looked puzzled.

Magda couldn't help the wide grin. 'On the last occasion you came home drunk, I took your boots off. Your socks smelled of Sunlight soap. Somebody was washing your socks for you.'

He grinned broadly. 'She always did take care of me, right from the first.'

'Like Danny. The man I'm marrying. Will you give me away, Uncle Jim?'

'You bet I will! Couldn't be more pleased, and if you're ever along White City way, we could go to the dogs together. Might even win a few bob.'

Chapter Forty-six

Magda and Danny

August and the austerity of a wartime wedding was counteracted by the balmy weather.

Danny had joined up just as he said he would, and German bombers had dropped their first raid on London. The phoney war and the days of testing air-raid sirens was over. The war was now for real and affected everybody.

Doctors as well as fighting men were being conscripted at lightning speed and emergency hospital stations were being established anywhere that could take over a hundred beds. More doctors were needed and those in authority didn't care much about gender – just about having enough.

Evacuating Dunkirk had resulted in a flood of injured men. And now there was bombing and the prospect of civilians injured in huge numbers. Never had trained staff been so in demand.

Their wedding was to be at eleven o'clock. There were so many things on Magda's mind that she just didn't have the time to be nervous. With the exception of Michael, her family were reunited. She'd received a letter from her father explaining that he couldn't possibly come back to England. The postmark had been Montevideo.

'You always did want a proper uniform.'

Magda brushed her hand over his shoulder. There was nothing there to be brushed away; she just wanted to touch him, to make sure that this wasn't all a dream and that Daniel Rossi, now an army lieutenant, was not an apparition.

He smiled at her nervously, his fingers drumming against her arm before handing her over to Uncle Jim who was looking big, bluff and happy to be there with his wife, Sally.

He was about to head to where the best man and the vicar awaited, when Magda grabbed his arm.

'You do have the ring?'

He nodded vigorously. 'Oh yes. That is, Stanley has it.'

Stanley was one of his police officer friends who had also left the force to take up an appointment as first lieutenant on a Royal Navy corvette.

'You don't mind that it's a bit dusty and that there's no music . . .'

'I don't mind at all.'

The truth was that a falling bomb had blown off one of the flying buttresses that had supported the nave of St Mark's for centuries. The dust had been cleared in time for the service but a residue remained.

A slim figure in black slid into the church before they did, pausing only briefly to glance at her before going in.

'That must be the vicar. I'd better go.'

He held onto both her shoulders as he kissed her, a warm, considerate and gentle kiss, almost fearful.

'You look grand,' said Uncle Jim.

She slid her arm through his and thanked him.

The dress was Venetia's, of a lovely cream colour with vague impressions of pink rosebuds. The corsage nestling on her shoulder was courtesy of Uncle Jim who boasted a garden at the back of his terraced house and an allotment beyond that.

'It'll be cabbages not roses I'll be growing from now on,' he said to her. 'Can't eat roses. But war or no war, there'll always be brides wanting roses.'

'Well,' said Magda taking a deep breath. 'Are you ready?'

'Once I get me vocals in order. Can't walk down the aisle unaccompanied now can we?'

Jim Brodie cleared his throat and began to hum the wedding march.

Magda laughed.

The church was indeed a little dusty and piles of rubble blocked what extra light would have been coming in from the west wing.

She kept step with her uncle's humming halfway down the aisle where breathlessness and a tickly throat caused her uncle to start coughing.

'Sorry, Father,' he said to the vicar who awaited them in front of the altar.

'No apology is needed, my son,' the vicar responded. 'Unfortunately my organist, as well as the church, has sustained a slight injury, hence we are unable to air Mendelssohn's wedding march as we should be doing.'

'Perhaps I could help.'

The voice was unrecognisable and had come from one of the back pews.

Magda recognised the slim young man whom both she and Danny had presumed was the vicar. On closer inspection he seemed too young, even though he was dressed in black.

He swept past them both, head down as though embarrassed by his brazen interruption at such an important time in their lives.

'You are an organist?' asked the vicar.

The young man nodded. 'You could say that.' He paused before taking his place. He looked directly at Magda. 'I'm sorry to spring this on you, but my name is Michael Darby. I'm a theology student. I also believe I'm your brother.'

A rush of subdued conversation and surprised looks ran between Venetia, Anna Marie and their respective menfolk.

With an air of confidence – as though presenting himself to his long lost-family was something he did every day – Michael sat himself at the organ and began to play, the stirring notes of the wedding march soaring up into the Norman rafters of the church.

Magda looked up at the stained-glass windows filtering colours along beams of sunlight. All her family were here. Everyone she'd ever loved. Her sisters. Her uncle, and now it seemed also her little brother. And Danny of course.

Her throat was dry as parchment. She only hoped it would recover long enough for her to say the words, 'I do.'

Her uncle delivered her to Danny's side. Danny took her hand and slid her arm into his.

'Ready?' he whispered.

'Yes,' she murmured back as the vicar began to address the congregation.

'Dearly beloved . . .'